Aurore

Graham Hurley

W F HOWES LTD

This large print edition published in 2017 by
W F Howes Ltd
Unit 5, St George's House, Rearsby Business Park,
Gaddesby Lane, Rearsby, Leicester LE7 4YH

1 3 5 7 9 10 8 6 4 2

First published in the United Kingdom in 2017
by Head of Zeus Ltd

A CIP catalogue record for this book is available
from the British Library

ISBN 978 1 51007 448 4

Typeset by Palimpsest Book Production Limited,
Falkirk, Stirlingshire

To Chris

With thanks for Civray-sur-Esves

'À la guerre comme à la guerre . . .'

Baron Hans Günther von Dincklage,
lover of Coco Chanel

PRELUDE

August 1930. A new decade. High summer in Bristol and a storm in the offing after three days of searing heat wave. Daytime access to the theatre was through the battered stage door, the one the actors used.

Billy had spent the morning polishing the brasswork in the dress circle. Now, he gazed at the rickety ladder that led into the roof space above the wings. He could hear the murmur of voices on the main stage, two actors in rehearsal, one of them Irene, the woman who would change his life forever.

He got to the top of the ladder and stepped into the darkness. It felt mysterious, enveloping, impenetrable. The borrowed torch was all but useless. He gave it a shake, then another, and in the dirty yellow light he was finally able to look round.

Huge wooden trusses above his head, heavily cobwebbed. A tiny splinter of sky where a slate had shifted. And off to the left his first glimpse of what he'd come to find: the long wooden gully, gently inclined, supported on trestles and tarred inside for reasons he could only guess at. At

1

fourteen years old, Billy Angell was in love with magic, with make-believe. And here it was: the device they called the Thunder Run.

The cannonballs were backed up behind a little rectangle of wood that fitted into a slot at the top of the run and served as a stopper. Lift the stopper and gravity would do the rest.

The actors on the stage below were rehearsing a scene from a costume drama built around a marriage in difficulties. An earlier incident had sparked a crisis and the wife had finally run out of patience. After an exchange of muted banalities, Irene had lost her temper.

'*The situation is intolerable*,' she shouted. '*Be honest for once in your life, what is it you want from me?*'

'*Nothing at all.*'

'*I don't believe you. You want all of me. Every last morsel.*'

'*That's not true.*'

'*Then leave me in peace, I implore you.*'

Perfect, Billy thought, imagining Irene and her stage husband locked in a moment of silence, awaiting a sign from the gods. He reached for the stopper and released the cannonballs. They started to roll down the gully, a gathering rumble that could only be the approach of a summer storm. Billy watched them as they began to slow where the gully flattened out. The support trestles were still shaking. This close, he could feel the thunder deep in his bones.

Below, on stage, the actors had abandoned the

script. Billy heard the scrape of a chair as one of them stood up. It must have been Irene.

'Damn and blast,' she sounded even angrier. 'I left my bloody washing out.'

The torch flickered and died. Billy was grinning in the hot darkness. Magic, he thought. Make-believe.

PART I

CHAPTER 1

R AF Wickenby was declared operational in September 1942, one of a network of airfields across the east of England that served as a springboard for Bomber Command. The climate was harsh, the landscape was flat and the scouring winds were merciless.

Aircrew arrived from everywhere. A handful of Australians who'd grown up on the beaches of New South Wales reported thin beer and thinner pickings among the local women. Fed on a rich diet of folklore about the Battle of Britain and the golden generation who'd chased the Luftwaffe across the skies of southern England, the newcomers discovered this was a very different kind of war.

Flight Sergeant Billy Angell arrived from Bristol on 4 April 1943. In July he'd be celebrating his twenty-seventh birthday but no one he was to meet over the coming months believed for a moment that he was that old.

His first day on the operational front line was sobering. He was to join an established crew flying an Avro Lancaster, call sign S-Sugar. The Wireless Operator he was replacing had been hosed out of the aircraft on its return from a raid over Essen after he'd been torn apart by a chunk of shrapnel. The explosion had also peppered the thin metal skin of the Lanc but the airframe and control surfaces were intact, along with three of the four engines, and S-Sugar had limped back across the North Sea before being towed to a maintenance hangar for assessment and repair.

By the time Billy reported to RAF Wickenby, work on S-Sugar had only just begun. A spare half-hour at lunchtime took Flt Sgt Angell to the maintenance hangar. Against the advice of a fitter working on the wrecked engine, Billy climbed the metal ladder propped against the fuselage and ducked inside. The gloom was pricked by daylight through dozens of shrapnel rents. Apprehension smelled of the kerosene the erks used as a disinfectant but something else – a metallic, slightly coppery smell – grew stronger as he struggled over the main spar and made his way forward towards the cockpit.

The Wireless Op sat at a tiny desk on the left of the aircraft, immediately above the bomb bay, facing forward. An observation window giving him a view out could be curtained to preserve night vision and he could count on the nearby heating vents to keep him warm. All this Billy knew already. He'd been through the Lancaster Finishing School only last month as his training came to an end. He felt at home at the heart of this enormous aircraft. He understood how to encode wind speed

8

reports and send them back to base, how to log the half-hourly target updates from Group, how to be the Navigator's eyes and ears when it came to cross-checking a DR fix against faraway radio beacons. What was new was the coppery smell. It was blood, with a thin top-dressing of something more visceral. Even a couple of days after his predecessor's war had come to an abrupt end, traces of the poor bastard still remained.

Billy stared down at the desk, at the stains beneath the panel of dials and switches, shuddering to think what a closer inspection might reveal. Nine months of training had taught him a great deal about the importance of his role in taking the battle back to Germany. But never this.

The father he'd never known had given his life in another war. Despite the questions he'd asked, his mother had always refused to talk about it and so he'd turned to books to find out what little he knew. His dad had served in the trenches. There'd been a huge attack. Everything had gone wrong and thousands of men had been killed. Billy was still looking down at the desk, still trying to imagine what it must have felt like. Would dying on the Somme have been preferable to this? Was it better – *cleaner* – to die at ground level with a bullet through your chest rather than suffer the agonies of a lonely death at 20,000 feet? He shook his head and turned away. Down on the hangar floor the fitter wanted to know whether he'd seen enough.

★   ★   ★

S-Sugar was retired to a training role and never returned to active service. In her place, the crew were presented with a newly minted Lancaster, flown in from the production line near Oldham by a diminutive Auxiliary Pilot called Daphne. S-Sugar's crew spoiled her with a cream tea in the Sergeants' Mess before her return to Lancashire and Flt Sgt Angell was sent to sweet-talk the cook into another plate of home-made scones.

By now, with a handful of successful ops under his belt, Billy was beginning – however dimly – to understand the strange chemistry that had kept these six men together. The pilot, or 'skipper', was a taciturn young Welshman called Harry Williams with a savage haircut, bitten nails and an astounding ability to roll cigarettes one-handed. He'd left school to work as a clerk at Swansea Town Hall and already looked a great deal older than his twenty-one years.

The Navigator was a Somerset man, Simon Meredith. He occupied the bed next to Billy. He'd taught French and Latin at a minor public school in the Mendip Hills and had a passion for the works of Leo Tolstoy. He regretted not being able to read *War and Peace* in the original Russian but was halfway through the first volume of what he told Billy was a decent translation. This book, with its worn cover and tiny print, accompanied Meredith on every operation but it was weeks before Billy realised that it also served as a good-luck charm. Tolstoy's 1,200-page masterpiece would see him through. Or so he hoped.

The rest of the crew were, by their own account, mongrel offerings from every corner of the kingdom. The Flight Engineer was a Glaswegian who'd joined Rolls-Royce. The Bomb Aimer, London-born and bred, was a private detective. The upper mid-gunner was a jobbing painter and decorator with a complicated love life and a pending divorce, while the rear-gunner, little Johnny Phelps, was a professional jockey with a passion for chess. On the final stages of the return leg of the longer expeditions over Europe, with the skipper's blessing, he and Simon Meredith would continue games over the intercom that they'd started earlier in the Mess. Bishop to A4. Queen to E2. Is that the coast I see down there? *Checkmate.*

The new Lancaster was call-signed V-Victor. By now, Harry Williams' crew had completed a dozen operations. A tour took you to thirty ops, after which you were excused active service for six months and joined a training squadron. This left Billy playing catch-up but over the weeks to come he quickly sensed that these men's experience, and the very fact that they'd survived, served as a form of protection and for this he was more than grateful. Rookie crews, he knew already, were the ones most liable to be posted FTR. FTR meant Failed To Return.

The quarters where Billy slept housed a dozen men. Returning from an op, you de-briefed, wolfed a plateful of eggs and bacon in the Mess and then got yourself to bed. All too often, hours later, you woke up to find that the possessions of other men in the dormitory had already been collected for despatch to their families. Barely half the crews on base would survive a full tour.

The memory of the empty beds and 'FTR' chalked against the names in the Briefing Room would never leave Billy, but joining an experienced crew could be doubly unnerving. On his first couple of ops, over the intercom, the pilot would occasionally address him as 'Dingo', which had apparently been the nickname of the dead Wireless Op. Billy didn't think there was any mischief in this but one chilly morning, after returning from a raid on Düsseldorf, he clambered out of the aircraft, had a stretch and then made the mistake of telling Harry Williams that it felt like flying with a ghost. Billy was pleased with the thought but the image sparked fits of laughter on the tarmac and from that day on Billy became 'Ghost'.

Not that it mattered. On 7 June 1943, the crew of V-Victor flew their thirtieth op. Harry Williams steadied V-Victor on the bombing run over the target flares, deposited six tons of high explosive and incendiaries on the bonfire that was Wuppertal, added thirty seconds of straight and level for the aiming point photos, and then made a hasty exit through the forest of searchlights to the darkness beyond.

Job done. On the return leg over the North Sea Billy clambered up to the astrodome, a bubble of

Perspex on top of the fuselage, and gazed at the dying stars while Johnny Phelps's bishop and castle harried the Nav's queen in the milky dawn over Skegness. V-Victor's aiming point photos, when developed and pinned to the ops board back at Wickenby, drew a quiet round of applause from fellow aircrew and that night Harry Williams dressed Billy in a white sheet for the end-of-tour celebrations in a pub called the Saracen's Head in nearby Lincoln.

By now, Ghost had become truly part of the crew. They recognised how different he was from anyone else they'd ever flown with. Physically he was an imp of a man, always watching, always listening, always on the move. They couldn't believe his gift for recalling some of the speeches he'd had to memorise in the theatre and on the longer ops they'd sometimes make specific requests. Shakespeare was always a favourite and Billy worked on a selection of party pieces from *Macbeth*, *Romeo and Juliet* and *Richard II*, selecting whichever felt most suitable at the time. The crew, to Billy's surprise, developed a real taste for blank verse and rarely interrupted. Ghost, they agreed, had the gift of keeping reality at arm's length, and at 20,000 feet on a dark night that could be more than useful.

One evening in the Mess, with the end of their tour in sight, Billy had told them stories about his pre-war years in the theatre, about the stars he'd met, about the long weeks on tour playing rep to

13

audiences of a dozen in draughty venues in God knows where. These yarns of his made them laugh and they even half believed him when he talked about recording a production of *Desire Under the Elms* for wireless broadcast, and later taking that same production to New York, but it happened that Simon Meredith had heard the play on a BBC transmission and complimented Ghost on his performance. Eben, he'd said, was a tough role for any young actor but Billy had more than done it justice.

Praise was as rare in bomber crews as in any other corner of British life but the realisation that Ghost might have been briefly famous, as well as a half-decent Wireless Op, definitely won their approval. And so at dawn beside the cathedral in Lincoln, after a night's celebration of surviving thirty ops, the crew of V-Victor raised their stolen glasses to the rising sun and assured Billy Angell that completing his own tour would be a piece of cake.

Wrong.

His new crew inherited V-Victor. That made Billy the elder statesman. These were airmen fresh off the assembly line and it showed. Adding Billy to their ranks was an odd thing to do because once again he'd be out of sync. To date, he'd flown sixteen ops, which left fourteen to go. After that, if they all survived, Billy himself would depart to a training squadron, saddling V-Victor with yet another stranger behind the Wireless Op's desk.

Billy's last outing was to take place towards the end of July 1943. By the third week of that month, the new crew of V-Victor had flown on twelve raids, most of them over the industrial heartlands of the Ruhr, a flak-laden hell hole dubbed 'Happy Valley'. The next trip would put Billy within touching distance of the magic thirty but by now he knew that he had a problem.

Even with a dozen ops under their belts, the new crew were still in the process of bonding and Billy was uncomfortably aware that the chemistry wasn't quite right. The skipper, unusually, was an older man and when Billy could hold his attention for just a few seconds in the Mess he sensed that his nerves had gone, that he was running out of steam, that he no longer believed in his ability to survive. Something about his eyes. Something about the way he refused to engage in any real conversation.

In civilian life Les Hammond had been an insurance clerk. He was long-faced and intensely serious. He walked with a pronounced limp and complained quietly of rheumatism when there was rain in the air. He had a wife and two children, he was twenty-nine years old, and he thought far too hard about all the ways the Germans could kill him. If you were looking for a real ghost, here he was.

Billy's twenty-ninth op took him deep into Germany, all the way to Berlin. The flak on the approach that night was unusually heavy. V-Victor had already suffered two near misses. The air-craft had been tossed around by the force of the explosions but everything was still working and there were no reports of injuries from the crew. The Bomb Aimer, who had nerves of steel, was sixty seconds from the release point when a searchlight swept briefly over a neighbouring aircraft, drifted away and then returned. Moments later came a second searchlight, a distinctive blueish-white.

Billy froze. This was the master beam and once it locked on, you were in real trouble because your radar co-ordinates were being automatically fed to the rest of the searchlights. Coned, you were easy meat for the flak batteries.

Pinned by the master beam, the nearby Lancaster dived into a tight corkscrew and disappeared, still pursued by the pencil of blueish light. At that point, inexplicably, V-Victor's skipper did exactly the same thing, wrecking the Bomb Aimer's calcu-lations as the aircraft plunged earthwards. The Bomb Aimer, who happened to be Australian, curtly requested another run over the target and the Navigator was still trying to calculate the new heading when the skipper announced he was returning home. Dump the bombs now. And that's an order.

Six tons of assorted ordnance tumbled into oblivion and nearly four hours later V-Victor landed safely back at Wickenby. At the debrief in front of the Intelligence Officer, Hammond blamed the incident on a false reading from the engine instrumentation. In the belief that two engines had caught fire, he'd aborted the bomb run and decided to turn back. It was a pitiful excuse. A single glance out of the cockpit would have established that there was nothing wrong with the engines.

No one else said a word while the Intel Officer nodded and made a couple of notes. Moments later, the debrief was over. That evening, after everyone had slept, the crew met up in the Mess as usual. There was no discussion of what had happened over Berlin, but when the skipper tried to buy a round of drinks, the Bomb Aimer eyeballed him for a moment or two and then left the building without a backward glance.

Billy, watching, felt nothing but dread. The next op would complete his tour. But if the Intel Officer neglected to press the issue and remove Les Hammond from operational flying then Billy's final op might well turn out to be just that.

That night, Billy returned to his sleeping quarters to find the Bomb Aimer alone, sitting on his bed. They both knew the skipper had become a liability. At first, neither said a word. Then Billy voiced the obvious question.

'So what do we do?'

'Mate, we fly with him. They'll probably give him one more chance.'

Billy nodded. They wouldn't be operational again for a couple of days. Maybe the Bomb Aimer was wrong. Perhaps the Intel Officer had recognised all the symptoms of a nervous breakdown and would be taking the appropriate steps. Perhaps.

The Bomb Aimer hadn't finished. Targeting was a closely guarded secret but he had his ear to the ground and he'd picked up some rumours. Billy wanted to know more.

'I hear Chopburg.'

Chopburg was aircrew slang for Hamburg. Chopburg was where the Germans had things properly organised. Chopburg was where the night fighters and the searchlights and the flak batteries ganged up on you and made things extremely ugly. Getting the chop was when they blew you out of the sky.

Billy swallowed hard. It was at moments like this that he thought helplessly of Irene. Twenty-nine missions completed. Searchlights dodged. Flak survived. Night fighters outfoxed. Every prospect of getting back to Bristol, of leaving some flowers on her grave, of seeing out the rest of the summer. Now this.

The Bomb Aimer was fumbling for a cigarette. For reasons Billy couldn't fathom there was a smile on his face. He lit the cigarette and expelled a long plume of blue smoke towards the ceiling before glancing across at Billy.

'One day at a time, eh?'

CHAPTER 2

Early the following morning, in a modest chateau 240 kilometres south-west of Paris, Hélène Lafosse stepped out into the still of dawn. A heat wave had settled over northern France: nearly a week of unbroken sunshine, of cloudless skies, of temperatures soaring beyond anything the older folk in Neaune could remember. The villagers, especially the women, had taken to staying indoors, grateful for the coolness afforded by the thick stone walls, and the handful of German soldiers that garrisoned the area had even been permitted to remove their shirts as they ambled through their working day.

Madame Lafosse was a newcomer to the Touraine. The Château de Neaune, like more or less everything else in her life, had been a gift from her husband, the Jew Nathan Khorrami. He'd presented it to her in the spring of 1938, knowing that war was around the corner. Khorrami was an art dealer of rare taste and iron nerve. With his easy charm, he was a negotiator of genius and he'd acquired a dense web of social and business connections in Paris: well-placed politicians, wealthy bankers, men of substance. Many of these individuals were clients of his and a number of conversations – increasingly troubled – had taught him to expect nothing from the French Army once Hitler deigned to make his intentions clear.

The Maginot Line, Khorrami had come to understand, was a joke, more a state of mind than a serious military obstacle. A small army of *soldats* squatted in semi-darkness on the eastern frontier beneath thirty metres of reinforced concrete, performing their drills, attending their periscopes, waiting for an enemy who'd never appear. 'Look at a map and pretend you're a German,' one industrialist had murmured at a French Government reception for Joachim von Ribbentrop, the German Foreign Minister. 'There are a thousand other roads that lead to Paris.'

The industrialist had been a Jew, too. And, like Khorrami, he'd sensibly packed his bags, despatched the best of his furniture to a friend's chateau in the south and bought a ticket to Lisbon within days of the first German units bursting out of the forests of the Ardennes and spearing into France. Hélène had missed her husband, especially the laughter and surprises he brought to her life, but accepted that it was prudent on his part to leave.

Now she walked across the cobbled courtyard to inspect the water level in the biggest of the wells. She was thirty-nine years old, Norman stock, tall, loose-limbed, pale complexion, big hands, fiercely practical. She had a physical presence that had always been a challenge for certain kinds of men and Nathan Khorrami had been one of them. She'd met him at a party at the Hôtel Meurice to celebrate the opening of his second art gallery, a small, stocky figure, immensely powerful. He wasn't handsome in any way, far from it, but he had a wit and an intelligence that she'd found irresistible and after the soirée they'd spent the night together in his apartment on the Île de la Cité.

The following morning, he'd brought her coffee. She was sitting in the window, enjoying the view. It happened to be raining but she'd never seen Notre Dame look more impressive. Nathan had handed her a cup of coffee and kissed the back of her neck. Already she knew that she was falling in love with a man who'd turned hyperbole into a way of life. 'You have the face of Jeanne d'Arc,' he'd told her earlier, 'the body of a goddess and the soul of my maternal grandmother.'

Nathan's maternal grandmother, she was later to discover, had owned a substantial palace on the Caspian Sea. By that time, though, he'd given his new lover another name, infinitely shorter, and the name had stuck. He called her Mustafa, Arabic for the Chosen One, an appellation all the more curious for being male. Was she upset at being given a boy's name? Did she mind the countless other little ways that Nathan had found to make her his own? *Pas du tout.*

The water level in the well was higher than she'd

expected. There was an old iron cup on a chain and she lowered it into the semi-darkness. This was cool, sweet water from reservoirs deep in the limestone and she took a sip or two before tipping up the cup and letting the rest trickle down her face. Even at this hour she could feel the warmth in the sun and she crossed the courtyard to enjoy the early morning shadows cast by the plane trees that lined the road to the village.

The chateau estate included a farm, a smallish wood and a lake that Nathan had stocked with carp and perch. One of his parting gifts before he'd left for Lisbon had been a book of his mother's recipes – things Persian housewives did with fresh-water fish – and three years later Hélène was still using it. Only last night she'd conjured pickled carp with a dressing of fresh herbs for her little *ménage,* drawing nods of approval from most of them, and she smiled to herself to think of her Persian art dealer one day back in France. Would Nathan Khorrami ever have the patience for life in the country? Somehow, she doubted it.

The tall windows in the chateau were open. From deep inside came the chime of Malinowski's precious clock. Six already. The old man would be up, pottering round the kitchen. On the far side of the courtyard was a line of stables. Valmy, her star performer, was corralled behind the blue door at the end. She'd ridden him only last night, for nearly an hour, hacking along the trail that led through the woods towards the water, and afterwards, rubbing him down in the courtyard before filling his bucket with oats, she'd nuzzled the blaze on his long face and whispered about the pleasures he could reliably expect once the people from Paris arrived. They'd be here by nine at the latest. That's what Klimt had promised, and in the matter of time Klimt was very seldom wrong.

She unlatched the top section of the stable door and swung it open. The horse was waiting for her. Valmy was another present from Nathan, a down-payment – he'd promised – on surviving life under the inevitable occupation. As a two-year-old, this lovely creature – so leggy, so brave – had been a three-times winner at Longchamps before taking the Prix de l'Arc de Triomphe in 1938. That victory, said Nathan, gave Valmy a stud value beyond rational estimation and the prospects were even sweeter because the very name commemorated the battle in which the French had sent the Prussians packing. In a letter from London posted after he'd taken the flying boat from Lisbon, Nathan had told her that the Germans wouldn't be able to resist helping themselves to Valmy's bloodline. Treat them like clients, he'd written. And insist on payment in Louis d'or. Gold trumps currency. Especially in times like these.

He'd been right, of course, but it was never that straightforward because the Germans had a habit of helping themselves. The polite term was requisitioning but to the rest of France it was simple theft. How, therefore, to keep her precious Valmy out of German hands?

She kept a bucket of last year's apples in the cool of the cellar and she'd slipped a couple into the pockets of her dress before leaving the chateau. This had become an early morning ritual and the moment the horse caught the movement of her hand towards the bulge of the apple it ducked its head and gave a sharp little whinny of expectation. She offered the apple on the palm of her hand, enjoying the rough warmth of the horse's mouth. Then she became aware of a presence behind her and she sensed at once that it was Klimt. Half an hour ago she'd left him in her bed, fast asleep. Now here he was. No footsteps. No greeting. Not a single clue that he'd stolen up on her. So typical.

She half turned. Well over six foot, he was even taller than her. Light blue eyes, curiously depthless. A mane of blond hair, lightly oiled. And, with the exception of an English cellist with whom she'd once been briefly in love, the most beautiful hands she'd ever seen on a man.

'Here. Before it gets cold.' Klimt was carrying a bowl of coffee. His French was perfect.

'And you?' She took the coffee.

'Malin is making another pot. He thinks we should have breakfast before they arrive.' Malin was their pet name for her resident Pole. In French it translated as 'smart' or 'shrewd', both close to a perfect description.

'Malin's right. I'm famished.'

Klimt nodded, reaching beyond her and stroking the horse. There wasn't a crease out of place on his green *Abwehr* uniform and the knee-length leather boots might have been brand new. She had no idea how he always managed to look so immaculate, especially in weather like this, but she knew him far too well to ask. There were parts of this man's life that she'd never share and she'd learned to prefer it that way. *Oberst* Bjorn Klimt, her precious key to a Paris that Nathan would barely recognise.

'Are they still coming for nine?' she asked.

He shook his head. Otto Abetz's attaché had telephoned the chateau a couple of minutes ago. The horsebox and escorts were already in Tours. Madame Lafosse was to expect them within the hour.

Otto Abetz was the German Ambassador to France. He lived in some style with his beautiful French wife in the Hôtel Beauharnais behind the Gare d'Orsay. Hélène wanted to know if the expected mare was his.

'Not at all. It will be a present, *une douceur.*'

'From whom?'

Klimt named a prominent French businessman, someone Hélène recognised from her pre-war outings to the patrons' enclosure at Longchamps.

'And he's paying?'

'Of course.'

'In gold?'

'I'm afraid not. He wonders whether US dollars will be acceptable.'

'How much?'

'He's promising $50,000 once she's in foal.'

Hélène frowned, trying to do the sums in her head. The village school was desperate for a new roof. The Packages for Prisoners' Fund was under-subscribed. Nathan was asking for $40,000 to conclude a deal on a Picasso canvas smuggled out of Paris only the previous month.

'I'll need three times that.'

'One hundred and fifty thousand dollars? *Aucun problème*. I'm sure the Frenchman will be happy to pay.' The smile again. Ways and means. A pleasure to be of service.

CHAPTER 3

T he Bomb Aimer had been right about Chopville. Billy Angell sat in the Wickenby briefing room, along with the rest of the crew of V-Victor, watching the Wing Commander striding towards the tiny spot-lit stage. Behind him, a black curtain masked the display map that would reveal that night's target, a small moment of theatre that Billy had always found rather comforting. The room smelled of tobacco and damp raincoats, and there was a feeling of intense anticipation, two memories that took him back to his pre-war days.

Billy was sitting between Les Hammond and the Nav. The previous evening he'd accompanied the skipper to a showing of *Casablanca* in the Sergeants' Mess. The prospect of Ingrid Bergman and Humphrey Bogart had attracted a full house and the Station Commander had taken advantage by starting the programme with a Road Safety film in the 'Crime Does Not Pay' series. The presentation offered a stern list of 'do's' and 'don'ts', and ended with the presenter eyeballing the camera. 'I can tell you people in the audience,' he'd said, 'that at the present rate of road accidents one out of every ten of you will be killed within the next five years.' The Mess erupted. These were odds you could only dream about. At Billy's side, V-Victor's Nav was rocking with laughter. Then Billy stole a look at Les Hammond. He was stone-faced. His hands were knotted tightly in his lap. And he couldn't take his eyes off the screen.

Now he was fidgeting nervously with his pencil as the Wing Commander mounted the stage. The news that V-Victor would be heading for Hamburg came as no surprise. Rumours of a 1,200-gallon fuel load had ruled out both Berlin and the Ruhr, leaving Kiel or Chopburg as favourites. Tonight, though, was to be a raid with a difference. Operation Gomorrah, he promised, would be seen as a turning point in the brief history of Bomber Command.

The Wing Commander was warming up. The map behind him extended deep into Europe. Lengths of red cord marked the outbound track to the target. Landfall on the other side of the North Sea would be the Frisian Islands that strad-dled the Dutch/German border and red and green celluloid overlays indicated flak and searchlight concentrations as the track dog-legged between them. This, said the Wing Co, was to be an outing in some force. Tally up the first, second and third waves and you were looking at nearly a thousand bombers. Vital, therefore, to be constantly mindful of other aircraft. Wickenby Lancasters would form part of the third wave. Time over target would be 02.10. Bomb the red TIs, and, failing that, go for the cluster of green flares.

TIs were target indicators, flares dropped by the Master Bombers who flew ahead of the bomber stream and orchestrated the entire raid, not a role for the faint-hearted. Billy gazed around at the upturned faces, the half-darkness pricked by the glow of cigarettes. He was one op away from saying goodbye to all this, six hours of flying that could – all too literally – save his life. Return to Wickenby intact and he'd be back in the real world.

He'd only been flying operationally for four months but by now he was a great deal wiser about what it took to survive. Crew chemistry was all-important but the key was the skipper. The best ones, the ones who made it through, had a gruff self-belief you could recognise within seconds. Harry Williams, barely twenty-two, had it. Other skippers in this room, all survivors, had it. It came from the conviction that you were bloody good, that you had luck on your side and that you were therefore invulnerable. On all three counts, alas, Les Hammond would never belong to this select little group of press-on skippers. In his own mind, he was already a statistic. He wasn't made for a war like this and sooner or later that same war would find him out. But not, please God, tonight.

The Met brief had started. A warm front was moving out over the North Sea but crews were to expect clear skies over the target. The forecaster began to detail expected winds at various altitudes and Billy watched the Nav beside him scribbling the figures on his notepad. Already, Billy had attended a separate brief for Wireless Operators and his own pad was full of jottings that would ease V-Victor's passage through the thicket of transmissions over the coming hours. Operationally, he lived in a world of codes. They were all changed daily and if you got them wrong the consequences could be fatal.

The Met man had finished. Supplementary briefings followed before the Wing Commander returned to the stage and summed up. We have, he said, a real opportunity to take the war to the enemy. A thousand aircraft. Six thousand tons of ordnance. And the targets for all that high explosive? German shipyards mass-producing U-boats. Munitions factories. Training facilities. Dozens of other key installations. Hamburg, tonight, was a place you wouldn't want to be.

The silence that followed wasn't the reaction the Wing Commander had expected. He peered into the spotlight, gathered up his papers and then nodded towards the door. The flight meal would be served in fifteen minutes. Take-off at 11.30. Good luck and God be with you.

Indeed. Billy made it his business to stick to Les Hammond as they hurried through the rain towards the Mess. He liked this man but he could feel a loneliness, or perhaps an uncertainty, that seemed to have taken him close to despair. The sanest option would be to report him, or to simply refuse to fly unless they found another skipper, but that smacked of betrayal and in any case Billy suspected that, deep down, Les Hammond had far more courage and far more self-belief than he gave himself credit for. Maybe he should try again to get closer to the man. Maybe that's where survival lay.

Tonight was cauliflower cheese and fatty chunks of what might have been beef. Billy and his skipper sat together. Hammond barely touched his food.

'Too greasy, Skip?'

'Not hungry, I'm afraid. Maybe I'll try and cadge a sandwich for later.'

Later they'd be en route to Hamburg. Eating a sandwich while wearing an oxygen mask and flying a Lancaster could be tricky.

'I get nervous, too, Skip. Who doesn't?'

Hammond shot him a look.

'Did I say I felt nervous?'

'Just a thought.'

'Then why bring it up?'

Hammond sounded irritated. The conversation was beginning to attract an audience. Rumours spread quickly on bomber bases. Les Hammond, said some, needed more lead in his pencil.

Billy had decided to change the subject. He knew Hammond's eldest daughter was mad about ballet. Here was a chance to offer a little career guidance.

'I used to be in the theatre, Skip. I was crazy about it. All I ever wanted to be was an actor. It's hard to get in when you're young but if you're really determined the chances are you'll make it.'

'You think that's true of flying, too?'

'No. I did the pilot training course down at Paignton. I thought I was the Red Baron at the time. Couldn't wait to get in a Spit.'

'Really?' At last a gleam of interest in Hammond's eyes.

'Yep. You get ten hours' instruction. You probably remember. After that you go solo. Do or die.'

'And?'

'Die. I stalled in. Bent the bloody Tiger Moth beyond recognition. You don't get to be a Wireless Op without running up a bill or two.'

It was true. Billy Angell had left the Initial Training Wing for the Wireless Op course with his personal file carefully stowed in his only suitcase. Under *Course Assessment* his flying instructor had written 'Appears unable to judge heights. Unsuitable for further pilot training.'

Hammond was laughing now. His hand strayed to his fork. He took a tiny mouthful of cauliflower cheese. Then another.

'I loved it,' he said. 'The minute I got into an aircraft I knew it was for me.'

He told Billy he'd abandoned his legal studies and volunteered for the RAF the day after war broke out. He'd scored the maximum in the aptitude tests, blossomed under an instructor of genius and gone solo after just seven hours. He was on the old side for a fighter pilot – twenty six, for God's sake – but he'd flown Hurricanes in the closing stages of the Battle of Britain and lived to tell the tale. Just.

Billy wanted to know what happened.

'I got shot down over Folkestone. Bailed out way too low. I was trying to miss a row of houses.'

'And?'

'Broke both legs. Fractured pelvis. Crushed vertebrae. Not nice.'

'I meant the houses.'

'They're still intact. A lady in one of them brought me a bunch of flowers in hospital.'

'That was nice of her.'

'That's what I said. She's now my wife.'

A navigator from another crew across the long refectory table mimed applause. Billy thought his skipper was joking at first but then realised he meant it.

Hammond seemed embarrassed by the sudden attention. He pushed his plate away and stood up. Billy was nowhere near finished. He eyed his plate, then offered to accompany Hammond back to their billet.

Hammond shook his head. He said he was off for a brisk walk to clear his head. His hand was on Billy's shoulder.

'Appreciate it,' he said. 'Thanks for your company. See you later.'

33

Billy watched him leave the Mess. A Nav leaned across the table as if he wanted to share a confidence.

'So who goes walking in the rain?' he said. 'On a night like this?'

CHAPTER 4

The rain crept south and east into Europe, on the back of a weather system laden with storms. In the rolling hills of the Touraine, with clouds massing over the last of the sunset, Hélène Lafosse decided to skip her nightly rounds with the watering can and save the precious water in the well. At night, in the chateau, she tried to make do with candles, partly because of the shadows they cast, and partly because she hated the thick blackout curtains. Not that anyone important was watching.

She found Malinowski in the kitchen, peeling the last of the potatoes for the evening meal. According to Nathan, who'd known him most of his life, the little clockmaker had been the handsomest man on the Île de la Cité, never appearing in public without a pretty woman on his arm. He was also – and remained – a craftsman of genius, with a repository of skills he'd picked up from his Polish father in Lublin and brought to Paris after the Great War.

Hélène had no doubt that her husband had been right. Even now, in his early seventies, Abel

Malinowski retained an aura that could fill any room. He was always direct, always spoke his mind, never backed down in the face of ignorance or intimidation – three reasons why Nathan had spirited him away from Paris and installed him in the chateau just days before he'd made his own exit to Lisbon.

Hélène, who'd got to know Malin well by then, had been both flattered and comforted by his company. He was an excellent houseguest with a fund of stories and cooked far better than she did. He'd also arrived with the pick of his collection of long-case clocks, a handsome Louis XV specimen in hand-crafted fruitwood bought by a wealthy aristocrat and handed down from generation to generation until the family had gone bust and Malin had arrived on the train from Paris to bid for it. The clock now sat at the foot of the stairs to the first floor and at Malin's insistence it had never been reset to Berlin time. Always an hour behind, you could hear the chimes throughout the house. Time will never be a friend of the Germans, Malin told Hélène. Exactly so.

This morning the party from Paris had arrived late, delayed by a puncture on the road south of Tours. The mare in the horsebox, a beautiful chestnut called Éclairage, with an impressive record of her own in Europe's top races, was beginning to suffer in the heat and it had taken nearly an hour to settle her down. Only then did the stable boy who was looking after her lead the mare to the cool stone granary which Malin had swept bare the previous day.

Malin had helped Hélène coax Valmy out of his stable and take him across the courtyard to serve the waiting mare. Klimt was there, too, talking to the officer from Abetz's security staff who'd travelled down from Paris. With the mare in season, the stallion had caught the scent the moment Malin opened the big wooden doors to the granary. The mare was still in the hands of the stable boy and he stood beside her head, gentling her as Valmy bucked and whinnied in the yard outside.

The coupling, as ever, looked perfunctory. The stallion mounted and – with Hélène's assistance – entered the waiting mare. Less than a minute later it was over. Klimt, who'd been present on previous occasions when Valmy performed, told Hélène that her damned horse had broken all records. He put it down to the weather. She blamed Éclairage. Show any male a body that beautiful, she said, and what do you expect?

Klimt had left within the hour, returning to Paris at the wheel of his gleaming new Mercedes. With the horsebox also gone, Malin had retreated to the cool of the big kitchen and helped himself to a tumbler of water before retiring upstairs for a nap. Now, half a day later, he was back downstairs, the potatoes peeled, nursing his second glass of wine at the long kitchen table. For once, the regular presence of Klimt at the chateau seemed to bother him. He wanted Hélène to tell him what next he might expect.

'I'm a Jew,' he reminded her. 'You want me to end up in Pithiviers?'

Pithiviers was a transit camp where the Germans held Jews before shipping them east. Pithiviers was where you started to disappear.

Hélène shook her head.

'Klimt's not interested in you,' she said. 'He's not interested in all the Jewish nonsense, either.'

'That's very comforting. But I need to know why. And while we're on the subject, how about our Spanish friends? And that sulky girl with the wireless who turned up last week? Do they matter? To your gorgeous *Oberst*?'

'Our Spanish friends' were a pair of anarchist refugees who'd fled from Franco after the civil war in Spain. Maria and Pablo had spent years living at a camp down near the Pyrenees and now they occupied a smallish room on the chateau's top floor, venturing out only for meals in the big kitchen below. They said they were married but no one knew whether it was true or not and in any case it didn't matter. As for the girl with the radio set, she was Belgian and belonged to a Resistance *réseau* from Lille. Just now she was on the run from the Germans, which gave a certain edge to Malin's question.

Hélène was trying to do something ambitious with a leg of lamb she'd had butchered in the village. She could see that Malin was serious but she didn't know how to respond. What had brought on this anxiety of his? How come a man as tempered by life as Abel Malinowski was suddenly so concerned about the permanence of their lives in the country?

'Everything's fine', she said. 'Everything's always the way it was. Since when have I let you down?'

'You've never let me down but that's not the point. The point is that no one's bigger than this fucking war. Not even you.'

'You think Klimt's going to make trouble? Is that what you're saying?'

'I'm saying what any sensible man would say. I'm saying I don't know. Which is the same as asking you for an explanation.'

'About what?'

'About Klimt.'

'You know about Klimt. We're close. It's an arrangement.'

'Of course. But you know the first rule about arrangements? They're subject to change. You tell me he lives in that apartment of yours. Nathan's apartment. In the rue de Corneille.'

'It's true. Klimt looks after it for me.'

'They call that requisitioning, don't they?'

She shook her head, trying to explain. Three long years ago the Germans had occupied Paris. The moment they'd secured the heart of the city they headed out towards the west. They knew exactly what they wanted and they knew exactly where to look. With Nathan already in London, Hélène was living alone in their apartment. The 16th *arrondissement* was an expensive area, wealthy neighbours, most of them gone. The Germans had moved from street to street, requisitioning entire buildings for senior officers. Hélène was the only owner to have stayed on in her block and she'd met Klimt beside the *loge* on the ground floor.

'And?' Malin wanted to know more.

'The lift didn't work. The power kept going off. Klimt fetched some people and fixed everything.'

'Why?'

'Because I asked him. Nicely. Firmly, if you will. That's what Germans like. Respect is a currency, Abel. It works both ways.'

'And you fucked him? That night?'

'The night after. Once we'd met properly.'

'How respectful was that?'

'On his part, very. This is a man with manners. On mine, the question is immaterial. Paris was in shock. France was in chaos. I suspect I was the first French person Klimt had met who knew how to keep her head.'

'You mean a woman?'

'I mean a person. Man? Woman? It made no difference. Back then the French were barnyard animals. There were herds of them, flocks of them, all on the road, all heading south. I'd chosen not to leave. That mattered to people like Klimt. Maybe that's what I mean by respect.'

Hélène paused. She must have had a million conversations with Abel Malinowski but she'd never let him this close. The sensation, to her surprise, was far from unpleasant.

Malin wanted to know more.

'About what?'

'About this relationship of yours. I can see what's in it for him. You're a very unusual woman. Men can smell that. We're all the same. We're animals. And I can see what's in it for you, too.'

'Really?' She wasn't smiling anymore. 'Care to tell me?'

'He gives you protection. He looks after your apartment. He makes things sweet down here in the country. He looks after you, too. That's not a bad deal if he has the right friends in the right places.'

'You make him sound like a concierge.'

'You're telling me there's more?'

'I'm telling you he's never let me down. I'm telling you there's a very large hole in my life and he fits perfectly. Why? Because he's a decent man, and he makes me laugh, and he knows a great deal about the things I think matter.'

'Such as?'

'Such as art, and music, such as half-civilised conversation, and just how ridiculous this whole thing is.'

'This whole thing?'

'The war. Hitler. The Thousand Year Reich.'

'He's not a believer?'

'Of course he isn't. So few are, once you get to know them. Their world has been taken over by gangsters but that's only something you'd say in bed, to someone you think really matters.'

'Like you.'

'Like me.'

'And Nathan?'

'Put Nathan and Klimt in the same room and they'd be brothers after the first glass. They wouldn't even need the whole bottle, Abel. Just the one glass.'

'And does Nathan know?'

'Know what?'

'About this German lover of yours?'

'Of course he does.'

'How?'

'I send him letters, through Lisbon. Ask me how. Go on, ask me.'

'Klimt makes it happen?'

'You're right. He has a channel through Lisbon. The British take care of it. They go to London in the diplomatic bag.'

This arrangement sparked a gleam in Malin's eyes. It might even have come close to approval.

'And does Klimt *read* the letters?'

'Of course he does. He's *Abwehr*. They read everything.'

'Does that bother you?'

'Not in the least.'

'And these are intimate letters? Letters between a man and his wife?'

'Extremely intimate. But unlike Klimt I have no secrets. He knows I love my husband and he has to make room for that fact. That's always been the deal. I belong to my husband. I've always belonged to my husband. And after the Germans are defeated, we'll be together again. Klimt understands that. In some ways it probably suits him. Does he strike you as a man I make unhappy?'

'Not at all. You've turned him into a puppy.'

'Far from it. That would wreck everything.'

'What then? What does this . . .' one hand drew a loose circle in the air, '. . . arrangement say about him? About your *Oberst* Klimt?'

'It makes him very clever, and quite complicated, and if you think that's exciting for a woman, you'd be correct.'

Malin nodded and fell silent for a moment, eyeing his glass. Then his head came up again. The expression on his face – quizzical, slightly confused – suggested he needed to clear something up.

'You say you both think this war is ridiculous.'

'I do.'

'Because . . .?'

'Because it's needless and stupid and brutal and not at all the way we should be with each other. Klimt goes to work every day and fights his little wars, and maybe thinks about the big war beyond the little wars, and at night when we're together we're in another space entirely. You want to guess which space, which life, is more agreeable? Or have I got this wrong?'

'I have no idea.'

'But you think it matters?'

'Of course it does. As long as you have the choice.'

'Otherwise?'

'Otherwise you're in the camp at Pithiviers, my child. Wondering what happens next.'

CHAPTER 5

Aircrew milled around in the soft drizzle at RAF Wickenby, waiting for transport to the dispersal areas. The final thing you were supposed to do was to leave your locker key with the NCO in charge in case you didn't come back. On the last twenty-nine ops Billy Angell had done the NCO's bidding but on this occasion he decided to break ranks and pocket the key. If he died in the next six hours, he'd be past caring. If he survived, there was no way a little mistake like that would matter.

He could see the line of vans approaching from the Transport Compound. As ever, Les Hammond stood slightly apart from the rest of the crew. A last cigarette spared him the torments of conversation, and he ground it beneath his flying boot as the WAAF driver brought the first of the vans to a halt on the wet tarmac.

V-Victor was parked up on the northern edge of the airfield beside a tall line of poplars. Hammond's crew got out of the van. Billy had been handed a packet of sandwiches by one of the girls in the mess but he hated fish paste and tossed the sandwiches to one of the ground crew before clambering up the ladder and getting himself into the aircraft that towered above them.

Movement inside the fuselage was a nightmare. Parcelled up in his flying suit, fleece-lined boots and heavy leather jacket, Billy groped his way forward, barking his shins on the cold metal of the main spar, and then settled himself at his wireless desk. He was sweating already and he knew that once the props were turning it would get worse. The heating ducts were right beside his desk. Airborne, especially at altitude, every Lancaster crew was the same: six frozen bodies plus a super-heated Wireless Op.

Billy plugged himself into the intercom and tested the system. Hammond, forward in the cockpit, grunted an acknowledgement. Moments later, the port outer coughed and caught, followed by the other three engines. The thunder of the props settled down and then, with a burst of throttle, the aircraft began to move. The rain was suddenly heavier, drumming on the fuselage above Billy's head.

He carefully stored his caffeine tablets, chocolate bars and orange juice. The latter could become a hazard if Hammond was forced to corkscrew to avoid flak, as could the empty screw-top bottle Billy always used if he needed to take a piss. In the early days with the old crew he'd filled the bottle but forgotten to secure it properly, a mistake he'd never make again.

The aircraft was rumbling around the perimeter track now, part of an ever-lengthening queue of Lancasters, and the Nav was confirming the heading they'd need for the climb-out after take-off. The Germans routinely monitored all operational radio frequencies for early clues about impending raids and so at this launch stage Flying Control communicated by means of lights. A green light from Control cleared you for take-off. A red one, for whatever reason, signalled a scrub.

Was Les Hammond praying for a scarlet Very flare to soar into the darkness? Was he waiting for the moment when dozens of Lancs throttled back and returned to their dispersal pans? Was he dreaming of a warm bed and the certain knowledge that he'd see the sun rise again? Billy didn't know, couldn't even hazard a guess, but as he checked again through the window at his elbow he saw the flash of green from control and felt the slow press of acceleration as Hammond released the brakes against the roaring props.

It took nearly a mile, always tugging to the left, for the Lanc to unstick. Then came the moment when the tail lifted and the blur of gooseneck runway flares gave way to darkness as the bomber lumbered into the air. Climbing slowly, still at maximum power, V-Victor entered cloud minutes later and the view from Billy's window offered nothing but the fiery red glow of the port engine exhausts.

At 9,000 feet, without warning, they burst

through the last of the cloud and emerged into a starlit night. Billy had been tuning in to the first of the half-hourly radio transmissions from Group Headquarters in case of a change of target or a last-minute scrub but there was no indication of either. Just the string of Morse 'V's – *dit dit dit dah* – that told the bomber stream to maintain the briefed heading.

Billy struggled to his feet. Above him was the astrodome. He wedged his head against the cold Perspex and took a look round. It was a beautiful night. The bomber stream stretched around him in every direction, hundreds of heavy black Lancasters hanging in the darkness above the rumpled grey eiderdown of cloud. According to the Nav, they'd left the English coast over Mablethorpe. Ahead lay a 230-mile transit across the North Sea before they hit the Dutch coast.

The bomber stream was still climbing. At 10,000 feet, Hammond ordered the crew to go onto oxygen. Billy, back at his desk, was noting down a transmission from Group detailing the frequency currently being used by Luftwaffe night fighters operating out of airfields on the Dutch/German border. In an hour, as they approached the coast, it would be his job to tune his transmitter to this frequency, and then return to the astrodome to play sentry. With luck, he'd be able to jam the night fighter transmissions and throw them off the scent.

It worked. As the Nav calculated their track,

confirming the coast beneath the thinning layer of cloud, the sky remained empty of enemy fighters. Billy, still in the astrodome, was desperately resisting the impulse to fart. At this height, 20,000 feet, the reduction in air pressure played havoc with your guts and he was beginning to regret the second helping of cauliflower cheese when he saw the first nest of searchlights lying in wait maybe sixty miles ahead. We're running out of cloud, he thought. Exactly as the Met man had predicted.

Minutes later he was groping his way back down the fuselage to help the Flt Engineer shovel handfuls of Window into the chute at the rear of the aircraft. This stuff was new to the bomber crews but the boffins swore that the little strips of aluminium would cascade down through the night, playing havoc with the enemy radar screens below. With the slipstream blasting up through the chute, the temperature had plunged way below zero and once the strips had gone Billy was glad to get back to the warmth of his desk. So far, so good.

He tuned to Group again to catch their latest transmission and stole a glance through the window. He could see the glitter of ice on the port wing and the looming silhouette of another aircraft beyond. The bomber stream appeared to have changed course to dog-leg around the searchlights, for which Billy was grateful. Give it another hour, he thought, and we might be on our way home.

Hammond reported a glow on the horizon minutes later. The first wave had already bombed and Chopburg was on fire. The Flight Engineer, perched in the cockpit beside Hammond, had a grandstand seat. He was a Yorkshireman, blunt to a fault, and he never bothered to hide his views on area bombing. Billy heard the click on the intercom as he opened his microphone.

'It's a right bonfire,' he said. 'The bastards had it coming.'

Hammond was on next, reporting heavy flak and a picket line of searchlights. This close to the target, the bomber stream was committed to a straight run-in but Billy could detect no flutter of nervousness in his voice. Good, he thought. Maybe the skipper's finally got a grip.

Minutes ticked by with occasional updates from Hammond in the cockpit. Then came a burst of static in Billy's headphones before the Rear Gunner reported night fighters climbing to meet them.

'Two of them, Skip. Your seven o'clock. Maybe a thousand feet below.'

Hammond grunted in acknowledgement and then told Billy to get back in the astrodome. Another pair of eyes on a night this clear could make the difference between life and death. Billy struggled to his feet again. The sweat beneath his flying suit quickly cooled once he'd left the furnace of the desk. Back in the astrodome he hunted in vain for the incoming night fighters. They're below us, he thought. Lurking with intent.

'One's coming at us, Skip. Astern and below.' The Rear Gunner again.

Billy heard the chatter of the .303 machine guns as the gunner hosed bullets into the night. Of late, the German fighter pilots had been working on a new tactic, stationing themselves below the target, using a remote cannon mounted in the fuselage to blast shells vertically upwards. This way they could target the bomb bay with consequences Billy shuddered to contemplate. The biggest of tonight's payload was a two-ton 'cookie' that could flatten half a street. At least it would be quick.

Hammond wanted an update on the fighter.

'Broken off, Skip. I think he's gone.'

'And the other one?'

'Can't see him.'

The Rear Gunner, a soft-spoken infant from Northern Ireland, never betrayed an ounce of emotion. Like Johnny Phelps in Billy's last crew, he seemed to have no fear. Billy knew how hard it was to pull off a trick like this. Once they started to approach the target, everyone was frightened. All the time.

Billy thought, quite suddenly, of his dead father, the way it must have been in the trenches, awaiting the blast of the whistle. The men poised to scale the ladders, ready to surge into no man's land. The hurricane of enemy machine-gun fire that awaited them. And the dad he'd never met battling onwards, only to fall.

V-Victor was close now. In a couple of minutes the Bomb Aimer would take control, flat on his belly in the aircraft's nose, calling tiny course corrections to Hammond as the Lancaster headed for the red glow of the target indicators. The bomber stream had tightened formation. Angels of death, Billy thought. No way back.

Billy struggled down to his desk. A small hatch at his feet opened directly into the bomb bay. After the Bomb Aimer pressed the release it was Billy's job to check that the ordnance had gone. Normally he didn't bother with the hatch because the big cookie fell nose first and the tail always clunked against the floor of the fuselage, but on this occasion he'd decided to do it by the book. God willing, he might never get to perform this action again. Chopburg, he told himself, would be a sight to cherish for the rest of his life.

The flak was evil now, streams of golden tracer climbing faster and faster to tear them to pieces while the searchlights stabbed at target after target. Billy, dry-mouthed, watched a Lanc off to port caught by the master beam. Within seconds, the aircraft was coned, pinned like a giant black insect by at least three searchlights. Then came the puffs of dirty grey smoke as the flak shells exploded around her. Committed to the bombing run, the pilot held his nerve until a huge chunk of the starboard wing cartwheeled into the darkness. First one engine caught fire, then another, and seconds later the aircraft erupted as a flak shell burst beneath the half-open bomb bay. V-Victor bucked in the violence of the explosion. Thrown backwards in his chair, Billy prayed that the master beam might linger for a second or two on the remains of the Lancaster. Not us next. Please God, not us.

By now, Hammond had wrestled V-Victor back on track for the beckoning target indicators. The Bomb Aimer was talking Hammond in.

'Steady . . . steady . . . that's nice. That's good.'

'OK?'

'Perfect . . . bomb doors open . . .'

'Roger that.'

'Steady . . . right a bit . . . right . . . right . . . steady . . . bombs gone . . .'

V-Victor leapt upwards as six tons of high explosive left the aircraft. On his knees beside the desk, Billy tugged the hatch open. The blast of icy night air took his breath away. As did the sight below.

It was like looking into the mouth of a volcano. The firestorm must have been several miles from edge to edge, deep reds and yellows and thick coils of smoke inset with tiny twinkling diamonds as yet more bombs added to the misery that had once been Chopburg. With his eyes half closed against the roaring slipstream, Billy told himself he could feel the heat, smell the charring timbers. He and his mates had turned the city into a furnace. From 20,000 feet this was a place you could warm your hands on. Hell, he thought, was too small a word.

He shut the hatch and confirmed bombs gone. The Bomb Aimer had taken his impact shots for the Intel debrief and Hammond had pulled the aircraft into a tight starboard turn when the master beam finally caught them.

'Shit . . .' Hammond was a man who never cursed.

Billy shut his eyes. There was nothing he could do now, no transmissions he could make, no warnings he could yell from his perch in the astrodome. They were in the hands of God and the flak gunners below. If it happens, he told himself, let it be swift.

Hammond had wrenched the Lanc into the tightest corkscrew dive Billy could remember. His entire face beneath the oxygen mask seemed to be squeezing sideways. He tried to fight the force of the turn, pushing hard against the fuselage, but it was hopeless. Through the window, when he dared look, he could see nothing but a blinding white light suffused with blue. His eyes hurt. His lungs hurt. Everything hurt. How could a man fly an aircraft under pressures like these? How could he keep control? Remember where the turn had taken him? Try and find somewhere to hide? Pilots back in the Mess were right to say that sometimes the sky can be the smallest place in the world. And here was the living proof.

The flak gunners had the range. A shell burst aft with a red-hot spray of shrapnel and the aircraft was suddenly full of coiling smoke from the explosion. It must have taken out a lump of the fuselage because the roar of the engines was suddenly much louder and there was another noise, too. It was high-pitched, an animal scream of pain, and it took Billy – still dazed – a second or two to realise it must be the Rear Gunner.

He fought his way back down the fuselage as the force of the turn slackened. The Elsan toilet had taken a direct hit. He could smell shit in the freezing air, laced with cordite from the shell, and when he finally made it to the Rear Gunner he knew it was too late. A huge chunk of shrapnel had torn through the revolving turret and taken off one of his legs. Blood was pouring from the severed artery and Billy could see the jagged whiteness of what remained of his thighbone. The rest of him was a shape in the darkness, a flying jacket hunched over the machine gun. Billy reached out and gave him a shake, then another, screaming his name, but nothing happened. As he watched, appalled, the pumping flood of blood from the artery started to slacken, then stopped completely. On the intercom, Hammond was calling for news but Billy couldn't find the words. Gone, he thought.

Abruptly, the master beam left them. Hammond pulled the aircraft out of the dive and Billy fought again for balance as the airframe groaned around him. Back at straight and level, Hammond was calling for a heading.

'Fly two three zero, Skip.'

Billy hadn't a clue where they were. He'd lost all sense of time. All he could think about was the whiteness of the Rear Gunner's bone in the roaring darkness. He began to claw his way back towards the front of the aircraft. Then came another huge explosion and V-Victor reared like a horse before settling down again. This time it was the Nav on the intercom.

'The Skipper,' he yelled.

Billy had made it back to his desk. The Nav was on his feet, fighting a blast of icy air. Then he caught sight of Billy.

'Flak on the nose,' he said. 'I thought the skip was a goner but I'm not sure. Check him out.'

He gestured up towards the cockpit and then stood aside as Billy squeezed past. The whole crew were casualty-trained but only Billy had done the advanced course.

The first aid box was stowed behind the Flt Engineer's seat. The Engineer himself had engaged the autopilot and was now trying to wrestle Hammond out of his seat but Hammond, it seemed, had other ideas. What Billy could see of his face was a mask of blood. Two of the Perspex panels in the cockpit's windscreen had been shattered in the explosion and Hammond was trying to protect his head from the numbing blast of icy air.

Billy gestured to the Flt Engineer to get out of his seat. The aircraft appeared to still be intact. Billy knelt beside Hammond and extracted a wad of thick gauze from the first aid box. He wiped away most of the blood. Dozens of fragments of Perspex had torn into Hammond's face but the damage seemed to be superficial. The real problem was going to be his eyes.

Billy opened the intercom.

'Can you hear me, Skip? Just nod.'

Hammond nodded, raising a single gloved thumb.

'What about your eyes?'

The thumb again, and then a halting confirmation on the intercom.

'I can see. Just about.'

'How well?'

'Well enough.'

'Well enough to get us home?'

A nod this time but nothing on the intercom.

Billy stared at him for a moment. All he knew was that salvation, if it ever happened, would mean losing as much altitude as possible. The lower they flew, the less cold it would be.

'My goggles.' It was Hammond again, his voice barely a whisper. He was making a downward gesture with his right hand. Billy fumbled on the floor of the cockpit between the two seats. Almost immediately, he found a shape in the darkness. Hammond's goggles. Like most pilots he preferred to fly without them. Now he had no choice.

Billy fitted them gently around his head. The Perspex wounds were beginning to weep but the intense cold had sealed most of the damaged blood vessels. Every cloud, Billy thought grimly.

Hammond was reaching for the control column. Then, very slowly, he disengaged the automatic pilot and began to fly the aircraft again. Billy felt a tap on his shoulder. It was the Nav. He was nodding back towards the escape hatch, one eyebrow raised. The question was no less obvious for being mute. Was now the time to bail out?

Billy didn't want to, though he wasn't sure about the Nav. When he looked at the Flight Engineer, all he got was a blank shrug. The man was deep in shock and Billy realised for the first time that there was blood trickling down his face, too. We're all going to die from hypothermia, Billy thought, unless we get this aircraft lower.

He turned back to Hammond.

'What do you think, Skip? We jump or press on?'

'Press on.'

'Then we need to go down.'

'You're right.' He glanced up, then managed a wink. 'I might leave the landing to you, Billy. God help us, eh?'

CHAPTER 6

élène awoke in the darkness. Something had disturbed her but she didn't know what. The storm had broken over the chateau before midnight, long drum rolls of thunder creeping down from Tours, then a sudden wind that stirred the elms beyond the terrace followed by torrential rain. She'd dreamed of a waterfall in the high Alps, a memory from the days in her youth when her father had taken her skiing, and she thought she could still hear cow bells when she lay in the darkness, the rain and the thunder gone.

The noise again. A voice, definitely. A woman's voice. From the room next door. Agnès, she thought. Fat little Agnès with the staring eyes and the skin problem and the neat little transmitter she hid in her bag beneath a tired assortment of underwear. She'd arrived last week on the back of an ancient motorbike. Her driver, whom she'd never introduced, had given Hélène an envelope before clattering off in a cloud of dust, refusing even a glass of water.

The note was unsigned but Hélène had recognised the loopy script and the line of kisses at the end. Evangelina had been her husband's assistant at the first of his galleries. She was Italian, small and squat, a female version of Nathan, and what had sealed the bond between them was her passion for a man called Carlo Rosselli.

Rosselli was an anti-Fascist intellectual who had made his home in Paris after fleeing death threats in his native Rome. His various schemes to assassinate Mussolini had put a sizeable price on his head, and to Evangelina's distress his life had ended on a sunny day in 1937 beside a country road in Normandy. He'd been stabbed twice and shot.

Evangelina had never met Rosselli, never even laid eyes on him. But the man's fervour had won her heart and the year after his murder the football World Cup had come to France. By now, Evangelina was working for Nathan Khorrami, who adored her. He'd bought two tickets for the quarter-final between France and Italy, and when they returned from the stadium to the apartment Nathan was sharing with Hélène, Evangelina was still in tears. France, her adopted country, had been beaten by a bunch of thugs thinly disguised as Italians. Worse still, they'd disgraced her homeland by giving the Fascist salute throughout the singing of the national anthem. On both counts, she was unforgiving. One day, she promised, would come the reckoning.

Lying in the darkness, listening to Agnès, Hélène remembered the last time she'd seen Evangelina in the flesh. It was the morning Nathan was leaving Paris. He'd just seen his best pictures, securely crated, depart on the back of a lorry for Lisbon. He was to follow by train. Evangelina had come round to the apartment to say goodbye. Expecting more tears, Hélène was surprised to find her in the sunniest of moods. The Germans were a day away from Paris. Already Evangelina had made contact with what would soon become a sizeable resistance group. These people were young, like her. They despised the Fascists. They wanted to chase them out of France, out of Italy. They had faith in the working class. They wanted to use this terrible moment to start building a world you could be proud to live in.

About the small print, she was vague. But it was Nathan, minutes away from the arrival of the taxi that was to take him to the Gare d'Austerlitz, who'd pressed a thick white envelope into her hands, enfolded her in a bear hug and wished her luck. The envelope contained a million francs: a down payment, he later wrote to Hélène, on the dream world Evangelina so desperately wanted to make happen.

Since then, nothing. Until Agnès arrived, bumping up the road from the village with her single bag and her handwritten note. *Agnès is one of the bravest women I know*, Evangelina had written. *Like Carlo, she carries a price on her head. Please look after her. Please treat her like a child of your own.*

Hélène swung out of bed and reached for her dressing gown. So far, she'd yet to warm to this latest houseguest. The girl seemed withdrawn and somehow resentful. She resisted any kind of conversation. And the moment she'd lifted her head from a book in the kitchen to see *Oberst* Klimt emerging from his Mercedes, she'd disappeared upstairs, never to reappear. Malin, who'd taken her food, reported a blizzard of questions. Who was this man? What was he doing at the chateau? Who'd invited him? And why?

Now Hélène stood in the corridor, listening at the door to Agnès' bedroom. Whatever she'd been up to with the radio appeared to have stopped. Hélène knocked twice and stepped inside. Agnès was in bed, carefully returning the transmitter to its wooden box. On her arrival, in the absence of any other house rules, Hélène had made one stipulation. No radio transmissions. Why? Because the Germans had detector vans that would bring armed troops to her door and, under those circumstances, with a fugitive as wanted as Agnès upstairs, not even *Oberst* Klimt would be able to offer protection.

'I thought I told you not to use that thing?' Hélène nodded at the box.

'That's right. You did.'

'So why do it? Why put us all at risk?'

Agnès wouldn't answer. Just ducked her head and plaited her stubby fingers in her lap. Bitten nails, one of them varnished black.

'Are you going to answer me? Or am I going to take it away?' This was like talking to a child. Hopeless.

Hélène waited for an answer. When none came

61

she began to go through it all again. How she was welcome to stay. Why she must resist the temptation to use the transmitter. And what might happen if she did.

At length, her head came up again, her face expressionless. She wasn't angry. She wasn't contrite. Not a word of apology.

'That lovely old man . . .' she said at last.

'Malinowski?'

'Yes. He said it's your birthday tomorrow. Is he right?'

Hélène hesitated. She had no idea where this conversation was leading. Finally she nodded.

'Yes', she said. 'And I'll be forty, if that's your next question.'

Agnès was studying her hands again. Then she nodded at the radio.

'You want to know who I've been talking to?'

'Not really.'

'People in London.'

'I see.'

'Don't you want to know why?'

'Tell me.'

'Because one of them knows your husband. Evangelina gave me the contact. I thought you might like to talk to him. On your birthday.' At last she looked Hélène in the eye. 'Unless there's someone else in your life.'

V-Victor crossed the Dutch coast at 400 feet. Still over Germany, Hammond had nursed the aircraft down to virtually ground level in a bid to raise the temperature and avoid the awaiting night fighters. A longish detour had taken them around the searchlights and flak batteries defending Wilhelmshaven and Billy had remained at Hammond's side, lifting his goggles and sponging his eyes from time to time to maintain what vision he had left. He removed his gloves to be as accurate as he could with the dampened cotton wool and Hammond's flesh was icy to the touch. Mercifully, expecting stragglers from the returning bomber stream at a far higher altitude, the night fighters had never found them.

The Nav, who was clearly unhappy about their chances of surviving a landing, had twice suggested they bail out as close to the English coast as possible. Les Hammond wouldn't hear of it. His job, he quietly insisted, was to get them all home in one piece and that remained his intention. The least he owed the Rear Gunner was a burial on British soil.

Billy, when he stopped thinking about the cold, was deeply impressed. He had no interest in jumping into an early dawn and hoping to God that an air/sea rescue launch would turn up. Nor, he kept telling himself, would he ever get into an aircraft again. Survive this last op, feel the steel rungs of the exit ladder beneath his frozen fingers and he'd move heaven and earth to turn his back on flying of any description. Six long hours ago, he'd had real doubts about his skipper ever making it through. Instead it was he, Wireless Operator Billy Angell, whose nerve had finally gone.

'Coast ahead, Skip. It has to be Mablethorpe.'

The Nav was right. Mablethorpe on the nose. In the grey light of dawn, the beach and a line of houses on the low cliff were approaching fast. V-Victor swept over the thin white line of breaking surf and Billy glimpsed barbed wire and beach obstacles before the blur of rooftops filled what was left of the windscreen. Billy checked one last time with Hammond. They had twenty minutes to run. He needed to get back to his radio and request an emergency landing.

Hammond shot him a glance. He'd long abandoned his oxygen mask and mouthed a thank-you. Then his gloved hands flexed on the control yolk and he pulled hard to gain the altitude he needed for a safe approach.

Back at the radio desk, using the Morse key, Billy raised Control at Wickenby. One dead. Two wounded. When the WAAF asked about the state of the aircraft he tapped back and said it was serviceable.

'No damage?'

'Lots. A windscreen would have been useful.'

Billy waited for a response but none came. V-Victor was at 2,000 feet now and dangerously low on fuel. Flying so low had been emptying the tanks at an alarming rate and Hammond knew he needed to get the aircraft down on the first attempt. Otherwise the last three hours would have been for nothing.

Billy abandoned his desk and wedged himself in the cockpit behind Hammond. He felt an inexplicable pride at what this man had proved to himself and if it all went wrong on landing then he wanted to be able to be there with him before they piled in.

He needn't have worried. Hammond nursed V-Victor down the glide path, selecting full flap as they wallowed over the fields of wheat that led to the familiar triangle of runways. The Sonia lights offered a welcome-home tent over the airfield and the gooseneck flares receded into the misty dawn. Billy could just make out a couple of fire tenders and an ambulance parked at the far end of the runway and he was aware of other aircraft in the circuit, awaiting their turn to land.

Half a mile to run. Juggling the throttles with his right hand, Hammond cheated the crosswind by crabbing the aircraft towards the perimeter fence, only kicking it straight with a bootful of rudder at the very last moment. Watching, Billy shut his eyes. Then he felt the first impact, absurdly gentle, as V-Victor settled on the racing tarmac.

At the end of the runway was a dispersal point for emergencies like these. Hammond brought the aircraft to a halt and then shut down the engines one by one. The sudden silence was overwhelming. The Nav was the first to peel off his gloves and clap.

'Outstanding,' he said. 'Thank Christ we didn't jump.

PART II

CHAPTER 7

It took several days to analyse the photographs from Operation Gomorrah. Bomber Command and the US Eighth Air Force revisited Hamburg and by the end of the week the consensus was clear. Whole areas of the city had been blown apart by high explosive and then drenched with incendiaries. The resulting firestorm had raged all night. Wireless intercepts described hundreds of yards of asphalted roads melting and then catching fire. The canals, coated with burning oil, proved death-traps. The surrounding countryside was full of refugees, leaving unknown numbers of incinerated bodies under millions of tons of still-smoking rubble. There was no certainty about the final death toll but it had to be close to 40,000. In short, thought Billy numbly, a real success.

He was on the stopping train from Paddington to Bristol. He was wearing RAF uniform and carrying a standard-issue kitbag. Before him lay the unimaginable luxury of a bedroom of his own and two solid weeks of uninterrupted peace. No cities to lay waste to. No master beams and night fighters to dodge. None of the gut-wrenching terror he'd experienced over Hamburg.

He got off the train at Bath. His mother, on the telephone, had told him to look out for a black Humber Super Snipe. It was, she said with a hint of pride, brand new. Billy joined the flood of passengers on the stairs down to street level. The whole world seemed to be in uniform. Emerging from the station entrance he spotted the Humber at once. There was someone behind the wheel he didn't recognise but his mother was standing beside the gleaming bonnet, a slightly uncertain figure in a long mauve summer dress that came as another surprise. He waved to her as he crossed the car park and she answered with a tiny flutter of her hand.

'Mum . . .' He put his arms round her and then gave her a kiss. She'd never been this thin. She also smelled different. Someone else. Almost a stranger.

Billy was looking beyond her, into the car. The man behind the wheel wouldn't meet his gaze. He looked much older than his mother. He was thickset with heavy black glasses and Brilliantined hair and he must have been hot in the grey pin-stripe suit because he had the window wound down.

Billy had been able to buy a bunch of flowers at Paddington Station. They looked a couple of days past their best – probably the heat – but he didn't think that mattered. He took a tiny step backwards and then, with a stage curtsey, presented his mother with the flowers.

Billy couldn't remember a time when she didn't love roses, especially red roses, but now she seemed embarrassed. She held them at arm's length, as if they might be infectious.

'You're mad,' she said, 'spending all that money. They must have cost the earth.'

'Everything costs the earth, Mum. I just thought . . . .'

'They're lovely. There's something I've got to tell you, something you need to know.' She nodded back towards the car. 'There's been a bit of a change around. I've been meaning to tell you.'

'Change around how?'

'I got married again. Last week. I know it's all a bit sudden but I'm really hoping you're going to like him. His name's Ralph. He's very nice, very kind.'

'And this is his car?'

'Yes. And it doesn't stop there. We're living out in the country. It's a lovely place. Wonderful views. It's got chickens, too. You can have as many eggs as you want. There . . .' she patted him on the arm and stepped aside, '. . . I knew you'd be pleased.'

They drove out of the station. Billy knew at once that this son of his new bride was the last person Ralph wanted to see. Billy perched himself on the big back seat, trying to make conversation. His mother's new world smelled of leather upholstery and cigar smoke. A bag from Jolly's, the posh Bath department store, lay at his feet.

The suburbs of the city sped by. Very little bomb damage, not at all like Chopburg. In fact, if you half closed your eyes, this wasn't an England at war at all.

Billy had always known his mum as Val. That's what everyone had always called her. In six brief months, since he'd last seen her, she seemed to have become Valerie. No warning. No mention of anything new in her life in the two letters she'd managed to write. Did that mean she was in some way ashamed of what had happened? Or was there a simpler explanation?

'You kept it very quiet, Mum. Any particular reason?'

'My fault, I'm afraid.' Ralph had a Midlands accent. 'My previous wife finds it exceptionally easy to take offence. The divorce, to be frank, was extremely difficult. We thought it best to keep the wedding to ourselves.'

Billy's mother half turned in the front passenger seat. She was doing her best to jolly the conversation along, to make her only son feel welcome in the bosom of his new family.

'We've got five spare bedrooms,' she said. 'You can take your pick.'

'I thought we agreed on the room at the back, Valerie?' Ralph shot her a look.

'Yes, but . . .' she shrugged, '. . . nothing, really.'

★   ★   ★

72

Blessington Manor lay among the rolling hills south of the city. The big wrought-iron gates on the road below the estate were already open and the drive wound up between stands of elm. The house itself was no more than a glimpse of pillars and white stucco in the distance. This was a long way from the terrace in the Bristol suburbs where Billy had grown up.

Billy wondered where this new stepfather of his had found the money and saw no point in hiding his curiosity.

'What line are you in, Ralph? You mind me asking?'

'Not at all.'

Billy caught the brief tightening of lips in the rear-view mirror. This was clearly a man who disliked direct questions. His new wife came to the rescue.

'Ralph has factories in West Bromwich,' she said.

'Making what?'

'Things for the war. Things we need to beat the Germans.'

'Like?'

'Military vehicles.' This from Ralph. 'Trucks. Ambulances. We're not small.'

'So how did you meet? You two?'

'Meet? Us? I suspect that's for your mother to explain.'

Billy cornered his mother an hour later in the kitchen. Val had domestic help, a fat old cook with narrow eyes and a double chin, someone she appeared to have inherited from Ralph's previous life. Val hadn't a clue how to cope with this situation and it showed. For the first time, Billy was starting to feel sorry for her.

'So what happened, Mum?' He'd taken her into a big panelled room that served as a library.

Val shook her head. She didn't want to talk about it. Not here. Not yet. Instead she wanted to know about Billy's war, about his new friends, about all the adventures he must have had. Billy winced at the nervous torrent of questions. He might have stepped in from a day at school.

'It was horrible, Mum. I was lucky to get out alive. That's all you need to know.'

'Horrible?'

'Worse. Tell me about Ralph. Or I'll ask him myself.'

'You can't. He's got an office upstairs where he shuts himself away. He's a man who works day and night, bless him. He tells me he's doing it for the war effort, for all of us, and I believe him. Without men like Ralph we'd be on our knees.'

'Who told you that?'

She wouldn't answer. Instead she just said that she wanted them all to be friends.

'Does he have kids of his own?'

'Three.'

'Have you met them?'

'No.'

'Why not?'

'She won't let them near me, his ex-wife. Two boys and a girl. One's nearly grown up. The others are still at school. She lives near Birmingham. She obviously hates me. She thinks what's happened is all my fault.'

'And is it?'

'No. Not at all. It takes two, Billy. Always. We met through Uncle Albert. He made the running, believe it or not.'

'You mean Uncle Bert?'

'I meant Ralph. He was looking for a personal secretary. Someone with the right skills. Someone he could depend on. That someone was your old mum.'

Billy nodded. It was slowly becoming clearer. Uncle Albert wasn't a real uncle at all. He owned hundreds of acres of Somerset apple orchards and had interests in the cider business. He'd been a friend of the family since before Billy could remember, something to do with the father he'd never known, and he'd been happy to play pretend dad to Billy when the occasion demanded. Billy always suspected Uncle Albert, who was single, had more than a passing interest in his mum and he'd certainly given them money when times were tough.

'So Uncle Bert knew Ralph already? Is that how it happened?'

'Yes. They're masons, Billy. I don't know whether you knew that. The masons are behind everything.'

'But you love him? Ralph?'

'I do, yes. He's much softer than he looks. I don't think he had much love before. It's hard to open men like that up. Your father was the same. I don't know whether it's shyness or maybe something terrible happened to them but they need a woman's touch.'

'Your touch.'

'Yes, Billy.' She looked him in the eye. 'My touch.'

Billy didn't know what to say. Was he the trespasser in this new relationship? Was he some kind of threat?

His mum wanted to know how long he'd be staying. Not because he wasn't welcome but just so she could get things straight in her head.

'Is that a question Ralph wanted you to ask?'

'Of course not. What a silly idea.'

She shook her head, tried to deny it, but her eyes were shiny with tears. Billy was about to say that it wouldn't be a problem, that he could find a million other ways of spending his next two weeks, when his mum put a hand on his arm.

'Ralph said something else, Billy. He wants you to be happy. He wants you to enjoy yourself now you've got this chance. He's got a place down in Devon. It's nice, really nice, not big like here. It's down by the water. It's cosy. You can have it until you have to go back. And he's got a little present, too. So you can give yourself a bit of a treat. That's him saying that, not me. Here . . .'

She stepped across to the biggest of the bookshelves and extracted a copy of *Bleak House*. Inside the front cover was a manila envelope. She gave it to Billy.

'Go on. Open it.'

Billy did her bidding. Inside was a fold of £1 notes. He counted them. Fifty quid. A fortune.

'Think of it as a wedding present, Billy. From both of us.' Val had found a handkerchief from somewhere. She blew her nose. 'You remember Nell? Irene's little friend?'

'Of course I do.'

'I got in touch with her yesterday once I knew you were coming. She'd like to go, too.'

'Go where?'

'To Devon.' She managed a smile. 'Where else?'

CHAPTER 8

Hélène wanted to take the radio and ride Valmy deep into the forest. She asked Agnès to come too, enquired with extreme politeness whether she didn't want to make the best of the still-glorious weather while it lasted, but Agnès had no taste for her company and saw through the invitation at once.

'You want me to work the transmitter,' she said. 'From somewhere safe.'

As it happened Agnès was right and Hélène told herself never to underestimate this woman. She'd been through a very great deal, that much was obvious, and she had no patience with Hélène's brand of lofty subterfuge. And so Hélène, slightly chastened, submitted to a brief lesson in how this thing worked. Fit the valves. Tune in to the desired frequency. And then transmit the message.

The message, as she expected, had to be in Morse code. Worse still, it was wise to limit the transmission to an absolute maximum of three minutes. Longer than that and you were inviting trouble. Even in the depths of the forest.

And so Hélène spent an hour in the morning

refining the birthday message she wanted to send to Nathan, her husband. Her skills in Morse code were non-existent and so the message had to be briefer than she'd have liked. Also, it had to be something distinctive, something original, something that would remind him of the times they'd spent together and the promise of the times to come. Nothing domestic. Nothing banal. I want to excite this man of mine, she told herself. I want him to want me.

She saddled up and led Valmy out of the courtyard. The transmitter had been slightly heavier than she'd expected. It was housed in a grey plywood box with a rusting metal clasp and she'd had to send Malin into the cellar to find the ancient game bag that had belonged to the chateau's previous owner. The transmitter was powered by a battery, itself surprisingly heavy, but there was room in the game bag for both.

Hélène urged Valmy into a canter. The horse had been bright this morning when she'd walked it round the courtyard, visibly enjoying itself, and she'd put this post-coital little dance down to the events of yesterday. After the oppressive heat, there was also a hint of freshness in the air and when the canter became a gallop she pressed herself low as she raced the stallion down the beaten path that led to the forest. After a kilometre or so, with the treeline looming ahead, a hare broke cover in front of them and zigzagged away towards a field of beets, but Valmy paid it no attention. Good boy,

Hélène thought, feeling the weight of the battery and the awkward edges of the transmitter's wooden box thumping against her back.

By the standards of other estates in the area, la Forêt de Neaune wasn't large. On the particulars of sale furnished by the *notaire* in Tours, it measured thirty-three hectares, but Nathan, after a day spent beneath the big old oaks, had apparently regarded the figure as an underestimate. What had especially attracted him, and brought negotiations to a rapid conclusion, was the lake at the very heart of the forest. He'd dubbed it l'Étang Mustafa in his wife's honour, and it said a very great deal about this marriage of theirs that she didn't set eyes on either the chateau or his precious lake until all the paperwork had been signed. When she'd taxed him about this, inquiring whether her own judgement might have played a useful role in the purchase, he'd gathered her in his arms and kissed her lightly on the lips. What kind of present doesn't come as a surprise, he'd asked her. And that was that.

Nathan had been right, of course. The forest had been the perfect complement for the chateau, somewhere deeply private she could make her own, and after the first year of living down here she couldn't imagine her life without it. Now, reining Valmy in to a modest trot, Hélène let the stallion find its own way down through the trees towards the lake. They came here often, normally in the cool of the early morning, and Valmy liked to drink from the lake. At first Hélène had been nervous of colic or something worse, but the water – a rich greeny-brown – seemed clean enough and the horse had never come to any harm.

The *étang* lay before them as the land fell away, bright splinters of sunshine through the screen of trees. The previous owner had built a wooden jetty at the toe of the path that wound down to the water's edge. The ancient punt that went with it had long since been submerged beneath the rain and the weather but the jetty, though wobbly and uncertain underfoot, was still capable of holding her weight.

She dismounted by the tiny crescent of muddy beach and held Valmy's reins while the horse splashed in and dipped its long neck to the water. Afterwards, as always, she harnessed the stallion to a nearby tree.

Unpacking the game bag, she settled in the shadow of the big oak. By this time in the afternoon the wind had died and she sat with her back to the broadness of the tree trunk, watching for the tiny ripples of fish rising to snatch insects. The warmth around her was full of movement – butterflies, bees, the occasional dragonfly – and she'd come to love these moments of solitude. The lake attracted a variety of ducks – mallards especially – but her favourites were a family of coots, tiny shy creatures that lived deep in the rushes beyond the pier. Coots, she'd once been told, mated for life and on the rare occasions they made an appearance she always cursed herself for not bringing the remains of the previous day's loaf. Back at the start of the summer they'd swum in a stately little line, the father and the mother with three tiny chicks bobbing in their wake, but it was a while since she'd last seen them.

Hélène lifted the lid of the transmitter box. A flock of pigeons exploded from the trees behind her and flew out over the lake. Curious to know what might have disturbed them, she half twisted, shading her eyes against the glare of the sun through the branches, but she couldn't see anything. She knew that men from the village hunted here, mainly with traps, but that usually took place at night. In the early days she'd put the word out around the village that she'd employ a gamekeeper if it didn't stop but as times got harder she saw no harm in allowing the odd poacher a rabbit or a hare for his pot.

Agnès, with a patience that had taken Hélène by surprise, had explained the workings of the transmitter. It was called a Paraset. First you inserted the three black valves. Then the aerial. Finally, you connected the battery and used the big dial to tune to whichever frequency you needed. She'd written down the frequency that would take her to her husband.

Hélène slipped on the headphones. Nothing. She stared at the radio, then checked her watch. Twenty-five past four. In five minutes' time she was due to transmit. Nathan, beside the radio operator at the other end, would be waiting. She had Agnès' word on that. He'd been alerted days ago, via an intelligence contact in London, the moment Malin had told her about Hélène's birthday. Hélène pictured him now, sitting beside the receiving equipment, waiting for her to come through. Except she was kneeling under a tree in the middle of rural France trying to fathom why the damned transmitter wasn't working.

She went through the sequence again – valves, aerial, battery. Again, nothing but silence in her headphones. Then her gaze followed the lead across the moss and she realised she'd neglected to plug the headphones in. *Putain.* She slipped the jack into the slot beneath the power lead and suddenly the machine was alive. She heard a whistling in her earphones, then a burst of static and a squeal or two as she inched the tuning knob around. Finally she found the wavelength that would take her to Nathan, the exact frequency, and a tiny bulb glowed red to confirm it.

She checked her watch again. Three minutes before she had to transmit. Don't wait for any kind of invitation, Agnès had told her. Just start with the Morse key the moment your watch hits half past four.

Hélène fumbled in the bag for her notes. She'd broken down each word in the message, depending on Agnès to pencil in the Morse code beside each letter, and under the *résistante*'s guidance she'd spent the early afternoon practising. She had neither the taste nor the aptitude for exercises like these but the thought of her waiting husband concentrated her mind wonderfully and the moment half past four arrived she bent to the machine and began to tap.

Dash dash dot

A brief pause, the way Agnès had told her.

Dot dash

Dot dash dot

Dash dot dot

Dot

She paused a moment, trying to relax, wondering how long this first word had taken her to transmit. *Garde*, she thought. One word done. Six to go.

The rest followed, deliberate key work, agonisingly slow, but free – as far as she could tell – from mistakes. This, she realised, was a difficult thing to do. There was no record of the transmission, nothing to confirm that she'd got the message right, just the busy void beyond the dots and the dashes. This afternoon, in the safety of her own forest, there were no pressures beyond her own clumsiness. But having to transmit from another setting, maybe a borrowed room in a busy city, would be something entirely different. She tried to imagine it – listening ears, a cough in the hallway outside, heavy boots racing up the stairs – and her respect for her new houseguest deepened.

Finally it was done. She'd asked Agnès whether or not Nathan would reply and Agnès said she didn't know. If a message came back it would obviously be in code and if that happened Agnès would be happy to provide a translation. That would mean transcribing the incoming dots and the dashes, and so now Hélène waited, the headphones still clamped to her ears, a notepad on her lap, her pen poised. But nothing happened. Just the crackle of static and a sudden howl as she tweaked the tuning dial, hunting for the husband she hadn't seen for three long years.

She began to relax, still waiting, still listening in case a message came through, wondering what it really meant to be stepping into her fifth decade. She hated the notion of getting old, of time passing, but these days the notion of time itself had been so warped by the *débâcle*, and the Armistice, and everything else that had happened since, that it was difficult to remember the way things had once been.

Because the truth was that France had remained frozen in a moment first of disbelief and then of something close to resignation, and if Hélène was to be part of that then so be it. Like everyone else she knew, she'd retreated inwards, making private accommodations of her own – some tiny, some not – and one consequence was that she paid very little attention to waymarks that would once have been so important. A birthday? Even the arrival of her fortieth year? Who really cared?

Malin, for one. He'd been waiting in the kitchen first thing that morning when she came down to put the coffee pot on. The present he'd so carefully wrapped was waiting for her on the table. Inside was the watch she was wearing now, a 1915 silver trench piece he'd picked up from God knows where and restored to full working order. And Klimt, too, hadn't forgotten. A huge bouquet of roses, delivered by a surly youth from the village, had arrived mid-morning. The accompanying card, featuring the swastika-clad Arc de Triomphe, wouldn't have done her reputation much good in the village but, once again, did she really care?

She closed her eyes for a moment as a sudden shaft of sunlight settled on her face. In these most difficult of times, she told herself that her conscience – if that's what it was – was clear, wiped clean by the knowledge that she was doing what she could for her little *ménage*. Having Spanish refugees, a Polish Jew and now Agnès under the same roof was never going to be less than a challenge, especially when you added occasional visits – rarely announced – from a senior *Abwehr* officer. Survival, as she was only too well aware, required juggling skills of a high order but so far, to her quiet satisfaction, she hadn't dropped a single ball.

A sudden flurry of birds again, rooks this time. She got to her feet. It was nearly ten to five. She bent to disconnect the battery and then set off round the lake to stretch her legs. A tumble of clouds had appeared in the direction of the chateau and when she paused to listen she thought she caught a distant growl of thunder.

Then came another noise, much closer. It was

Valmy. She glanced back. Something had disturbed him. He was pawing the ground, testing the rope she'd used to tether him to the tree. She turned on her heel and began to head back. Then she froze. A figure had emerged from the trees. It was a man. He was carrying something that looked like a crossbow. He was wearing a pair of blue dungarees and, after he'd inspected the radio, he picked up Hélène's notebook.

Hélène felt a surge of anger. This was double trespass. Her forest. Her notebook. He looked up from the notes she'd made and she recognised the broad, sallow face and the tangle of black curls. Benoit. A farmer from the rougher pastures on the far side of the village. Like Hélène, he was a newcomer to the area. She'd had very little to do with him but she'd heard from others that he was *insolite*. *Insolite* meant unusual. In Neaune, to be *insolite* was never a compliment.

'What are you doing here?'

Benoit was staring at her. His hands were soiled. He rubbed one of them on his dungarees, then nodded down at the radio. He still had the crossbow.

'I might ask the same question,' he murmured. There was a hint of education in his voice, even refinement.

'Have you been watching me, *monsieur*?'

'Yes. I had no choice, I was here before you arrived.'

'Doing what?'

'Looking for truffles.'

'There are no truffles, *monsieur*. And as far as I can gather, there never were. So let me ask you again. What were you doing? And why do you need that thing?' She nodded at the crossbow.

Benoit didn't answer. He still had Hélène's notes. '*Garde bien les heures volées. Mille bises. Mustafa.*' He looked up, swaying slightly. '*Les heures volées?* Very pretty.'

Hélène wanted the notes back. Benoit didn't move, a refusal that – to Hélène – felt full of menace.

'What do you want, *monsieur?* Apart from my truffles?'

'I want nothing. You mistake me.'

'Then let me ask you again: why are you here?' She gestured towards the crossbow. 'Is it the rabbits? The ducks? Whatever else you can shoot? Is life so hard you have to play the thief?'

She'd touched a nerve. She could see it in his eyes. Like most of the few men remaining in the village, Benoit was a drinker and it showed.

'Is there anything in this country people like you don't own?' he asked at length.

'Lots, if you're serious. But, like it or not, this is private property. If you want to come here to shoot game, there might be a possibility of some arrangement. Nothing regular, *monsieur*, but often enough to keep your pantry stocked.'

'And my mouth shut?' He was looking at the radio.

Hélène ignored the threat. 'You have a wife who knows how to cook?'

'I live alone.'

'I'm sorry.'

'Don't be. I cook very well. And I sleep like a baby.'

'Meaning?'

'No contact with the Boches. I keep myself to myself.'

'Then you're lucky, *monsieur*. Your life is a bubble. You want some advice? Make sure it doesn't burst.'

Benoit ignored the taunt. He wanted to know more about *les heures volées*. In French *voler* has two meanings, to fly and to steal. Benoit had opted for the first.

'*The hours that have flown?*' Hélène shook her head. 'No.'

'Then what does it mean?'

'Guess.'

'The *stolen* hours?' The frown made him look like a child. 'Why stolen?'

'Because the Germans took everything. Even the way we measure our day. Having our clocks on Berlin time might be a small thing, *monsieur*, but there are still people in this country who resent that kind of theft.'

He nodded, then consulted the notes again.

'*Take great care of the stolen hours. A thousand kisses.*' He looked up. 'So that's the message you sent?'

'Yes.'

'To your German friend? With that fancy car of his?'

'I think not.'

89

'Then to who?'

Hélène shook her head. She was angry again. She'd had enough. When he asked whether the message had been a code of some sort, she told him to get off her land. When he stepped closer, wanting to pursue the conversation, she snatched the notepad from his hand. She could smell the alcohol on his breath. Calvados, she told herself. A single man living a life scored for resentment and a wilderness of empty bottles.

'Go,' she said again, standing her ground. 'Unless you want the police at your door.'

'Or the Boches at yours?' He aimed a kick at the radio and missed. Then he made a visible effort to control himself before nodding across the lake towards the trees. 'A rabbit or two, *madame*?' He spat at her feet. 'You'll have to do better than that.'

Seconds later he was gone, a bulky shape in blue serge making his way up through the trees. Hélène steadied herself. She'd been too angry to be frightened but now he'd gone she realised how vulnerable she'd been. He could have done anything, she told herself. Forty's not too old to fight back but she had no illusions about where a struggle might have led.

The horse was restless again. It seemed to have sensed the tension in the air. Hélène glanced down at the notepad. Her columns of carefully copied dots and dashes had been dirtied with soil from Benoit's thick fingers but at least it was back in her own hands. If he went to the Germans she'd deny everything but she knew that was unlikely. Over another bottle or two he'd work out what he really wanted from her. And then her problems would begin in earnest.

She stowed the radio and the battery in the game bag and looped it over her shoulder. A different route back should keep them out of Benoit's path. About to untether the horse, she paused. Another rumble, much louder, out to the west. Thunder, she thought, for sure.

Merde.

CHAPTER 9

Bristol's biggest cemetery lay at Arnos Vale, about a mile from Temple Meads railway station. In peace time, burials normally ran at thirty a week. In a cold winter, especially when influenza galloped through the city, that figure might double, but nothing had prepared the taciturn men who dug the graves for 2 November 1940.

That night, the bombers came. The Luftwaffe unloaded a torrent of incendiary bombs and hundreds of tons of high explosive on the blacked-out streets below. Thousands of houses were destroyed or damaged and next morning the city's mortuaries were counting 207 dead. One of them was a forty-eight year old woman from Park Street. Her name was Irene Gallagher.

Billy's mum had dropped him off at the cemetery gates. He was carrying his kitbag, ready for the train journey down to Exeter, and he gave her a hug before he said goodbye. She'd made an attempt to keep him another couple of days at Blessington Manor but they both knew her heart wasn't in it. With Billy gone to the war, she had no taste for solitude. That had happened before, in an earlier conflagration, and the results had been catastrophic. Ralph, in his own gruff way, had brought her both company and the security of considerable wealth, but the truth was that he had no desire to share this new life of theirs with a son he'd never met before.

Now Billy made his way down through the maze of headstones and monuments. Two of the cemetery staff were sheltering from the rain beneath a willow tree: thin, gaunt-faced men, spared active service. If you were after a reserved occupation, thought Billy, then here it was. You could always rely on people dying. Especially in times like these.

'Irene Gallagher?'

One of the men remembered the name. He'd dug her grave himself after that second big raid, spaded the earth back onto her coffin after the interment, refilling the hole.

'Quaker lady,' he said. 'Wasn't she?'

'That's right. And a fine actress, too.'

'Relative, are you?'

'No, just a friend.'

'And a bit of a fan, I expect, seeing she was famous.'

'Of course. As you might expect.'

The grave was way down at the bottom of the cemetery, a plot protected from the wind by a neighbouring hedge. The ground had been returfed after the burial and someone had sown a drift of wild flowers in the moist grass. In mid-summer,

93

the swirl of colours – startling blues, soft yellows, dots of white and pink – was totally random yet to Billy it seemed to perfectly capture the essence of this woman he'd known so well.

After the formality of other graves, it offered something different, something alive, something spontaneous, everything he'd associated with the woman who'd taken him under her wing. Since her death that night, he'd often struggled to find the word that best described their relationship. On her part, he thought it was a question of belief. Belief and a magical kind of patience that seemed inexhaustible. On his part, it was much simpler. He worshipped her.

And the gravedigger was right. Irene had died a Quaker. He was gazing at her headstone. It still looked new. He loved its simplicity. Just her name, Irene Marigold Gallagher, her date of birth, and the date the bombers had arrived to take her away. Nothing else. Typical.

She'd once tried to explain her faith to Billy. She told him she'd been a believer since she was old enough to think things through for herself. Her family had been Methodists, occasionally fervent, often not. She'd had to accompany them to services when the mood took them but she'd had no taste for the horse-faced minister and his stern list of do's and don'ts. She'd wanted something different, something nobody else had mucked about with, something that didn't belong to the ministers and vicars and the bishops and all the rest of the palaver, and in the end it seemed to boil down to a room where she could meet with a handful of people she trusted in order to sit down and think.

This, as Billy now knew, was exactly what the Quakers offered. By then, he and Irene had enjoyed a million backstage conversations, many of which had helped seed Billy's dawning realisation that she might be right about the career that lay before him, that his talents might extend beyond selling programmes and sweeping up after the audience had gone.

This quiet determination, married to the natural bravado of late adolescence, had won him a trickle of walk-on parts that had quickly become a flood. In the late thirties, for whatever reason, the company had been short of decent young actors and it had been Irene who'd bullied the resident director into giving him a crack at a decent part. Playing Oliver Twist in a stage adaptation of the Dickens classic had been terrifying but the audience had liked it and so – as it turned out – did the management.

After Oliver Twist came a season of smallish classical parts, mainly Shakespeare and mainly comedy, coming to a triumphant end with *As You Like It*. Billy's take on Orlando – his first leading role – won him an admiring review in the *Bristol Post* but Irene, bless her, had refused to take an ounce of the credit she was due. Three weeks later, the actor playing Eben in *Desire Under the Elms* broke his leg and Billy, as understudy, stepped

95

into the breach. The performance was a smash hit, at least for Bristol audiences, and it was then – riding the crest of the wave – that Irene invited her young trouper to accompany her to an evening at the Friends Meeting House. This was where the Quakers gathered, an old timbered building down by the weir, and it was there that Billy discovered something even sweeter than applause: the blessings of silence.

Now Billy knelt at the graveside. Earlier he'd thought about flowers but decided against it. Too mundane. Too ordinary. Instead he closed his eyes and recited the lines that Irene had loved best of all. They came from *The Tempest*.

> *Be not afeard. The isle is full of noises*
> *Sounds, and sweet airs, that give delight and*
>   *hurt not.*
> *Sometimes a thousand twangling instruments*
> *Will hum about mine ears, and sometime*
>   *voices*
> *That, if I then had waked after long sleep*
> *Will make me sleep again; and then in*
>   *dreaming*
> *The clouds methought would open and show*
>   *riches*
> *Ready to drop upon me, that when I waked*
> *I cried to dream again . . .*

'Billy?'

He glanced round, recognising the voice. She

was wearing an old gabardine mac that must have belonged to someone much taller. She had a full figure and a soft, round face with dimples that Irene had once described as proof that God could be in a good mood. Her hair, still blondish, was longer than Billy remembered and she'd gathered it at the back with a twist of scarlet ribbon. The last time Billy had seen her was the night they'd celebrated her thirtieth birthday.

'Nell,' he said.

'That was beautiful, what you were saying. I remember it from the funeral. Do it again. For me.'

Billy obliged. The rain had stopped at last and after he'd finished he could hear the thwack-thwack of nearby shovels as the diggers deepened yet another grave.

Back on his feet, he wanted to know how Nell had known where to find him.

'Your mum picked me up. She said you'd be here.'

'You're still in Clifton?'

'Yes. Same room. Same view. Half-shares in the same cat.' She smiled. 'Do I get a kiss?'

Billy stepped close and kissed her on the cheek.

'You're still nursing?'

'Yes.'

'Up at the Infirmary?'

'Yes. We're on the go all the time. If you want the truth we could do with a few more men around the place.'

'Is that a hint?'

'You hated it.'

He kissed her again, properly this time, and held her for a moment. It was true about the Infirmary. By the time war broke out, Billy had already become a Quaker. Quakers didn't fight wars, didn't believe in them, and after protracted negotiations with the officer in charge of conscripts at the local yeomanry barracks, he'd registered as a conscientious objector. Conchies, he knew, might spare themselves the fighting but were obliged to take all kinds of other jobs. Thus the order to report to the Infirmary where he was to become a porter.

The hospital, for the first few days, had been all right but the work was heavier and more repetitious than he expected and the saddest of truths was that he missed the theatre. In the last month of peace, *Desire Under the Elms* had taken him to New York, an experience that had given him a taste for the brightest of lights. Playing Broadway, albeit briefly, he'd suddenly felt that literally anything might be possible, that a whole world out there was waiting for more of Billy Angell. Coming back to the night shift at Bristol Infirmary had been the hardest of landings.

Nell had a bag with her. She wanted to know whether Devon was going to be OK.

'With who?'

'With you.' The smile was less certain now. 'Only it's been a long time.'

★   ★   ★

The village of Topsham lay beside the water south of Exeter. The river became tidal here, abruptly widening, half a mile from bank to bank. Billy and Nell walked away from the station as the tiny steam engine and its three carriages headed down the branch line towards the sea. Miles downriver, a jumble of houses overlooked the estuary.

'Exmouth,' Nell said.

They were standing in a churchyard above the water, gazing south. It was early evening, the sun beginning to set. The tide was out and the glistening mudflats were busy with bird life. Billy absorbed the view. He'd never seen a landscape so gentle, so perfectly formed, so peaceful. Chopburg, and Cologne, and Essen, and the bare fields of Lincolnshire, might never have existed.

'Redshank, Billy,' Nell was pointing upstream. 'Oyster catchers. And look there, a heron.'

Billy looked. A bird was a bird. He wanted to know when Nell had been here before.

'When I was a kid. My mum came from Honiton. She had a friend who lived in the village here. This is where I learned to swim. You could only do it properly at high tide but I still remember the feeling of the mud all squelchy between my toes. Some kids hated it. Not me.'

Billy was impressed. Despite his mum's best efforts, he'd never learned to swim.

They moved on. Higher Shapter Street was a five-minute walk away. Glimpses of the river between the waterside houses convinced Billy he'd stumbled into paradise. Two old men in a rowing boat, drifting slowly with the tide. Distant yelps of laughter from a gang of kids kicking a leather ball. And then, in a moment of silence, a bird call.

Billy paused, his ear cupped. He wanted to know more.

'It's a curlew, Billy. Look, I'll show you.'

She led him down to the water's edge. Curlews, she said, were shy. Don't move.

'That one? The brown one? With the funny beak?' Billy, his eyes shaded with his hand, was peering into the setting sun.

'That's it.'

Billy nodded. Then came the call again. He'd never heard anything so sad. Irene, had she been alive, would have called it haunting. He closed his eyes, wanting the bird to call again, but nothing happened. Then, out of the darkness, swam an image of the Rear Gunner, his leg shattered, his upper body hunched in the roaring darkness. Billy shivered, reaching for Nell, but when he opened his eyes again she was already making her way back to the road.

Ralph's place lay in a terrace of narrow-fronted houses that climbed up from the river. The key in his pocket was carefully labelled: Number Seven. Billy pushed the wooden gate open and let them in.

The house smelled of damp. Ralph hadn't bothered with much furniture – a tiny settee and a single armchair in the downstairs sitting room, and two metal-framed single beds in the front room at the top. At first glance, the bedroom reminded Billy of the Infirmary.

'Honeysuckle Ward,' he told Nell. 'My mum says there's sheets and stuff somewhere.'

Honeysuckle Ward had been a room reserved for the terminally ill at the Infirmary, one bed for the patient, the other for a near-relative. Wake up in Honeysuckle Ward, he told Nell, and you knew your days were numbered.

'That's horrible, Billy. This is supposed to be a holiday.'

'For who?'

'For you. That's why your mum asked me in the first place. She wants me to make it nice for you.'

'You mean us.'

'Of course.'

She shot him a look he couldn't quite fathom and then disappeared to look for sheets and blankets before it got dark. Billy stepped across to the window and stared down at the cobbled street. On the train, coming down, he'd been dreading the inevitable questions about his last six months but to his relief she hadn't once asked about the RAF. Instead they'd talked about the hospital, about people they both knew, about the landings in Sicily, and about just how long this war could possibly last.

She was back with a couple of sheets and a blanket. Their eyes met over the single beds. Nell, like most nurses, could be extremely direct.

'We push them together?' she asked.

'If you want.'

'You're sure you're ready for this?'

'Yes, I think so.'

'Only think so?'

'I dunno. Let's find out.'

He helped her with the sheets. By now, the light was beginning to fade. It occurred to Billy that neither of them had eaten since breakfast. He was carrying more money than he'd ever seen in his life but where was he supposed to find food as late as this?

Nell told him not to worry. She'd already been through the cupboards downstairs. Tins of potatoes and processed peas. More tins of spam and something else in the meat line. Plus jars of fruit and pickles. In short, a feast.

Billy was grinning. He'd been unpacking his kitbag and at the bottom he'd found two bottles of wine his mum must have liberated from Ralph's cellar. With them came a note. *Dear Billy. I know it's not much but it comes with all my love. Your mum. XXX*

Nell found a corkscrew in a drawer downstairs. Billy was searching for wood beneath the lean-to in the tiny pocket of back garden. It was high summer but the house still felt damp and he yearned for the comfort of a real fire. A charred log in the grate in the front room told him the chimney probably worked and he'd spotted a pile of old newspapers on the bare boards beside the settee. Nell busied herself in the kitchen while

Billy built a fire. By the time darkness fell, they'd nearly finished the first bottle.

Nell arrived in the front room with the supper. Billy's fire was a huge success. She gave him a plate and switched off the light. Flames danced in the fireplace. Billy pulled the cork on the second bottle. After the chill of the evening, he felt warm at last.

They'd settled on the sofa, lightly drunk, gazing at the fire. Nell asked him why he'd ever volunteered for the RAF. One minute he'd been telling her how Quakers never killed anyone. The next he'd disappeared to bomb the hell out of the Germans.

Billy gave the question some thought.

'Irene,' he said at last.

'But she was a Quaker, too.'

'That's right. But they killed her. The Germans killed her. I was the one who took her down to the mortuary. I had to identify her. There was no one else.'

Her family, he said, lived in London. The theatre had closed. He knew she lived in Park Street and the morning after the raid there was nothing left. He'd been with her only a couple of days before.

'At the Quaker place?'

'Yes, at the Meeting House.' He nodded, the remains of his meal untouched. 'They brought her to the mortuary at the Infirmary, like all the other bodies. I'd seen plenty of dead people by then. You know I had. It was my job to get them

103

down from the wards. But I'd never seen anything like this.'

'Like what?'

'How damaged they were. You know how I knew it was Irene? By the ring she used to wear. The rest of her . . .' He shook his head.

'But you carried on working.' Nell's hand found his.

'That's right.'

'More dead bodies. And more raids, too.'

Billy nodded. After they'd killed Irene, the bombers had returned to claim more victims. Two raids before Christmas had brought the King and Queen to the city to inspect the damage. Then, after Christmas, yet another visitation, the Germans again. And then another. And a third. By the time spring came, nearly a thousand bodies had been through the mortuary.

Without Irene, Billy said, he was in trouble. He couldn't work it out, couldn't understand it. Where was God in all this? How would sitting in silence and trying to start some kind of conversation with God ever bring Irene back?

'You did that?'

'I did.'

'Tried to make God change his mind?'

'Yes.'

'And send Irene back?'

'Yes.'

'And you thought it would work?'

'I did. I was crazy. I admit it.'

'You never looked crazy. You never sounded crazy.'

'That's because no one ever asked.'

'Not your mum?'

'Not anyone. That's the thing about Irene. She'd made me so strong. She'd made me so calm. She'd once told me that if anything was ever to happen to her then I still had to believe, still had to go to the Meeting House, still had to be there for everyone else who was suffering. And I tried, Nell. I really did. But then that last raid happened, that following summer, just the one plane, and you know where the bomb dropped? Right by the Meeting House.'

'You make it sound personal.'

'It was. That's exactly what it was.'

Nell was gazing into the firelight.

'So that's why you joined the RAF?' she said after a while.

'Yes,' Billy nodded. 'It was revenge, really. I was so angry. Not just about Irene but about everything. All those raids. All those bodies. You've no idea how hard it is to stop being a conchie. It's all paperwork. They never want to believe you. But I think I was lucky. The Air Force seemed to have broader minds. As long as you qualify, pass the tests, all that, then you're in.'

'You told me you wanted to be a pilot.'

'Of course. Everyone wants to be a pilot. Except I was hopeless. That's why I ended up as a Wireless Op.' He lay back on the settee, closing his eyes. 'I've just done my thirty ops, Nell, and I'm still here. That makes me the luckiest bloke on earth. But I've seen some terrible things, some truly terrible things. You know what they never tell you? That we're very, very good at killing people. Not hundreds of people, not thousands of people, but tens of thousands of people. And that's in a single night. And you know something else? Way up there in the sky, where it matters, the Germans are very, very good at killing us. Does that bring me any closer to God? Will it ever? I don't think so.'

Nell put her arms around him. The fire was starting to die but the room was still warm.

'You're shivering,' she said.

'Am I?'

'Yes.' She kissed him again. 'And that's another reason why I'm taking you to bed.'

CHAPTER 10

Hélène was in the kitchen at the chateau when she heard a shout from upstairs. It was Malin.

'The Boches are coming,' he yelled. 'Tell the girl.'

'The girl' was Agnès. She was sitting at the long table, as moody as ever, dipping chunks of bread in her bowl of coffee. Getting her down from the room where she slept for something to eat had been the work of nearly a week. Hélène, weary of playing the waitress, had issued an ultimatum. Either you're part of this household or you move on. Now this.

Agnès was already out of the room. Hélène listened to her bare feet racing up the stairs. Then she collected the bowl from the table and emptied the contents down the sink. Germans had an eye for detail. They were hard to fool.

The big drawing room at the front of the chateau offered a view of the drive. Malin was right. She recognised the low-slung Citroën *Hauptmann* had requisitioned from a family in Tours. At least he was alone in the car, driving himself.

She stepped out into the sunshine, waiting at the top of the steps. She and Müller had met on a number of occasions and she'd always treated him with a chilly *politesse*. He was in charge of the soldiers down in the village, a pudding of a man, too old and too fat for the Eastern Front. He laughed easily, laughter that reached his eyes, and she rather suspected he could be convivial company. Not that she ever intended to put him to the test.

Her fear was the farmer, Benoit. Had he betrayed her? Had he slipped a note through Müller's door? Directed his attention to the mistress of the Château de Neaune and her surprising interest in short-wave radios? Somehow she doubted it but one of the lessons Hélène had learned in occupied France was never to make assumptions. These were the strangest of times and country folk could be the strangest of people.

'*Bonjour, madame.*' Müller offered a courtly little bow. His accent was execrable and the flight of steps had left him short of breath.

Hélène returned the greeting. She enquired how she might help him. Müller produced an envelope. The handwriting was as bad as his French but she recognised her own name.

'Is that for me, *Herr Hauptmann*?'

'No, *madame*. For me.'

He tore the envelope open. A single sheet of paper was typed on one side. He scanned it quickly, and then glanced up.

'SS *Oberst* Klimt? You know this officer?'

'I do, yes.'

'He presents his compliments, *madame*. He requests your company. He's in Paris. He also requests that you bring something suitable to wear at a formal occasion.'

'Really?'

'Yes, *madame*.'

'What kind of formal occasion?'

'I'm afraid he doesn't say.'

'Then I shall telephone him.'

'That won't be necessary, *madame*.'

'May I ask why not?'

'Because he wants you there this afternoon.' He beamed at her a moment, then took a tiny step sideways and nodded down at the car. 'It will be my pleasure, *madame*. I'm at your service.'

Müller waited in the kitchen while Hélène selected a dress or two. She had no idea what had sparked this sudden invitation. Klimt always phoned, always made a point of keeping their communications direct and intimate. It was one of the ways he had of telling her that she – they – were more important that all the other official nonsense. You owed people you loved a conversation. Not fat little *Hauptmann* Müller with a typed set of instructions.

Pausing at her dressing table to sweep her make-up into a bag, she glanced at her face in the mirror. She'd always been proud of her ability to mask her emotions. It was, after all, one of the tricks that men like Nathan, and now Klimt, appreciated. It spoke of strength, of dignity. But there were lines around her mouth and shadows under her eyes that she didn't recognise and for the first time she wondered exactly how long this *putain* of a war would go on. Her red beret hung from a corner of the mirror on the dressing table. Wearing it always made her feel better. She tucked it in her bag and headed for the door.

Müller, at her invitation, had helped himself to coffee from the pot on the stove. Agnès had left her borrowed slippers beneath the table but Hélène doubted that the German had noticed them.

'You look wonderful, *madame.*' He was on his feet already. 'Allow me to carry your bag.'

They drove back to the village. Müller apologised that standing orders forbade him to make a long journey alone. He was obliged to travel with an escort, a young infantryman who'd picked up a bullet wound in North Africa and had been posted to *la France profonde* to speed his convalescence. Young Norbert, he said, would be taking the wheel. That way he and Madame Lafosse could enjoy a proper conversation in the back.

Hélène's heart sank. Norbert turned out to be a lanky blond in late adolescence with playful eyes and much better French than his *Wehrmacht* boss. Hélène spent most of the first hour of the journey quizzing him about what he made of the village and the area beyond. By the time they were on the outskirts of Tours, Müller was asleep.

★   ★   ★

110

They reached Paris in late afternoon. Müller, awake now, showed off his knowledge of the city by directing his young escort to the headquarters of the Military Governor of Paris. When they pulled to a halt outside the Hôtel Meurice, Müller struggled out of the car and held the door open for Hélène. A word to the sentries at the foot of the steps got her into the hotel, and she waited in the reception area while Müller announced their arrival.

SS *Oberst* Klimt, it appeared, was busy. Another first. When Müller offered to stay and keep her company, Hélène extended her hand and told him that wouldn't be necessary. Doubtless they'd meet again before too long.

'A pleasure, *madame*.' Another little bow. 'As ever.'

Hélène waited for him to disappear before she sank onto a threadbare banquette within sight of the brisk young men at reception. In truth, she was worried. What if Müller took this opportunity to take half a dozen of his soldiers up to the chateau and have a good look round? Who would they find and where might that lead? And more troubling still, why was Klimt suddenly playing the senior *Abwehr* officer? With the kind of curt invitation he'd never have dreamed of sending before?

She let the questions swirl round her head, irritated that this sudden attack of uncertainty had got the better of her. Then she told herself to relax, to look on the brighter side. Klimt had never let her down. Not once. And she thought she knew enough about his kind of men to know that there'd be an explanation.

She was right. She sat waiting for nearly an hour. Before the war, she'd known this hotel well. Nathan had been on the best of terms with the maître d', a teasingly good-looking Austrian from Trieste, and they'd regularly entertained guests in the restaurant. She remembered the silky taste of the chef's *blanquette de veau* and her husband's insistence on ordering impossibly expensive bottles of Côtes du Rhône for clients whose taste he appreciated. Back then, even in the late thirties, it would have been impossible to imagine these elegant spaces peopled with an occupying army of busy Germans, no matter how well turned out, and she marvelled at how easy it had been to deceive themselves. Peace, if you have money, is something that will never end. How wrong could she have been?

'Madame Lafosse.'

It was Klimt. Not for the first time, he'd taken her by surprise. He extended a hand and helped her to her feet, escorting her across to the lifts. They went up to the third floor. Here, most traces of the hotel she'd known had disappeared. Wherever she looked there were signs in German. Every bedroom door appeared to open into an office. Even the fire extinguishers were a uniform grey.

Klimt stopped at a door at the end of the

corridor. He produced a key and let her in. She'd never been here before.

'This is where you work?'

She was looking round. A simple desk but not small. Piles of paperwork, neatly arranged. Three telephones. A long line of files on a single shelf. A street map of Paris, heavily annotated in Klimt's careful script. Evening dress had been laid on the single bed.

'You sleep here?'

'When I have to.'

The news surprised her. For the last year and a half she'd gladly surrendered her own place to Klimt. His first months in Paris had been spent in a neighbouring apartment, quickly requisitioned, but after they'd been together for a while she'd seen no point in Klimt not moving in. For one thing, he could keep the apartment secure. And for another, it put their whole relationship on a more intimate level. Relaxed, out of uniform, a drink in his hand, evenings with Klimt felt part of a life that had nothing to do with an office like this. Was that another act of self-deception on her part? And, if so, did that make her foolish, as well as wrong?

'You're looking surprised, Hélène.'

'I'm not surprised. I'm curious.'

'About this?'

'About me. I somehow . . .' She shook her head. '. . . It doesn't matter.'

He held her gaze for a moment or two and she

tried to imagine those eyes across a desk. This was becoming uncomfortable, and they both knew it.

'So what happens next?' she asked.

'Now? I order champagne. My aide-de-camp brings canapés. We make love.' He stepped closer and kissed her on the lips. 'That's a joke, by the way. I hope Müller played the gentleman.'

He made space on the bed and invited her to sit down. Then he drew a chair up until they very close. This evening, he said, Otto Abetz was throwing a party. His wife, the lovely Suzanne, had especially requested that *Oberst* Klimt and Madame Lafosse attend. He smiled. His hand found hers. Then he was suddenly on his feet.

'Excuse me. I have a call to make.'

Hélène stared up at him. He was gesturing towards the ceiling. Then he put his finger to his lips. Hélène, bewildered, watched him as he crossed to the desk. He picked up the telephone, that same finger anchored on the receiver, while he began to speak. A false call, she thought. A call to no one. The faux-conversation over, he lingered a moment, scribbling himself a note. Seconds later, she found herself looking at a single word. *Mikro*, he'd written, pointing to the ceiling again.

She nodded. She thought she understood. The room, probably every room in this warren of a hotel, was wired with hidden microphones. Someone, somewhere, was listening to everything. Even pretend conversations on the phone. The spies spied on, she thought. Only the Germans.

'About the rue de Lille,' she said. 'Tell me more.'

The rue de Lille was behind the Gare d'Orsay. It housed Abetz's sumptuous residence, the Hôtel de Beauharnais. As the German Ambassador to France, he deserved nothing less.

Klimt explained that Abetz had tired of the interminable days of high summer. Paris was too empty, too hot, too dead. He wanted to add a bit of style, a bit of movement, a bit of culture. And so he and his wife had decided to throw a little party.

Hélène suspected it was a lie. Was this for the *Mikro* or was Klimt trying to fool her too?

'Lovely. Exquisite.' She glanced down at her bag. 'Shall I get dressed?'

Klimt left the room while she stripped naked, braced herself for a cold-water wash in the room's hand basin, dried herself on a tiny rectangle of grey towel and then put on the dress she'd brought. She'd only worn it once before. It was a Coco Chanel design, part of her spring '38 collection, a stylish confection in black silk net that had been yet another *douceur* from her husband. Nathan had loved it, especially the effect it had on other men, but she'd never had the opportunity to wear it since.

Klimt was back. He closed the door carefully behind him then studied her for a moment.

'*Schoen*,' he said softly.

A uniformed driver took them across the river to the Left Bank. After three years of occupation she'd yet to get used to the absence of traffic, to the bareness of the Place de la Concorde. There were more bicycles than vehicles and some of the cars, with their bulky wood-fed generators, looked like props from a stage production that had never quite worked. The giant swastika flags, on the other hand, hung from every building; set dressing that robbed every glance of the Paris she'd once known. An entire city, she thought. Stolen.

The driver turned into the rue de Lille. Ahead, at the end of the street, Hélène could see guests embracing on the pavement outside the Ambassador's residence. Klimt told the driver to pull in.

'We'll walk the rest of the way,' he said.

Alone on the pavement, Hélène took Klimt's proffered arm. No *Mikro*, she thought. She was half expecting some clue to why Klimt was being so wary, but instead he told her the good news about Éclairage. The mare was officially in foal. The French businessman planned to present her to Otto Abetz at the Longchamps races at the weekend. One hundred and fifty thousand dollars would be with Hélène by the end of the month.

'How?' The Nazis had a habit of freezing French bank accounts.

'In cash. I'll bring the money down myself.'

'To Neaune?'

'Of course. It'll get me out of Paris.'

'You never needed an excuse before.'

'I know. But times are changing.'

'Should I be concerned?'

He paused on the pavement, just yards from the guests, and looked her in the eye.

'Trust me.' There was a slight lift at the end of the sentence. It felt like a question rather than an order. She didn't reply.

They joined the guests filing into the Ambassador's residence. Hélène knew many of these faces from her pre-war days with Nathan: leading industrialists, a banker or two, starlets from the movies, fashion designers, a chef she'd last met at a function in the Louvre. Some of them still lived in her own area, Neuilly, in the 16th, and she exchanged smiles and the occasional embrace.

Abetz himself was waiting in the mirrored hall, his French wife on his arm. He was a good-looking man with pale eyes and carefully parted hair and he had a talent for hiding the more brutal truths about the Occupation from occasions like these. Senior German officers were everywhere, immaculate in full dress uniform, and they circulated among the guests as if these people were old friends. The war, the invasion, the *débâcle*, might never have happened, thought Hélène. The German guests were obviously handpicked. Unless you were prepared to speak fluent French all evening, you didn't make it through the door.

Hélène was deep in conversation with a woman named Corinne she'd known through Nathan when the SS officer approached. She'd been aware of him watching her for a while.

117

He waited for a pause in the conversation. Then came a click of his heels and a word of introduction. In a setting like this, the man's formality was jarring.

'*Sturmbannführer* Johann Huber, *madame*.' Half expecting a Nazi salute, Hélène was relieved to accept the outstretched hand.

Hélène introduced Corinne. Huber summoned a passing waiter and insisted on more champagne. Hélène, unsure about the wisdom of accepting a third glass, was scanning the salon for Klimt, of whom there was no sign.

They talked about horseracing for a minute or two. Huber seemed very well informed. The previous weekend at Longchamps had, he said, made him feel positively French. The ambience. The company. And the fact that he'd made a little money.

Hélène asked whether he was new to Paris.

'I am, *madame*.'

'And what do you make of it?'

He seemed unaccountably surprised by the question. He said he'd had the privilege of visiting many cities over the last year or so, especially in Holland and Belgium. Rotterdam was a tragedy. Amsterdam, if you half closed your eyes, was still a treasure. Antwerp needed a great deal of what he called 'attention'. But Paris? Paris was untouched. Still luminous. Still beautiful. Still unique.

'That's because you didn't bomb us.'

'And that's because you opened the city gates

118

and made us welcome, *madame*. There's nothing in this world that can't be resolved with patience and good sense and to our immense relief Paris had plenty of both.'

'Had?'

'Has.' He tipped his glass. '*Touché*.'

Hélène said nothing. She wondered what he might have said had he been with the first wave of occupying troops. The empty roads. The boarded-up cafés. The shuttered houses. The mainline stations choked with families still desperate to escape. Was it some kind of comfort, years later, to tell yourself that Paris had been grateful for your company?

She wondered whether it was worth pursuing this conversation, if only to feel better about herself, but then she became aware of a hand on her arm. It was Huber. He'd be grateful for a word in private.

He led her out of the salon and up the staircase to a sitting room on the next floor. He seemed to be familiar with the house. He closed the door and invited her to sit down. Hélène felt a prickle of apprehension. First the *Mikro*. Now this.

'We need to talk about paintings, *madame*. About fine art.' His long pale fingers did a circuit of the room. Hélène had already recognised a Monet and a Degas hanging between the bookcases. Downstairs, she'd been within touching distance of a Pissarro she adored. *Le Louvre sous la neige* had been a favourite of Nathan's, too.

'You know my husband was a dealer?'

'Of course. That's why we needed to meet. Are you still in touch with him?'

The bluntness of the question startled her. How much did this man know?

'My husband's in London, Herr Huber. Under the circumstances, conversation is far from easy.'

'That wasn't my question. I'm asking you whether you ever make contact.'

'And how would I do that?'

'I imagine there might be ways and means.'

'Then the answer is no. I live in the depths of the countryside. I lead a very quiet life. I keep myself to myself. If you need to know more, then you might do worse than have a conversation with *Oberst* Klimt. He's downstairs. If you require an introduction I'd be happy to oblige.'

'I know *Oberst* Klimt, *madame*. This conversation has his blessing.'

'It has?'

'Of course. We're not quite as stupid as you might think.'

'And does *Oberst* Klimt believe I'm in touch with my husband?'

'*Oberst* Klimt believes you are a woman of rare intelligence. He also believes you sometimes take matters into your own hands. If I may say so, that makes *Oberst* Klimt a very lucky man.'

A smile played at the corners of Huber's mouth. Hélène realised he was enjoying this conversation.

'I'm flattered,' she said. 'Tell me how I might be able to help you.'

Huber crossed one leg over the other and then fingered the crease on his trousers. Part of his responsibility was, he said, to draw up a comprehensive list of holdings with regard to the leading European art galleries currently under German protection. In France, the task was complicated by the fact that the French authorities had evacuated many of the best pictures during the *drôle de guerre*. The Germans had arrived to find most of the walls in the Louvre bare. Which remained, said Huber, a disappointment.

Hélène permitted herself a smile. *La drôle de guerre* was the Phoney War. Huber was right. The best stuff had gone south.

'You know about these paintings, *madame*?'

'I know they were evacuated. Everyone knows that. All you had to do was go to an art gallery. There was nothing there. That's why they all closed.'

'So where did they go?'

'I have no idea. France is a big country. I imagine it's a question of *patrimoine*. A war breaks out, you do your best to protect your precious heritage. I'm sure Germany would do the same, no?'

Huber left the question unanswered. Nathan, he said, would surely have known.

'Why?'

'Because it was his business, *madame*. Literally. Talk to anyone in this city about fine art, about paintings, and Nathan Khorrami is a name that comes up. He knew everything about everything.

I find it inconceivable to believe that he wouldn't know where the best work went.'

Hélène shook her head. Herr Huber might be right. She accepted that. But if he also believed that her husband had shared any of this knowledge with his wife, then sadly Herr Huber was wrong.

Huber's face was a mask. He plainly didn't believe a word.

'We think many of the paintings ended up in chateaux,' he said. 'It doesn't take much to hide even a big canvas. It would save us a great deal of time and effort if we knew where to look.'

'And you still think I know?'

'I think your husband knows. In fact I'm certain he does. And I also think it might be wise for you to have a conversation with him. We can facilitate that, *madame*. There are ways and means.'

'By pigeon?'

'By telephone. You will doubtless have his number. Am I right?'

Hélène nodded. Klimt had acquired a number from sources he'd never revealed. She'd tried to get through on a number of occasions but calls out of France were always blocked at the exchange.

'So what am I supposed to say to him?'

Huber had produced a single sheet of paper. He flattened it on his knee, then glanced up.

'You will appraise him of this conversation, *madame*, and present my compliments. You will tell him that we believe he may know the whereabouts of this list of paintings.' He nodded down

122

at his knee. 'Maybe not the entire list but certainly some of them. You will ask him where they are and to whom we should direct our further inquiries. Does that sound reasonable?'

Hélène didn't know what to say. No wonder Huber had been spending so much time in Holland and Belgium. He must be systematically emptying northern Europe of centuries of priceless paintings.

'What if my husband just says no? What if he refuses to co-operate?'

'Then life might start to become . . .' he shrugged, '. . . difficult.'

'For whom?'

'For you, *madame*.'

Hélène nodded. Obvious, she thought. Abetz didn't want Klimt at his *soirée*. He didn't even want Hélène. He wanted Nathan.

The silence stretched almost audibly. Downstairs, Hélène could hear laughter. Huber was waiting for an answer. Finally Hélène asked to see the list.

Huber passed it across. Hélène got no further than the first painting. Then she looked up. She wanted to laugh.

'The *Mona Lisa*, Herr Huber? Are you serious?'

CHAPTER 11

Nell left next morning to catch the early train back to Exeter. Billy watched her through half-shut eyes as she packed her suitcase. When she went to the bathroom he slipped out of bed and folded a five-pound note beneath the top layer of clothes. They both knew the night had been a disaster and Billy, like Nell, had no appetite for a repeat performance. When she returned with her toothbrush, he pretended to be asleep. She left the room with her bag and moments later he caught the soft click as she opened the front door. Her footsteps receded down the street, leaving Billy with the squawk of the seagulls. If he felt anything, he felt relief. Better to be alone, he told himself, regardless of what happens next.

He drifted back to sleep. A vivid dream took him downstairs in the little terrace house he'd shared with his mum in Bristol. The postman had just paid a visit. A letter was lying on the square of spare carpet that served as a doormat. The envelope was brown. It looked official. He opened it, knowing already in the dream that this would be his call to arms. Report to the Initial Training Wing. Bring proof of identity and a toothbrush. He shook the single sheet of paper from the envelope and studied it. A shopping list. Sprouts. Beetroot. And calamine lotion for his mum in case it got hot.

He jerked awake, thinking of his mum. She'd always had reddish hair and the kind of milky complexion that burns easily. She loved the sun and every spring, when you could start to feel the heat, she'd come back from work at lunchtime and take a blanket into their thin ribbon of back garden and lie down for an hour or so before heading back. Next morning, without fail, her face would be scarlet with sunburn but she swore by the calamine lotion and within a week or so she'd have the makings of a proper tan.

Back then, when he was still a kid, Billy's mum had been the prettiest woman he knew. Most of the time she was soft with him, lots of treats, lots of attention, lots of love, and she saved the occasional smack for the rare moments when he really upset her. He'd cry, mostly from surprise, but they'd always make up afterwards and she'd tell him that it was hard being a woman and having to play father. What Billy really needed, she'd say, was his dad back again but thanks to the war that was never going to happen. Billy understood the logic, however dimly, but in truth he was more than happy to have his mum to himself. She'd always been his best friend, his trusted pal, a state of affairs he'd taken utterly for granted. Only in the last few days, since he had returned from duty, had he come to realise she had needs of her own.

He got up late, wondering whether Nell might have left a note downstairs. She hadn't. He found some tea in an old biscuit tin and made himself a brew. The last six months had taught him to do without milk when needs must and he took the scalding mug through to the sitting room at the front. The ashes in the grate were still warm and the smell of charred wood still hung in the dusty air. The house faced south and the room was full of sunshine. This was seaside weather. Bucket and spade weather. Babbacombe, he thought. And the view across the bay.

He took the train to Exeter, and then another to Torquay. Sitting in the half-empty compartment with the sun on his face, he felt himself floating, apart, cut off from the conversation between the two women opposite, from glimpses of the nearby river, from the sudden chequerboard of shadows as the train clattered past a line of trees. At first he blamed last night. They'd drunk a lot, a bottle of wine each. But then he recognised something else. That this feeling of numbness came from somewhere else. That he was truly alone. No Nell. No mum. No aircrew. No friendly WAAF faces waiting at the foot of the ladder when they returned from yet another op. Not a single living person to share the week and a half to come.

He walked the couple of miles from Torquay

station to Babbacombe. The RAF had taken over most of the hotels and in the early afternoon they were as busy as ever: officers with briefcases ducking into cars at the kerbside, recruits still in civvies trying to match hotel names to their joining instructions, uniforms in line abreast marching untidily towards the seafront.

Billy followed them. The Sefton Hotel overlooked a patch of greensward before the clifftop dropped away to the beach below. The view stretched across the blueness of the bay. In the far distance, beyond the line of ochre cliffs, he could just make out the smudge that was Exmouth.

Billy paused, looking back at the hotel. He'd spent eight weeks here barely a year ago, sharing a room on the second floor with three other lads. Everything had been packed up and stored away for when peace finally returned – furniture, curtains, even carpet – and he remembered the bareness of the place, its sense of grim purpose, and the feel of the floorboards beneath his bare feet.

In the services, they stripped you naked and remade you in their own image, exactly the way they wanted you. Like speeches he'd had to memorise in the theatre, he could still recite the standard issue kit that would shape the days to come. Knife, fork, spoon, shaving stick, hair brush, button cleaner, polishing stick. This was what turned you into an airman, an expert in the delivery of high explosive, but what had won his undivided attention were the dog tags. There were two. One was green and one was red. The green one was water-resistant. The red one would survive a fire. They were suspended on a 38-inch loop of cotton cord and you wore them round your neck. Stamped with your name, initials, service number and religion, they were all that would be left of you if it came to the worst. The red one, said the instructor, would be sent to your squadron for purposes of information. While the green one remained with whatever was left of you.

Whatever was left of you.

It was a phrase that Billy would never forget. So casual. So graphic. So laden with images too horrible and too unlikely to contemplate. Then, like everyone else, he'd shoved the thought to the very back of his mind because it served no useful purpose. Over the weeks to come, thanks to daily PT and hours in a classroom, he'd lost nearly a stone and learned a great deal about basic airmanship, every busy day taking him a step closer to acceptance as a trainee pilot. The flying hadn't worked out, not at all, but gazing at the hotel he knew that the instructor had been a great deal wiser than he'd ever realised. Only at 20,000 feet over a burning city, he thought, do you finally understand where all this may lead.

Whatever was left of you.

He walked back down the hill to the harbour. More memories. This was a drill you only did once. Flying suit. Boots. Helmet. Goggles. And your Mae

West life jacket. Standing on the edge of the harbour he gazed down at the murkiness of the water below. Felt the instructor's hand in the small of his back. Then came the whispered invitation. Just do it, Angell. Don't stand there. Don't think about it. Just jump. And so he'd launched himself off the edge of the harbour, anticipating the explosion of bubbles, the icy kiss of the water as it sluiced into his suit, how heavy everything felt, and that unlikely moment of salvation as he finally surfaced. Through his misted-up goggles, he'd just made out the upturned dinghy. It was barely a fingertip away. And it was his job, with a couple of pals, to right it.

One of them was a Scouser called Mick who'd later died over Wuppertal. The other was a thin-faced former choirboy from Reading who'd bailed out of a Halifax over the North Sea and was never seen again. Billy stared down at the water, at the blur of boats. Something to eat, he thought. Anything.

The café lay several streets away from the waterfront. It was small and empty. Billy was glad of the semi-darkness at the back. A little privacy, the way he was feeling, was more than welcome.

He asked for cake and a cup of tea at the counter. When the cake appeared on the plate it was a thin slice, wartime portions, and so he ordered two. The waitress, who was on the plump side, gave him a wink and then a grin but Billy wasn't in the mood for conversation. He retired to his table with his tea. The cake was tasteless and he couldn't even guess at the ingredients. He ate half the first slice and left the rest, staring glumly at a nearby poster.

An airman in full flying kit was appealing for waste rubber. The line drawing was good and the implications were beyond sensible. Waste rubber makes for more wheels, more take-offs, and – on a good morning – more landings. Who wouldn't dig out their worn bicycle tyres for the war effort? Swap their rubber doormat for another shower of bombs on some half-destroyed German city?

He thought about the deal, waste rubber for mass incineration, and stirred his tea. It was nearly a week since he'd returned from the Hamburg raid. He'd avoided the chop, just, but what stuck in his memory, what grew and grew like some hideous cancer, was the moment he'd opened the hatch above the bomb bay and glimpsed the bubbling furnace below. He was part of that. He was complicit. Despite Irene, despite their visits to the Friends Meeting House, despite his passionate arguments with more or less everyone else in his life, he'd finally bent to the wind, and appeared before the selection board, and taken the train down here, and doubled up and down to the beach, and mistaken jelly-legs for patriotism. In the name of democracy, and to revenge the death of the woman he'd worshipped, he'd mastered the dark arts of slaughter. It was wrong. Wrong, wrong, wrong. And yet he'd done it.

He stared down at the slices of cake. His appetite had vanished. His vision was blurring again. He felt a choking in his throat. People were right about war. It ate you up.

'Are you all right?'

The question gave him a physical jolt. In combat, you never see the one that gets you. And here it was. The killer question.

Local accent. Male. Soft. Concerned. Gentle.

Are you all right?

'No,' Billy wiped his nose with the back of his hand. 'No, I'm not.'

He was looking up now. Against the glare from the street it was hard to be sure about details. Middle-aged? Bald? Wide face? Full lips? Kind eyes?

'Here. Take it.'

Billy did as he was told. The handkerchief was white, unsoiled. He dabbed at his eyes and then blew his nose.

'I'm sorry.' He was looking at the handkerchief.

'Don't be. Keep it. You're on leave? Bit of a holiday?'

'Yes.'

'Alone?'

'Yes.'

'But something's happened? Am I right?'

A second killer question. Two in a minute. This wasn't a chat, Billy thought. This was an interrogation.

Something's happened?

Billy took his time. He was a believer in the comfort of strangers, always had been, just one of the instincts that had drawn him to Irene. You looked someone in the eyes. You listened hard to the tone of their voice. You absorbed all the signals. You tuned to their wavelength. And if you were brave, or desperate, you made that leap of faith.

'Have you got a moment?' He nodded at the other chair. 'I'd be grateful.'

They stayed in the café for the rest of the afternoon. The stranger's name was Don. He helped out in the kitchen odd afternoons during high summer. The café happened to be on the route from the station and he'd watched hundreds, maybe thousands of young RAF recruits make their way up the hill towards the requisitioned hotels at Babbacombe.

Money was always short, he said, and mornings and evenings he worked in a hotel along the way. The place was popular with the men in blue and he'd seen more than enough of these young heroes to be able to mimic their conversation. He was a good mimic. He caught the nervous edge of their excitement, of their shared glee to have avoided Army service, of their brash awkwardness when local girls turned up, and he drew a small round of applause from Billy when he described their anticipation of what awaited when they started flying in earnest.

'They all think they're in the movies,' he said. 'They can't wait to be famous.'

Billy knew about their kind of fame. About the endless cycle of ops. About the twice-weekly allotment of targets. About waking up to fog and praying for a scrub. About putting your life in the hands of the weather gods and the small army of radar technicians, flak gunners and night-fighter pilots all lying in wait to kill you. And finally about what happened to a pal of his over Hamburg who'd volunteered to be a Rear Gunner. His description spared Don none of the details.

'This is recently?'

'Last week. Did we win the war? No. Did he die? Yes. Did it hurt? Yes. Was he frightened? Very. And were there tens of thousands of people underneath us in exactly the same boat? Again, yes. It makes no sense, Don. So why do we do it?'

'Because we have to. Because we must.'

'Otherwise?'

'Otherwise we'll all be speaking German.'

'And is that such a bad thing? Compared to this?'

Don didn't answer. He was looking at the cake.

'Was it that bad?'

Billy shrugged. Then asked the time.

There was an old station clock on the wall behind the counter. Nearly half past six. The café would be closing very soon. Don retrieved the cake and the empty mug and headed back to the counter. Did Billy fancy a proper drink?

Billy did. They left the café and headed along the seafront towards Paignton. A side street took them inland. Don walked with a heavy limp and progress was slow. At last they got to the hotel. It was called the Palmview. It was small, wedged between a garage and a firm of undertakers, and it was badly in need of a coat of paint. Not a trace of a palm, no sign of a view. This, said Don, was where he spent most of his working hours. His boss was a man called Stan. He'd been with him at the hotel for a while and tonight was special because Stan's mum had just died, leaving Don in sole charge while Stan and his wife took the bus to Plymouth to sort everything out.

'How many guests?'

'Three. Two families and a bloke on his own. That's all the rooms we've got, apart from mine.'

'You live here?'

'Yes.'

'And Stan?'

'He and his missus live next door.'

They were still standing outside the hotel. Billy was staring at the coffins behind the big plate glass window.

'It's a funeral place.'

'That's right. That's where Stan says the money is. Death and taxes. What else can you rely on these days?'

The hotel smelled rank. Billy had identified drains, stewed cabbage, chip fat and the remains of the morning's toast by the time they made it down the narrow stairs to the basement bar. Here, at last, Stan had made an effort. The bar itself was dominated by a huge wooden propeller and squadron pictures, all in black and white, lined the walls. A blow-up photo of a Stuka served as a dartboard and a long list of names and scores were scrawled on the adjacent chalkboard. No wonder the recruits flocked here.

'I've come here to get away from all this,' Billy pointed out.

'No, you haven't. You came back for a look. You came back to try and understand how it all started. And then you met me.'

'That's true.'

'I'm asking for help, Billy. And I'm guessing that's something you need, too. The fun starts any time now. With luck it might get ugly.'

Ugly turned out to be an understatement. Losses in Bomber Command were stratospheric and here was the living proof. These recruits were kids, younger than ever, piling in from the street, clattering down the stairs, and they had no idea how to drink. The cider came off a farm in the hills behind the town. It was home-brewed, intensely cloudy and very strong. It was also very cheap. By mid-evening, glassy-eyed, drinkers were peppering the wooden panels around the Stuka with darts. They were also singing.

> *Poor old pilot's dead*
> *Poor old pilot's dead*
> *He's killed himself*
> *He's killed himself*
> *Poor old pilot's dead*

Billy tried to shut his ears to the lyrics, comforted by Don's presence behind the bar. Don was a natural with the kids, letting their brashness wash over him, and when a series of parp-parps from the road outside announced the arrival of the bus that was to return the recruits to Babbacombe, he had no difficulty getting them out of the door. One was sick on the stairs. Another threw up in the apron of parched grass that served as a front garden.

Billy watched the bus growling away towards the seafront.

'This happens every night?'

'Twice a week. Lucky me, eh?'

They cleared up in the bar. Then Billy watched Don at work with a mop and a bucket on the stairs. He wanted to know about the limp.

'I fell off a fairground ride as a kid. I think the bone man at the hospital must have been drunk that night. The thing never set properly.'

'Thing?'

'This.' Wedged sideways on the staircase, Don tapped his left thigh. 'They broke it again and had another go but that only made it worse. You want a piece of advice? From someone who knows? Never trust a Waltzer.'

Billy nodded. He wanted to know whether the limp had got him out of National Service.

'Of course it has. That's why I'm here. Mopping up after the nation's heroes.'

'And you don't mind?'

'Mind what?'

'Missing it all?'

Don didn't answer. Instead he handed the bucket to Billy and nodded at the nearby toilet. By the time Billy got back down to the bar he was looking at two huge balloon glasses on the bar. Something amber and fizzy.

'What's that?'

'Brandy and ginger. I'm sparing us the cider. Thank Stan for the brandy.'

They touched glasses. The last time Billy had drunk brandy was the end-of-run party on Broadway before the long voyage home. He took a sip, and then another. Lovely, he thought.

He found himself talking about those days. Don had the happy knack of listening. He also seemed to have an intuitive grasp of what was going on in Billy's head. How life had slipped out of focus after his return from New York. How he seemed to have parted company with everything he'd once taken for granted. How the war had blundered into his life and stolen everything that had once mattered. The theatre was closed, Irene was dead, and now even his mum, thanks to her new life, was equally beyond reach.

'So what's left?'

'Nothing. Just this . . .' Billy gestured round at the bar. He felt unaccountably tearful again. The laughter gone. Nothing left but the terror awaiting these young drunks.

He watched Don adding a hefty glug of brandy

to his glass. They'd run out of ginger ale but already he knew he was drunk.

'You know the way it is in the theatre?' he said. 'They pay you to be someone else. I never realised it at the time but that's a real privilege. Why? Because you don't have to be you anymore.'

'And that's the way you feel now?'

'Exactly. Except that now's worse. Because there's no script, no role, no play, no curtain call, no nothing. Now's real. And you want to know what I dread? That now is forever.'

'You want to be someone else?'

'Yes, please.'

'Some*where* else?'

'That's impossible. We are where we are. I can't stop the war. No one can. The war's like gravity, like the bloody weather. It just happens. It's who I am that bothers me. These last few days I feel nothing. Just nothing. Ask me to get up. Ask me to make a decision, open the door, turn the tap on, I can't do it. Nothing happens. Choice is meaningless. Choice is a tease. Choice will change nothing. Because *I* am nothing. Life's a game. I know that. I used to be a player. I knew the rules. I threw the dice. Sometimes I even won. That's all gone. And it's gone because I can't even *find* the bloody dice, let alone give it a roll.' He gazed across the bar at Don, tried to get that big warm face into focus. 'Am I making sense? Do you understand? Just a little bit?'

Don nodded. He'd barely touched his own glass.

'Do you ever read poetry?' he asked.

'Yes.'

'Did you ever come across a Persian poet? A man called Rumi? Thirteenth century?'

'No.'

'He was a wise man. I have a book upstairs. Here's a line to think about, Billy. Are you ready for this?'

Billy nodded. Reached for his glass. Nursed it in both hands. Waited.

'*A wound is the place where the light comes in.*'

Billy stared at him. Beautiful, he thought.

'Say it again.'

Don obliged. This was just a taste of Rumi, he said. He'd be happy to lend Billy the book.

'You'd do that?'

'Of course.'

'And you think that applies to me?'

'I know it does.'

'Because I'm wounded?'

'Because you're damaged. And because one day you'll get better. Live in the moment, Billy. Live in the breath. Let time have her way. It's OK to be frightened, to be upset, to cry. Just let it happen. And afterwards you'll be glad.'

Slumped on the bar stool, Billy nodded. Speech seemed to have deserted him. He emptied the glass, shut his eyes, felt the brandy scorching down his gullet.

'That's a promise?' he managed.

'It is.'

Billy felt a hand settling on his. Don, he thought.

Thank God for Don. He opened his eyes again. Gazed round.

'Where am I sleeping?'

'With me. Upstairs. Is that OK?'

Billy's gaze returned to the blur behind the bar.

'That's fine,' he said. 'That's perfect.'

CHAPTER 12

After the soirée in the rue de Lille, Klimt took Hélène to a nightclub. She said she needed a drink. For the time being she hadn't shared her conversation with Johann Huber but she was in no doubt that he meant what he said. Either assist the Reich lay hands on the best of French-held artwork or be prepared to face the consequences. Find the *Mona Lisa*? Crazy.

The club was called Le Poisson d'Or. She'd never been there before but Klimt seemed to know it well. She watched him moving from table to table, exchanging handshakes and gossip and fond little kisses for a succession of women. At first glance he seemed to be on home territory – relaxed, enjoying himself – but she sensed that Klimt, too, was under threat. How many of these people does he trust anymore, she wondered.

A saxophonist was playing on the tiny stage. Hélène watched him through the haze of blue smoke. He was black. He wore a greasy leather hat and he dipped and swayed as he played. Many of the men around the tables were in uniform and most of them had their backs turned to the music.

They were talking to each other, lots of hand gestures, lots of emphatic nodding, and Hélène watched them for a moment or two as the waiter arrived at the biggest table with yet another carafe. Officers at play after a busy day's Occupation, she thought. They've been here years and they control everything and that's the way they assume it's always going to be. Welcome to the New Order. No wonder Paris was so surly, so withdrawn.

Klimt ordered champagne. She wanted to talk to him. She wanted to be somewhere quiet, somewhere private, where they could be themselves again, but when she leaned closer and suggested they forgot the champagne and went back to her apartment for the night he shook his head. Believe it or not, he was still on duty. And duty compelled a return to the Hôtel Meurice.

'Do I come too?'

'Regrettably not.'

'*Vorschriften*?'

'I'm afraid so.'

Vorschriften meant 'regulations'. The whole of France had made this first step into the German language.

Klimt put his hand over hers. Then came a counter-suggestion. Might he ask her for a dance?

The dance floor was even smaller than the stage but they had it to themselves. At a discreet nod from Klimt, the saxophonist slowed the tempo, allowing Klimt to draw Hélène closer. He was dancing with real intimacy, the kind of closeness you can never confect. Hélène recognised the tune. It was the theme from *Casablanca* and as the saxophone dipped and soared Klimt began to sing the lyrics to her. In English.

Hélène was aware of turning heads, of abandoned conversations, of a stillness settling on the smoky club. And the quieter it became, the more justice Klimt was able to do to the lyrics.

His English was faultless, lightly accented with an American lilt. He might have been Humphrey Bogart. The music came to an end and Klimt took a tiny step backwards and kissed Hélène's outstretched hand. By now Hélène had realised that this was a show for the benefit of his countrymen, that Klimt was saying he didn't care about the rough protocols of Occupation, about *Vorschriften*, that in a Paris disfigured by a terrible defeat it was still possible to behave like a gentleman and a romantic. Love mattered. The music mattered. And maybe all will come good. As time goes by.

Was this a figment of Hélène's imagination? She stood with Klimt on the dance floor, gazing round. One of the younger officers at the back was the first to start applauding. He smacked the table with the flat of his hand. Then came another hand. And another. Until the room was swamped with applause and the saxophonist had taken up the tune again and everyone who knew any English was doing their best with the lyrics.

Back at their table, the champagne arrived. Klimt sorted out a two-hundred *Reichsmark* note to give to the waiter. The man was French. He wouldn't take the money.

'*C'est gratuit, m'sieur.*' His eyes drifted to Hélène. '*Avec nos compliments.*'

Klimt offered a nod of gratitude, then folded the note into the waiter's top pocket.

'*C'est pour vous, m'sieur. Travail, famille, patrie, n'est-ce pas?*'

Work, family and motherland were the three legs of the Vichy stool on which the whole of France now squatted. This was Marshal Pétain's prescription for the coming years, and Klimt's toast to the waiter had pushed a romantic gesture to its limits. If senior officers were present in the club, then Klimt could be in real trouble. These were martinets without a sense of humour or a moment to waste on mere sentiment. But that didn't matter. Because Hélène had understood the message Klimt was sending.

They left the club with the bottle of champagne and walked down through a maze of streets to the Seine. Now they were sitting on a bench on a *quai* beside the river. Klimt was staring at the blackness of the water. Hélène reached for his hand.

'That was for me, wasn't it? Back in the club?'

'Of course. And for my countrymen.'

'Why?'

'Because we have a terrible gift for taking ourselves too seriously. Not just us Germans. Everyone.'

'Including me?'

'Possibly not. You have different kinds of gifts,

talents I barely understand, except for one thing. Without them, without the knowledge that they exist, I would be nothing.'

Hélène put the champagne bottle aside and kissed him. From Klimt, this had the makings of a speech. He was good at little quips. His occasional jokes made her laugh. He knew how to choose a present. He made her feel wanted, protected. They pleased each other in all kinds of ways. But never this.

'Tell me more.'

'There is no more.'

'That sounds very final.'

'It needn't be.'

'Then tell me why you've changed.'

The fact that he didn't deny it told her a great deal. She wanted to know who he'd upset, and how serious the consequences might be.

'You think I'm in trouble?' he asked.

'I think we're in trouble.'

'Because I might not be around to look after things?'

'Things' made her wince. Not once had their relationship sounded so mundane, so utilitarian.

'Is that what it is for you? A question of management?'

'Sadly not. I love you.'

He wouldn't look at her. He was watching a pair of uniformed *Wehrmacht* on patrol. They'd been past once already and he'd dismissed their demand for papers with a terse word or two she hadn't understood.

Now she tried to coax his face around. She wanted him to look at her. She wanted to know that it was true.

'You think I'm lying?' he said. 'You think this is some kind of game?'

'No.'

'Then believe me.'

'But I need to know.'

'Know what?' At last he looked at her. He was angry. She could see it in his eyes. 'That I love you? That I really love you? That I don't make these things up? Is that it? Is that what you want to know?'

'No. I want to know what's happened in that world of yours. I want to know what's going on, what's made you so . . .' she shrugged, '. . . different. And I want to know when it might stop.'

'Ah . . .' he forced a smile, '. . . stop. Now there's a question.'

There was a long silence. The soldiers were on their way back, their boots echoing on the cobblestones. In her heart, Hélène knew that the conversation was over. Back to the Hôtel Meurice. A car for Madame Lafosse to the 16th.

'Might we meet tomorrow?' It was a question she had to ask.

Klimt was on his feet. He looked down at her. The soldiers were very close.

'*Sturmbannführer* Huber will be at your door by midday,' he said. 'My compliments to your husband.'

CHAPTER 13

Billy spent four days in Torquay. He kept company with Don, first at the hotel, then at the café, then back to the Palmview for more decorous evenings in the bar without the company of the Babbacombe recruits. He'd never been with a man before, not like this, and it felt completely natural. No shame, no guilt, not an ounce of embarrassment.

In ways he couldn't quite explain, Don seemed to have known him for years. Nothing Billy could say about himself appeared to come as a surprise. Neither did Don seem the least bit bored by his fund of stories. With aircrew, Billy had always been careful to rein himself in from his wilder fantasies. Flying was a very grown-up occupation, as was survival. It was also, in the exact sense of the word, overwhelmingly male. Feelings like these, feelings he had for Don, had no place in either a heavy bomber or the succession of freezing billets where they lived. For a quiet life, you pretended to be as normal as you could. For an actor, that wasn't difficult. For the real Billy Angell, as he was coming to recognise, it had taken him close to madness. Thank God, once again, for Don.

'Be who you are, Billy. And be proud of yourself.'

They were standing on Torquay station. The train from Paignton had just arrived and the carriages were being mobbed by recruits. When Don suggested he get a move on to secure a seat Billy shook his head. The kids would be travelling way up the line. After two months of jelly-legs they deserved a sit-down. Billy, on the other hand, had just enjoyed what felt like the holiday of a lifetime. And one of the things he wanted to say was thank you.

Don was taller as well as older than Billy. Billy reached up and kissed him. A woman with two spaniels on a lead stopped in mid-stride, then headed for a different carriage. Billy toyed with an apology, then had second thoughts. Don didn't seem the least bit upset.

'You don't mind?'

'Mind what? You kissing me?'

'Yes.'

'Do I look like I mind?'

'Not at all.'

'So don't worry. You're a lovely man. And you're much braver than you think. Come back any time. Come back for good. Either way, I'll be here for you.'

I'll be here for you.

Billy stood on the train, wedged between a couple of sleepy recruits, trying to sort out his feelings.

That Don had strayed across his path was a stroke of extraordinary luck. That they'd been so natural together, and so close, had been another blessing. In the theatre, had Don been a character on the page, he'd have been a privilege to play. Billy loved his patience, his wit, his big lopsided face, his absolute faith in the goodness of others. In some ways, it felt like being with Irene again, except Don's blood pressure seemed to be even lower. That someone so wise, and so sure of themselves, could find even a splinter of promise in a battle-damaged Wireless Op was an immense relief. There might, thanks to Don, be some prospect of getting through.

Getting through what? Billy walked the half-mile back from Topsham station. It was still the same village, still quaint, still full of heart-stopping glimpses of the river but, shorn of the terrible burden of trying to pretend he was someone else, he seemed to be seeing it through new eyes. He'd been grateful for Nell's company. It had been kind of her to try and ease some of the pain he'd been feeling. But what she wanted from him, the Billy she thought she knew, had gone. God knows, she'd tried hard enough. She was an accomplished lover. She had a repertoire of tricks. She knew what worked with him and on previous occasions they'd done OK. But now was different. Now, for what-ever reason, he'd become the real Billy Angell. And that realisation had warmed him in ways he'd only ever dreamed about.

He let himself into the house. Waiting on the mat was an envelope with his name on it. He recognised his mother's handwriting. The postmark was Bristol. The door still ajar, he ripped the envelope open. Expecting a letter of some sort he found himself looking at a telegram. Beneath it, in pencil, his mum had scribbled a single word. *Sorry*.

The telegram had been sent by the Station Adjutant at RAF Wickenby. Billy must have read dozens like these: the same flat prose, the same blunt sympathy. REGRET TO INFORM FLT SGT SIMON MEREDITH KILLED IN TRAINING ACCIDENT.

Billy closed the door and took the telegram through to the kitchen. It had been kind of the Adjutant to trouble himself with sending a telegram but the house was suddenly cold. Not just cold but arctic. The rest of V-Victor's lads had presumably been scattered among the other training crews, imparting little seeds of experience to help them towards the front line. The fact that they were still alive, still airborne, was some consolation. But not much.

Why Simon? And how come he survived a full tour, cheated impossible odds, and then hit some Scottish mountain with a bunch of amateurs who didn't know what they were doing? Billy sank into the kitchen's single chair. He wanted Don here. He needed a listening ear. He wanted someone wise enough, and big enough, to make sense of it all.

There was a phone box down at the end of the road. He had the Palmview's number. He could put a call through, and maybe later that's exactly what he'd do. But for now he knew he needed to confront this news on his own. No props. No Don. Nothing but the ticking silence and the sigh of the wind in the eaves.

He made himself a cup of tea. The last time he and Simon had been alone was at the start of the summer. They'd slept until mid-afternoon thanks to a dawn return from a long trip to Stettin. It was a glorious day and they'd cycled away from the airfield and found a patch of woodland on the other side of the village.

Harry Williams, V-Victor's skipper, had been there before them. He'd said there was a pond with kingfishers at the heart of the wood. He'd been right. Billy and Simon had abandoned their bikes and lolled in the warm grass beneath the trees, watching for the sudden flash of orange and blue over the brackish water. Simon knew about kingfishers. He said they hunted for prey from riverside perches. One of the tiny birds hovered inches above the pond, waiting for a fish to rise, and Billy watched it, fascinated. He understood about flying, about cheating gravity, about the freedom of the skies. But never this.

When the kingfishers had gone, Billy lay back on the grass, his eyes closed. Simon was talking about a walking tour he'd taken in Greece, a whole month in the Peloponnese. Successive waves of conquests had given the rugged landscape Venetian fortresses and Ottoman architecture and he said he'd trekked alone from site to site with everything he needed on his back.

Each stop on his route had shed fresh light on a winter's reading and in September he'd returned to the school in Somerset where he taught with the feeling that he'd become someone else. It was partly, he said, the experience of sleeping rough. Out in the open, especially high in the mountains, it could be cold after dark but the huge bowl of the night sky was pricked with stars and he'd spent hours getting to know the constellations.

Leo was his favourite, the lion poised to leap, and he was also fascinated by Orion. Orion, he said, belonged to Greece. It was visible from any point on the earth's surface but the hunter's real home was here, among the olive trees and the rough mountain pastures. Quite how Simon had made the connection was lost on Billy but the Nav's fascination with the night sky had stayed with him, and once Billy was flying with his new crew he spent more time than he should in V-Victor's astrodome, scanning the heavens.

Was Simon up there with them now? A celestial presence among the teeming stars? Was this where every Nav was destined to end his days? Reclaimed by the constellations they'd befriended in the name of Bomber Command? The thought was strangely comforting and Billy folded the telegram back into its envelope.

Hours later he went to a pub in the village, looking for something to eat. Stale bread, mouldy cheese and a glass of flat beer did nothing to brighten his mood but before he left the pub he got himself a pocketful of change for the phone box. Don was on bar duty at the Palmview and the Babbacombe recruits had just got off the bus. Billy could hear laughter in the background and after a stumbling attempt to share his news with Don, he gave up. Maybe later this evening, he thought. Or maybe tomorrow.

He slept badly, tormented by images of Simon's Lanc spearing in through thick fog, of the violence of the crash, of licks of yellow flame devouring everything inside the broken fuselage, and of the search parties trudging up the mountainside with their body bags and their stretchers. The instructor at Babbacombe, he'd decided, had probably got it right. Death in this war left nothing but a set of dog tags. And that's if you were lucky.

He woke at dawn. He was in a sweat. Imagination had once been his best friend but these days it stalked him day and night. He lay in bed under the dampness of the single sheet, counting the days until he had to take the train north and report, once again, for duty. He knew that instructing with training squadrons could be as dangerous as ops. Aircraft retired from front-line service and barely fit to fly. Novice aircrews. English weather. Flying at night. Plus countless other factors that could gang up to snuff you out. That was fine. That was the chatter in the Mess. But downstairs on the kitchen table was the proof that all this bar talk was true. That even an airman as competent as Simon Meredith could disappear at dusk, never to return.

He shuddered and closed his eyes. Was this fear that he could feel? Was it as simple as that? Was he a coward? Was he yellow? Did he lack moral fibre? Or had Don been right that first night when they'd slept together? That deep inside himself there existed another Billy Angell, the real Billy Angell, who knew that war was wrong, that killing was obscene, and that somehow the bloodshed and the terror had to end?

He was back in a place he didn't know, couldn't make a sane decision, and he must have drifted off to sleep again because the next time he opened his eyes it was full daylight with sun streaming in through the uncurtained windows and he could hear the clump-clump of footsteps coming up the street from the river. The footsteps paused. Then he heard a rap on the door. The postman, he thought.

He wound a towel around himself and made his way downstairs. The tiles in the narrow hall felt icy on his bare feet. He opened the door. Another telegram. He signed for it and then stepped back inside. Telegrams all came in the same brown envelopes. And they all carried news you never wanted to hear.

Billy thought about ignoring it. He toyed with

ripping it to shreds or holding one corner over a burning match. Was this the old V-Victor mob again? Was it Harry Williams this time? Or Les Atkinson, the Bomb Aimer? Or little Johnny Phelps back there in the rear turret? Was it their turn to lay down their lives in the service of Training Command? Did you really survive thirty ops to end up in a brown envelope on someone else's door mat?

He picked up the telegram and took it through to the kitchen. Nell had found a dressing gown when they'd first arrived and he went upstairs to fetch it. Back in the kitchen, he slipped a knife under the flap of the envelope and spread the message on the kitchen table. For a moment, the words made no sense. No name. No regrets. No one killed. Then he read it through a second time.

PLEASE PHONE SHE 4987 AT EARLIEST CONVENIENCE. ASK FOR URSULA BARTON.

CHAPTER 14

*S*turmbannführer Huber appeared at the concierge's desk shortly before noon. Thunderstorms had been rolling over Paris since dawn and his long leather greatcoat was pebbled with rain when Hélène stepped out of the lift to meet him. There was the same coldness in his eyes that she'd noticed the night before and the perfunctory nod of greeting gave nothing away. A car was waiting at the kerbside. The business they had to transact wouldn't take long. With luck, she could be back in the 16th by early afternoon.

Hélène followed him onto the pavement. Across the road, a queue had formed outside a private house that served as a distribution point for bread. One of the women, recognising Hélène, gave her a discreet wave and mouthed *bonne chance*. You wouldn't wish a visit from the SS on anyone.

Hélène climbed into the back of the car with Huber. He sat with his hands carefully folded on his lap, his eyes fixed on the road. Twice he corrected the driver on his choice of route but apart from that he remained silent. This is a man who's died already, Hélène thought. He belongs in the mortuary.

Half expecting a return to the Hôtel Meurice, Hélène was surprised to find herself outside a gated house in the 12th. A soldier saluted Huber as he escorted Hélène into the courtyard, and another figure awaited them at the top of a modest flight of steps. This was an older man, short, thin-faced. He wasn't in uniform but he obviously knew Huber.

They followed him into the house. Twice he checked his watch as they mounted the stairs to the first floor. The house was light – huge windows – and beautifully furnished. Hélène had the feeling she'd been there before but couldn't remember exactly when. Maybe friends of Nathan's, she thought. Back when Paris belonged to the people who lived here.

'Come in, please.'

The older man spoke good French. He held the door open for Hélène. The room was small, even intimate. Bookshelves, an armchair, a pretty little banquette, and a desk beneath the window. Pre-war, thought Hélène, this would have served as a study or a room where you might read undisturbed in the quiet time before the shops opened again and Paris gathered up its skirts for the evening's entertainments.

There was a single telephone on the desk. The older man had lifted the receiver and was dialling a number he checked from a sheet of paper. A muttered question from Huber brought no response except a lifted finger. Patience, please.

Hélène couldn't take her eyes off the telephone. Would Nathan really be at the other end? And, if so, how on earth had they contacted him? Her relationship with Klimt had taught her a great deal about the power and reach of the intelligence services but there was still a kind of sorcery about what was happening. The husband she hadn't spoken to for three long years. The husband whom she'd tried to contact only days before.

She wondered whether he'd ever received the coded birthday greetings, and if so whether he'd thank her. That, given the circumstances, could be worse than awkward. The last thing she wanted to hand Huber was any kind of reason to extend this encounter into a formal interrogation.

The older man was talking on the phone. Huber had folded his greatcoat over the banquette and settled himself in the armchair. He looked attentive and expectant, and he had a pad on his knee. He might have been at the theatre, Hélène thought. He might have been a first-night reviewer tasked to pass judgement on some controversial new play.

The older man gestured for Hélène to take the chair at the desk. He gave her the phone and apologised for the quality of the line. Cross-Channel calls could be troublesome, he said. He'd tried to secure a better connection but he'd failed.

'Is my husband there?' Hélène was holding the phone at arm's length.

'Yes. You might have to shout.'

Hélène nodded. She brought the phone to her ear. All she could hear was the thin rasp of static.

'Nathan?' she ventured. 'Are you there? Nathan?'

'Louder,' it was Huber. 'Shout.'

'Darling?' She'd raised her voice just a little. Not once in her life had she shouted at her husband and now, she told herself, was no time to start.

She adjusted the phone, using her body to shield this conversation from Huber. She thought she caught just a hint of a voice at the other end. A man, certainly, but her husband?

'Nathan? Is that you?'

Abruptly, for whatever reason, the static cleared and her husband was suddenly there, close enough to touch, his voice unmistakable. She'd always loved his voice. It was the first thing she'd noticed about him. It was a deep voice, beautifully modulated, a voice that belonged in a much bigger body. It bubbled with all the things she held dear. With irony and laughter and a rich enjoyment of other people. Nathan never made conversation. Instead he cast spells and his voice was key to that. Just now he had a question.

'What are we speaking? French? English? German?'

Hélène checked with Huber. French. She bent to the phone again. A game like this required rules of engagement and she was determined to spell them out. No subterfuge. No pretence.

'Listen, darling. I'm sitting in a room with an

SS officer. His name's *Sturmbannführer* Johann Huber. He's probably recording this conversation. I simply don't know. We're somewhere in the 12th. It's a nice house. For once our new friends haven't wrecked it. Should I say thank you? What do you think?'

Nathan roared with laughter.

'Huber I know,' he said. 'His father used to run a decent gallery in Berlin. It was called the Galerie Turschmann. He had an eye, that man. He had a collection of Koenigs including *Der Magic Lantern-enpfahl*. You'll remember that painting, Hélène. The crazy figures in the lamplight? The faces at the window? Well, that belonged to Père Huber, probably still does. Ask Huber if he'll take an offer. I have friends in Sweden. Anything is possible. Tell him dollars, if he insists. Twenty-five thousand but not a cent more. Are you still there?'

Hélène stole a look at Huber. His face was impassive. He'd yet to take a note.

'Still here, my darling,' she confirmed. 'Happy birthday. I'd have loved to send you a message, a card, a letter, caviar, anything, but our new friends don't encourage that. How do you feel?'

'Older.' The laughter again. 'And you?'

'I feel nothing. This war does something funny to time. I feel like one of those flies trapped in amber. Everything has stopped. Including me. You remember the amber we brought from Poland? That trip we made to the Vistula delta?'

'Sorrel soup every night? *Zupa szczawiowa*? With

dumplings? You loved it.' Nathan had a gift for languages and a prodigious memory. A month in Poland and he could hold his own with the locals in any bar.

Huber was on his feet now. Their time on the phone was obviously limited. He'd scrawled two words on his pad. *Mona Lisa?* The message couldn't have been plainer. Move the conversation along.

Nathan was still reminiscing about their time in Poland. How they'd made a friend of the young Jewish artist in Lublin who'd worked only in charcoal, producing small masterpiece portraits of old women in his neighbourhood. How they'd celebrated St Wenceslas night in Warsaw with a boisterous army of Czech students and danced until dawn.

'I seem to remember Huber has a brother,' he said. 'I think he was on that crappy old battleship when they shelled the Polacks in Danzig. September '39. First day of the German invasion. I wonder if he ever knew what he was starting?'

Huber was tapping his pad. *Mona Lisa?*

At last, glad that the conversation had strayed so far, Hélène did his bidding. She could picture her husband sprawled at some desk in the middle of London, his feet up, his tie loosened, the buttons on his waistcoat undone in anticipation of a decent lunch. The clue, as ever, was the voice. Nothing, to her immense relief, had changed. Nathan, regardless of the circumstances, was enjoying himself.

She told him about the previous night's conversation with Huber. The French had emptied galleries across Paris.

'Very wise. I did the same.'

'But you took your stuff with you. I know you did. It's the rest Herr Huber wants to know about.'

She'd brought the list Huber had given her last night. She went through it, line by line. Specific galleries. Specific paintings. She saved the *Mona Lisa* until last.

'So what's your question?' The laughter had gone from Nathan's voice.

'Not my question, darling. Huber's. He wants to know where all this stuff has ended up.'

'And he thinks I know?'

'He's certain you know.'

'How?'

'Because he thinks you were friends with these people, with the people at the Louvre, and all the other galleries. And he assumes they let you into their little secrets.'

'Does he really?'

'Yes.'

'And he thinks I know where these pictures, these paintings, are hidden?'

'Yes. France is full of chateaux. He has men standing by. He wants to know where to start.'

'Then tell him I don't know. Tell him any chateau. It makes no difference. It's a lottery, like everything else in life. Maybe he's lucky, maybe not. You want a tip from me? The *Mona Lisa* is probably treble-wrapped in waxed paper inside some little wooden crate and buried in the middle of some farmer's field. Tell him to start at Calais and work south. Dig it all up. The Pas-de-Calais. Picardie. Normandie. Bretagne. The lot. He'll be an old man by the time he gets as far as Paris but at least he'll have the satisfaction of knowing he's tried. Blood and soil. The Germans love it. Our soil. Their blood. That sounds like a deal most gentlemen could live with. Tell him to try it. Let's see what happens.'

Hélène glanced at Huber again. The older man had given him a pair of headphones. He was obviously monitoring every word of the conversation.

There was silence on the line. Then Nathan asked whether she was still there.

'I am, darling.'

'And Huber?'

'Him, too.'

'Good. Something else he ought to know. In fact, three things. Tell him to write them down. Is he ready?'

Huber was back in the armchair. Not a flicker of response.

'Go ahead, darling,' Hélène said. 'I think he's listening.'

'All right, so it's 1940. The Germans are on the move. They're in France. They've found an open window. They've climbed into the boudoir. And they're about to screw us, every single one of us. That's a fact. That's what they did. Now Huber happens to be right about the galleries. Most of them moved stuff out much earlier because in real life that's what you do. I happened to be late because I happen to be a gambler. You know that and so do all those important people Huber mistakes for friends of mine. Alas, that's not true. For three reasons. One, I'm a Jew. Two, I'm very successful. And three, I know how to look after myself. So does Huber, of all people, who knows a lot about Jews, really imagine that any of these important people would share their secrets with a fat little Persian kike who's made so much money? Has he ever lived in that country of ours? Does he know about Dreyfus? About Léon Blum? And how about the camp at Drancy? Let me tell you something about Huber and his pals. They've emptied all the galleries in Paris run by Jews. Every single one. And you know where all those paintings have gone? The Jeu de Paume. The Rothschilds, the David-Weills, the Bernheims, Paul Rosenberg's stuff, it's all gone there. Put him on, Hélène. Let me talk some sense into the man.'

The Jeu de Paume was a gallery on the north corner of the Tuileries Gardens. There were tens of thousands of looted pictures stored there. All Paris knew.

Hélène was staring at the phone. Even she was taken aback by the venom of her husband's outburst. She'd seen this side of Nathan before. In business he could be tougher than anyone she'd ever met. That's what had earned him his standing in the city's art world. That's what had led to the

164

opening of his second gallery. People admired his taste, appreciated his negotiating skills. But there was something else he had to understand here, something she'd yet to share with him.

'They're making threats, darling.'

'Who's making threats?'

'Huber. He thinks you know what he needs to know. And he thinks I can make you share that knowledge.'

'He really thinks I'm privy to all this stuff?'

'Yes.'

'Then he's crazy.' A longish pause. 'Threats, you said.'

'Yes.'

'What kind of threats?'

'It could be anything. These people have total control. They can do whatever they like.'

'To you?'

'I'm afraid so. I don't want you to worry, my darling. I just want you to know.'

'And you think there's a difference? Jesus fucking Christ.'

Nathan rarely swore. This was suddenly a whole new conversation. Hélène checked on Huber again. For once, there was a smile on his face.

'Tell your husband he has a week,' he murmured. 'One week. Then you have another conversation.'

Hélène nodded. Nathan was back. He'd been thinking about what she'd told him. And he'd come to a decision.

'Put Huber on the line,' he said again.

Hélène looked at Huber. Huber shook his head. 'You can tell me,' she said.

'Fine. These people are crude. They take a hostage. It happens to be you. They know you're my wife. They assume you're precious to me and for once they're right. So the deal is simple. We swap. I come to them. You come here. Then I can tell them in person what I really feel. Put it to him. Ask him. Tell me what he says.'

'He's listening, darling. He knows already.'

'And?'

Hélène let the question hang in the air. She was looking at Huber. He scribbled something on his pad and then got to his feet.

'One week,' he said, heading for the door.

CHAPTER 15

B illy took the train to London. He'd telephoned Ursula Barton, the signatory of the telegram, and learned nothing beyond his summons to an interview. When he'd enquired whether this might be connected to his imminent posting to a training squadron, she'd been non-committal. But what was odd was her accent. Billy was good with accents, and he was certain she was German.

Despite it being high summer, London was wet and dispiriting, a study in grey. The war was eating away at these people, Billy thought. You could see it in their faces, gaunt, unsmiling. They were preoccupied, withdrawn, locked inside a world of someone else's making. The top of the bus was packed as it made its way out towards the western suburbs yet there was little conversation. Even the servicemen had nothing to say.

The woman on the telephone had told Billy to get off at Shepherd's Bush. Stanlake Road was a five-minute walk away. He was to look for number 49. It had a brown front door. Billy set off from the bus stop. The directions took him into a terrace of substantial properties, handsome double-bay windows, modest first-floor balconies. Even a spindly tree or two dripping rain onto the flagstones in the front gardens. The gate at number 49 had been secured with a loop of binder twine. Cracked black and white tiles led to the front door. Brown. Just as the woman on the phone had promised.

Billy hesitated. He'd been expecting something more official, less interesting. This house couldn't belong to any branch of the RAF. He pushed through the gate, then paused again. From deep inside the house came the sound of a woman singing. It was a recording. It had to be. Billy stood motionless, listening to the sweep of the music, then the moment of near silence that brought in the soloist. Simon Meredith had owned the recording. He'd once played it in the Mess on a particularly rowdy night, to universal bewilderment.

Billy looked for a door knocker. There wasn't one. He rapped on the single pane of pebbled glass. Waited. Tried again. At length a shadow appeared behind the glass and the door opened.

It was a woman, medium height, patterned dress, nice legs, sensible shoes, thin face, good features, blonde hair carefully gathered with a tortoiseshell comb.

'Bellini,' Billy said. '*Casta Diva.*'

'Excellent,' a hint of a smile. 'A very good start, if I may say so.'

She invited him inside and shut the door. The

house smelled musty. At the end of the tiled hall Billy could see a kitchen through an open door.

'Ursula Barton,' the handshake was brief. 'We will talk in here.'

Billy had been right about the accent. Definitely German. It went with the face, naturally severe, and with the hint of sternness in her bearing. This was a woman used to being in a man's world, Billy decided. And in all probability she didn't live here.

The front room was badly in need of redecoration. The wallpaper was beginning to peel in one corner where the damp was getting through and the fireplace had been roughly bricked up. A scattering of books brightened a low shelf on the back wall and there was a fading reproduction of Constable's *The Hay Wain* hanging drunkenly above it.

The gramophone lay on a table in the bay window. The woman lifted the needle and slowed the turntable with her finger until it stopped altogether. In the sudden silence Billy could hear the clip-clop of a horse coming down the street. The milkman, he thought.

The woman tidied a wisp of blonde hair and asked Billy to sit down. Two armchairs, both leather, both showing their age.

'Bel canto is like a box of Belgian chocolates,' she said. 'Very rich. Very tempting. But sometimes you can have maybe too much. Do you find that?'

'Never,' Billy nodded at the gramophone. 'Leave it on if you want to.'

She favoured him again with the same faint smile but made no comment. She wanted to know about his days in the theatre. She'd listened to the performance of *Desire Under the Elms* on the radio and thoroughly approved.

'Elan is a difficult character. You caught him perfectly. Accent. Manner. Everything. A fine performance, Mr Angell. In fact I went to Bristol to find out more.'

Billy was staring at her, caught completely off guard by the compliments. Was this some kind of audition? Was she part of the London theatre world? Had his luck suddenly changed? Was this the beginning of some kind of fairy story?

'So what did you see?' he asked.

'*As You Like It*. And you didn't disappoint.'

'That was just before we went to New York. With the Eugene O'Neill.'

'So I understand. Selling the Americans their own work. That takes nerve as well as talent. Did you enjoy it?'

'I loved it.'

'No nerves?'

'Of course. If you're not frightened you'll never do yourself justice.'

'You believe that?'

'I do, yes.' The expression had come from Irene. Billy had never forgotten it.

'And it works for you? On stage?'

'Absolutely.'

'And off?'

'That can be harder.'

She nodded. This conversation had already become an interview and Billy suspected that most people would have been taking notes by now. But he sensed that this woman didn't need paper and pen. She'd remember everything.

She changed the subject. She asked him about his Quaker beliefs.

'How did you know about that?' Billy felt the first flutter of alarm.

'You were a registered conscientious objector, Mr Angell. It's a matter of record.'

'But is it relevant?'

'Everything is relevant.'

'Why? How?'

'Just answer the question please, Mr Angell.'

Billy, aware of a sudden hardening in her voice, struggled to formulate an explanation. Anything too formal sounded wrong and so he decided to make it personal.

'I was a bit lost at the time,' he said. 'And then I met a woman at the theatre. An actress. She was a wonderful person. And she also happened to be a Quaker.'

'She converted you?'

'She made me see life differently.'

'Are you an easy person to change?'

'I'm a person who trusts people I like, people I look up to. Irene was older than me. She was also wiser than me and she knew how to listen. You don't meet many people like that.'

'You make it sound like a love affair.'

'It was. On my part.'

'And hers?'

'She looked after me. I owe her everything.'

'Have older people always mattered in your life?'

'Yes.'

She nodded, turning to briefly swat at a fly buzzing in the heavy air. The rain had stopped now and a shaft of sunshine caught the planes of her face. Billy had rarely met someone so intense, so direct.

'Tell me about your family,' she said. 'Your father. Your mother.'

'My father was killed in the last war. My mum brought me up.'

'Your father's dead?' The news appeared to surprise her.

'Yes. He was killed before I was born. I never knew him.'

'So your mother brought you up?'

'Yes.'

'And how was that?'

'Fine. Lovely.'

'No men in the house?'

'None. We were pals, Mum and me.'

'And now?'

'Now's different.'

'How?'

'She's remarried. Her new husband is very wealthy. In some ways I think she deserves it. Having no husband all that time must have been hard.'

'And has it changed her?'

'I think it's changed us.'

'For the better?'

'Probably not.'

Billy left it at that. He hadn't come all this way to talk about his mother, to explain about the new life she was sharing with a man too rich and too selfish to make room for a stepson, to describe a house with so many rooms that his poor mum would need a map to locate them all. That conversation belonged elsewhere. He'd had it only days earlier with Don.

'Why am I here?' He did his best to warm the question with a smile. 'Do you mind me asking?'

'Not in the least. And in due course I might explain. But first I need to know why a conscientious objector joins the Air Force. Thirty operations, am I right? And the last one over Hamburg?'

'That's right.'

'So what happened? What made you kill all those people? Given that you were a pacifist?'

For a moment Billy wondered whether she had relatives in Hamburg, or maybe in one of the countless other cities he'd helped destroy. Then he dismissed the thought.

'Irene died in an air raid,' he said simply. 'And that made me think.'

'About what, Mr Angell?'

'About God.'

'Because He wasn't there that night? When your Irene died?'

'Yes.'

'Did you expect Him to be there?'

'Yes.'

'Because Irene told you?'

'No. Because Irene introduced me to Him. We went to meetings together. I like to think I got to know Him. I like to think I got to trust Him.'

'Trust Him to do what?'

'To look after us all.'

'And?'

'I was wrong.'

'How do you know?'

'I was working in the big hospital in Bristol. I was a porter. It was my job to take bodies down to the mortuary.'

'And one of them was Irene?'

'Yes.'

'How was she?'

'In pieces. Literally.'

'And you.'

'Much the same. Ever since.'

He'd said exactly the same thing to Don, the result of another recent conversation that had lasted for hours. Then, like now, he knew it was true. After Irene nothing had made any sense.

Billy heard footsteps in the hall outside. The door opened and a man stepped in with a couple of mugs in one hand. He was immensely tall, middle-aged, military bearing, stiffly erect. He was wearing an old pair of flannel trousers and a grey cardigan over a check shirt. Beautifully polished brogues.

He left the mugs on the table beside the gramophone, then glanced down at Billy.

'No sugar, I'm afraid.'

He turned on his heel and stumped from the room. Billy picked up his mug. He hadn't smelled coffee like this since New York. He took a sip, and then another.

'Delicious,' he said. 'Where did you get it?'

'Lisbon. They import the beans straight from Brazil. We regard it as a rare perk, Mr Angell.'

We? Billy was tempted to enquire further but sensed this wasn't the time or the place. There was a script here, a tacit protocol, and his role was to sit tight and do his best to answer whatever questions came his way.

'Tell me about RAF Wickenby, Mr Angell. Are you glad to have left?'

'I'm glad to have survived.'

'That wasn't my question. Would you be happy if you never returned there?'

'You mean Wickenby? Or operations?'

'Both.'

'Do I have a choice?'

'We think you may.'

'You mean leave the Air Force?'

'Yes.'

'To do what?'

The question seemed to amuse her. She took another sip of coffee. Long fingers. Carefully trimmed nails. No rings. Then she looked up again.

'What took you into acting, Mr Angell? Why the stage?'

'I sort of fell in love with it. I liked the show. I liked the make-believe. It was amazing to watch people have to become someone else.'

'You mean actors?'

'Of course.'

It was true. The first time Billy saw two strangers in rehearsal playing a warring old couple after half a lifetime in a bad marriage had been a moment of revelation. He'd believed every gesture, every line of dialogue, every howl of despair, and when the scene was over he couldn't believe how completely he'd been drawn in. He tried to share this feeling with Ursula. Once you knew how the trick worked, he said, then you couldn't wait to try it for yourself.

'You make it sound like a spell.'

'It is, in a way. That's exactly what it is. It's magic. It's a conjuring trick. It's illusion. It also puts you in charge.' He smiled, thinking of the hot summer's day when he'd discovered the Thunder Run. 'Until I went on the stage I was a shy little boy,' he said. 'Acting changed all that. You can be whoever you want, whenever you want.'

'And wherever you want?'

'Of course. We toured as a company. New York was wonderful. They had proper heating as well as decent food. England's not like that at all. Especially in the north.'

'You're telling me you travel well?'

Billy didn't understand the question. Ursula said she wanted to know whether he was resourceful, whether he could look after himself, whether he could adapt to difficult circumstances. In all three cases, the answer was yes.

'And do you speak French?'

'No. Is that a problem?'

'Not at all. Quite the contrary, in fact.'

She studied him for a long moment and then finished her coffee. She wanted to know where Billy was staying and for how long. When he mentioned Topsham a smile briefly warmed her face. She knew the village. In fact she had friends there. A truly beautiful place. And so very English.

'But I thought you were staying with your mother? That's the address we got from Wickenby.'

'That was what I intended.'

'But it didn't go to plan?'

'No.'

She nodded. There was a briefcase tucked down beside her armchair. She extracted a long brown envelope and shook the contents onto her lap. Then she handed Billy what looked like a form.

'Read it, please,' she said. 'Then I'll be back.'

She collected the mugs and left the room. Billy scanned the form. It came in two parts. The first was a shortened version of the Official Secrets Act, spelling out the penalties for non-compliance. Without much effort, it seemed to Billy, he could be facing the death penalty for divulging state secrets. The second part of the form ran to a couple of brisk paragraphs. By signing on the bottom line, Billy pledged himself to denying that this morning's meeting had ever happened, and that he'd never paid a visit to 49 Stanlake Road.

He was reading the material a second time when Ursula Barton returned. She had a pen in her hand. She stood over him. Billy was aware of his own name typed beneath the dotted line at the bottom of the form. She said that she'd enjoyed their meeting and that he was free to return to Devon to resume his leave. She made a note of the address where he was staying and said it would be helpful if he would let them know if he moved on. Use the phone number on the telegram. In the meantime she'd be happy to meet his travel expenses.

'Do you have any questions, Mr Angell?'

Billy nodded, ignoring the proffered pen.

'Just one,' he said. 'Who exactly are you?'

'Sign on the dotted line, Mr Angell. I'm afraid you have no choice.'

'You're not going to tell me?'

'Alas no,' the smile again. 'At least not yet.'

CHAPTER 16

Hélène spent another two days in Paris in the hope that she might be able to see Klimt again. Twice she phoned the *Abwehr* number at the Hôtel Meurice and both times they said he wasn't available. That evening she stayed at the apartment, hoping he might come home. When he didn't, she tried the Meurice again and this time she found herself talking to someone prepared to be a little more helpful.

Oberst Klimt, he explained, had been called at short notice to a number of important meetings in Berlin. He might be back in Paris by the end of the week. Alternatively he might be absent for a great deal longer. He'd be happy to pass on any message and perhaps a telephone number if that might be useful. Hélène was tempted to supply both but knew that might not be wise. *Important meetings in Berlin? Absent for a great deal longer?* She'd been right. Klimt was in deep trouble.

The following morning she took the train back to Tours. She had a friend in the city, someone she'd met that first summer when she and Nathan had taken possession of the chateau. They'd attended a function at the Musée des Beaux Arts three days after the signing of the German/Soviet Non-Aggression Pact and she remembered a conversation with a couple of Tours' more nervous *citoyens*. They were anticipating that the Germans would pounce on France the moment war was declared and they were already making plans for a decorous, unhurried move to the Spanish island of Mallorca. Better that, said one of them, than to drown in the inevitable flood of refugees.

In retrospect their advice might have been sound, but Hélène's friend had ignored it. Her name was Danielle. She was a palaeontologist working at the Department of Pre-History at the local university. Aside from her knowledge of fossils she had an inexhaustible passion for primitive cave paintings and made frequent visits to the Chauvet caves in the Ardèche. The fact that her conception of time stretched back dozens of millennia had always fascinated Hélène. Here was someone, she always told herself, for whom the Thousand Year Reich would be a mere blink.

Once Nathan had departed for Lisbon, the two women had begun to meet regularly. Danielle occupied a cluttered third-floor apartment over-looking the Loire. She lived alone with three cats. As long as she had access to gasoline, Hélène could leave the chateau in mid-morning and be in Tours in time for lunch. Danielle cooked robust dishes which depended on game from Hélène's estate.

Beneath a torrent of conversation she conjured magical tastes from rabbit and hare, washed down with choice red wines from Hélène's *cave*, and Danielle somehow managed to lay hands on drinkable bottles of calvados to follow the cheese. The cheese, all of it locally made, came from the father of a student of hers. These regular feasts, for both women, had become a kind of lifeline. Even under the New Order, there was still room for laughter, and a brief reunion with gluttony.

Hélène arrived unannounced. Danielle, immersed in a treatise on the Francevillian group fossils, was still in her dressing gown. Hélène had bought two hundred and fifty grammes of coffee from the concierge who looked after her apartment building, the best connected woman in the 16th. It was early afternoon. Hélène stood by the window, watching a barge emerge through the arches of the nearby bridge, while Danielle brewed the coffee. This friend of hers had an almost telepathic gift for other people's moods.

'What's the matter? What's happened?'

Hélène told her about Huber, about the telephone call to Nathan, and worst of all about Klimt. She had never mentioned his name before. The news that Hélène had a relationship with a serving *Abwehr* officer – someone with a finger in everybody's pie – would have come as a profound shock to most women. Not Danielle.

'You love this man?'

'Sometimes, yes.'

181

'Very wise. Just a piece of yourself. And never the best piece, eh? Here—'

She'd poured the coffee. Made a space for Hélène among the drift of papers on the floor. The apartment had no proper furniture. Just a collection of huge stuffed cushions scattered randomly. This was a woman who lived at knee-level, Hélène had always thought.

'So he's what kind of man, this Klimt?'

'He's nice. And *sympa* when you get to know him.'

'He looks after you?' Danielle's little hand flapped at her belly. 'All of you?'

'Very well.'

'And in other ways? He keeps his countrymen in order? So they don't bother you?'

'Yes.'

'Good. A relationship with logic. Never as common as one might like. Put it on the mantelpiece, *chérie*. Give it a dusting from time to time. Along with your favourite clock.'

'This man's not a clock. He'll never be a clock. The clocks stopped three years ago.'

'Lovely, *chérie*. A lovely image. But nothing lasts forever. Not even your precious Klimt.'

Hélène smiled. Danielle had always been ruthless in her private life. Men were attracted to her intelligence, and her wit, and something Hélène had begun to recognise as a kind of madcap courage, but she rarely let them stay in her bed for more than a month or two. She had a tireless interest in good sex. The two women often compared notes. But men's minds bored her quicker than their bodies and once that happened she simply moved on. Life, she told Hélène, was *une confiserie.* The moment you've had enough of one sweetie is the moment to try another.

'So what about Nathan? You think he's serious about coming back? They'd throw him in a cattle wagon. He must know that.'

'He does. He must do. Nathan knows everything about everything.'

'So does he mean it?'

'I don't know.'

'Do you want to put him to the test? Find out?'

'No.'

'Why not?'

'Because you're right. I'd never see him again.'

Danielle nodded. The round-up of Jews was taking place everywhere, all over the country. In Tours the first clues had been there from the start: the queues of shuffling Jews awaiting registration, the big yellow stars they pinned to their overcoats, the arrival of trucks to seize their possessions, and finally the long march to the railway station to await transportation to God knows where. The rest of France had developed a nasty habit of looking the other way and that, in Hélène's view, was regrettable.

'Understatement, *mon petit lapin.* I love you for it. But what else do we do?' Danielle was eyeing the litter of paperwork, notepad after notepad black with her own jottings. 'Me? I'm a submarine. I just submerge and do what I do and wait for the storm to pass. It means I understand the weather. It means I have some respect for the ocean. It also means I'm probably a coward, one of those timid little *moi d'abord* our new masters depend on. But it's not an answer. Not if you're facing a dilemma like yours.'

Hélène shook her head. *Moi d'abord*? Me first? In her opinion Danielle was the least selfish of women.

'Dilemma?' she wondered aloud. 'Is that what it is?'

'Of course. You have two men in your life. Both appear to be in mortal danger. Make sure the next one is more settled. You need a gardener or perhaps a priest. Food for your belly and comfort for your soul. Our German friends understand neither but that's a different issue.'

'So what do I do?'

'*Rien*. You do nothing. You wait for the enemy. The enemy is Huber. Life is a game, *ma petite*, and you always hold better cards than you think. Last night I was listening to the BBC. In weeks, the British and the Americans will be in Italy. Musso is a balloon. By September he will have burst. You bring me more game and we celebrate. By then your little dilemma will have resolved itself.' She tipped her coffee cup in salute. 'Trust me.'

CHAPTER 17

Billy found himself waiting in hope for the telegram. He'd no idea where this strange encounter might lead but the approach of the postman's boots was no longer a threat. He wanted to find out more. He wanted to meet Ursula Barton again, if only to convince himself that he hadn't been making the whole thing up. And on the third day back, at eight in the morning, the telegram appeared.

ARRIVING EXETER CENTRAL 11.04.
PLEASE MEET US. URSULA.

Us? Billy performed a courtly little dance around the kitchen chanting another favourite speech from *The Tempest*:

Our revels now are ended. These our actors,
As I foretold you, were all spirits and
Are melted into air, into thin air . . .

Was that the truth of it? That real life and make-believe were separated by the thinnest of divides?

That – come the afternoon – the last six months of his life, all those faces, all those memories, all those moments of first bewilderment, then despair, then blind terror, would simply vanish? Fizz away? Evaporate? All that heartache? Gone?

He was at Exeter Central station half an hour early. He descended to the platform, waiting for the tell-tale curl of smoke and piping whistle that would announce the arrival of the Waterloo train. When it arrived it was ten minutes early. The carriage doors burst open and the empty platform was suddenly a sea of young faces. This was still holiday season. Torquay, he thought. Paignton. Maybe even the Palmview Hotel.

Ursula Barton was among the last to step off the train. Billy didn't know whether or not to extend a hand. In the event he was spared the decision. Ursula was already leading the way up the long flight of stairs to the street.

A black saloon was waiting outside the station entrance. At the sight of Ursula the driver snapped a salute and opened the back doors. He was wearing an Army uniform and the moment they were both embarked he slipped behind the wheel and eased the car into the thin afternoon traffic. They motored west, towards the soft green hills that announced the approach to Dartmoor. The road grew narrower by the mile, scabbed with mud and cow dung, threading past a succession of farms. Finally, they arrived.

The house would have been easy to miss. It lay

some distance from the road, hidden by a screen of trees. It was Georgian, two-storey, white stucco, tall windows, and sat comfortably in the plumpness of the landscape. To Billy it might once have been a rectory. The scale of the property was perfect, neither grand nor humble. This is where my mum should have ended up, he thought.

The car came to a halt on the crescent of gravel beside the house. The journey from Exeter had passed in silence. The driver opened the rear doors and Billy followed Ursula up the steps. A woman was waiting inside to greet them. She might have been Ursula's sister – same manner, similar age, same fierce sense of purpose, except that she was most definitely English.

'In there if you please. Eats when you're ready.' She nodded at an open door at the end of the hall.

It was a big room bathed in sunlight. The windows were open and Billy could smell the sweetness of newly cut grass. Two horses were grazing in a meadow beyond the white timber fence.

Billy looked around. The room was beautiful: deep green walls, tasteful country prints, a lovely Adam fireplace. It was a room that managed to marry comfort with good taste and it was dominated by a long antique dining table, highly polished, obviously loved. Three places had been set out at the head of the table.

'Have you eaten, Mr Angell?'

Billy glanced round. This was the man with the beautifully polished brogues he'd briefly met in

London. He had a long, bony outdoors face and eyes made for laughter. There was a persistent hint of Scots in his voice.

Billy admitted he was hungry. A meal, it seemed, would be served in due course. But first, down to business.

The man folded himself into the chair at the end of the table. So far he hadn't bothered to introduce himself and neither had Ursula offered any clues. Billy, in the spirit of this adventure, decided to think of him as McTavish, partly because he'd once known a stage manager of the same name and partly because he liked the sound of it. McTavish. His master of revels.

Like Ursula, McTavish had a briefcase. He extracted a file and laid it carefully on the table. Billy recognised his name on the front cover, typed on a sticky white label. Below it was a hand-scrawled word he couldn't read. It carried a question mark.

'Miss Barton has shared with me the interview she conducted the other day,' McTavish began, 'and I must say we're all gladdened by what she managed to dig out of you.'

Dig out of me? Billy allowed himself a smile. What was he, an allotment? Or the rumour of buried treasure? Or what? And who, exactly, were these people?

McTavish hadn't finished. He steepled his long fingers, shot a glance in Ursula's direction and then addressed himself to Billy.

'You remember the form you signed? The Official

Secrets Act? I'm afraid the same house rules apply on this occasion. What we're about to share with you is officially secret. More secret than secret. In fact Top Secret.' There was a glint of amusement in his pale blue eyes and Billy wondered how often he had to make a little speech like this.

'That's fine,' Billy said. 'It's the same in the Air Force. Officially nothing much happens. Sometimes I think we get to kill all those people by accident.'

'Nicely put, Mr Angell. I suspect we're kindred spirits. It's all a game, of course. But, then, it has to be.'

He leaned forward across the table. Billy's eyes settled on a tiny nick on his chin where he must have cut himself shaving.

'We're in the spy business, Mr Angell. Or, more precisely, we're in the counter-spy business. If you want the label on our tin it's MI5. MI stands for Military Intelligence which some of our brethren regard as a contradiction in terms. It gets more complicated after that but I imagine you get bored as easily as I do so I'll spare you the details. Suffice it to say that we're immensely devious, chronically underfunded and largely left to our own devices. Happily, we find ourselves getting quite remarkable results because we have a habit of breaking the rules. Breaking the rules, young man, can be fun. In fact breaking the rules is a dependable source of rude delight.'

Billy had heard of MI5. It was a sister organisation of MI6 and belonged to a sprawling intelligence empire that no one in uniform quite understood. These were the faceless men – and now obviously women – who patrolled the darkness beyond the castle moat and plainly got up to all kinds of mischief. Billy wanted to know more. These people, he told himself, belonged in the theatre. They were larger than life.

'Are you with us so far, Mr Angell?' Ursula this time. Billy badly wanted her to use his Christian name but couldn't think of the best way of asking.

'I think I understand,' he said. 'So how can I help?'

'Interesting question, young man.' McTavish again. 'Let me start with a spot of scene setting. As I've just explained, we're in the intelligence business. Our job is to make life hard for our German friends but we don't like guns very much. That means we have to find another way and, believe it or not, most of what we do comes from up here.' He tapped his skull. 'We dream up games, Mr Angell. We make it our business to play with the enemy. We do lots of pretending. We win his confidence. We earn his trust. We feed him little snippets of information, some of them so small and so unimportant that you or I would probably lose them down the back of the sofa. But the key thing about all this information, all those snippets, is that you plant them in such a way that the enemy ends up doing all the work. In short, young man, we make our German friends believe what they want to believe, and we do that because the final picture – the jigsaw, if you like – will serve our purposes, too.'

Billy was lost. 'I'm not sure I understand,' he said.

'No shame, young man. These are the darkest of arts but, believe me, we're exceptionally good at them. The people we use, our agents if you will, have to be a certain breed. They have to have a certain predisposition. They have to be blessed with certain talents. And you're here with us today because we think you may be one of them.'

'Talents?'

'You've been an actor, young man, and according to Miss Barton a decent one. An actor, by defin-ition, is someone we welcome with open arms. Why? Because he spends his working life pretending to be someone else. In our business, believe me, that's an asset beyond price. We exist to fool the enemy, to make him believe something that isn't true. And in our little world it's people like you who can make that happen.'

Billy stole a glance at Ursula. Her face was half turned to the sunshine streaming in through the window and her eyes were closed. She suited this room perfectly, he thought. She might have been the vicar's wife enjoying a quiet afternoon deep in the country. But was she acting, too? He didn't know.

He turned back to McTavish. He still needed to understand exactly what was on offer.

'We have a role for you, laddie. Pretend you're in a new play. Here's the plot. Are you ready? Ears peeled?'

Billy nodded. He liked that 'laddie'. Very much. 'Tell me more,' he said.

'All right, so let's imagine you're flying with the RAF. You're a Wireless Op in a Lancaster squadron. Twice a week you sally forth to drop horrible things on the Germans. So far, so good. We think you can manage that role. In fact we believe you'll be word perfect. But here's where it gets a little trickier because we're going to supply you with a brother, a pretend sibling who doesn't exist. It will be your job to give him a name and a face, because in general we find it works better that way and, between us, we're going to dream up his life history. He'll be older than you, maybe by a couple of years, and you'll have worshipped him all your young life. Why? Because he'll be strong and wise and handsome and patient and we think you can imagine a relationship like that because I understand you experienced something similar with a woman called Irene.'

'Irene was real.'

'Precisely. And this brother of yours isn't.' He paused. 'Name? Anything come to mind?'

'Douglas.'

'Why Douglas?'

'Because I've always wanted a brother called Douglas.'

'And is that true?'

'Of course it isn't. I just made it up.'

'Excellent, laddie.' McTavish roared with laughter, thumping the table with the flat of his hand, making the cutlery dance. 'All you have to do now is remember the bloody name.'

'Douglas,' Billy repeated. 'It's printed on my soul.'

'Right. Onward. This is what happens to your precious Douglas. You're at liberty to interrupt at any time if you think you can improve on the story. This is a collective enterprise, which is one of the reasons we have such fun.'

A discreet knock on the door admitted the woman they'd met earlier. She wheeled in a trolley laden with food. Billy caught the tang of mint sauce. Steam curled from the joint on the carving tray. How did these people know his favourite meal was roast lamb? And where did the meat come from? He liked this giant at the head of the table. And so he put the question.

'I believe we've been in touch with some of your people at Wickenby,' McTavish was loading Billy's plate.

'About roast lamb?'

'Of course. Life is all small print, laddie. Get one detail wrong and the rest of the story falls apart. My name's Tam, by the way. Tam Moncrieff. Tuck in.'

Billy did his bidding. The lamb, in a nest of fresh vegetables, was delicious. He'd already noticed that the table setting included a dessert spoon.

'Afters?' he enquired through a mouthful of runner beans.

'Guess.'

'Treacle tart and custard?'

'Correct. Detail, laddie. Never fails. We need wine with this. Miss Barton?'

Ursula disappeared in search of a bottle. Moments later she was back with apologies from the kitchen.

'It's been uncorked for a while. I'm guessing it's up to blood temperature by now.'

Tam examined the label and pronounced himself content. Mouton Cadet. Most satisfactory. He poured three glasses and passed one to Billy.

'*Salut*, laddie. Here's to mayhem.'

They ate, at first in silence. Through the open window Billy could hear the cawing of rooks. Then Tam wiped his mouth with a serviette and took up the story again.

'This brother of yours was in the Royal Navy. They taught him how to dive. Last year he volunteered for special service. A bunch of lunatics had formed something they christened the Combined Operations Pilotage Parties. Call it COPPs for short. Everyone else does.' He paused for another gulp of wine. 'All this is true, by the way. No need to make it up.'

'So what do they do, these people?'

'Excellent question. Answer? They creep onto enemy beaches at the dead of night, right under the noses of our esteemed enemy, and take samples, beach samples, core samples. They have little corkscrew things, very technical, very clever. They bore down like termites and then take the samples home.'

'How?'

'They come and go by submarine. Midget submarine. That still leaves a sizeable swim, if you're wondering.'

'And the samples? The sand?'

'That goes for analysis. The boffins are clever. All boffins are clever. They take a look at these samples and they have ways of telling how soft or firm the beach is. God knows how but apparently they're never wrong. Give a boffin a tube of sand and he'll tell you whether the beach is suitable or not.'

'For what?'

'For an invasion.'

Tam reached for his glass again and raised it in a silent toast. 'Invasion' had been the word on everyone's lips for months. First North Africa, back last year. Now Sicily. Soon, the mainland of Italy. And after that, the coast of northern France. Only by crossing the Channel in force and driving inland towards Germany could the Allies bring the Third Reich to its knees.

'So what happened to my brother?'

Tam ducked his head and stabbed at a glistening morsel of lamb. Then he described the night Douglas Angell swam ashore on a French beach with his core driller and got to work. It was a moonless night. The tide was low. The wave heights were negligible. In short, perfect conditions.

'So what happened?'

'No one knows. That brother of yours made it off the beach. We're certain of that. He wasn't spotted. He wasn't captured. He was back in the oggin, making for his midget submarine and maybe a spot of very welcome cocoa.'

'How do we know?'

'Because divers always work in pairs. They have a buddy. The buddy lost all contact. Your precious Duggie?' The hand again, reaching for the glass. 'Gone.'

'Dead?'

'Lost at sea'.

'So where was this beach?'

'Ah,' Tam raised his glass a second time. 'Dunkirk.'

CHAPTER 18

It was nearly dark by the time Hélène got back to the chateau. A friend of Danielle's had been visiting a relative in Descartes, the nearest town, and had made the detour to Neaune. Hélène got out of the car at the gates of the estate and began to walk the 600 metres to the house. It was a fine evening, warm and cloudless. Insects buzzed around her head when she paused to enjoy the last of the sunset, and she never heard the footsteps until they were upon her.

It was Malin. He was in his slippers. The old clockmaker had seen the lights of the car from the house and come down to investigate. At first she thought he was fooling around. Being stern was a game he sometimes played. But she was wrong. This time he was genuinely angry.

'You're out of your mind,' he was out of breath. 'The car could have brought you all the way.'

'But I didn't want that. It's a beautiful evening. I wanted to walk.'

'At this time of night? The way things are?'

Hélène stared at him. Was he talking about the

war? The Occupation? Was she never again to walk alone?

He'd taken her by the arm. He was hurrying her up the drive towards the house. She shook herself free. He was mumbling to himself in Polish and it began to occur to her that something must have happened.

'What is it?' she said. 'Why are you behaving like this?'

He wouldn't answer. At the chateau, exhausted, he paused at the foot of the steps. She waited for him to catch his breath. He kept looking over his shoulder as the darkness crept towards them.

'What's out there? Who are you expecting? Tell me, Malin.'

He shook his head. The kitchen, he muttered. Everyone's waiting in the kitchen.

It was true. Hélène couldn't remember when the entire household got together like this. That wasn't the way her little *ménage* worked. Even the Spanish couple had descended from their quarters on the top floor. Pablo was slight, olive-skinned, and wore a permanent look of alarm. Maria was his wife. She was physically bigger, plumper, braver, and had always seemed to steady the relationship. They'd fled their home in Barcelona after the fascist victory in 1939 and walked across the mountains to France. They'd barely survived a winter in a refugee camp among the sand dunes south of Perpignan and still had no illusions about what they might expect at the hands of the French authorities. Jews? Gypsies? Communists? They were all ending up on the trains heading for the east.

Hélène had always liked Maria. Her husband barely said a word to anyone but in her halting French she always welcomed a conversation.

Now, Hélène asked her what had happened. Malin was bolting the front door.

'You don't know, *madame*?'

'No.'

'In the village, they talk.' She gestured vaguely towards the window.

'About what?'

'About the farmer.' She frowned. 'Benoit?'

'Ah . . .' Hélène was beginning to understand.

Malin was back. The old clockmaker settled into a chair at the table. Agnès, so far, hadn't said a word.

Hélène helped herself to a tumbler of wine from the carafe on the table and then sat down. The wine was rough but more than welcome. Her call on Danielle seemed suddenly all too brief. She looked up.

'Malin? You want to tell me about this? About Benoit?'

'Of course. The man is crazy. Everyone knows it. But maybe he means it.'

'Means what?'

'Means to burn us out. Means to kill us all. You think that wouldn't be easy? Two o'clock in the morning? Everyone asleep?' He levelled two fingers at Hélène. 'Bang. Bang. Sleep well.'

Agnès stirred. 'He's seen the radio. He knows about it. How did that happen?'

The question had the force of an accusation. Hélène sensed denial was pointless. She explained about Benoit watching her in the forest. He'd seen everything. He'd even read the message she'd sent her husband. He'd had this thing with him, this contraption with him. The Pole was horrified.

'A contraption?' Malin was staring at his hands. Already he seemed resigned to an early death.

'A crossbow, Malin. Farmers normally have guns. Maybe Benoit prefers the old ways. But I still don't understand.' She was looking at Agnès again. 'How do you know all this? You never leave the house so who told you?'

'I got a message. On the radio. A warning. Benoit belongs to the crazies. My people know about him. This man has a big mouth. He doesn't believe in secrets.'

'These people are mad.' This from Malin. 'First they boast. Then they kill. Then they boast again. Is that what this war is about? Dying at the hands of a madman?'

At first Hélène had been inclined to treat this outbreak of panic lightly. Village gossip never killed anyone. But the sight of Malin's face across the table told another story. This was a man who'd survived the attentions of the Jew-haters in his native Poland, who'd outrun the Brownshirt thugs as he'd made his way across Germany, who'd managed to build a decent living in Paris, who knew about the lethal consequences of misreading a glance in the street or a whispered betrayal by a neighbour. If Malin was taking Benoit seriously, she said to herself, then so should I.

'So what else do you know?'

It was a question open to everyone.

'Benoit has a code name,' Agnès again. 'He calls himself *le Corbeau*.'

Le Corbeau. The Crow.

'And?'

'He's killed before. In Nantes there was a battle between the FTP and the crazies. He shot two men to death. The FTP offered money for his corpse. Maybe that's why he's here.'

Les Francs-Tireurs et Partisans were left wing, fiercely committed, and controlled by the Communists.

'Your people told you this?'

'Yes.'

'On the radio?'

'Yes.'

'Tell me about the crazies.'

'They act like gangsters. They hate everyone. Vichy. The FFI. The FTP. The Armenians. They behave like kids. They love attention. They think life is a movie.'

'There are lots of them?'

'Not so many.'

'They're well organised?'

'No. These people belong in an asylum. Or maybe the graveyard.'

'And Benoit's definitely one of them?'

'So my people say.'

Agnès' people, to the best of Hélène's knowledge, were FFI, followers of the exiled madcap colonel, Charles de Gaulle. They were well-funded and enjoyed a certain respect, even among the Germans. In Paris, at the apartment late at night, Klimt had occasionally talked about them. In his view you could only be a resistant if you'd always been a misfit in society but he accepted their sincerity, and their courage, and had once told Hélène that one day France would wake up to find de Gaulle in the Elysée Palace. That small revelation had warmed her heart. Just another reason she'd made room in her life for Bjorn Klimt.

'Your German friend,' Agnès again. 'Benoit wants to kill him, too.'

Hélène stared at her. This was almost telepathic. Did this young *résistante* really need a radio?

'You're sure about that?'

'Not me. My people. Benoit likes an audience. One day it will be the end of him. The FTP? The Milice? The Germans? Who knows? But one day someone will knock on his door and put a bullet in his head.'

'That would solve everything,' Malinowski growled. 'Can you make that happen?'

Agnès didn't answer. She was looking at Hélène.

'Well?' Hélène asked. '*Can* you make that happen?'

'It might be possible but nothing is easy. One death always leads to another. The Germans love us killing each other. It spares them a lot of time and effort.'

'So you won't pass the word? Is that what you're saying?'

'I'm saying nothing. I'm just telling you the way it is.'

Hélène nodded. A rogue *résistant* with debts to repay. A known killer with madness in his eyes. Add a bottle or two of home-brewed spirit and anything could happen. Malin was right. The situation deserved Hélène's serious attention.

She reached for her glass and enquired whether anyone was hungry. There was silence around the table. Food was the last thing these people needed. Her little *ménage* wanted an answer.

'Leave it to me,' she was looking at Malin. 'And get some sleep.'

The faces round the table drifted away. Malin was the last to leave. He wanted to know that Hélène really understood about Benoit and was going to do something about it. Hélène put a hand on his shoulder and told him not to worry. The old man was getting thinner by the week. His face was gaunt in the candlelight. He badly needed reassurance.

'The situation will be resolved, Malin. You have my word.'

Hélène slept badly. She was thinking of Klimt. She couldn't get him out of her mind. She'd begun to take his presence and his support for granted.

This was a man who was in love with her. He'd never admitted it, not until a couple of days ago, but she'd seen it in his eyes, in the thousand ways he attended to her, in the moments of near-intimacy when he shared his contempt for the regime he was obliged to serve.

Klimt, her Klimt, could think like a Frenchman. Maybe that was a qualification for his job. Maybe that was why he seemed to be so good at it. He could understand the anger of a nation forced to pay for its own occupation. Having a third of a million Germans on French soil cost twenty million *Reichsmarks* a day. That had been Klimt's figure and Hélène knew it was true. Thus the sullen faces on the streets of Paris, and the blank resignation in a deeper, more secret France. That money came from French pockets, from French pastures, from French pantries, and everyone knew it. Twenty million *Reichsmarks* was two billion francs. A day. And all of it going to Berlin.

Merde.

She lay in the darkness, wondering whether she'd ever see him again. All the signs were ominous. The listening ears in the Hôtel Meurice. The cold-eyed attentions of *Sturmbannführer* Huber. The little tableau Klimt had staged afterwards in the night-club. Serenading her. In English, for God's sake. In front of an audience of drunken Germans, certainly, but Germans of some rank, of some significance, Germans with power and influence. Klimt didn't take risks like that. It wasn't his style. This was a man who locked everything down tight, bolted every door, let no one close unless it suited his purposes. Had Hélène suited his purposes? She hoped so. She had no idea how or why but she hoped so. A good man, she thought. Gone.

She rose at dawn and dressed. Thinking about Klimt, about what she'd probably lost, about Nathan, and about Huber . . . all that helped when it came to Benoit. This affair was something she'd have to sort out by herself. If the crazy chose to take a crossbow to her, so much the better. That kind of death she could understand. Clean. Quick. Simple.

Vas-y.

CHAPTER 19

Mid-afternoon, Tam proposed a walk. The treacle tart, a disappointment after the miracle of the roast lamb, sat heavily on Billy's stomach, and he was glad to get into the fresh air.

They set off alone, Billy hurrying to keep up with the older man's long stride. He'd collected a shotgun on the way out of the house, and a handful of shells he stored in a shoulder bag. He'd also whistled a dog from an outhouse at the back of the property. It was a spaniel, young, lively, and it answered to the name of Rabbie. It seemed to know Tam well which suggested he must be a regular visitor.

They crossed the meadow, and a stream beyond, and then climbed through the trees towards the crest line of the nearby hill. Twice their progress disturbed pigeons. On the first occasion Tam raised his gun but didn't fire. On the second, he gave the flock both barrels, just a beat in between. The spaniel vanished into the woodland and returned with both birds. Tam took a copy of *The Times* from the shoulder bag and knelt to wrap the limp little bodies in newsprint. It seemed the lady of the house was partial to game pie.

At the top of the hill the trees thinned and Tam paused to show Billy the view. In front of them lay a vast expanse of moorland under the wideness of the sky.

'Know Dartmoor at all, laddie?'

Billy shook his head. The only time he'd been anywhere near the moor had been on a navigational exercise in a Halifax bomber before he'd started operational flying, an experience he was happy to share with Tam. On that occasion the Nav had made a couple of errors, bringing them way too far to the east, and Billy could still remember the instructor looming over the charts, bracing himself in the narrow fuselage as the pilot dropped a wing to fly the new course. The Hallybag was far too low and for a handful of moments Billy's window was a blur of brown heather as the pilot fought for more height.

'Enjoy the flying, did you, laddie?'

'Not much, if I'm honest.'

'Won't miss it, then?'

'Not in the slightest.'

Billy wanted to know more about this assignment he appeared to have been offered. So far Tam had only discussed his fictitious brother but Billy knew there was more to come. Tam, though, was in no hurry.

'Hay Tor, laddie.' One bony finger was pointing to an outcrop of rock a couple of miles away, black against the scudding clouds. 'This is God's country, believe me. Bare as a badger's arse. The Cairngorms without the bloody midges. I was in the Royal Marines once. Can you believe that? They marched you right across the moor, top to bottom, full kit. After that they told you there wasn't a war you couldn't win. Nice views but bloody hard graft.'

They walked on. The dog raised a hare but Tam didn't bother to go for the shot. The animal bounded away, a brown zigzag in the heather, and Rabbie waited beside the path for them to catch up. Tam found a scrap of something edible in his pocket and tossed it to the dog.

'We have it in mind,' he said, 'to drop you in France. I understand you don't speak the language.'

'That's right.'

'No matter. No sane Englishman ever does. Helps immeasurably with your cover.'

'Cover?'

'You're a Wireless Op in a bomber crew. You're returning from a raid on the U-boat pens. Saint-Nazaire, we think. The aircraft's in serious trouble. We'll work on the details later but the long and the short of it, laddie, is that you bail out.'

'For real?' Billy was staring at him. Bailing out was a nightmare he never wanted to experience.

'Sadly not. We have to get you into the right company on the ground. Bailing out's too hit and miss. I understand your people sometimes have enough trouble finding the right city, let alone the corner of some bloody field.'

'So how do I get there?'

'Lysander. We'll fly you in. There'll be people waiting. You'll have a parachute, of course, and you'll need to leave it somewhere obvious for them to find.'

'Them?'

'Our German friends.'

'And the bomber? Won't they expect wreckage?'

'The bomber made it home. You were the only one to jump.'

Billy nodded. He knew about Lysanders, the tiny two-man aircraft that flew into occupied France at the dead of night. They could land pretty much anywhere and be gone within minutes. Flying a Lysander called for steady nerves. Being a passenger was probably even worse.

'So what am I doing in France?' Billy asked. 'What happens next?'

They were walking on again, keeping to the crest of the hill. The wind was sluicing up from the valley below and Billy could just make out the shape of a buzzard, riding the thermals over the bareness of the landscape.

Tam was talking about the reception committee awaiting Billy in France. These people would come from a known and trusted resistance network. One of them, in all probability a woman, would accompany Billy south. The end of his journey would be the Pyrenees and the Spanish border but en route he'd pause for breath at a series of houses judged to be safe. One of them was a chateau in the Touraine.

'Where's that?'

'In the countryside south of the Loire. It's the middle of nowhere, laddie. And there you'll be staying a while because the whole journey so far has been deeply unpleasant. Why? Because you made a silly landing with the parachute.'

'You're telling me I'm injured?'

'Yes.'

'But I'm not.'

'Of course you're not. But that's what the story calls for. That's what you've got to make everyone believe. And you know how you're going to do that, laddie?' He was beaming now. 'You act.'

They were back at the house in time for tea. It was Ursula with the trolley this time. Billy eyed the scones and the brimming dish of clotted cream. Tam had disappeared to sort out his dead pigeons, leaving Ursula to sketch out the rest of the mission.

The Château de Neaune, it seemed, was the property of a French woman, Madame Hélène Lafosse, married to an art dealer, a Jew. The art dealer was safe in London but she'd elected to stay in France. According to a resistance network operating in the western suburbs of Paris, Madame Lafosse had a German lover, highly placed in the *Abwehr*. He'd moved into her apartment in Paris and surveillance had established that he made regular visits to her chateau down in the Touraine. The couple had been together for nearly three years.

Which meant that Madame Lafosse had indirect access to some of the top names in Berlin.

'What's the *Abwehr*?'

'German military intelligence. These people are always at each other's throats. The *Abwehr* have had the upper hand so far. It's run by a sly old fox called Admiral Canaris but he hasn't got much time for Hitler and everyone knows it. The SS have had their eye on him for a while and they're starting to make some interesting moves. Our money is on Himmler. We think he'll be top dog pretty soon, which won't be the best news for Madame Lafosse and her *Abwehr* man. So it might be wise to use this channel while we still can.'

'You know all this? You're certain?'

'Yes.'

'Am I allowed to ask how?'

'No.'

'So what do you want me to do?'

'We want you to step out of the Lysander. We want you to have sustained a credible injury. We want you to go with the escort they supply. And when you get to the Touraine, we want you to make a very special friend of Madame Lafosse.'

'How?'

'Just do it. She may be very personable. We've seen photographs. She's certainly striking. Whatever happens, she has to like you. And beyond that she has to be interested in you.'

'Why?'

'Because you're going to be sharing confidences.

Let's call it friendship. You'll be talking about your war. About Irene. About your Quaker faith. About what happened when you started flying in earnest. This won't be hard for you, Mr Angell, because you take things to heart. It's an endearing trait. It's impossible to miss. She'll like that. That's why she'll trust you.' She paused, spooning cream and then jam onto another scone. 'I understand you turned down the offer of the gun this afternoon. On the way back.'

'That's true.'

'And why was that?'

'Because I've done enough killing.'

'My point exactly.' She offered Billy the scone. 'And that's what she'll recognise. You're very sincere. Maybe that's why you put your heart and soul into every part. Maybe that's what I recognised the night I listened to the Eugene O'Neill. My guess is you're thinking all this is a game. Am I right?'

'Yes.'

She nodded. She seemed pleased. Billy had the feeling he was being coached through a particularly challenging script.

'So what happens when the conversation comes round to your dead brother?' Ursula asked.

Billy thought about the question, toying with the scone.

'I'm sad,' he said finally. 'And I'm angry, too.'

'Why?'

'Because they lied when they told me he was

dead. They said he'd been lost at sea in a training accident. No body ever recovered. No funeral. No chance to lay him to rest. Nothing.'

'And did you ever find out the real story?'

'Yes.'

'How?'

'Douglas had a wife. Or maybe a fiancée. She got the same lie. But then my brother's diving buddy, the pal he was with that night, came and told her the real story. Maybe he was drunk. Maybe he'd always liked the look of her. In any case, he told her what really happened. Why they went. And where.'

'And she told you?'

'She did.'

'And how did you feel?'

'Lied to. Taken for granted. Made a fool of. And robbed of the brother I loved.'

'Good. Excellent.' There was a new expression on Ursula's face. Not surprise, or even relief, but something close to admiration. She brushed crumbs from her lap and then looked up. 'So what do you do with this story of yours? About your brother? And his night on a beach at Dunkirk?'

'That's easy.' Billy picked up the scone. 'I tell Hélène.'

CHAPTER 20

Hélène made her way around the village, avoiding the gaggle of requisitioned houses where *Hauptmann* Müller's men were quartered. It was still early, barely half past six in the morning, and the streets were empty. She'd dressed carefully, a pair of work trousers she used to clean out the stables, and an old shirt of Nathan's, far too baggy and buttoned to the neck. To anyone stealing even half a glance she must have looked like a farmhand on the way to the fields. Nothing must provoke this man, she told herself. Nothing must light even a flicker of excitement.

Benoit's farmhouse was a wreck. As far as she knew from local people in the village, the low brick dwelling had been extended by a succession of owners but the soil was poor, the drainage inadequate, and none of them had managed to coax a living from the handful of soggy fields. As a consequence, Benoit had paid a pittance for his new home and those few who had seen him at work were bewildered by his lack of basic skills. He didn't know one end of a horse from the other.

His single bid to take the borrowed plough to the gluey clay hadn't lasted a full day. And most of the scrawny chickens he'd acquired from the market at Descartes had been taken by the fox.

Benoit *le pauvre*, they muttered. And Benoit *l'ivrogne*.

His drinking was legendary and Hélène had seen the effects for herself. The scarlet face. The watery eyes. The sudden eruptions of temper. Here was a man it was wiser to visit in the early morning before the alcohol fired him up again. Benoit with a bursting head she might handle. Benoit emptying yet another bottle she probably couldn't.

There was no gate on what passed for a farmyard. She picked her way through knee-high thistles, wondering what he used for a path. An old Renault van was parked outside the house. Eventually she found the front door of the house. To her surprise, it was open. She could hear the buzzing of flies inside and there was an overpowering sweetness in the stale air that she preferred not to think about. They've been here already, she thought. One of the countless enemies this man must have made had paid him a visit and put him out of his misery.

She stepped inside the house, already anticipating what she might find. The room was empty except for an untidy pile of badly sawn timber heaped in the fireplace, a single threadbare rug on the wooden floorboards, and a tiny half-painted chair he might have stolen from the schoolhouse beside the church. A chipped cup had been abandoned on the window sill. She picked up the cup and sniffed it. Coffee, probably ersatz.

She looked round, finding no explanation for the smell, wondering about the rest of the house. A pair of wooden stairs led upwards into near-darkness. On the other side of the room, another door. She went across, applied a little pressure with her fingertips, felt it give. The smell was suddenly much stronger. More flies. She covered her nose with her hand and stepped inside.

This was the kitchen. A single tap was dripping onto something red and viscous in the sink but her gaze went to the stone-flagged floor where the flies were thickest. There must have been hundreds of them, thousands, crawling over the carcase. The deer had been ripped open from its throat to its belly. Entrails spilled onto the flagstones. Blood had crusted over a deep wound in its flank and the head lay at an odd angle, the bones of the long neck nearly severed.

Hélène stared down at the wreckage of the beast. She had deer like this in the forest. She knew of nowhere else it might have come from. Its eyes were still open, filmy with death, and a tiny triangle of grey tongue protruded from its mouth. It must have been young, no more than six months. Had he killed it with the crossbow? Trapped it? Separated it from its mother and hunted it down?

She shuddered, taking half a step backwards, knowing she had to get out of this place. It stank of death and of dying. Benoit the poacher, she thought. Benoit the thief.

'Madame Lafosse . . .'

She hadn't heard him come in. He was naked except for a towel around his waist. His face was dark with stubble and he needed to lose a kilo or two but his eyes were clear and there was no smell of drink.

'Is that my animal?' She nodded at the floor. Take control, she told herself. Show no fear.

'Yes.'

'How did you kill it?'

'With this.'

He gestured her aside and stepped round the carcase. She hadn't seen the crossbow. It was propped in the corner. It looked crude.

'Did you make that yourself?'

'I acquired it.'

'Stole it?'

'Bought it. Two hundred francs and a cut of whatever I kill. This was the leaf suspension from an old car.' He showed her the bow at the front. 'The mainspring comes from a lorry. The man who made it was a mechanic. As well he writes poetry. Good poetry. Poetry the way poetry used to be.'

'He lives locally, this man?'

'He's my brother, my brother in arms. He loves country broth and alexandrines. Difficult times demand a sensibility like his, don't you agree, *madame*?' He tipped back his head and rolled his eyes and cackled with laughter and in that one moment Hélène realised he was crazy. Not drunk. Not the burned-out husk of the man she'd been imagining. Not the member of some lunatic *réseau*. Not even *le Corbeau*. Just crazy.

He was also, to her bewilderment, a man of some education. Alexandrines? Sensibility?

He was offering her the crossbow for inspection. She took it. The weapon was heavier than she'd expected and he was right about the leaf spring. She could see the stampings in the black metal. She gave the cord on the bow a tug. You needed strength to use something like this.

She glanced up at him. Oddly enough, she felt no fear.

'Two hundred francs? A bargain, *m'sieur*. For two hundred francs you can barely buy a loaf of bread.'

'My friend is a poet. I told you. Men of letters have no time for petty advantage, for bargaining, for avarice, for the habits of the peasantry. They despise wealth.'

'As do you.'

'Do I?'

'That's what you told me. When we met in the woods.'

'I was drunk. My apologies, *madame*. It won't happen again.'

Hélène nodded. She felt comfortably stern. 'I hope not,' she said. 'Is this the first beast you've taken?'

'Yes. I've tried before but failed. Then the poet

made this.' He retrieved the crossbow and gave it a stroke. The stock was made of wood, crudely planed and sanded. Then he put it back in the corner and knelt to the open belly of the deer. Hélène watched him extend a finger deep into the carcase. When it came out it was glistening with blood. He examined it for a moment and held it out as an offering.

'For you, *madame*.' Hélène shook her head.

'But it's yours, *madame*. Your animal. Your property.'

'No, thank you.'

Benoit nodded, accepting the refusal. When he licked the finger he looked meditative, thoughtful, then he coated it with blood a second time and drew a cross on his own chest. His finger lingered over the intersection of the two lines.

'You know what lies beneath, *madame*?'

'Your heart, Benoit.'

'*Exactement*. My heart. That's where the firing squad will aim. Just there.'

'You mean the Germans? The Boches?'

'The French, *madame*. These days we fight a war of our own.'

'They say you're in the resistance. They say you've killed two men. Is it true?'

'No.'

'So who spread the rumour?'

'I did.'

'They also say you want to kill me. And the people I live with. And that German friend of mine.'

'The officer? With the car?'

'Yes.'

'It would be a privilege, *madame*. And a pleasure. Is there much meat on that German lover of yours?' He was examining his finger. 'Would he look good if I took the knife to him? Would the flies feast on his eyeballs?' He paused, struck by a sudden thought. 'And does God speak German? Or only French?'

'God is nowhere, Benoit. God is the sickest of jokes. God is the shortest cut to madness.'

'You believe that?'

'I believe nothing. Show me a priest who doesn't believe you can buy your way to heaven. We are what we are, Benoit. We make our own hell here on earth. You can hunt on my property whenever you like. I simply ask that you use a gun.'

'Why?'

'Because it's cleaner.' She nodded down at the crusted wound in the animal's flank. 'How did you kill it in the end?'

'With a knife, *madame*.' He drew the bloodied finger across his neck. Another roll of the eyes.

'Then use a gun.'

'A gun is noisy.'

'It doesn't matter. You have my permission. But one animal at a time. Are we in agreement?'

Hélène backed out of the room, leaving Benoit in silent contemplation of the deer. She left the main door open exactly as she found it and made her way through the thistles. She didn't run.

She didn't even hurry. When she got to the road she turned left and retraced her steps through the village. There were people on the move now, all of them women, but they didn't spare her a second glance. Within the hour, she was back in her own kitchen. It was still early but Malin had the coffee pot on.

He asked where she'd been. She told him. Only when he'd poured the coffee and sat down at the big table did he enquire what had happened.

'The matter has been settled, Malin.' She gave his gnarled old hand a squeeze. 'To my entire satisfaction.'

CHAPTER 21

Billy was in Exeter by early evening. Ursula had accompanied him back from the house on the edge of the moor and the uniformed driver had dropped them in the heart of the city. The Royal Clarence Hotel overlooked the western end of the cathedral. The doors were open and Billy could hear the muted thunder of the organ as worshippers hurried in for evensong.

Ursula told the driver to wait. Then she nodded up at the hotel.

'We're a little early,' she said. 'But I don't think it'll matter.'

Billy had no idea why they'd come here. When he'd enquired in the car she'd simply said there was one last person he needed to meet. Billy got the impression that this was yet another part of the recruitment process but when he tried to press her for details she'd said very little. Now they stood at the reception desk among a swirl of guests. There were uniforms everywhere, no one lowlier than a full colonel, and many of the officers were accompanied by women who wouldn't have been out of place in the pages of *Tatler and Bystander*.

222

Everyone seemed to have a drink in hand and laughter bubbled from a bar down the corridor. Billy recognised the sense of slightly frenzied eagerness from his days on the stage. This might have been the launch of a new production, he thought. Back when the Bristol theatre was still open.

Ursula had met someone she knew. The full-dress uniform told Billy he was a General. He stooped to kiss Ursula and then nodded towards the staircase that led to the upper floors. Billy caught mention of the word 'Director'.

'Room 328, Mr Angell.' Ursula nodded towards the nearby stairs. Briefly, towards the end of the afternoon, she'd begun to use Billy's Christian name. Now they were back on more formal terms.

Billy followed her across the lobby. The buzz of conversation dimmed as they climbed the staircase. The hotel was plush, opulent, apparently untouched by the war. Billy stood aside for a waiter returning with a tray from one of the bedrooms upstairs. Three slices of beef and most of the vegetables on the plate hadn't been touched. Unthinkable.

Ursula tapped on the door of Room 328 and announced herself. Billy heard a voice from inside, male, softly authoritative.

'Come.'

Ursula opened the door and Billy found himself in a spacious bedroom. It felt like a theatre set: the four-poster bed, the plush velvet armchairs, the ornate dressing table, and a glimpse of a huge enamel bath through the open door in the corner. The cathedral filled the view from the tall sash windows, the honeyed stonework glowing in the evening sunlight.

A man in evening dress was standing in front of a full-length mirror, making adjustments to his white tie. He was Billy's height, five foot ten. He was almost completely bald and, when he turned round and extended a hand in greeting, Billy warmed to the smile on his face. It was unforced, genuine. Late middle-aged, Billy thought. And in need of a good night's sleep.

'May I offer you a drink, young man?' He nodded at a selection of bottles on a silver tray. 'They seem to be spoiling me.'

Billy asked for a brandy and ginger. Ursula, unbidden, sorted out the glasses. Gin and tonic for herself and their host, the brandy for Billy.

'Is soda acceptable, Mr Angell?' she enquired. 'No ginger, I'm afraid.'

Billy took the proffered glass. A cello stood in the corner of the room, propped against the chair from the dressing table. There was a score of some kind on the music stand beside the chair and Billy began to wonder about the milling guests downstairs.

'How was the rehearsal, sir?' Ursula passed the gin and tonic across.

'Patchy, I'm afraid. We never meet as often as we should. Fingers crossed and let's hope it works.

Much like everything else, eh?' He lifted the glass, eyeing Billy over the rim. 'Here's to Vivaldi. I just hope he's not listening tonight.'

Billy raised his glass. He knew nothing about Vivaldi but he liked this man's sense of humour. Tam had it, too. These were definitely people used to taking risks.

The three armchairs sat comfortably on the thick pile carpet. Once again Billy had been offered no name, no formal introduction, but 'Director' seemed more than fitting.

'Miss Barton has told me a little about you, young man. We're more than happy to have you on board.'

Billy didn't know what to say. Was this it? Were his RAF days over? And, if so, where was the paperwork? The endless formalities you might expect with a change of direction this abrupt? A week ago, he'd been bracing himself for a return to flying duties. Now he was out of uniform entirely.

The man he chose to cast as the Director hadn't finished. He was waving his glass in the air, a gesture that appeared to indicate the world across the Channel.

'No one's pretending an excursion like yours is going to be easy, young man, but we'll do our best to take care of you. Tell me about Hamburg.'

'Hamburg, sir?' Billy blinked.

'That last op. I understand things didn't go well.'

'That's right, sir. They didn't.'

'But you coped?'

'We got back, sir.'

'In one piece?'

'Not entirely.'

'I think I understand. A very good friend of mine has a son in Bomber Command. Lancasters, like you. His father was in the trenches in the first war. Gazetted at Loos. Gassed on the Somme. Got himself the MC in Flanders. Busy old time. And you know what his son says? His son tells him they should have made a better job of the peace. Then all this nonsense wouldn't have been necessary. I suspect he's got a point, though I'd blame the politicians.' He paused. 'Do you resent having to risk your life?'

Billy stared at him. No one had ever asked him a question like that before.

'I resent feeling so helpless,' he said carefully. 'I resent the fact that no one seems to have a choice anymore. Everything happens at the point of a gun. And that's before you ever meet the enemy.'

'Indeed,' he gestured towards the window. 'Where we're sending you will be dangerous. But you know that already, don't you?'

Billy shrugged. He said he'd no idea what awaited him. He'd been given a script and he was happy to play it the best way he could.

Ursula was on her feet. A briefcase with two locks lay on the carpet beside the bed. She extracted a beige file and gave it to the Director.

There were photographs inside. He selected two and handed them across to Billy.

One of the photographs showed a woman stepping onto a pavement. Against the passers-by she appeared tall. She had blonde hair, neatly arranged, and she was wearing a long winter coat. Her face, half turned towards the camera, suggested a woman in a hurry. Good features. A hint of sternness. Someone used to making her own way in life.

'This is the woman at the chateau?'

'Hélène Lafosse. Yes. Now look at the other one.'

The second photograph was taken at a different location. Summer, this time. Among the women sitting on the terrace of the café was the same Hélène Lafosse. With her was a German officer. The camera angle didn't offer much detail but the clue to the relationship was the expression on the woman's face. The sternness, the sense of purpose, had gone. Her hand lay lightly on her companion's forearm. She was laughing. She clearly enjoyed this man's company.

'This is her German friend?'

'We think he's her lover.'

'And she doesn't care who else knows?'

'Obviously not. The man's name is Klimt. He's extremely well connected. He will offer Madame Lafosse a great deal of protection as well as a number of other things. Alas, Herr Klimt's days may well be numbered. Which is why we're having to be a little hasty. Opportunities like these are extremely rare, young man. Today is Wednesday. Within a week, we intend to have you in France. After that . . .' he spread his hands wide, and smiled, '. . . *bonne chance.*'

'And afterwards?'

'Afterwards, God willing, we get you out. Retrieve you safe and sound.'

'How?'

'Miss Barton is still working on the details. Exits can be as tricky as entrances, as you doubtless know from your theatre days. Either way, we're doing our best to keep you in one piece.'

'And after that?'

'After that, the war will be coming to a close.'

'For me?'

'For all of us.'

'But no more flying? No more bombing? No more RAF?'

'No.'

Billy nodded. He was trying to imagine what this new life of his would be like. He was, after all, a qualified Wireless Op.

'Do I carry a radio? Keep in touch?'

'That won't be necessary.'

'Keeping in touch?'

'Having a radio of your own. There are ways and means, young man. I'm afraid you'll have to trust us.' The Director drained his glass, and then checked his watch. Time, he said with some regret, spares no man. Vivaldi awaited him downstairs. It had been a pleasure to make Billy's acquaintance and he looked forward to meeting him again.

They all stood up. The interview, if that's what it had been, was evidently over. Then the Director was struck by a final thought.

'I imagine you might want to say adieu to your mother.' He turned away. 'Miss Barton?'

'It's in hand, sir. Mr Angell will be coming up to London the day after tomorrow. Plenty of time to say his goodbyes.'

'Excellent.' The Director was smiling. His handshake felt, to Billy, like a benediction. 'Welcome aboard, Mr Angell.' He glanced at Ursula. 'Agent Thesp? Am I right?'

'Yes, sir.'

'And the operation?'

'Aurore.'

The uniformed driver was waiting beside the car outside the hotel. Ursula was catching a train back to London. She gave Billy another address, more central this time, and a travel warrant. The warrant was in two parts. The first would take him to Bath. The second, the following day, would bring him to London. A couple of days of intense training and then he should expect a late-night departure from an airfield on the south coast.

'As far as your mother's concerned, you're still in the RAF,' she said. 'Do you mind awfully?' The phrase sat uncomfortably with her German accent.

Billy shook his head. 'As long as I never see Hamburg again,' he said.

'That would be impossible, Mr Angell.' She wasn't smiling. 'There's nothing left of it.'

Billy stared at her. The train's guard had his whistle to his lips but something was bothering him.

'Aurore?' he enquired. 'What does that mean?'

'It's French for 'first light'. Operation Aurore. We'll be using it on all communications.'

The uniformed driver took Billy back to Topsham. He sat in the car, trying to get his thoughts in order. What he'd seen of these new people in his life had deeply impressed him. They seemed to have found a space for themselves that he'd never dreamed existed. They played games with the enemy. Their armoury of weapons extended a great deal further than the blunt cosh of a two-ton cookie and a torrent of incendiary bombs. They sharpened their wits on each other and laughed a lot. Best of all, they seemed to have identified a talent in young Billy Angell that only Irene had found before. They trusted him. They thought he could do this new role justice. And on what felt the slightest of evidence they were prepared to spare him the rest of the war if he got it right. He smiled to himself. Operation Aurore. Agent Thesp.

They were in Topsham now. The driver dropped him by the river. Billy waited until he'd gone and then slipped into the telephone box. He'd done the sums in his head in the back of the car. According to the charges displayed behind the reception desk, a double room at the Royal

Clarence Hotel would be his for seven pounds and twelve shillings. He still had £46 from Ralph's money. After next week, his life would be in the hands of the gods. These weren't the odds he'd face during a normal operational tour. These weren't risks he could calculate and try and come to terms with. This, in every sense of the word, was the unknown. Dimly he understood that he might get captured. Interrogated. Tortured. Shot. On the other hand he might deliver the performance of his life and return scot-free. He might even learn the language, stay in France forever and play the role for keeps. He simply didn't know.

He found the coins for the call and dialled the number of the Palmview from memory. When Don answered he asked him whether he had a proper suit. Don said he could borrow one. Why?

'Because we're having a night out tomorrow.' Billy was gazing at a raft of ducks drifting on the tide. 'All you have to do is say yes.'

CHAPTER 22

Hélène spotted Agnès on the path that led to the woods. It was mid-evening, perfect for a ride. The last of the sunset threw the oncoming trees into silhouette and the warm air was thick with midges.

Hélène dismounted and tethered Valmy to a nearby sapling. She'd been trying to have a conversation with Agnès all day but she'd refused to come out of her room, refused to talk, refused to discuss any of the questions Hélène wanted answered. Now, to her visible irritation, the girl had no choice in the matter.

Hélène wanted to know about Benoit. Where had Agnès got her information? Who had told her that the man had anything to do with any resistance network? Where did this fairy tale come from?

Agnès wouldn't meet her gaze. She'd been worrying her spots. The lower part of her face was scarlet and angry.

'We don't tell anyone anything,' she said.

'So why all the stories about Benoit?'

'That was different. He was going to kill us.'

'And were the stories about him true?'

Agnès didn't answer. Hélène put the question again. Agnès shook her head, tried to step past. Hélène blocked her path, then lost her temper and pushed her roughly to the ground. The girl's bulk cushioned the fall. She lay on her back in the long grass beside the path, her face dark with anger. Hélène straddled her, pinning her shoulders with her knees. Above them loomed the horse.

'What else have you lied about?'

'I don't lie. I never lie.'

'So explain about Benoit.'

'Benoit's dangerous.'

'How do you know?'

Again, no answer. Hélène bent low.

'Have you met this man? Just tell me. Otherwise I'm going to hurt you.'

'You're hurting me already.'

'This is nothing, I promise you.'

Agnès stared up at her. Hélène recognised something new in her eyes. Fear.

'Do you know Benoit?' Hélène asked. 'Have you met him?'

'Yes.'

'When?'

'When you borrowed my radio.'

'You mean you met him in the woods? That afternoon when I sent the message?'

'Yes. I came down to find you just in case you needed help. That's where you said you'd be.'

'And?'

'I met this man. He was coming up from the lake.

He said his name was Benoit. He had a crossbow. And he was very drunk.'

'So what happened?'

Agnès didn't want to say. Hélène asked the question again. Then slapped her hard. The horse flinched, whinnied, pawed the ground. There were tears in Agnès' eye.

'He raped me,' she turned her face away. 'Twice.'

Hélène took her back to the chateau. She'd return for the horse later. Agnès was crying now and Hélène began to suspect that this story of hers was true. She had it on the best authority that Agnès had done something brave, or perhaps foolhardy, for a *réseau* in Lille. Evangelina had told her in the note that arrived with Agnès. She remembered the phrase she'd used, the exact words. *This girl carries a price on her head. Please look after her. Please treat her like a child of your own.* A child of my own, Hélène thought. If only.

Back at the chateau, she led Agnès to the privacy of her bedroom. The room looked out over the courtyard at the back and she caught sight of the old clockmaker mucking out after Valmy. It was nearly dark now. Malin had hung a lantern in the stable and in the throw of light across the cobbles the warm air was busy with bats.

Hélène opened the window and called out. She told Malin where to find the horse. Perhaps he could bring him back.

Malin gone, Hélène pulled the curtains against

the night. Agnès was lying on the bed, her back turned away. Hélène settled beside her. A child of my own, she thought, stroking the girl's hair.

'I'm sorry I hurt you. These are difficult times. Forgive me.'

Agnès said nothing.

'Why did he rape you? Did you provoke him? Did you upset him? What happened?'

'Nothing. He was drunk. Otherwise he wouldn't have bothered.'

'What?' Hélène was staring at her. At last Agnès rolled over. Her eyes were swimming with tears. Or maybe anger.

'Who'd rape me? You don't have to be kind. All you have to do is look. Maybe he did me a favour. Maybe that's what I wanted, needed. Maybe I should have said thank you. Twice makes me lucky. Isn't that the way to think?'

'You were a virgin? This was the first time for you?'

'Yes. He knew that. I know he did. Maybe that's why he stayed so excited.'

Hélène rocked back on the bed. All she could think about was the carnage in Benoit's kitchen, the sink overflowing with entrails, the sweet coppery tang hanging in the grey dawn, and the sheer madness of a man who first licked his blood-soaked finger and then scrawled himself a message on the bareness of his chest. This was someone obsessed by blood. Poor Agnès.

Hélène reached for her hand. Tiny stubby fingers. Bitten nails.

'What are these?' Hélène traced a pattern of thin scars that criss-crossed the inside of her forearms. 'Is this the Boches? Is this their work?'

'No,' Agnès shook her head. 'It's mine.'

'You did this yourself?'

'Yes.'

'Why?'

Again no answer. She tried to roll over again but Hélène held her tight. This time she didn't fight back.

'Didn't you think of telling someone? About Benoit?'

'Like who? Like the police? Like that fat German who took you away the other day? I was watching, *madame*. I saw his face. I knew what he wanted from you. I know what they all want.'

'You mean Germans?'

'I mean men. All men.'

'And you think he got it? Müller? You think I'd give it to him?'

'No. But you give it to your other German. I know you do. Malin says his name's Klimt. Is that true?'

'Yes.'

'So what's he got that the fat one hasn't? Apart from a nicer belly?'

'Maybe we're close. Maybe that makes all the difference.'

'Of course. And maybe he can do more for you than Müller ever could.' She blinked, rubbed her arms. 'Life in this country has become a negotiation.

You see it everywhere. What do I have that might be valuable? What might make my life easier? I'm lucky. And you know why? Because I have nothing. No money. No appeal. Nothing that any man could ever want. Except when he's very drunk and he finds himself raping a virgin. Here's something else for you, *madame*. I killed two men in Lille. I shot them to death outside a bar. It was very late. And you know why I did it? Because they were both with French women. I told my *réseau* they were mercy killings.'

'For who?'

'For the women. And you know what my boss said? How he reacted? He laughed in my face. Because it turned out that both the women were whores. Business is business, is what he told me. And so is war. *À la guerre comme à la guerre.* Get by any way you can. And fuck the consequences.'

Hélène nodded. Her own mother had once used the same phrase. Take things as they come. If God gives you lemons, make lemonade. If Germans have money, and you're drunk or desperate enough, sell them whatever they want. Was she – Hélène – any different? Hadn't the mistress of the Château de Neaune turned this hideous war to her own advantage?

She put the question to Agnès. Be honest, she said. Tell me what you think.

'I'm the wrong person to ask, *madame*. Without you, without this place, I'd probably be dead.'

'That's Klimt's doing. Not mine. Thank him.'

'He knows I'm here?'

'Probably not. I've never told him and he's never seen you. But he knows I offer shelter and he respects that.'

'But what if he *did* know? What if you told him, if you gave him my name, if he took it back to Paris or wherever he comes from and checked his records and found I'd killed two of his precious soldiers? What then?'

'I like to think it would make no difference.'

'Why?'

'Because he loves me. And because we all fight our separate little wars.'

'*À la guerre comme à la guerre?*' For the first time she managed a bleak smile.

'Exactly.' Hélène gave her hand a squeeze and apologised again for what had happened beside the bridle path. 'I just had to do it,' she said. 'I just had to find out what's going on with Benoit. You wouldn't have told me otherwise. This war is here to stay and the least we owe each other is the truth.'

Agnès nodded. She seemed more relaxed. Hélène found a cushion for her head. Downstairs she heard the kitchen door open and close. Agnès drew her knees up, the way a child might. A thought seemed to have struck her. It was a real smile this time.

'You know something, *madame*?' Her fingers had strayed to her mouth. She began to gnaw a curl of nail. With as much gentleness as she could muster, Hélène took the hand away.

'Tell me,' she said.

'That man, Benoit.' Agnès was staring out towards the window.

'Yes?'

'Maybe I'm right. Maybe I really should thank him.'

'For raping you?'

'For making me less ashamed of my own body. I think he enjoyed me. In fact I know he did.'

'And you?'

'Second time was all right. Second time it didn't hurt at all.' Her eyes found Hélène. 'What should that tell me, *madame*?'

Hélène didn't answer. Her fingers traced the line of Agnès' chin.

'You're beautiful,' she said. 'Just remember that.'

The girl nodded. She wanted to believe it. She found Hélène's hand and gave it a squeeze.

'Thank you,' she said.

Hélène bent low and kissed her on the forehead. She could hear footsteps on the stairs. Then came a knock on the door. It was Malin.

'Valmy, *madame*.' The old man was gasping for breath. 'He wasn't there. He's gone.'

CHAPTER 23

Billy was back in Exeter late afternoon the following day. He'd booked a double room at the hotel in the name of Mr and Mrs Angell. His wife, he explained, would be arriving late from London. He paid for the room and made a reservation in the hotel's restaurant before giving Don a ring.

'Half past six,' he confirmed. 'We start with something special.'

The Zodiac Bar at the Royal Clarence was famous for its cocktails. It served fifty-one concoctions, many of them invented by the hotel's resident genius. According to the woman on the reception desk, who'd taken a shine to Billy, Mr Ginger Wood was the toast of every officer who'd ever made the Royal Clarence his last port of call before returning to front-line service. She especially recommended a Gloom Chaser, the cocktail that had made Ginger's name, and Billy gave it a trial run to get himself in the mood. Don arrived ten minutes later, by which time Billy knew he was already in trouble.

The cocktails took them through to dinner. Even

the third plate of canapes made little difference. Two more Glooms had landed on the emptiness of Billy's stomach and by the time they sat themselves down at the table by the window everything tasted of Grand Marnier and curaçao.

Don fingered the menu. He'd borrowed a suit from his boss at the Palmview who kept a wide selection for every possible funeral, but he must have been a much smaller man than Don because the suit was short in both the arms and the legs. Billy, who was wearing his service uniform, told him it didn't matter. They were here to toast Billy's return to the front line. Who cared if they caught a glimpse of Don's skinny white ankles?

They were still waiting to order when a big party arrived to fill a long crescent of reserved tables that occupied most of the restaurant. Even drunk, Billy recognised that this was a celebration. Maybe a wedding anniversary. Maybe a favourite son home from some distant campaign. The guests straddled three generations. The host, a man in his late forties, was wearing the uniform of an RAF Group Captain while a much older man carried the gold rings of a Vice Admiral on the cuffs of his jacket.

The Group Captain spotted Billy in his uniform by the window. There followed a chilly nod of acknowledgement and Billy knew at once the question he'd be putting to his lovely wife. How come a bloody flight sergeant can afford a place like this? Billy didn't care. When his wife sneaked a look towards the window, Billy lifted his glass in salute. He might have been sworn to silence by his new friends at MI5 but it was comforting to know that he'd never again be under the command of a man like this.

The waiter arrived to take their order. Don wanted fish. Billy went for a rack of lamb. From the enormous wine list he chose a bottle of Pol Roger, half hoping the wine waiter would linger beside the Group Captain before arriving with the ice bucket. The price of the champagne would have kept him and his mum in groceries for at least a month.

Don had yet to fathom the real reason for Billy's largesse. When he enquired for the third time, Billy repeated that he was off to fight the war again from the innards of some bloody bomber, training rather than killing, but Don had a real gift for putting the clues together and didn't believe it.

'So what's happened? You're different. Down in Paignton you were a bag of nerves. You'd got to the point where nothing made any kind of sense. Now you're like a kid on Christmas Eve.'

It was a lovely image. The waiter had poured the champagne. Billy reached for his glass and covered Don's hand with the other.

'You should see the bed.' He didn't bother to lower his voice. 'It's a four-poster. Crisp white sheets. Lovely view.'

'The cathedral?'

'You.' He clinked glasses. 'Here's to tonight. And all the nights to come.'

'Amen to that. Should I apologise for Paignton? The bed could have been bigger.'

'Never. Tonight's a thank-you.'

Billy was aware of a lull in the conversation behind him. A glance told him that a couple of the women were taking a stern interest in the table by the window. He put it down to Don's suit and told him not to take any notice. Don wasn't fooled.

'Discretion, my friend.' He withdrew his hand. 'Eat now, play later. Never fails.'

The food arrived. Billy had lost all interest in the rack of lamb but still sawed away at the chops. His right foot was wedged cosily between Don's ankles. He wanted to touch this man. He wanted to make sure he was for real. Nothing, as he'd later confess to Hélène Lafosse, was ever more important.

Don wanted to know when Billy was next due leave. Billy played vague. He waved his fork in the air, invented lies about the flying schedule when it came to training squadrons, said he'd be back within weeks unless fog or a mountain got in the way.

Don leaned forward. His plate was nearly empty.

'You're making it up,' he said. 'The question I want to ask is why?'

Billy tried to get him into focus, to keep him in the very middle of this gently spinning room. Never had he felt so close to another human being. Even with Irene this kind of intimacy would never have been possible. This man read him like a book.

He kissed his forefinger and settled it lightly on Don's lips.

'I love you,' Billy announced. 'Am I allowed to say that?'

Billy heard the scrape of a chair behind him. Then came the sudden weight of a hand on his shoulder.

'My friend, you have just one minute to get out of this restaurant. Do I make myself clear?'

Billy looked up. It was the Group Captain. He had two faces. Then three. Billy could still feel the warmth of his breath against his ear.

It was Don who got him out of the restaurant and steered him across to the single lift. Mercifully the lift door was open. Billy closed his eyes, clutching Don, feeling the world rise beneath his feet. Take-off, he thought vaguely. Hamburg again.

The lift doors opened. Don hadn't moved.

'You've got the key?'

'Key?'

'To the room?'

'Ah . . .' the realisation that the op had been magically scrubbed put a big smile on Billy's face. '. . . left trouser pocket. Gently, if you please.'

Don found the key, checked the number and manoeuvred him down the corridor. Once inside, he deposited Billy on the big double bed and locked and bolted the door. Billy splayed his arms and his legs and invited Don to help himself. Seconds later, he was asleep.

The rap on the door came shortly after midnight.

Billy, still fully clothed, didn't move. It was Don who slipped into one of the hotel's dressing gowns and opened the door. Outside were two uniformed policeman and a civilian in a well-cut suit who announced himself as the night manager.

'We have grounds for believing Mr Angell has falsified his reservation,' he announced. 'Are you his wife, sir?'

Don stepped aside. The smaller of the two policeman had already drawn his own conclusions. He stood by the bed and shook Billy awake. Then he hauled him to his feet and pushed him roughly towards the door. Billy had time to be sick on the carpet before asking the obvious question.

'What's going on?'

'You're under arrest, Mr Angell.' The bigger of the two policeman this time. 'And so are you, Mr . . .?'

'Hennessey. Why the arrest?'

'Contravention of the Offences Against the Person Act, sir. Buggery's still a crime if you were wondering.'

'You think we were making love? In his state?' Don nodded at the spreading pool of vomit on the carpet.

'That's for the court to decide, sir,' he paused. 'I suggest you get changed.'

A police van was waiting in the darkness outside the hotel. Billy sat in the back, wedged against the bulk of his minder. The policeman stared into nowhere. Billy could feel his unease. The bloody Group Captain, he thought. A word to the hotel management and Billy's glittering new career was going down in flames.

He asked the policeman what he might expect. No response. It was the driver in the front who replied.

'Two years hard labour, mate,' he grunted. 'And that's if you're lucky.'

With Don aboard, they drove to the city's police station. The sergeant appeared to be half asleep. He was an enormous man, overflowing his uniform, and spoke with a soft Devon accent. Nothing appeared to surprise him.

'Friends are you, gentlemen?'

'Always.' Billy was reaching for Don's hand. 'Am I allowed a phone call?'

'Depends. Does your mum know you're up late?'

The question put a smirk on the faces of the two policemen. Billy ignored them. His brain was beginning to function at last. Never again would he put his trust in Grand Marnier with curaçao.

He had the London number on a scrap of paper in the breast pocket of his tunic. He laid it carefully on the desk in front of the sergeant. The sergeant reached for a pair of glasses. He had trouble with Billy's handwriting.

'Who's this, then?'

'Ask for Ursula.' Billy frowned. 'Or Miss Barton.'

'Who are they?'

'She. Just ask, please. Can you do that?' Billy ventured a smile. 'Tell her it's about Agent Thesp.'

'Who?'

'Thesp.'

The sergeant stared at him for a moment then eased his bulk into an office behind the desk. With the door open, Billy could hear him lifting the receiver and dialling the number. Then came a muttered conversation, difficult to follow, before the sergeant returned. This time he wasn't quite so sure of himself.

'Someone will be phoning back,' he nodded down the corridor. 'You'll wait in the cells.'

Even in summer, the cells were freezing: bare walls, a wooden bench, a single, barred window. Billy was alone in the darkness. Don was in the cell next door. Twice he tried banging on the wall but there was no response. Slowly, the hours went by. Billy was suffering now, and his head had begun to throb. By the time the sky outside the window was pinked with dawn, he was shivering with cold. They've abandoned me, he thought. I've had my one chance and mucked it up. With luck, a two-year sentence might see him through to the end of the war but he had no taste for breaking rocks in some quarry on Dartmoor.

He thought of the walk he'd shared with Tam, up through the trees until they'd emerged on the crest of the hill. He could taste the wind. He could see the distant buzzard. And he could still feel that stir of anticipation sparked by the conversation over lunch. He should have listened to Ursula. He should have taken the train to Bath and said a proper goodbye to his mum. Room 328 had been a crazy thing to do.

The sun was up when he caught the approach of footsteps outside. Then came the turn of a key in the heavy metal door and the moment when the gaoler stepped aside to allow another figure into the cell. Billy looked up. It was Tam.

'Laddie . . .' he sounded amused, '. . . just what do we have here?'

PART III

CHAPTER 24

M15's 'B' Section appeared to be head-quartered in a slightly run-down country house north of Aylesbury. The house, brick-built, had worn steps and wired glass in the panels of the Edwardian front door. Flt Sgt Billy Angell was allotted a room on the second floor that had once belonged to the owner's youngest daughter. Rabbits, in the style of Beatrix Potter, still featured on the fading wallpaper, and a child's globe occupied the top shelf of the room's only bookcase. For two days, chastened after a difficult interview with Ursula Barton, Billy Angell retired to the room between bouts of what Tam called 'full submersion'.

They taught him how to make secret ink using a match head impregnated with a headache tablet. A Welsh instructor who looked like a Spanish bullfighter coached him in close-combat knife drills, a thick towel wrapped round his right arm. A woman from some outpost of the intelligence empire, petite and French, spent an entire after-noon teaching him a handful of phrases that just might help him to evade the ever-present possibility of arrest. And Tam himself arrived with a variety of pistols to test his shooting skills.

To Billy's immense surprise, he turned out to be good. A cardboard target at twenty-five paces was infinitely preferable to anything with a pulse and by lunchtime Billy's live rounds were creeping steadily towards the scarlet bull's eye.

'I don't know about the enemy, laddie, but you've certainly frightened me.'

They'd driven to a nearby pub for lunch. It was a sunny day and Tam had found a table outside, shielded from both the wind and listening ears.

Billy wanted to know whether he'd be carrying a gun in France.

'The jury's out, laddie. Maybe yes, maybe no. Before this morning we thought it might be a handicap. I'll have to take soundings.'

'But what do *you* think?'

'I think you're probably best off without one. Play to your strengths, laddie. You're a fine shot but you're better thinking on your feet. In our game you need steady nerves and a knack for taking the right kind of risks. Tell me about that friend of yours. Hennessey? Have I got the name right?'

Billy nodded. Don had also been released from custody. Pledged never to discuss the incident at the Royal Clarence, he was back at the Palmview Hotel, preparing for yet another onslaught from the Babbacombe recruits. Outside the railway station, Tam had allowed the two of them a moment of privacy before the departure of the Paignton train. Billy had briefly embraced Don. When Don asked how on earth he'd managed to get them released down in Exeter, he'd just grinned.

'Put it down to magic,' he'd said. 'That's what I'm best at.'

Now Tam wanted to know where this Hennessey fitted in Billy's life.

'Important chap, is he? Close?'

'Very.'

'Long-standing? Known him all your life?'

'Eight days.'

'Magnificent. And I understand it was a four-poster. Shoot for the moon, laddie. God never cares if you miss.'

Billy laughed. In the cells he'd been close to consigning this new life of his to the dustbin. He'd had his chance and wasted it. Now, in ways he didn't quite understand, the risks he'd taken sat perfectly with how these people operated. Ursula Barton, as implacable as ever, had warned him that there was no room for showmanship, for drawing attention to yourself, but Tam seemed to be saying something very different. People who make things happen come out of a different mould, he'd told Billy earlier. Wars have no respect for caution or the commonplace. Godspeed to Operation Aurore.

Was that a compliment? Billy had no idea. What mattered just now was getting himself back on track. He wanted to know about the reception he could expect in France.

'Couple of blokes on the edge of a field. Plus the good lady who'll take you in hand.'

'Do you have names?'

'Lots. They're code names, of course. And they change by the week. I gather you're liable to be making the acquaintance of a woman called Alice. That's her real name. I'm told she's good. You'll be her intended.'

'Intended?'

'You're her fiancé. Marriage in the offing, laddie. Lots of canoodling when you get on the train. Start working on your body language.'

'She speaks English, this woman?'

'She does, laddie, but never in public. Bit of a clue, speaking English.'

At the end of the week, Tam drove Billy out of London. They arrived on the south coast in time for curling sandwiches and a mug of lukewarm tea at an airfield outside Chichester. Billy pumped Tam's outstretched hand, said his goodbyes and killed the evening with a game of solitaire in the draughty hut that served as a kind of Mess. He was being looked after by a sullen woman of uncertain age. She wore a pair of oil-stained dungarees and spent most of her time stripping out an aero engine in the neighbouring hangar.

At dusk she reappeared to announce the imminent arrival of the Lysander. The little monoplane performed a perfect crosswind landing and came to a halt on the apron of cracked tarmac. The woman wiped her hands on a rag and greeted the pilot as he climbed out of the cockpit. They appeared to be old friends and Billy found himself wondering how many other men and women Tam had brought down here for delivery to France.

'His name's Stanislaw,' she announced, before heading back to the hangar.

A Pole, Billy thought. The RAF was full of them. They made the best pilots and often the best company. Given any kind of choice, they tended to favour Fighter Command because that way they got to kill Germans at close quarters, but he'd met a number of Polish bomber crews and got to recognise their trademark mania. On the ground they drank like fish. In the air they flew like angels.

Stanislaw. Perfect.

They took off at a minute to midnight. Billy sat in the passenger seat. He was wearing faded blue work trousers, a grey smock and a stout pair of leather boots badly in need of new soles. Also a beret, black, with a greasy leather rim. The parachute Billy was to hide beside the landing strip was wedged behind his seat, together with a small scuffed bag of French manufacture, containing a change of clothes, all French. Billy was carrying forged documentation including French identity papers in the name of Guillaume Berliot and the people in 'B' Section had acquired a wad of *Reichsmarks* that Billy was assured were genuine. Somewhat to his relief, he'd been spared a gun.

Better to rely on your wits, Tam had told him. Good luck and good hunting.

The little plane soared into the darkness, quickly enfolded in cloud. The passage across the Channel was bumpy. Used to flying at 20,000 feet, Billy found himself hunting for glimpses of the full moon as the clouds briefly parted above his head. The weather over the landing zone, according to Stanislaw, was perfect: low cloud base, plenty of wind, a pitch-black night scored for the briefest of visits. With luck, thought Billy, his new Polish friend would be in and out within less than a minute and back in bed before the sun came up.

They began to lose height over Laval. Billy had the map spread on his lap. France was under blackout and when they finally broke free of the clouds he could see nothing beneath him except a thin ribbon of what looked like water. Stanislaw was grinning. A leather-gloved finger settled an inch or two south of the chinagraphed cross on the map. He's been here before, thought Billy. Probably hundreds of times.

Stanislaw kicked the plane into a savage bank and then pushed hard on the control stick. Billy felt his stomach coming up to meet his gullet and then he caught a tiny white light through the smeary Perspex of the windshield, bang on the nose. Two flashes. Then nothing. Then three more. Stanislaw was singing now. The words meant nothing to Billy but that didn't matter. These blokes flew like homing pigeons, he thought. Point them in the right direction and they'd never let you down.

A field was coming up to meet them. Billy saw a line of trees. Stanislaw cut the engine, hauled back on the control stick and settled the little plane on the racing turf. All three wheels. Perfect. Moments later they'd bumped to a halt. Two figures had materialised from nowhere. One of them opened the passenger door. After the fug of the crossing, it was suddenly cold. The wind tasted of pine needles.

'*Venez!*' urged the two men. '*Allez-y!*' encouraged Stanislaw.

Billy gave Stanislaw a squeeze on his arm. The Pole winked back, already reaching for the throttle. Billy grabbed his bag and the parachute and heard the door bang shut behind him. Then came the howl of the engine and the furious wash of the propeller as Stanislaw dragged the plane around. Seconds later it was gone, climbing away into the darkness.

Billy followed the two men towards the trees. One was young, maybe even a teenager, the other middle-aged. The older man made the running, hugging the treeline for a hundred metres and then finding a path that took them deep into the woods. The trees were in motion, bent to the wind. Once they paused while Billy found a hiding place for the parachute under a fallen bough, then they pressed on again.

After what felt like an eternity they came to a

clearing. An ancient Citroën van was parked at the end of a track through the woods. Painted across the side, *Jacques Perez, père et fils.* Neither of the two Frenchmen spoke English.

'*Montez.*' The younger one already had the rear doors open.

Billy climbed in and lay flat while the Frenchman covered him in blankets. The engine coughed into life and suddenly they were bouncing down the track between the trees. Minutes later, the squeal from the suspension eased and there was the hiss of tarmac beneath the wheels. It had started to rain and Billy shifted his head to avoid a steady drip from a leak in the roof.

Time was hard to judge but at least an hour must have gone by before the van slowed and finally came to a halt. The boy was first out. He pulled the rear doors open and helped Billy get out. It was still dark but a thin smudge of light on the horizon told Billy that dawn couldn't be far away. They were in some kind of farmyard. The arrival of the van had triggered a frenzy of barking from two tethered dogs and it was the older man who silenced them.

'*Suivez-moi.*' The boy led Billy towards the open doors of the barn. The yard was muddy underfoot after the rain. Inside the barn the boy moved silently towards a ladder that led to an open loft. At the foot of the ladder he gestured upwards.

'*Servez-vous.*' He mimed sleep. '*Dormez bien.*'

Billy offered a whispered '*merci*'. There was a

flash of white teeth as the boy grinned in the darkness, and then he was gone. Billy climbed the ladder. A thick layer of straw covered the bare boards. From somewhere close came a thin mewing. A cat, he thought. With kittens.

He heaped up the straw and made himself a bed. The floor of the loft lay under the eaves and a tiny rectangle of grey suggested a nearby window. On hands and knees he crept across. He was right about the cats. As the light grew stronger he could see the mother eyeing him from the nest she'd made in the corner. She was a tabby. Billy counted three kittens playing around her, a tumble of arms and legs. He returned to his makeshift bed and used his bag as a pillow. Within minutes, he was asleep.

He awoke to the cackle of a motorbike. Daylight flooded the barn. Alarmed, he rolled over and checked below. One of the doors was half open but he could see nothing. Back beside the window he peered out. The motorbike lay parked below. It was field-grey. Germans, he thought. After a while he heard laughter. Then a young soldier appeared. Bareheaded, he was carrying a paper bag with some care. With him was a woman Billy judged to be in her late twenties. She watched while the soldier stowed the bag in one of his panniers and kicked the motorbike into life. A pantomime salute drew another peal of laughter from the woman and then the soldier was gone, easing the bike through the maze of ruts that criss-crossed the yard.

'Our friends love eggs, *monsieur*. Welcome to France.'

Billy spun round. All he could see was a face at the top of the ladder. She must have climbed like a ghost, he thought.

'Alice?' he said uncertainly.

'*Oui*.' She was smiling. 'You like omelettes?'

They left the farmhouse after breakfast. Alice could have been the sister of an actress Billy had known before the war. She was slight and pretty and moved with the awkwardness of delayed adolescence. A mass of red curls framed a face that would burn easily in the sun and among her repertoire of hats was a wide-brimmed straw confection she'd decorated with a green velvet ribbon. The station, she said, was half an hour away. At this time in the morning, this deep in the country, they'd be unlikely to encounter any Germans.

Wrong.

The outskirts of the town were a straggle of brick-built houses, most of them shuttered against the sun. Paths led off the road towards the fields beyond.

Alice saw the German first. It was the soldier who'd called for the eggs. He was straddling his bike while inspecting the contents of the petrol tank. He had his back to them.

'There,' Alice was pointing to a copse off the road. 'Wait until I come.'

Billy did her bidding, resisting the urge to look back and check on the soldier. Nor did he run. Alice is in charge of this production, he told himself. She gives the stage directions. She makes the calls. Act naturally. Pretend you belong here. Attract no attention.

The far side of the copse looked out across the field. Billy sat on the damp earth with his back propped against the tree, enjoying the sun on his face. Above his head, he recognised the call of a blackbird. He sought to find it among the tangle of leaves and then caught the single tiny movement that gave the bird away. The turn of the head. The tiny adjustment. The melting sweetness of the bird's song.

'He's gone. You were good. Very good.'

She'd done it again. Not a single giveaway footfall as she made her approach. Just those same green eyes shadowed by the hat.

'Sit down,' Billy patted the grass beside him.

She laughed and shook her head. The train was due in twenty minutes. The one thing this war had left intact were the timetables. *Allons-y*.

Wrong again. The train was more than half an hour late. Billy had settled on a bench near the end of the platform, his eyes closed, pretending to be asleep. Alice fetched a couple of stale baguettes from a woman in the waiting room who eked a living from the line. Billy wanted to pay for them.

'No need,' Alice ate at breakneck speed. 'The woman is my aunt.'

The train steamed in. Three carriages, already full. Alice had said the trip would last a couple of hours. Their destination was a town called Sainte-Maure. From there, they'd face another walk.

Billy found a space beside the lavatory door. Alice was with him. When he nodded at the nearby compartment, and whispered in her ear that one of the men might surrender their seat, she shook her head. Her job was to deliver Billy in one piece. What if there were Germans on the train? What if he was asked for his papers?

Just as well. They were slowing for the next station when the guard appeared from nowhere. He was French: neat moustache, impeccable uniform and a hint of impatience in his eyes. Alice had bought tickets for both of them. She nodded at Billy to indicate she knew him.

The guard studied Billy for a long moment.

'*Vos papiers, m'sieur?*'

Billy understood *papiers*. It was the first word he'd been taught. His ID was deep in his pocket. He fetched it out for inspection. Under *occupation*, it read *bibliothécaire*. Librarian.

'Fascinating, M'sieur Berliot. You have some favourite books perhaps?'

He was speaking in English. Billy knew it was a trap but Alice was standing on his foot just in case.

He shrugged, spread his hands wide. The guard looked at him a moment longer, said something in French that Billy didn't understand, then moved on down the corridor. Eyes settled on Billy. He began to sweat. Another giveaway.

The train came to a halt. This wasn't Sainte-Maure but Alice appeared not to care. She eased him towards the door. Billy had never been so relieved to get off a train.

It was a tiny halt. The handful of passengers were already making their way off the platform.

'What did he say?' Billy nodded at the departing train.

'He said you have to do better than that.'

'He thought I was English?'

'Of course.'

'And now I expect he knows it.'

'You're right. But there may be Germans on the train. And he may need a favour or two in the future.'

'That's the way it works?'

'Of course.' She linked her arm through his. 'What did you expect?'

They walked for the rest of the day, taking a series of back roads that Alice seemed to know by heart. Once, she knocked at the door of an isolated house and waited for the door to open. When the woman appeared she gave Alice a hug and they both disappeared inside in a flurry of sing-song patois. When Alice emerged, minutes later, she had a bag of fruit and some pastries still warm from the oven.

'She wants to know whether we'd like to stay the night.'

'Does she know who I am?'

'No, but she knows me and I think she's guessed the rest.'

'You think it's risky?'

'It might be. Her husband is a brute. He's out at the moment but he hates the English.'

'Why?'

'Because they're not French. And because they killed a brother-in-law of his at Mers-el-Kébir.'

Billy nodded. Mers-el-Kébir was in Algeria. Earlier in the war the Royal Navy had sunk half the French fleet there to keep them out of the hands of the Nazis. More than a thousand French sailors had died.

'Let's keep walking,' Billy said.

An hour or so later he was beginning to regret it. His arms ached from the weight of his bag and his boots were giving out. Two blisters had burst and the back of his heel was bleeding where the leather pinched. At this rate, he'd have no problem feigning injury.

'How much further?' He'd paused to take the weight off his feet.

'An hour. Maybe more. We should arrive in daylight. People get nervous after dark.'

And so on they went. Alice walked with the grace of a young antelope. Her long legs swallowed kilometre after kilometre and when, for the umpteenth time, she offered to carry the bag, Billy finally said yes. Months of sitting on his arse and bombing Germany had done nothing for his stamina and he was beginning to doubt whether he'd make the chateau before nightfall. Then they came to a bend in the road and found themselves looking across a valley. They hadn't seen a soul since they'd left the house and Billy was beginning to suspect that France was empty.

'There. You see the white towers?'

Billy followed her pointing finger. On the far side of the valley, nestling in the trees, was a chateau. It was unmistakable. Two white towers and a glint of the dying sun in the upstairs windows.

'That's it?'

'Yes.'

'Is she expecting me?'

'She's expecting someone. Our people in Paris sent a message.'

'How much does she know about me?'

'She knows nothing. As I know nothing. As everyone knows nothing. The evenings are long these days. You've plenty of time.'

Billy hesitated a moment, still looking across the valley at the chateau. The light was fading fast now and he wondered exactly how much Alice, with her near-perfect English, really knew about his mission.

'Are you staying there with me?' He nodded across the valley.

'Just tonight. Tomorrow I go to Nantes.'

'Another Englishman?'

'No. I have a friend there.'

'A Frenchman?'

'Yes.'

'Lucky man.'

He meant it. She blushed prettily and ducked her head. Then she told him they had to keep moving. Long shadows were creeping up the valley and the first stars pricked the darkening sky.

The trudge across the valley was longer than it looked. From the road, a track led up towards the chateau through an avenue of plane trees. The first dog started barking when they still had a way to go. Billy stopped. He hated dogs.

'Don't worry. It's old. It won't hurt you.'

He knew he had no choice but to believe her. Minutes later, he was limping slowly up a flight of steps towards the big front door. She knocked three times, paused a moment, then knocked again. A land of codes, Billy told himself. Perfect for the Wireless Op. *Dot dot dot . . . dash.*

At length there were footsteps, brisk, approaching the door. Then a harsh metallic rasp as the bolts were drawn back. Finally the door opened an inch or two.

'*Alice? C'est toi?*' A woman's voice, older and deeper than he'd expected.

'*Oui.*'

'*Avec . . .?*'

'*Oui.*'

'*Entre.*'

Alice slipped in through the open door. Billy pushed it a little wider, thrust his good leg forward and extended a hand. He'd last seen this woman sitting at a café table in the middle of Paris with a man who'd put a smile on her face. Since then she seemed to have aged.

'Your name, *m'sieur*?' She ignored the proffered hand.

'Billy. Billy Angell.'

'Angel as in *ange*?' She extended her arms and offered a little flutter with her hands. '*Excellent. Parfait.*' She forced a smile. 'An angel would be most welcome.'

CHAPTER 25

The three of them ate in the kitchen. Billy, to his relief, had left his boots beside the front door. Alice wolfed the cold lamb, pausing between mouthfuls – Billy imagined – to catch up on the local gossip. The fact that these two women obviously knew each other was deeply comforting. It meant that in this new world of mirrors Hélène would appear to be the person he'd anticipated, a woman of some standing who seemed to have fashioned a space of her own deep in rural France, largely beyond reach of the Occupation. The strangeness of the language, on the other hand, put him equally beyond reach. Why weren't they speaking English?

He asked the question over the empty plates. Hélène seemed amused.

'We're lazy, *m'sieur*. And we're handicapped.'

'By what?'

'By our nationality. Some people think our language is all we've got left. Maybe they're right. What happened to your leg?'

'I fell out of an aeroplane. Made a bad landing.'

'The plane was crashing?'

'I don't know.'

'You were careless? You had some kind of quarrel? You didn't want to go home?'

'Not at all. We were told to bail out. Orders are orders. I did my skipper's bidding.'

'And the rest of your crew?' Hélène nodded towards the hall and the front door. 'Should I have prepared more food?'

The thought made Billy laugh. He liked this woman. Something told him that life had taken her places he could scarcely imagine. She was brisk, ironic. Billy guessed she took nothing at face value. Least of all him.

'We were coming back from Saint-Nazaire, *madame*. You know about the U-boat pens?'

'I know about the ice creams. Before the war, Saint-Nazaire was famous for ice creams.' She turned to Billy's guide. 'Your favourite, Alice?'

'I've never been to Saint-Nazaire.'

'*Dommage*. Then let me choose on your behalf. Pistachio. Always pistachio. With a little curl of cream on top. No. *Attends*. Maybe *two* curls.' She giggled and for the first time Billy wondered whether she'd been drinking. Her gaze left Alice and returned to Billy. She would welcome more information about the U-boat pens.

Billy did his best. He'd only bombed Saint-Nazaire once in his life and the impact photographs had tracked a harmless line of explosions in open water hundreds of yards from the target. That was with his new crew in V-Victor and marked the moment

269

he began to suspect that Les Hammond might be a wobbler.

'The pens are made of concrete, *madame*. They're metres thick. Only a direct hit will do any damage and you need a very big bomb.'

'And what happened? After you made a very big hole?'

'I'm afraid we missed.'

'*Dommage*,' she said again, pulling a face. 'All that way and not even an ice cream.' She turned back to Alice. 'You're taking Monsieur Ange south tomorrow?'

Alice shook her head. She said they'd driven all the way from Laval to spare Billy's leg. Her brother was taking the car back. Tomorrow she was off to Nantes.

'To see Didier?'

'*Oui.*'

'And Billy will be with you?'

'Alas, no.' She nodded towards Billy. 'A few day's rest? Maybe a week?'

Billy gazed at her, impressed by the fluency of the lie. Maybe Alice knew everything. Maybe she was best pals with Tam and the indomitable Ursula.

Hélène was studying Billy with a new interest.

'You need a doctor, Monsieur Ange? For that leg of yours?'

'No. I don't think it's too serious. Just a day or two in bed.' He risked a smile. 'If that might be possible.'

'Anything's possible, *monsieur*. That's the beauty of these days. You never know what might happen next. It's like being in love without the compensations. I hope for your sake that bomber of yours crashed. Because otherwise you might have made a very costly decision.'

'Jumping out?'

'Coming here.' She offered him an icy smile and enquired about cheese. In the countryside, she said, a civilised life was still a serious proposition. She could offer a brie past its best or a slice or two of Sainte-Maure. *La France profonde*, the butt of endless peacetime gibes, was quite the place to be just now. Even certain Germans preferred it to the bigger cities.

Billy told her food was scarce in England. Thanks to the U-boats, people lived in a world of ration cards. One fresh egg a week. Four ounces of margarine. Even bread had become a luxury.

'Here, too, *monsieur*. The Germans allow us twelve hundred calories a day. Scarcely enough for a baby.'

'What do they expect you to do?'

'They expect us to cheat. And they're seldom disappointed. Occupation is the mother of bad faith. We get by as best we can, a modest lie here, a bigger one there. I recommend the Saint-Maure, *monsieur*. We have our local goats to thank. It's inexpensive, as well as delicious.'

The cheeses were in the pantry. She stepped out of the kitchen to fetch the Sainte-Maure and returned, in addition, with a bottle of red wine. She poured three glasses, and then hesitated in front of Billy.

'You prefer a *digestif*, Monsieur Ange? A little cognac perhaps?'

The mention of spirits reminded Billy of the Grand Marnier. He settled for red wine even though the stuff was barely drinkable.

'You live alone, *madame*?' Billy dabbed at his mouth with the back of his hand.

'No.'

'Children? Kids?'

'One. Her name is Agnès. I expect you'll meet her.'

'How old is she?'

'Twenty-four some mornings. Eight, others. Sometimes even younger.'

Alice obviously knew about Agnès. She said something in French that drew a mirthless laugh from Hélène. Then Alice turned back to Billy with an explanation.

'Agnès is like me. A *résistante*.'

'And she lives here?'

'She's in hiding, much like you, *monsieur*.' This from Hélène. 'In her case I'm not sure her parachute opened properly. In fact I'm not sure it opened at all. Maybe you two should compare notes.'

'She's a flier?' Billy was lost.

'Only in her imagination, monsieur. I offer the thought as a figure of speech. Life becomes more interesting by the day. Are you good with horses?'

272

'I know nothing about horses.'

'Excellent. A fine place to begin. I have a very precious horse. Precious financially. And precious here.' One large hand settled briefly on her chest. 'The horse has gone. Stolen. In the right hands it will be worth millions of francs. Billions of francs. In the wrong hands it will end up in a casserole. This is rural France, *monsieur*. Which outcome do you favour?'

'The casserole.'

'*Exactement.* Tomorrow we will address the problem of my horse. I will value your opinion.'

There was a long silence. Hélène took another sip of wine. Billy's foot was throbbing. When Hélène invited Alice to show him to the room he'd be occupying, he hauled himself upright. He began to thank Hélène for the meal, and for taking him in, but she appeared to have lost interest. Her hand returned to the bottle and Billy suspected there'd be more to come.

He limped out of the kitchen and followed Alice upstairs. On the first landing he became aware of a door an inch or two open and a pair of eyes in the darkness beyond. Up another flight of stairs, he paused on the landing.

'Agnès?' he nodded at the door below, now shut.

'No.'

'Someone else?'

'Yes.'

'There are more people here?'

'Of course. The place is a zoo, Billy.' She paused

beside the adjacent door and pushed it open. 'This will be your room. After midnight, the power goes off. *Dormez bien.*'

Billy had flying dreams, everything in Polish, towers of cloud in the bright moonlight, everything on fire below. He fought the heavy blankets, determined to save the Rear Gunner, failed completely. He couldn't breathe, couldn't swallow. Then came a trickle of blood seeping from beneath a lavatory door, and he felt the sway of the train beneath his aching feet, and saw the guard pushing through a crowded Mess with a leer on his face. The guard marched him out into the rain for execution. He tripped over rubble in the wet darkness. Hauled upright, he was shoved backwards. Half collapsed against a wall scabbed with rough plaster, he tilted his face to the rain, praying for it all to be over. The sound of the firing squad drawing back the bolts on their rifles jerked him awake. He was lying in total darkness. Heavy blackout curtains hung at the window. His mouth was parched. His bladder was bursting. He badly needed the bathroom.

Slowly, with infinite care, he manoeuvred himself out of bed. Everything hurt. He had a mental picture of the room from the moment before he'd turned off the light. He remembered about the power. Until the mains supply resumed there was no point switching anything on.

He was naked but for a pair of pants. He groped

his way towards the door, remembering the big oak wardrobe en route. Somewhere down the landing, he'd find a bathroom, a tap, cold water, relief. He opened the door. The wind had got up and the house ticked and sighed in the darkness. Left or right? He stepped left, his hand to the wall. He found the handle on the first door. It was locked. He crossed the landing, both hands outstretched. Another door. This time it opened. He waited on the threshold, trying to make sense of the noises inside. Someone breathing? He wasn't sure. Then came a soft grunt, male, and the sound of bedsprings as he turned over.

Billy eased the door shut and moved on. By now he judged that he must be nearly at the end of the landing. His fingers found the frame of yet another door. The handle turned and the slightest pressure eased it open.

The drip-drip of a tap was the sweetest sound. A bathroom, he thought. Water. A lavatory. He stepped inside, moving very slowly, trying to map the room in his imagination. The leaking tap lay ahead, slightly to his right. He could feel tiles beneath his bare feet, another good sign. Then came an open doorway, the tap within touching distance, the silky smoothness of a basin beneath his fingertips. Beside it, lower, a lavatory bowl. He stood in the darkness, voiding his bladder, oblivious to the noisy splash of urine. When he'd finished, he stepped sideways to the sink. His fingers found a tap. Hot or cold? He didn't care. Just as long as it was water.

The water was cold, almost icy. He cupped both hands beneath the tap and drank greedily. Then came the rasp of a match behind him and he half turned at the sink. The bigger space he'd just crossed was a bedroom. A woman was reaching out to light a candle on the table beside the bed. The wick flared, then settled down. In the soft yellow light Billy found himself looking at Hélène.

'It's me. Billy,' he said at once. 'I'm sorry, I thought this was a bathroom.'

She was rubbing her eyes. She sat up properly, peering towards him.

'Monsieur Ange,' her voice was low. 'A visitation. How fitting. There's a glass on the table beside you. Some water would be more than welcome.'

Billy found the glass. Filled it. Then hunted for a towel to wrap around himself. Hélène was following his movements in the half-darkness.

'Come in here, Monsieur Ange. No need to be shy. There's plenty to wear in the wardrobe. Help yourself.'

Billy delivered the water. It was a big bed, antique. The last time he'd seen a bed like this was in a production of a pre-Christmas farce.

'Behind you, Monsieur Ange.'

'Behind me what?'

'The wardrobe.'

Billy interpreted the prompt as an invitation to stay. The wardrobe was huge. He pulled out a long garment that looked like a greatcoat.

'Is this OK? Do you mind?'

'Perfect, Monsieur Ange.' She was smiling. 'You might take a look in the mirror. A promotion at this time in the morning? *Oberst* Ange? Most unexpected.'

Billy was trying the greatcoat on. It was dark green, military in both weight and cut. It belonged to a much bigger man and it smelled lightly of cigars.

'You may sit down, Monsieur Ange,' Hélène patted the bed. 'Take the pressure off that leg of yours. Thank goodness there was a car to bring you here.'

Billy perched himself on the edge of the bed. Her partner at the café table would have fitted a coat like this, he thought. How many other items in this room belonged to him? How often did he make it down from Paris? And when might she next expect a visit?

Hélène was rolling herself a cigarette. Aside from the need for water, she seemed untouched by the evening's drinking.

'Tell me more about the car, Monsieur Ange. What sort of car was it?'

The question carried an edge of menace. Billy blinked.

'It was black,' he said. 'A black car. Not big.'

'Make?'

'I've no idea.'

'You didn't look? All men look. Cars are toys. Men love toys. A Citroën, perhaps? Some other make?'

'I don't know.'

'Which route did you take? Were you on the big roads?'

'I've no idea. I was asleep most of the time.'

She nodded, examined the cigarette, then lit it from the candle. When she offered it to Billy, he shook his head. He was still disturbed by the drumbeat of questions.

'Why do you want to know about the car?' he asked.

She looked at him for a long moment and then sucked at the cigarette. A plume of blue smoke curled into the surrounding gloom.

'Show me your right foot, Monsieur Ange.'

Billy hoisted his leg onto the bed. A single glance at his heel was all she needed.

'You walked, Monsieur Ange. There was no car.'

'How did you know?'

'I had a look at your boots. Fresh stains. Blood.'

'Does that matter?'

'You mean the car?' she asked. 'Or the blood?'

'Both.'

'Of course it matters. Are you denying that the car was a fiction?'

'No.'

'Then why the lie?'

'I don't know.'

'Are you blaming young Alice?'

'Of course not.'

'Then why invent the story?'

Billy gazed at her. He'd never expected an interrogation like this. So deft. So merciless. He remembered Tam at the airfield. His parting advice. *Think on your feet, laddie. It may save your life.*

'You want the truth?' he said at last. 'About the car?'

She nodded. Said nothing.

'I wanted to pretend I had a serious injury,' Billy said.

'Why?'

'Because I want to stay here a while.'

'But you already have an injury . . .' she nodded at Billy's blistered foot and the raw flesh where the boot had rubbed, '. . . wouldn't that be sufficient?'

'No. Blisters heal quickly. I could be gone in a day or two.' He paused, biting his lip. Confession time, he told himself. Make it hard. Play to the audience.

'You want to know why I really jumped from that plane?'

'Because you were told to. That's what you said last night.' She raised an eyebrow. 'Another fiction?'

'Yes.'

'So what really happened?'

Billy stared at his hands. Under these circumstances shame came easily. Caught in someone else's bedroom. Caught taking a piss. Caught out in a lie.

'I'd had enough of the war, *madame*. I'd been thinking of doing something like this for weeks. Normally we bomb targets in Germany. I didn't want to bail out there. The op to Saint-Nazaire

279

was perfect. There's an escape hatch at the back of the aircraft. It's near the lavatory. You push it open and jump. It's something we have to practise. So that's what I did. For real.'

'That's desertion, Monsieur Ange. In this country you get shot for that.'

'In mine, too. If they ever catch me.'

'You think they won't? Maybe after the war? If you're still alive?'

'I have no idea. War is madness. It makes you crazy.'

'You're right, Monsieur Ange. It makes all of us crazy. The whole world is crazy. The man who stole my horse is crazy. But you have to live with that.'

'Why?'

'Because there's no other option. War brings you face to face with yourself, Monsieur Ange. Look in the mirror and the results can be alarming.'

'You think I'm a coward?'

'No one who jumps out of an aircraft is a coward.'

'Then what? What do you think?'

'I think there's a lot more to your story.'

'You're right. How did you know?'

'Because people never tell you the whole truth. Sometimes it's because they don't know it themselves. And sometimes it's a little more . . .' she studied the end of her cigarette, '. . . complicated.'

Billy nodded. He'd spotted his opportunity. He'd never dared believe this could be so easy. The script was unfolding in front of his eyes. All he needed to do was pace himself. He could hear Irene, that first moment back in Bristol when he'd realised she believed in him. *Take your time, Billy. Build the expectation. Let the audience wait.*

He told Hélène about his days with the Quakers, about his visits to the Friends Meeting House, about the hours sitting in silence trying to disentangle his confusions about the coming war. He tried to share the torment he'd felt about registering as a conscientious objector. He described the long nights at the Infirmary, wheeling Blitz victims down to the mortuary. And then came the moment when the next wrecked face on the slab belonged to a friend of his.

'A close friend?'

'Yes.'

'Someone you loved?'

'Yes. She was a Quaker, too. She brought me to God.'

'And that worked for you?'

'Yes. Until she died.'

'And so you got rid of your conscience? Became a flier?'

'Yes. I wanted to be a pilot but that was hopeless. I became a Wireless Operator.'

'You know about radios?' Her voice had quickened. 'You can make these things work?'

'Yes.'

'Excellent.' She nodded in approval. 'So what happened next?'

Billy told her about the training, about the

transfer to Wickenby, about replacing a Wireless Op who'd just been killed. He went on operation after operation. Do thirty of those and your life was briefly your own again.

'You did it? You did your thirty?'

'No. The last time I flew we went to Hamburg. We destroyed it. It was deliberate. It was a very clever plan. You blow the place to pieces and then you set what's left alight. The fire does the rest. You know how many people we killed? Tens of thousands. And you know what they called our night's work? Operation Gomorrah.'

Hélène removed a curl of tobacco from her lower lip. She was smiling.

'Gomorrah, Monsieur Ange? That makes you God, doesn't it? A visitation on the city of the damned? Divine retribution? All those dead Germans? How did you feel?'

'I felt nothing. I'd run out of feelings.'

It was true. Billy stared into nowhere and then pulled the greatcoat more tightly around him.

'It doesn't end there,' he said softly. 'There's something else.'

He told her about Douglas, his brother, someone else he'd loved.

'He was a Quaker, too?'

'Far from it. Douglas never had much time for God.'

He told her about his brother joining the Navy, becoming a diver, volunteering for special service.

'Doing what?'

Billy looked at her for a long moment, then shook his head.

'You're not going to tell me?'

'I can't.'

'Why not?'

'Because . . .' he was frowning now, '. . . it just wouldn't be right.'

'I don't understand, Monsieur Ange. This is some kind of secret?'

'Yes, I suppose it is.'

'State secret? Government secret? Something the Germans might want to know?'

'Yes.'

'Then tell me.'

'I can't.'

'Wrong, Monsieur Ange. You can. You're a deserter. You've turned your back on the war. You have no more responsibilities in the matter. Except, perhaps, to help bring all this craziness to an end.'

Billy's head came up. He wiped his eyes on the sleeve of the greatcoat. He owed her a small round of applause. The perfect audience, he thought.

'You're crying, Monsieur Ange. Have I offended you? Insulted you? This brother of yours . . . he's still alive?'

'No. And that's the point. He's dead. He went missing. And they never even bothered to tell me. This is my brother, *madame*. Someone I grew up with. Someone I loved. Someone who'd do anything for me. And now he's gone and I never had the chance to say goodbye.'

'This happened recently?'

'A month ago.'

'Where?'

'Off Dunkirk.'

'What was he doing there?'

'Testing the beach.'

'For what?' She was leaning forward now. 'Tell me, Monsieur Ange. Trust me. Tell me why he was there.'

Billy held her gaze. Then shook his head and got to his feet.

'I can't,' he said, limping towards the door.

CHAPTER 26

Next morning Billy found himself alone in the kitchen with an old man who seemed to be in charge of the coffee. He'd heard Hélène lift the phone earlier but since then she'd disappeared. The old man ignored Billy's attempts at conversation. Maybe he doesn't speak English, he thought. Or maybe he can't be bothered.

Wrong on both counts.

'You want some of this coffee? Any more hot water and it'll taste of nothing.' Good English, heavily accented.

He was right about the coffee. A precautionary sip told Billy it was even worse than last night's wine. His eyes followed the old man as he limped about his tasks.

'You're working here?'

'Always. Also I live here. Hide here. Maybe die here.'

'You think the coffee's that bad?'

'The coffee's the best of it, my friend. All we need is a reminder of what real coffee should be,' he nodded down at his mug. 'It's hot and it's black.

Let your imagination do the rest.' He shot Billy a look. 'You're a flier? Like the other boys?'

'Yes.'

'Spain, is it?' He jerked a thumb towards the sunshine outside the window. 'Ten days heading south and you can see the mountains. Four days to walk across. Another week to get to Madrid. Then home, maybe. Afterwards you climb back in your aeroplane. And then you get shot down again. Isn't that the way it goes? I had a shop once. In Paris. I made clocks. For company I kept a rat. She was black. I called her Coco and she lived in a cage in my workshop. During the day the cage was open. She could go anywhere, my Coco. But I only ever fed her in the cage and always at the end of the day she came back. We do that, all the time. Life's a cage my friend. Don't be fooled by freedom.'

Billy thought he understood. He said he was in no hurry to walk to the Pyrenees. This corner of France looked more than promising.

'For what? You want to *stay* here?'

'Yes.'

'You know what it's like? The Germans helping themselves to everything? The women happy to oblige? The black market thieves? The curfew? We wander round in the dark, my friend. And that's before we dare to step outside.'

Billy nodded. He wanted to know what had happened to the rat. The old man had started washing last night's plates at the sink.

'I had to leave her with my neighbour.' He didn't turn round. 'I expect she's been eaten by now.'

Hélène and Alice ghosted in. Hélène had obviously caught the end of the conversation.

'Did Malin tell you his occupation?'

'He said he was a clockmaker.'

'That's right. Malin knows about time. Keeping time, marking time, that was his business. You know what the Germans did when they arrived? They put all the clocks forward. On to Berlin time. They stole a whole French hour, all of it, every single second. And you know the worst of it? Within days, no one noticed anymore.'

She muttered something to the old man in French. He nodded, and wiped his hands dry on the dish cloth before leaving the kitchen. Billy enquired whether he was off on some errand or other.

'Malin never leaves the estate, *monsieur*. Jews have a habit of never coming back.'

'Is that why he lives here?'

'Of course. The rest of his family are history. Most of them never left Poland.'

'You have more Jews in the house?'

'No. We have a couple of Spaniards. We have the girl Agnès. And now we have you.'

'And the Germans?'

'The Germans mind their own business. We mind ours.'

'We?'

'Me.'

'All by yourself?'

'Mostly. I have a little help from time to time. It keeps me sane.'

Bjorn Klimt, Billy thought, remembering the tang of cigar smoke in the folds of the greatcoat.

Alice was on the point of departure. A friend from Sainte-Maure was meeting her at the foot of the drive. They'd be driving together to Nantes.

'Are you sure you don't want to come, Billy?' The invitation sounded playful but Billy wasn't sure. Had Hélène had words about their arrival last night? About the car journey that had never happened? About a story based on a lie?

Apparently not. Hélène was escorting Alice towards the front door. Monsieur Ange, she insisted, was welcome to stay as long as he liked. She'd offered him a little job and he'd been pleased to accept.

Billy said goodbye to Alice at the front door. She'd looked after him on the journey and he was genuinely grateful. He held her hand a moment longer and wished her luck.

'You, too,' she grinned. '*Prenez garde.*'

He watched her tripping down the steps, the straw hat in her hand. She turned to give Billy a final wave and then made for the line of trees that marked the drive.

Billy stepped back into the house. Hélène was waiting in the shadows.

'*Prenez garde?*'

'It means take care.'

'I see,' Billy nodded. 'And the little job I've accepted?'

Hélène was heading for the kitchen. She glanced back.

'You can be my guardian angel.' She wasn't smiling.

The Mercedes arrived in the late afternoon. Billy was asleep upstairs, his curtains pulled against the fierce afternoon sunshine. Hélène met Klimt in the courtyard. He's lost weight, she thought. He offered a brief nod of greeting, his eyes already on the empty stable. Malin had left the stable door open in case Valmy wandered back but there'd been no sign of the stallion since he'd disappeared.

'You're sure he's been taken?'

'As sure as I can be. The tether was fast. It needed someone to untie it. Horses can't undo knots. Not even Valmy.'

'And you think Benoit? This farmer?'

'I know it. I'm sure of it.'

So far she hadn't had the chance to explain about the poaching, about the mutilated carcase on Benoit's kitchen floor, about their earlier encounter in the depths of the forest, about how crazy the man was. Now she explained what had happened.

'He threatened you?'

'He was very drunk. He was armed. There's a girl upstairs who says he raped her that same afternoon. I don't know whether I believe her but it's possible.'

'Girl upstairs?'

'A guest, *Oberst* Klimt. A wandering soul.'

'Do I need to meet her?'

'Definitely not.'

Klimt permitted himself a smile. It was hot in the courtyard. He followed Hélène into the cool of the kitchen. Hélène closed the door. They kissed this time, and held each other. Hélène asked how he was. Valmy and Benoit could wait.

'I'm fine. *Alles gut.*'

'I don't believe you. How was Berlin?'

'Berlin is Berlin. The British come every night. That's the way it feels. The people are shocked. It was never going to be this way. It's hard for them. They believed every word for years and years and now they sit in the bunkers and hug their knees and wait. Was it bound to happen? Of course it was. Are they surprised? No. They're just frightened. And maybe a little bit angry.'

'That's not what I meant. I meant *you*. What's going on? What's happened?'

Klimt looked at her, then shook his head. He didn't want to talk about it.

'Tell me about Huber,' he said.

'That man has given me a week to find the *Mona Lisa*.' She rolled her eyes. 'And I thought Benoit was crazy.'

She explained the call she'd had to put through to her husband in London. Huber was certain that Nathan could supply the key information. There were rumours that *La Gioconda* was on the move from hiding place to hiding place and Nathan

290

would know because he was still in touch with figures in the *Résistance*.

'And is that true?'

'Quite possibly. Nathan is a real expert when it comes to networks.'

'So what did Huber say?'

'Not much. Nathan wanted to talk to him on the telephone but Huber refused. A week is what he gave me. A week to tell him where to find the *Mona Lisa*. Nathan offered to swap places with me but Huber doesn't seem interested in that, either.' She paused. 'You want the truth? I hate the bloody picture. Nathan does, too. He says it's an essay in bad taste. Why Leonardo ever chose to paint a woman like that is a mystery.'

'Has Huber been in touch since?'

'No.'

'Does he know where you live? Does he know about this place?'

'He's a German, darling. Germans know everything.'

'But he hasn't appeared?'

'No, not yet.' She paused. 'Huber made one of those delicate little threats. You know the sort.'

'Against who?'

'Me. He said things might get difficult. He also said this whole exercise, this *Mona Lisa* farce, had your blessing.'

'That's a lie,' Klimt was staring at her. 'Huber is a true believer. He's got Himmler imprinted on his soul. Do you really think I keep that kind of company?' He turned away, shaking his head. Then he was back again, inches from her face. 'This isn't about your husband. It isn't about the *Mona Lisa*. It's about me.'

'You?'

'Of course. Can't you see that? Intelligence is a rough business. You have to learn to look after yourself. I was good at that. Once.'

Klimt rarely lost his temper. His face was pale with fury. Hélène couldn't remember seeing him like this. Worse than I ever imagined, she thought. She reached for his hand, drew him towards her.

'I think I can help,' she said.

'With Huber?'

'With you. There's an English flier upstairs. He appeared last night. He's got an interesting story. It might be good for you to talk to him.'

'Why would I want to do that?'

'Trust me, darling. A conversation might change everything. But first we need to get my horse back. I think I know where he is and I think our English flier should come with us.'

'Why?'

'Because he needs to see you in action.'

CHAPTER 27

Hélène shook Billy awake. He was to come downstairs and meet a friend of hers. Billy, rubbing the sleep from his eyes, enquired why.

'That's not a question you should be asking, Monsieur Ange. You're a guest in my house. You do my bidding.'

Billy got dressed and followed her downstairs. The figure at the kitchen table was all too familiar. Hélène's companion at the café table. *Oberst* Bjorn Klimt.

'Mr . . .?' He got to his feet and extended a hand. Impeccable English.

'Angell, Herr Klimt.' Hélène was already at the door. 'I call him *mon ange*.'

They went out into the courtyard. Klimt ushered Hélène into the front of the Mercedes and then held the rear door open. Billy settled himself in the back. The smell of new leather carried a faint hint of cigars.

Klimt drove down to the main road, braking to avoid a pair of pheasants scuttling across the shadowed gravel track. Billy was curious to know where they were going but was reluctant to ask. This man radiated power. You could see it in his bearing, in the crispness of his uniform, in the way his eyes drifted up to the rear-view mirror, holding Billy's gaze. Was this the beginning of the end? Were they setting out for Paris? For some underlit basement reserved for novice spies? Had Billy put too much faith in his new masters? He didn't know. Relax, he told himself. And remember your lines.

They drove to the other side of the village. The sight of the Mercedes with Klimt at the wheel drew smart salutes from a squad of passing soldiers. Hélène was supplying directions. Beside what looked like a beaten-up old farmhouse, she told Klimt to stop.

She was talking to him in French, nodding at the farmyard, at the near-derelict car, at the outhouse with the sagging roof. Billy didn't understand a word. Then he saw the eyes in the mirror again.

'You will come with me, Mr Angell. Do exactly as I say. We understand each other?'

Billy nodded and got out of the car. It was still hot. Hélène hadn't moved.

The farmyard was overgrown with thistles. Klimt strode through them. A pistol, a Luger, had appeared in his right hand. He checked first in the outhouse, slipping past what was left of the door. Billy peered inside. The place was musty, full of cobwebs, and there was a bale of hay propped against the nearby wall. The twine encircling the bale had been cut and hay lay scattered on the mud floor. Klimt was squatting in the gloom. He put the gun to one side, slipped off his glove and extended a finger to something on the floor. Then he lifted his finger and sniffed.

'*Gut.*'

Horse shit, Billy thought, recognising the smell. He might be spared Paris after all.

Moments later, they were back in the sunshine. The door to the house was open. Klimt stepped inside. For a big man he made no sound.

He glanced back at Billy, motioning him in. The room was bare and airless in the heat. Billy had never smelled anything so vile, so overpowering, in his life.

Klimt was already at a door on the other side of the room. He pushed it lightly with his fingertips and looked inside. Whatever he saw drove him physically backwards. When Billy wanted to look too, he shook his head, then gestured silently at the ceiling.

Billy followed him upstairs. Step by step the rumble of someone snoring grew louder. At the top of the stairs a narrow landing led to three doors. The closest was an inch or so open. Klimt paused outside a moment, listening intently. Someone asleep. Probably a man. Klimt hesitated a moment longer, and then stepped inside.

Billy was behind him. The room was tiny. A man lay naked on the single bed. The bottle of wine on the floor beside his limp hand was nearly empty. No glass. Klimt picked up the bottle, sniffed the contents, then held it out and slowly tipped it until a thin dribble of red wine splashed down on the face below. The man awoke with a start. Klimt let go of the bottle. It hit him under the right eye. The man tried to lash out but Klimt had a boot planted on his chest. Slowly, the blood-shot eyes fought for focus. The Luger was inches from his face.

Klimt was talking in French. There wasn't an ounce of aggression, or even urgency, in his voice. He wants information, Billy told himself. He wants to find the horse.

The man was shaking his head. He wanted no part of this little piece of theatre. He wanted these strangers out of his life. He wanted to go back to sleep and wake up to find it had all been a bad dream.

Klimt was talking again. Billy had no idea what he was saying but when Klimt drew the slide back on the gun there was fear in the man's eyes. Klimt put what sounded like a question. The man nodded, answered, gestured out towards the yard with a nod of his head.

'*Vraiment?*'

'*Oui.*'

Klimt turned to Billy.

'Go round the other side of the outhouse. You'll see another building. He calls it a hut. We're looking for a horse. It has a white stripe on its nose.'

'Is the hut locked?'

Klimt turned back to the man on the bed. Another question. A shake of the head.

Billy made his way back down the stairs. The pain in his foot, he suddenly realised, had gone. He waded through the thistles and found a path that led around the outhouse. On the other side, as Klimt had promised, was the hut. It was windowless, the kind of hideaway shed you might find at the bottom of any English garden. The door was secured with a loop of rope.

Billy untied the rope and peered in. The horse was huge, much bigger than he'd expected. It stirred and then whinnied at the smell of fresh air. There was barely room for it to stand up. Billy stared at it, overwhelmed by the sheer size of the beast. Huge brown eyes. And a splash of white, exactly as Klimt had said.

Billy wrestled the door shut and returned to the farmhouse. Nothing had changed in the upstairs bedroom, except the man's eyes had closed.

'Well?' Klimt didn't look round.

'It's there. Just like you said.'

'And is it all right?'

'I couldn't say. It's certainly alive.'

'A big hut?'

'Tiny.'

'Feed? Water?'

'Not that I could see.'

Klimt nodded, said nothing. His boot was still on the man's chest. He muttered something in French and the man's eyes opened, staring up at the gun. The first bullet took him in the mouth, the second put a neat hole in his forehead. Billy flinched. The roar of the gun was deafening. Klimt removed his boot and shot him twice more, this time in the chest. Klimt picked fragments of teeth from the front of his uniform and then stepped back and holstered the Luger. Blood was dripping onto the bare floorboards and there was a faint buzzing as the first flies settled on the stickiness of the man's face. So businesslike, Billy thought, still staring at the bed. And so pitiless.

Back outside, they returned to the car. Klimt hadn't said a word. Hélène watched them approaching and then opened the door.

'Herr Klimt . . .?' She was shading her eyes against the sun.

Klimt knelt beside the car. For the first time, Billy noticed the dark stains on the front of his trousers. Blood, he thought.

'In there, *madame*,' Klimt was indicating a compartment beneath the dashboard. 'It's unlocked.'

Hélène opened the compartment. Inside was a thick parcel, brown paper, carefully taped.

'Take it out. It's yours.'

Hélène extracted the parcel, weighed it in her hand, then looked up.

'Thank you,' she said. She was smiling.

'Not at all, *madame*.' Klimt was standing up now. 'Mr Angell will take you to your stallion. He's lucky not to have been killed and eaten. I suggest you ride him home.'

Billy had anticipated the session with Klimt. Still shaken by what had happened out at the farm, he lay on the bed in his room, waiting for the knock at the door. The stallion was safe. Hélène had brought him back to the chateau, relieved that her precious Valmy had suffered no visible damage. A little thinner, she'd said, and more highly strung than ever, but the stallion had moved sweetly beneath her and seemed pleased to be back in its own stable.

'Mr Angell?' It was the old man. He pronounced his name with a hard 'g'. Angle.

Billy rolled off the bed and got to his feet. Everything was happening much faster than he'd anticipated. First the small hours heart-to-heart with Hélène. And now the abrupt arrival of Klimt. The phone call she'd made this morning, he reasoned, must have been to Paris. Come quickly. We have a visitor. Talk to this man.

Klimt was waiting in his car. He eyed Billy through the open window and then patted the passenger seat. We need to take a little ride, Mr Angell. I promise you no stallions.

They drove for nearly an hour. Keeping track of the mid-afternoon sun, Billy estimated they were heading north-west. Klimt, apart from a quiet volley of abuse when an old man on a bicycle weaved across his path, said nothing. His silence,

Billy decided, was deliberately unnerving. At length they appeared to be close to their destination. Klimt slowed for an impressive pair of gates. Three sentries stood guard outside. One of them obviously knew him. Another shouted *Heil Hitler*, arm thrust high, and the gates opened.

Klimt didn't even bother to acknowledge the salute. He glanced across at Billy.

'You want to see a proper chateau, Mr Angell? It's entirely my pleasure . . .'

The chateau lay at the end of an ornamental drive. The gardens on either side were immaculate: carefully geometric plots bisected by gravel paths. The plantings were in full bloom and Billy assumed the Germans must have retained most of the French gardeners to keep order amid this riot of colour.

The Mercedes growled to a halt outside the chateau's imposing entrance. Billy by now was resigned to facing arrest. Whatever Klimt's standing in the intelligence world he was hardly able to parade a downed member of Bomber Command without having to face difficult questions. At best, a roughing up and then a billet in some far-flung *Stalag*. At worst, a day or two of indescribable pain followed by a merciful release. He'd read magazine accounts of what these people were capable of. Discount most of it as propaganda and you were still facing the world's experts in making you talk.

Inside the big entrance doors, long galleries

stretched in three directions. Klimt paused by a desk which appeared to control access. A young clerk in civilian dress listened to his question, shot a brief glance at Billy and then got to his feet. They followed him down the central corridor. Apart from a distant glimpse of a hurrying uniform or two, the chateau appeared to be even emptier than the gardens outside. They climbed a staircase to the first floor, their footsteps echoing on the gleaming marble. A more modest flight of steps carried them higher. Most of the doors they passed had been badged with German signs and where pictures should have hung on the gallery walls there were empty oblongs, a richer colour than the rest of the fading yellow paint.

Finally, on what Billy judged to be the fourth floor, the clerk paused outside a door, knocked twice and waited. After a while the door opened and Billy found himself face to face with a man Klimt appeared to know. He was smaller than Billy, slender build. He had a crooked smile in a handsome face and a tangle of blond curls framed the kind of tan you didn't acquire by accident. He was wearing what Billy recognised as a flying suit, dark grey, unzipped to his waist. His feet were bare. Billy had met people like this before. And they'd always been fighter pilots.

'Dieter Merz,' Klimt explained. 'He's flown down specially to meet you. We will all speak English, *ja*?'

Dieter nodded, and extended a hand.

'Pleased to meet you, Herr Angell.' Like the old man at Hélène's chateau, he used the hard 'g'.

Klimt and Dieter exchanged glances. Then Klimt nodded towards the window.

'Outside?'

'*Ja*. Of course. Always.'

Merz stepped aside. The room was small and appeared to serve as an office: a desk pushed untidily against the wall, two filing cabinets and a wall map that carried dozens of multi-coloured pins. Klimt was heading for a door in the corner. He seemed to know his way around. The door opened into a bedroom, as spartan as the office next door. The blankets on the single bed were rumpled and a pair of flying boots had been discarded in one corner. Klimt was still on the move. Yet another door led onto an open-air terrace. The grey stone tracery that contained the terrace was waist-high and the afternoon sun threw crazy shadows on the flagstones underfoot.

Klimt beckoned Billy closer. He wanted to show him the view. Billy stepped towards him. The stone tracery was warm to his touch. Billy peered over. He was happy in aeroplanes but he loathed heights like these. They made his head spin, but worse still they sparked an inexplicable urge to jump.

'What do you think, Herr Angell?' It was Dieter.

The view, Billy had to admit, was breathtaking. A river, close enough to touch. The spread of gardens on either side, the patterns suddenly making perfect sense. The dizzy splashes of midsummer colour from the flower beds. Even at this height, Billy swore he could hear the buzzing of bees.

'Look . . . you see how small people are?' Klimt this time. Billy felt a pressure in the middle of his back. An invitation to peer over again? Or a reminder that Billy – should he prove difficult – might find himself surrendering to gravity?

Billy did Klimt's bidding. Immediately below, two officers in peaked caps were locked in conversation as they hurried along. Klimt was right. Ants, Billy thought. As much at the mercy of the regime as he was.

Merz had fetched three fold-up chairs. He arranged them in a loose triangle and asked Billy to sit down. Billy's chair, he noticed, was closest to the drop.

At a nod from Klimt, Merz opened the questioning. He had no notes, no checklist, but from the start he knew exactly what he wanted to ask.

'You were with a bomber crew, *ja*?'

'Yes.'

'What kind of aircraft?'

'Lancasters.'

'Which squadron?'

'101.'

'RAF Scampton?'

'Wickenby.' It was a trick question and Merz acknowledged the fact with a smile.

Next he wanted to know about Billy's last

operation. Billy described the trip to Saint-Nazaire, the flak and the nests of searchlights they'd avoided en route, the outer and inner rings of anti-aircraft fire around the target itself, the flak barges moored on the estuary, and the relief they'd all felt after the climb-out. Tam had commissioned a full written account from a Wickenby crew that had bombed the target the previous week and Billy had committed it to memory.

'Night fighters?'

'None that I saw, thank God.'

'Was that unusual?'

'It depended on the target. The Ruhr was always horrible. Hamburg, too.'

'You bombed Hamburg?'

'A number of times.'

'But recently? Back last month? The night of the firestorm?'

'Yes.'

'My parents were there. My home was there. You did a good job, Herr Angell.'

'What do you mean?'

'They're all dead. All gone. Even the house. Even the next door house. You left us nowhere to run, Herr Angell. Which I imagine was the point of the exercise.'

'And you?'

'I was on the Dutch coast. Trying to shoot you down.'

Billy stared at him. The conversation had ceased to make any sense. Thanks to Bomber Command, this man had lost most of his family, most of his previous life. Yet here he was, still smiling at someone who'd helped fuel that carnage. Was this a professional thing, a doff of the cap, airman to airman, an acknowledgement that Billy and his mates had done well? Was there no particle of regret that his family had been reduced to ashes?

Klimt wanted to move the conversation on. He needed to be sure that Billy was exactly who he claimed to be. There followed a barrage of questions from Merz. About operational radio frequencies. About the success of the recent experiment with radar-bluffing aluminium strips. About layering the bomber stream as it closed on particular targets. About the latest tactics to avoid German night fighters. About sustaining aircrew morale in the face of constant losses.

Billy answered each question as best he could, knowing that he'd stepped way out of line. Name, rank, number. That's all he was obliged to volunteer. Yet here he was, betraying operational secret after operational secret, much to Merz's surprise. Destroying Hamburg was one thing. Handing all this windfall information to the enemy quite another.

Merz had come to the end of his mental list of questions. He was looking at Klimt.

'He's an aviator,' he said simply. 'He's telling the truth.'

'So ask him why he ended up in France. See if that sounds right as well.'

Merz put the question. Billy guessed that Hélène had already shared last night's conversation with Klimt. He knows about me bailing out, he thought. All I have to do is remember the script.

Billy went through it all again. The moments in the air when his will, his belief, his motivation, began to weaken. The long days back at Wickenby when he thought too hard about the people he'd slaughtered tens of thousands of feet below, and the Rear Gunner he'd watched die barely a fingertip away. All of it was needless. And all of it took him to a place where he knew he'd become a liability. Not just to himself but to his crew as well.

'So what happened?'

'I jumped from the aircraft.'

'It was on fire? Crashing?'

'No.'

'You just jumped? Did it?'

'Yes.'

'Why?'

'I'd had enough.'

This, to Merz, was clearly inexplicable. Everyone was frightened. All the time. War wouldn't be war if you weren't shitting your pants.

'OK.' Billy shrugged. 'You asked the question. That's my answer.'

Merz nodded, still bewildered, then said something in German to Klimt. Klimt permitted himself a brief smile and then turned back to Billy.

'He's checked the records for that night,' he

explained. 'Now he knows why no one found any wreckage.'

The interview on the terrace ended within minutes. Merz, after a brief conversation with Klimt, tugged on his flying boots, zipped up his flying suit and collected a map from the desk in the office. Billy had time to register a blue chinagraphed line from north-west France to the Dutch border before Klimt ushered him into the corridor. There was no farewell handshake from Merz.

Back on the ground floor, Klimt steered Billy through a maze of corridors until they emerged through a door at the corner of the building. A fenced-off area overlooked the river. Zinc-topped tables and metal-framed chairs suggested that this was where the garrison made time to relax, but late afternoon there was nobody around.

Klimt chose a table at the water's edge. Billy wondered whether he could expect waiter service.

'We need to talk a little more, Mr Angell.' Klimt had taken his jacket off. 'My apologies for Dieter Merz.'

'Apologies?'

'Socially, Dieter moves in very small circles. As you can imagine, he loves the company of people like himself. At heart he's a warrior. So far, this war hasn't let him down, not even his year in Russia. I suspect people like yourself upset him.'

'And you?'

'Mine is a different kind of war. We interest

ourselves in motive. With Merz it's far simpler. The best man always wins.'

Billy turned away to gaze over the river. Just who won at Hamburg, he wondered? And how could Dieter Merz possibly forgive a thousand bomber crews for robbing him of pretty much everything?

'Madame Lafosse told me an interesting story, Mr Angell. It involves your brother. Might you care to repeat it?'

Billy had readied himself for this moment. He shook his head.

'No,' he said. 'I owe Madame Lafosse an apology. I got carried away last night.'

'You're telling me it never happened?'

'I'm telling you nothing.'

'Why on earth not? You've just spent an hour sharing every secret you know with Merz. If you were in the Luftwaffe, they'd have you shot. Why this shyness about your brother? The damage is done, Mr Angell. Just do me the courtesy of repeating the story.'

'No.'

Klimt nodded. Said nothing. Billy was watching a fat carp nuzzling a clump of weeds in the limpid water. Having this view to himself was something he'd never expected. A pair of ducks were drifting down the river, untroubled, serene. Rooks bickered in a stand of elms. Bees gorged themselves on pollen in a nearby flower bed. Bliss, he thought.

Klimt hadn't finished. If Billy found difficulty in

telling the story in detail, perhaps he'd like to confirm the points that really mattered.

'Your brother was in the Navy. Am I right?'

'Yes.'

'They taught him to dive?'

'Yes.'

'He became a specialist?'

'Yes.'

'So what kind of man was he? This Douglas?'

The question took Billy by surprise. Clever, he thought. How could his thoughts about his dead brother add to the damage he'd already done?

'He was older than me. I worshipped him.'

'Does worship come easily to you, Mr Angell?'

'I'm luckier than most. So the answer has to be yes.'

'You need someone to look up to?'

'I need someone to respect, and maybe to follow.'

'You were similar? Similar people? Similar thoughts? Hopes? Dreams?'

'Not at all. Douglas was brave. Courage was something I had to borrow from others. Maybe that's another reason I jumped. My courage ran out.'

'And now? You're in a very difficult situation, Mr Angell. You're in a foreign country. You don't speak the language. You're depending on the kindness of strangers. And just now you're also depending on me. I could have you locked up in five minutes.' He clicked his fingers. 'Just like that.'

'I know.'

'So give me one reason why I shouldn't do that thing.'

'I can't.' Billy held his gaze. 'But it hasn't happened, has it? You haven't done it. We're sitting here. We're having a civilised conversation. You haven't threatened me. You don't appear to regard me as the enemy. So maybe you should be the one telling me why.'

Klimt acknowledged Billy's little speech with a tilt of his head. He hadn't finished with Douglas.

'Describe him, this brother of yours. Taller? Thinner? Paint me a picture.'

'He was smaller than me but more compact. We used to wrestle as kids. He always won.'

'But you told me he was older.'

'Two years. I had weight on my side but Doug was the athlete. He knew about balance. He lived in his body.'

'And you?'

'I always wanted to be someone else. Maybe that's why I became an actor.'

'In the theatre, you mean?' A perceptible spark of interest.

'Yes. I loved it. And I was good as well. My brother thought acting was for cissies. Maybe he was right.'

'Cissies?'

'Not real men. Doug was a real man. He loved being physical. He loved risk. War gets through a lot of men like my brother.'

'And you think that's a waste?'

310

'Of course I do.'

'You have a girlfriend, Mr Angell? A wife, perhaps?'

'No.'

'No interest?'

'I didn't say that.'

Klimt slipped his watch off and laid it on the table. The metal strap glinted in the sunshine. He closed his eyes, tipping his face to the sky.

'I think you're right, Mr Angell,' he murmured at last. 'You and this war were never made for each other. Madame Lafosse mentioned the Quakers. That doesn't surprise me at all.'

'You know about the Quakers? You have them in Germany?'

'Of course.' His eyes were still closed. 'My father was living in Berlin after the first war. Your Quakers were feeding half a million mothers and children. It was a terrible time. These people would have starved otherwise. We Germans even had a word for it. *Quäkerspeisungen.*' He smiled. 'Quaker feedings.'

'And now?'

'Now we still have Quakers. The Gestapo don't trust them but the Gestapo don't trust anyone. They go to all the meetings but the Quakers don't care. Before the war they helped us with the Jews.'

'How?'

'By getting them out to other countries, by helping them flee. That's the way we like to do things, Mr Angell. Get someone else to do the work. And get someone else to pay for it.'

'You mean the Quakers?'

'Of course. And the Jews themselves.'

Billy nodded. He thought he caught a hint of contempt in Klimt's voice but he couldn't be sure. Either way, it didn't seem to matter. This man, for whatever reason, had a great deal of patience. Every minute that passed, Billy felt a little safer.

'Is your father still in Berlin?' he asked.

'My father is dead.'

'And you? You live in Berlin?'

Klimt didn't answer. A pair of swans had appeared overhead. They circled once then came in low over the nearby stone bridge and splashed down on the river.

'Do I have to explain the meaning of Dunkirk or will you?' Klimt hadn't taken his eyes off the swans.

'I don't understand the question.'

'Yes you do, Mr Angell. Your brother was lost off Dunkirk. That's what you told Madame Lafosse last night. You said he'd been digging up the beach. The question is why.'

Billy shrugged, said he didn't know, said it was nothing to do with him. Then, faintly at first, came the throaty rasp of a piston engine. It grew louder and louder until the aircraft appeared over the treeline. It was tiny, even smaller than the Lysander. The sight of Klimt and Billy sitting by the river drew a waggle of the wings and Klimt lifted a hand in salute as the shadow swept over them.

'Merz,' Klimt said quietly. 'You know about this plane?'

'No.'

'We call it a *Storch*. It can take off in a car park, a meadow, a country lane. Merz loves it.' He fell silent, watching as the little plane disappeared towards the east. Then he closed his eyes again. 'One day the *Storch* will be all we have left, Mr Angell. No more 109s. No more Focke-Wulfs. Just the *Storch*. And you know who will fly our leaders out of Berlin? When there's nothing left to destroy? Dieter Merz.'

CHAPTER 28

K limt drove Billy back to the Château de Neaune. Expecting him to turn in at the gate and drive up to the house itself, he was surprised to be dropped on the road. Klimt announced that he was returning to Paris. Herr Angell would please present his compliments to Madame Lafosse.

Billy watched the Mercedes roar away in a cloud of dust. It was a lovely evening, still warm, though Billy could see a tumble of clouds in the east. Six months on a bomber crew, sitting through briefing after briefing, had taught him a great deal about weather patterns and he recognised the onset of the warm front. Rain later, he thought. And then sparkling sunshine and a drop in the temperature as the wind shifted round to the north.

He set off up the drive, taking his time. In some ways, he thought, his job was done. He'd planted the lie about Dunkirk, first with Hélène and then with Klimt. He sensed that they'd both believed him, in part because it seemed to serve their purposes. For whatever reason these people were in serious trouble and the longer he'd listened to

Klimt beside the river the more obvious became the man's disillusion. You didn't have to be a Quaker to realise that the war, from everyone's point of view, was madness. The fact that Klimt appeared to believe that this madness extended to the Reich itself was additional comfort.

So what would Klimt do with his windfall tip about Dunkirk? What kind of space would Billy's phantom brother occupy in the files of *Abwehr* intelligence? Where did information like this belong in the jigsaw of Allied intentions? Would Berlin, above all, really believe that the invasion forces would swarm back over those same beaches that had witnessed the evacuation? Barely three years ago?

It was an arresting thought, a neat twist to recent history, but Billy doubted whether it was true. Why plant information like this when you needed, above all, to maintain total secrecy? Why invite German reinforcements to a coastline you intended to attack? The blow has to fall somewhere else, he told himself. All I have to do is avoid the attentions of anybody who'd put my story to a serious test.

Easier said than done. During the final briefing, Billy had pressed Tam for a radio. He was fully trained. He understood how these things worked. But Tam had turned him down. The kit was too bulky. Travelling in public, he said, would draw the wrong sort of attention. Communication from the chateau, he'd hinted, wouldn't be a problem.

Just let matters unfold. At the time, barely days ago, Billy had been happy to accept Tam's reassurances but now he wasn't so sure. How was he supposed to trigger the return of the Lysander? Did Hélène keep pigeons? And, if so, did they have MI5's address?

He was back at the chateau now. Malin, the old clockmaker, let him in and took him through to the kitchen. The blackout curtains had already been drawn and the candles threw a dancing light on the thick stone walls. Billy counted the faces around the table. There were three, a man and two women. They looked sombre, fearful. None of them answered Billy's smile of greeting.

Malin was fiddling with the bolt on the kitchen door.

'Hélène?' Billy asked.

'Madame Lafosse has been arrested.'

Billy stared at him.

'A couple of hours ago. Müller came again. He had soldiers with him. I was upstairs. I heard it all.'

He said a farmer had been killed in the village. Witnesses had seen Madame Lafosse outside his property. She'd been waiting in the Mercedes belonging to the man Klimt.

'That car will kill us all,' he said. 'They know who that car belongs to. They know who drives it. And they hate Madame Lafosse.'

'So what happens next?'

'We don't know. Maybe Madame Lafosse still

has protection from the Germans. Maybe not. Maybe Müller will come back. Search the place. Arrest all of us. Maybe not. For three years we've had a kind of life here. The mistake is to believe that anything lasts.'

Billy nodded. The image of the dead farmer lying naked on the bed had been with him all day. He couldn't get it out of his mind.

'Good news about the horse, though,' he said brightly.

'Fuck the horse.'

They sat in silence. Billy's gaze drifted from face to face. This was bad. Worse than bad. The man he'd never seen before had his arm round the woman beside him. Billy suspected she'd been crying. The other woman was much younger, much fatter, her face cratered with acne. Slumped in the chair, she was biting her nails.

At length she met Billy's gaze. She looked resentful, angry.

'Ask him why he chose this place.' She'd glanced at Malin, putting the question in French. She obviously didn't speak English. Malin obliged.

'I didn't choose it,' Billy said. 'I found my way to good people. They put me in touch with the *Résistance*. They brought me here.'

'You didn't know about us before?'

'No. How could I?'

'Because maybe you're a spy.'

'I'm a flier,' Billy said. 'Ask Madame Lafosse.'

'We've had other fliers here. They were never

like you. They came at night. By next day they'd gone. You? You stay.'

'Who says?'

'Madame Lafosse. She says you're injured. Another lie.'

Billy could feel suspicion spreading around the table. A nod of the head from the woman. A rap on the table from her companion. At times like these, people needed someone to blame, someone to answer for their worst fears.

'I'm in the RAF,' Billy said quietly. 'I flew in a bomber crew. I worked the radio. Something went wrong. I had to bail out.'

'Agnès has a radio set.' This from Malin.

'She has?' Billy was staring at him.

'Of course. She's a *résistante*. The Germans want to kill her. That's why she's running. That's why she's here.'

Billy nodded. Tam knew about the radio, he thought. Because Tam also knew about this woman. Maybe that's how he knew about the chateau, too. About Hélène and her German lover. Maybe he has Agnès to thank for his abrupt change of career.

'Does Agnès's set still work?' he said carefully.

Agnès didn't need a translation. She nodded.

'*Oui*,' she said. '*Ça marche.*'

'May I use it?'

A translation this time. Agnès wanted to know why.

'Because I need to tell people at my airbase I'm

318

still alive. They'll pass the message on to my family. It's a favour, that's all.'

The old man was staring at him. It was hard to read his face in the candlelight but Billy knew he wasn't smiling.

'You think you'll be getting out of this alive? Good luck, my friend.'

Hélène returned shortly before midnight. The couple at the table had retired hopelessly to bed with a candle, resigned to whatever might happen next. Through the open door, Billy had watched the woman pausing at the foot of the stairs. First she stared at the front door. Then she crossed herself.

Agnès was still at the table when Billy heard the growl of an engine and the crunch of gravel outside. She'd talked no more about the radio despite Billy's best efforts and had ignored his questions about what exactly had brought her to the sanctuary of the chateau. Now, Malin was on his feet, braced for the worst. When the knock finally came it was remarkably light, even gentle.

Billy watched the progress of his candle to the front door. The bent old figure wrestled it open and then peered into the darkness. Hélène stepped past him. She appeared to be alone.

Billy was on his feet. Agnès hadn't moved. Hélène gazed round the kitchen. No one had touched the carafe of wine from last night.

Hélène poured herself a glass and settled at the

table. She looked exhausted. She sat in silence, the glass as yet untouched. From time to time her fingers found her wedding ring and she twisted it round and round, a gesture as revealing as it was unconscious. A moment of crisis, Billy thought. A moment when the life you've led taps you on the shoulder, and a life to come appears all too unlikely.

At length she looked up at Malin.

'I have no news,' she said. 'But at least they let me go.'

'For now?'

'Until tomorrow. Tomorrow they tell me they will have more questions. It's a game, Malin. They're playing with me.'

'With us.'

'Indeed. You have my fullest sympathy.' She reached for her glass. 'Please leave me alone, now.'

Malin wanted to continue the conversation, to find out more, but Hélène waved him away. All three of them got to their feet. Billy was about to head for the darkness beyond the open door when she nodded at his empty seat.

'Not you,' she said. 'Not yet.'

Billy sat down again. He could hear footsteps receding up the stairs. Then an abrupt silence.

'Go to bed, Malin.' Hélène was shouting. 'Do as I say, for God's sake.'

She went to the kitchen door, listened for a moment, and then shut it. Back at the table she swallowed the rest of the wine. Billy fetched the carafe.

'You'll need a glass, *monsieur*. And another bottle.'

She kept the wine in the *cave* below. Billy descended with a candle and selected what he thought might be a promising vintage. Back upstairs, the carafe was empty.

'The Bouchard Châteauneuf-du-Pape.' Hélène was eyeing the bottle. 'Excellent. There's more. We might as well drink it up.'

Billy opened the bottle. Hélène watched him pour two glasses. The Boches, she said, had posted men around the estate. It might still be possible to get out but you'd need cat's eyes in the dark and somewhere to head for afterwards.

'They've bottled us up, *monsieur*. They've sealed us in. We're just like the rest of France. Solidarity, *quoi*.' She lifted the glass. 'A toast, perhaps?'

'Solidarity . . .' Billy mumbled.

He wanted to know why she'd been arrested. Had she made enemies?

'You want a list? Everyone hates me.'

'But someone in particular?'

'Of course. The local man in charge is called Müller. He's an oaf. Perfectly reasonable in his own way but a fool. I have no difficulty with Müller. Put Müller in a uniform and he gets ideas above his station, especially where women are concerned, but he's also a realist. No . . .' she shook her head, '. . . Müller is a puppy. I have no problems with the man.'

'Who, then?'

Hélène gazed at him for a moment. Her eyes were pouched in darkness.

'His name's Huber,' she said quietly.

'And he hates you?'

'He hates someone close to me. Huber is also SS so his kind of hate matters.'

'And he's here? In the village?'

'Of course not. The SS always play to an audience. They prefer cities to places like this.'

'Paris?'

'Yes. And Brussels. And Amsterdam. And Berlin. And Vienna. And wherever his journey takes him next. Someone once told me the SS are pilgrims, sworn to the faith. There you have it, *monsieur*. Huber the pilgrim, Huber the zealot. Huber the crusader. Men like Huber are only interested in the next step forward, the next bend in the road. The view never interests them. Only the destination.'

'Where did you learn your English, *madame*?'

'Call me Hélène. I like it better.' She frowned, staring at the glass. 'I studied in Oxford. Before the war. It was a privilege and a pleasure. I have a husband, Nathan. He likes the English even more than I do. Which is probably why he's in London.' She lifted her head. 'You like art, *monsieur*? Fine art?'

'A bit. I like a landscape.'

'You know the *Mona Lisa*, of course?'

'Of course.'

'Huber wants me to find it, to lay hands on it.

322

Can you believe that? A grown man? It's nonsense, of course, a pretext, an opportunity to break me, and he knows it.' She shook her head, despairing. Then she reached for the bottle again.

They drank in silence. Hélène was brooding.

'Everything goes back to the *débâcle*,' she murmured. 'Our army may have done brave things in the field but we made the Germans a present of Paris. This is our jewel, the most precious thing we possess, and we handed it over to the burglar with a pretty curtsey and a smile. Most people I know went south, took to the roads, fled. That first winter I stayed. But to survive in Paris you had to become invisible. This is something for which no Parisian was prepared. We're pavement people. Café people. Outdoors people. And then all of a sudden, *monsieur*, you find yourself locking your shutters, and filling your bath, and hiding the good linen. That's terrible. That's hopeless. That turns us into people we're not. We used to be compassionate with each other. We used to help each other out. Now my friends in Paris huddle at home and don't allow themselves to know anyone anymore. Because it's too dangerous. Because it's too depressing. And because defeat brought out the worst in us. You know what happened to the Germans the moment they arrived in Paris? They were swamped with paperwork. It was all denunciations. And it was all in French. No wonder the Germans smile and salute while they rob us blind. They have no respect. Because they know who we really are.'

323

'And here? In the countryside?'

'Here is different. People are tougher. They understand time. They live by the seasons. They know that one day the Germans will be gone so all you need to survive is somewhere to hide your beets. A great deal of patience is also useful. These people are bred to be patient. They're good at it. And they're hard to fool, too. There was an old lady down in the village who watched the Germans arrive. They drove through in their lorries, tossing bonbons to the children. She thought that was kind until her husband picked one of them up and realised they came from a sweetshop they'd looted in Tours. Thieves in uniforms, *monsieur*. And all the handsome ones have gone to Russia.'

Billy nodded. He wanted to know about Agnès. About the *Résistance*. And about the decision to turn the chateau into a place of sanctuary.

'That happened by accident. Malin was the first. I decided to leave Paris in the end and when you do that you take your most precious possessions. Malin was precious to us. My husband loved him. He's a Jew, just like Nathan. Jews had to register by now but Malin was too old and too wise to do that. He was Polish but he'd lived in Germany in the years before the war when they were making life hard for the Jews. He knew how much the Germans depended on their paperwork. He knew where registration led. He knew it would never be just a question of wearing a yellow star. And so he ignored all the rubbish they stuffed under his door and when the time was right he came down here. The Spanish couple were next. They just appeared one morning. It was the middle of the winter. They'd walked from the Pyrenees. They were like ghosts. They had nothing. And so I took them in. Agnès was more recent. She's still a child, which perhaps makes her more difficult.'

'She told me she was with the *Résistance*.'

'That's true. And she still is. Those people are like the Jesuits. Once they have you, you're theirs forever.'

'She says she has a radio.'

'That's true. She does.'

'She's still in touch with her people? With the *Résistance*?'

'I don't know. I expect so.'

'Have you heard her tapping at all? Sending a message?' He mimed an imaginary Morse key on the table.

'No. But that means nothing. It's a big house, *monsieur*. You might have noticed.'

Her glass was empty again. She poured another. Billy wanted to know what questions she might expect tomorrow.

'I have no idea. The Germans know a lot about me and so do the French. I lead a charmed life, *monsieur*. I have no secrets and that may be the end of me. If they want to put me against the wall and shoot me they could do it tomorrow, tonight, whenever. A wine like this, I probably wouldn't mind.'

She contemplated the glass, then took another mouthful.

'So why don't they?'

'Why don't they what?'

'Shoot you?'

She didn't answer. Her eyes were moist now but her words were clear and Billy guessed she'd need a great deal more wine to soften the memory of the last few hours.

Billy put the question again.

'Why do they let you get away with so much? Why weren't you arrested long ago?'

'Because I'm a woman. Because I'm as clever as they are and because certain kinds of men find me attractive and because luck had one of these men cross my path. I liked him a great deal. I still do. Do you call that love? Maybe you do. Does that make me a *putain*? No.'

There was a long silence. Far away, Billy could hear the hooting of an owl.

'Klimt?' he said softly.

'Yes.' She smiled. 'For a man you have good instincts, Monsieur Ange. Was it that obvious?'

'He's in trouble, isn't he? Like you?'

She nodded, fingering the glass. Then she peered round, as if the kitchen was suddenly new to her.

'We got to know each other in Paris. We shared the same apartment block. I paid my rent. He'd evicted the previous owner. For a while we stayed in our separate apartments but then the time came for me to be down here and I asked him to move into mine. That's where he lives now. My foreign lodger, *n'est-ce pas*? Paying the bills and fighting off the mice and keeping everything in good order. Collaboration? Of course. But of the very best kind.' She was smiling again. 'I remember the first time he came down here. The chateau was a present from my husband. He knew about that and he knew about my husband, too. And so he arrived and I brought him in through the front door and he took a long look round, room after room, floor after floor, upstairs, downstairs, even the cellar, and watching him it was as if he'd come to buy the place, as if he'd come to make it his own. And, in a way, that's what he's done. Without Klimt, I wouldn't be here. Without him I'd probably be dead.'

'So what next?'

'I have no idea.'

'It must depend on your friend?'

'On Klimt? It does. And in ways you probably can't imagine.'

Another silence, longer this time. Billy listened hard for the owl but heard nothing. The wind was beginning to stir the nearby stand of trees and he'd been right about the rain. He imagined the Germans in their capes standing guard around the estate. At least he wasn't out in the open.

He asked about radio detector vans. Were there any in the village?

'There was talk of one recently but I think it's gone. This afternoon Müller asked for another.'

'Has it arrived?'

'No. It was coming from Nevers. It broke down near Chinon.'

'How do you know?'

'Müller told me. I think it was a bid for sympathy. He likes to tell me how hard he has to work to keep us all in order.'

'Are you sure he's not lying? Not laying a trap?'

'Müller?' She laughed. 'My fat little Hans? He wouldn't have the wit. Or the imagination.'

'Are you sure?'

'I'm certain. Why do you ask?'

'Because I'd like to send a message.'

'A radio message?'

'Yes.'

'To who?'

Billy repeated the story about getting in touch with his airbase in England. There were people who might want to know he was still alive.

'Including your mother and father?'

'I never knew my father. He died in the first war.'

'In France?'

'Yes.'

'Just as well, perhaps. How will your mother view your desertion?'

'My mother has remarried. She has other things on her mind.'

'You have a wife of your own? A girlfriend, perhaps?'

'No.'

'Someone else?'

'Yes.'

'A man?'

'Yes.'

'Someone who matters to you?'

'Yes.'

She looked at him, a new expression on her face. Billy knew she wanted to trust him. He sensed a thousand and one questions she wanted to ask, but she was a gambler as well, and it showed. She'd been lucky all her life. One last throw of the dice.

'The radio's in the cellar,' she said. 'I'm sure you know what it looks like.'

Billy found it without difficulty, hidden in a cobwebbed corner of the cellar beneath an old blanket. He hauled it out and took it upstairs. It was a Paraset of a kind he'd never seen before but relied on the same principles he'd mastered in training.

Hélène watched him as he unravelled the aerial and plugged in the valves. They'd given him frequencies and time slots during his preparation but there was a procedure for emergency calls and he used it now. He'd been careful to memorise every detail, just the way he'd always taken a script and turned words on the page into flesh and blood on the stage.

He gave some thought to the message he'd be sending. Agent protocols limited any message to no more than a minute. His keying skills were excellent, way above average, and unless she knew

Morse code there was no possibility of Hélène making any sense of what was to follow.

The transmission was routed through a central control room in a rambling old country house north of London, manned twenty-four hours a day. Priority Black would take it straight to Tam. Billy made a last adjustment to the aerial, slipped on the headphones and then hit the keypad. *Agent Thesp in place*, he tapped. *Principals in jeopardy. Script delivered. Intense pressure. Ends.*

Billy sat back from the set. He'd checked the battery and he could afford to keep the radio in listening mode. He'd no idea what Tam might be doing at half past midnight but he'd been assured that Priority Blacks earned a swift response. It came within minutes. He noted down the letters. A single word. *Jeopardy?*

He bent to the radio again, unsure how much detail to include. You tried to avoid real names or places in case of interception. *Principals* was the agreed code for Hélène and Klimt. Hélène was *Female Lead*, Klimt *Male Lead*. The chateau was *the Theatre. Script* was the news about Dunkirk.

Male Lead under threat. Female Lead facing arrest. Situation critical. Curtain call?

Curtain call was code for immediate extraction. It meant that Billy had done his job and would like to come home. Tam, a master of understatement, would, he hoped, understand. Another trip with Stanislaw would be more than welcome.

He waited for a response. Nothing. He poured

himself another glass of wine. Still nothing. An hour later, he returned the radio to the cellar. When he got back to the kitchen Hélène was at the sink, sluicing her face with cold water. When she turned round, her face was shiny in the candlelight.

'Your friend is relieved?' she enquired drily.

'I don't know.' Billy nodded at the radio. 'That was the operator at my airbase. He needed to check something.'

'He'll pass the message on?'

'I hope so.'

She nodded. Her face was a mask but Billy sensed she'd seen through his tissue of small deceits.

'It would be good to meet this friend of yours one day,' she said at last.

'Then maybe you will.'

'You could make that happen?'

'I could try.'

'In England?'

'If that's what you wanted.'

'Both of us?' She reached for a towel at last. 'Myself and Klimt?'

CHAPTER 29

Hélène, to everyone's relief, never left the house next morning. There were no military vehicles grinding up the drive, no invitations to attend another session in the village, not even a phone call. Hélène lifted the telephone herself at midday and put through a call of her own. The phone was in the hall. Billy heard her from the landing above. He had no idea whether it was a Paris number, nor did he understand a word she was saying, but he assumed the conversation was with Klimt. The call at an end, she announced her intention to exercise Valmy. She appeared to believe the soldiers around the estate had been withdrawn.

From an upstairs window, Billy watched her lead the horse across the courtyard and out to the bridle path that led away towards the forest. She adjusted the reins, gave the stallion a pat and then swung herself into the saddle. Moments later she was away, raising a pair of pheasants hiding in the hedge.

The radio was exactly where Billy had left it. He could have sent another message from the cellar but he didn't want to be disturbed. Malin was tending a rose bed out in the sunshine. Of Hélène's other refugees there was no sign. He carried the radio up to his bedroom and wedged the door shut with a sliver of wood he'd found in the cellar. Setting up the radio, in broad daylight, was a piece of cake. Priority Black again.

Male and Female Leads request immediate curtain call. Thesp.

Again he waited, sitting on the bed, crouched over the radio. Again, nothing. The battery was beginning to run down. He waited another five minutes and then disconnected the power feed. At this time of day, Tam should be at his desk. So why the lack of response?

One more try, he told himself. Half an hour went by before he tried again. He double-checked the aerial and the seating of the valves, and then sent the same message, same priority. Time and again, he made tiny adjustments to the frequency tuner, raising bursts of static, searching in vain for some ghostly evidence that Tam had picked up the message. As an experienced Wireless Op, Billy knew there were dozens of reasons why a message might not get through but silence after two attempts was unusual. Atmospheric disturbance over the Channel? Maybe some kind of jamming operation? He didn't know. One more try later, he promised himself.

He packed the radio away and thought about a walk in the sunshine. The flower beds were a riot of colour after the overnight rain and his right foot was almost back to normal. He picked up the radio and stooped to release the wedge beneath the door before opening it. Agnès was sitting on the floor across the landing, her back resting against the wall. With her was Malin. He was carrying a shotgun.

Agnès didn't move. Just stared up at Billy.

'*Espion*,' she hissed. Spy.

Malin gestured him back into the bedroom. The shotgun was inches away from his chest.

'Sit,' Malin nodded at the bed. 'Explain to us about the radio.'

Billy couldn't, didn't. He shook his head.

'No,' he said.

'Why not?'

'Because it's complicated. And because it's none of your business.'

'Everything that happens here, my friend, is our business. You're a flier. Your leg is better. You need to get to Spain. You need to escape. And yet you're still here. Why?'

Good question. Just now Billy would have paid any price for another thirty miles on the road with Alice. Anywhere but here in this madhouse, he thought.

'You're talking to the Germans?' It was Agnès. Malin translated.

'No. Never. Why would I do that?'

'Because Madame Lafosse has been betrayed. Because we've all been betrayed. And you know the penalty for that? For selling us to the Germans?'

334

Agnès wanted to search him. Malin stood aside, the gun still pointed at Billy's chest. From a pocket in his trousers she extracted a thick wad of notes. She counted them on the bed.

'Seven thousand three hundred.' She looked up. 'Do English fliers always carry *Reichsmarks*?'

Billy knew he was in trouble. He shook his head. Said nothing. Hopeless, he thought.

Agnès wanted to shoot him. The expression on her face – vengeful, contemptuous – needed no translation. Malin shook his head. He wanted to know more. And he wanted to wait for Madame Lafosse.

It took Hélène more than an hour to ride to the Deschamps' farm. This was the first time she'd given the stallion a proper workout since bringing him back from Benoit's place and she was pleased with his performance. From the moment she'd slung a bag over her back and urged him into a gallop, he'd lunged ahead and she'd flattened herself against his flying mane, hearing the thunder of hooves beneath her, enjoying the rush of warm air as she spurred him faster and faster down the bridle path.

They skirted the forest, the trees a blur in the sunshine, and then they were out into open country, greens and yellows rolling north towards the Loire, towers of cloud on the far horizon. There was thunder in the air. Fields of wheat shivered in the gathering wind and the sight of women with baling hooks told Hélène that the harvest was already upon them. Not once did she see anyone in uniform.

Georges Deschamps had a handful of meadows on rich soil near the village of Moines. More ambitious than most farmers in the area, he bred fine cattle for beef, and he also ran a flock of sheep on the higher ground where the vegetation was sparser. Hélène had got to know him through a local butcher during the long summer before the war broke out. Nathan, who loved her version of Chateaubriand, had taken a single mouthful of Georges Deschamps' beef and insisted they pay him a visit. Since then, thanks to Nathan's charm, they'd become friends.

The track to the farm was puddled from a recent shower. Hélène slipped out of the saddle and led the stallion towards the cluster of outhouses. The lush meadows lay beyond but Hélène could see no cattle.

Georges emerged from the barn he used as a workshop. He was in his late sixties, a giant of a man, stooped, gruff, weather-beaten, with a mane of white hair and – according to Nathan – a crushing handshake. The sight of Hélène put a hint of a smile on his face. A retired boxer, she'd always thought. Battered but indomitable.

She embraced him and asked how things were going. Georges ignored the question.

'He needs a rubdown,' he said, looking at the stallion. 'You're working him too hard.'

He disappeared into the barn and returned with an old towel. Valmy moved gently against him as he mopped the sweat from his gleaming flanks.

Hélène wanted to know about the cattle.

'Gone.' Georges was bent double, working on the stallion's legs. 'The Germans don't even ask anymore. Just help themselves.'

'When?'

'Last week.'

'*All* of them?'

'Every last animal. Get yourself to Paris and there might be some left. I'm sure you know the right hotels.'

There was no malice in his voice, simply an acknowledgement that in this matter, as in many others, a man was helpless.

'They took the sheep as well?'

'Not so far. Maybe next week. You want to come in?'

He tethered the stallion and led the way to the farmhouse. He'd lost his wife recently to a heart condition. His only son, Marc, had helped around the place until the war took him to the eastern frontier. He'd manned the Maginot Line and made it back with minor injuries but since then he'd been shipped to Germany as forced labour, like every other young man in the area.

'He's still in Essen? Marc?'

'As far as I know. The last letter I got was at Christmas. He said things weren't too bad.' He shook his head, looking for the coffee pot. 'That boy always knew how to lie.'

Hélène put her bag on the table and watched him grind the coffee beans. Real coffee was as rare as gold these days. If she was looking for a sign of Georges' respect, then here it was.

'How's that husband of yours?' he asked.

'He's in London. He's well.'

'You've talked to him? You're in touch?'

'Yes.'

Georges shot her a look. No more questions.

'You've come for a reason,' he said.

Hélène sat down. The sheepdog under the table nuzzled her ankle. She explained that life had become difficult. She had to get away from the chateau and she had to take people with her.

'How many people?'

'Maybe six, including me. Maybe less.'

'Where will you go?'

'I don't know. Paris?' She shrugged.

'Are you in trouble?'

'Yes.'

'You can come here. You know that.'

'Thank you, Georges. I appreciate it.'

'No?' He held her gaze.

'No.'

'As bad as that?'

'Probably worse.'

She reached for her bag. Inside was the package from Klimt. She hadn't even opened it. She began to tear at the wrapping. One look told her that

Klimt had been short-changed. Not American dollars at all but *Reichsmarks*. From the owner of the mare that had gone to Otto Abetz.

'That ambulance of Marc's?' she asked. 'The one he brought back before the Armistice.'

'The Renault?'

'Yes.'

'It's in one of the barns.'

'And it works?'

'Perfectly. Marc did everything before they took him to Germany. I haven't used it since.'

Hélène nodded. Marc had driven the ambulance after the collapse of the French Army. Outrun by German armour, he'd ferried casualties to hard-pressed casualty stations along the route. After the surrender, he'd managed to nurse the vehicle all the way back to the Touraine. Hélène remembered the first time she'd laid eyes on it: the neat line of bullet holes through the thin metal skin, the smashed windscreen, the sagging suspension, the rag stuffed in the fuel tank where someone had stolen the cap. At the time Marc's ambulance, with its fading red cross, had perfectly summed up everything that had happened to France during those terrible weeks and she'd retained the image in her mind ever since. Georges called it *le corbillard*. The hearse.

'You want to borrow it?'

'I want to buy it.'

'It's not for sale.'

'Then I'll hire it. You tell me how much.'

She extracted a fat handful of notes and began to count them out. They were in denominations of fifty. She'd got to seven hundred *Reichsmarks* when he told her to stop.

'I don't want your money. *Le corbillard*'s yours. Just bring it back when you've finished.'

'That might not be possible.'

'Then *tant pis*. Cattle? Sheep? They matter. No one ever ate an ambulance.'

Hélène smiled. Instead of money, perhaps he'd take Valmy.

'You want me to look after him? While you're away?'

'I want you to have him. Forever. And if times get really tough . . .' she shrugged, '. . . maybe you can put him in the pot.'

'I don't want your horse.' Georges was pouring the coffee. 'Of course I'll look after him but he's yours.' He looked up. 'He was a present, wasn't he? From your husband?'

'Yes.'

'Then show the man some respect.' He nodded at the notes on the table. 'And don't insult me again.'

Hélène was back at the chateau within the hour. She'd left Valmy with Georges, and she'd tucked a couple of thousand *Reichsmarks* under a plate in his kitchen when he wasn't watching to help cover feed costs. She'd like to think it was a loan, a favour on the part of Georges, but in truth she'd no idea whether she'd ever see the stallion again.

Once again, there were no signs of field-grey uniforms on the narrow country roads around the estate. For whatever reason, the threatened patrols must have been withdrawn. She parked the ambulance at the back of the chateau and walked through the courtyard towards the kitchen, doing her best to ignore the sight of Valmy's empty stable.

The moment she stepped into the kitchen, she knew something was wrong. Everyone was there: Malin, Agnès, the Spanish couple. And then she caught sight of Billy. His hands had been roped to the back of his chair. Malin sat opposite, eyeing him across the table. Nathan's shotgun lay on the table within reach.

'What's going on?' Hélène shut the door.

No one answered. Hélène picked up the gun, broke the barrel, and extracted the shells. She asked Billy whether he was all right. Billy nodded silently.

'Show her,' said Agnès, looking at Malin.

Malin dug into the pocket of his dungarees and extracted a thick wad of *Reichsmarks*. He laid them carefully on the table in front of Hélène.

'More than seven thousand. I counted every note.' He nodded towards Billy. 'And you told us the man's a flier.'

'Billy?'

Billy looked up. Hélène had never used his Christian name before.

'I am a flier,' he said.

'He's not. He's a spy.'

Billy recognised the word *espion*. He shook his head. He hadn't taken his eyes off Hélène.

'Ask me anything about the RAF, about what I've been doing, about the targets we bombed. You know it's true. Ask Klimt. He knows.'

'Klimt?' Malin threw his head back and laughed. 'Is that man your defence? You're relying on a *German* to get you out of the shit? Agnès was right. I should have let her shoot you.'

'Thank God you didn't.' Hélène was unpacking her bag. She put Klimt's package on the table in front of Malin. More *Reichsmarks* spilled over the table. 'Count them,' she told Malin.

'Where did that come from?' Malin was staring at the money.

'You know where it came from. It came from the mare Valmy covered. It came from a French businessman. And you know why? Because the man wanted a favour from the Germans. The mare is in foal. The mare now belongs to Otto Abetz. And Otto Abetz is Berlin's man in France.'

'That's collaboration.' This from Agnès.

'No it's not, my child, it's business.' Hélène rounded on her. Billy couldn't follow this conversation but he'd never seen her so angry. 'You think this world we live in is simple? You think killing a couple of Germans outside some bar in Lille is going to solve all our problems? It didn't, did it? They were still there next day. Hundreds of them. Thousands of them. They were looking for you. And the moment they found you, they

342

were going to take you somewhere very dark and make you cry for your mother and betray all those brave friends of yours and when they were done they were going to take you out and shoot you. A single bullet in the back of your pretty head. And that's if you were lucky. So you ran. You ran and you ran. And in God's good time you ended up with us. We were a place of safety. We looked after you. You're still here. You're still alive. And you know who you have to thank for that? Klimt. Yes, Klimt. *My* Klimt. The man who looks after me. The man who looks after all of us. And you want to guess what made that possible?' She was looking at Malin now. 'The fact that he was well placed. And the fact that he was a German.'

'Our protector.' Malin rolled his eyes. 'A fucking German.'

'You knew that, Malin. You've known it for years. You've taken advantage of it for years. Not because I told you but because you worked it out. Agnès has an excuse, Malin. She's a child. You're not. You know how the world works.'

'This world.'

'Of course. You want to try another? You want to see what happens when Klimt's not around anymore? When there's no one standing between us and a different kind of German? Be my guest. Because, like it or not, it's about to happen.'

The Spanish couple had been listening hard to Hélène's outburst. The woman's French wasn't

343

good. She whispered in her husband's ear. He said something in Catalan and she looked horrified. Agnès ignored her. She still wanted to know why Billy was carrying German currency.

Hélène said she didn't care. It didn't matter. Nothing mattered any more except getting away.

'Getting away? You mean from here?' Malin was staring up at Hélène. 'Why would we want to do that?'

'Because otherwise the Germans will come for us.'

'And Klimt?'

'There is no more Klimt. He did his best. And now he's gone.'

'They've killed him?'

'I've no idea. All I know is that he's in big trouble, the worst kind of trouble, and so are we. We're lucky, *mes enfants*. We still have a choice. Stay here, and life will get extremely difficult. Leave, and there may be some kind of future.'

'We do this thing now? You're serious?'

'Tomorrow morning.'

'How?'

'I've bought a vehicle. It's big enough for all of us. It used to be an ambulance. Maybe that's what we deserve. Maybe that's what we need. An ambulance.' Hélène hadn't finished. She reached down and pushed the pile of notes towards the old man. 'Count the money, Malin. Nothing in this world comes cheap.'

In all, including Billy's contribution, they had

just over 120,000 *Reichsmarks*. Hélène knew she'd been cheated over the deal with Otto Abetz's mare but just now she didn't care. By dawn, they had to be ready to leave. What they had to decide now was where they might go.

Determined to share the decision, she went slowly round the table. An agreement on the destination might ease the days to come.

'Agnès?'

'I don't care.'

'You want to stay here?'

'I didn't say that.'

'So where do we go?'

She was chewing her fingernails again. The fact that Hélène had untied Billy seemed to have deflated her. She lived in a world of blacks and whites. The English spy should have been dead by now.

'Well?' Hélène still wanted an answer.

'Anywhere. I don't care.'

Hélène moved on. Pablo said the Pyrenees. He named a pass he knew in the mountains. If they had to they could dump the ambulance and walk. The path led to Andorra, and then into Spain. There were people he knew on the other side. It would be hard going but this time of year there was no snow. At the mention of Spain, a flicker of a smile appeared on his wife's face. When Hélène enquired how she felt, she nodded.

'*Si,*' she whispered. '*España.*'

'Malin? You agree?'

The old man had piled the notes into neat blocks. He'd never seen so much money in his life.

'Why not Paris?' he said. 'We could lie low. We could buy anywhere we like.'

'Paris is full of listening ears,' Hélène pointed out. 'Money attracts attention. And so would we.'

It was true. She was tempted by Paris herself. Her apartment was still there, and maybe Klimt was, too, if he'd managed to keep his enemies at arm's length. Had she been alone she'd have gone north without a moment's hesitation. But she wasn't alone. She had responsibility for these people. And she knew the moment had come when she had to put their safety above hers. Any other decision, and Agnès would be right. *Collabo. Putain.* Just another survivor keeping the skin on her back.

'The south? The Pyrenees? Spain?' She was still looking at Malin.

'It's a long way. The Germans are everywhere.'

'I know. But it's going to be the same wherever we go. The south is emptier. We keep to the country roads. We take food, water, bedding. Less than a week and we could be in the mountains. You think you could manage that? The mountains?'

While this decision was being made, something had changed in Malin. The fire had gone out of him. He had an air of contrition. He was staring at the money. His voice was low. Hélène, he muttered, was the one with a head on her shoulders. She'd never let him down, not once. In his opinion she was woman enough to have any man and if her choice had fallen on Klimt then *tant pis*.

He'd been angry, earlier. He admitted it. He hated the Germans and he hated what they were doing to France and if the English flier was part of all that then it was shameful. But Hélène was back now. The quarrel was over. This was her place, her property. She'd kept him safe for three years and he didn't care to enquire how. Klimt was obviously part of it and without Klimt their door was wide open. At this point, he looked up. His eyes were shiny with tears. He fumbled for a handkerchief and blew his nose. If things were really that bad for Klimt, he growled, then he'd follow her anywhere.

Malin seldom made speeches. Hélène thanked him for his support. She'd bring the ambulance round to the courtyard. Everyone was allowed a single bag. They'd empty the kitchen of provisions, take plenty of water and wine. A couple of saucepans, matches, all the candles they could find. The money would keep them supplied en route. Bread, milk, cheese and eggs from farmers deep in the country. Fuel wherever they could buy it. They'd live like gypsies and by the time they got to the mountains they'd be a couple of days away from freedom.

She was about to fetch the ambulance when Malin raised a hand.

'A favour, *madame*,' he said.

'What?'

'My clock, if you please.'

'You want to take it with us?'

'Of course. And it's still on French time.'

The loading of the ambulance, to Hélène's surprise, took less than an hour. The back of the vehicle was empty but Georges had used it to store sacks of wheat and oats and Agnès fetched a broom to sweep the floor clean. Malin stopped his precious long-case clock and disconnected the pendulum before Agnès and Billy carried it out of the house. Agnès, surprisingly strong, avoided Billy's gaze as they manoeuvred it into the yard. Billy thought she might have put the earlier scene to one side but he couldn't be sure. The clock was the size of a grown man. It was awkward and heavy and they laid it carefully on a couple of blankets Agnès had found for the back of the ambulance. The Spanish couple had disappeared upstairs and took no part in ferrying supplies out into the darkness.

Box by box the back of the ambulance began to fill until Hélène called a halt. In her judgement they had enough to get by for a couple of days before the *Reichsmarks* bought them fresh food. At this point, close to midnight, the Spanish couple reappeared. Pablo was carrying a single suitcase, very old, secured with a length of rope. He offered it to Malin, who stowed it next to the big jars of water. When they'd gone again, Hélène moved it closer to the front where it nestled beside the radio.

'That's exactly how they arrived,' she was looking at the suitcase. 'Three years ago.'

It was nearly midnight. Exhausted, Hélène said she was going to bed. Billy accompanied Malin back to the kitchen. Of Agnès and the Spanish couple there was no sign.

'You need a drink.' The old man's gaze had drifted to the carafe of red wine on the dresser. It was an order rather than an invitation.

Billy fetched glasses and poured the wine. The evening had become surreal. He'd lost his place in the script and he had no idea what might happen next but his admiration for Hélène was unbounded. Not only had she probably saved his life but in her brisk, unsentimental way she appeared to have found a chink of light in the enveloping darkness.

'To *madame* . . .' Billy raised his glass in a toast.

Malin didn't move. His gnarled old hands lay knotted on the table top, skin and bone against the grain of the wood. Billy stared at them, knowing there was something missing in the house. Then he had it. The ticking of the clock.

'You think it'll work? Leaving?'

'I have no idea, my friend. If anyone can make it work, she can.' His head came up. 'She could have left us. You know that? She could have left us all.'

Billy nodded. The thought had occurred to him, too.

'She's brave,' he said quietly.

'You're right. And she's unusual, too. I knew her

husband. He was the same. A fine couple. Unexpected. He was always laughing but he was steel inside. *Madame?* She doesn't laugh so much. Not these days. But she's maybe even stronger than him.'

He talked about the ambulance. He'd seen it before, within weeks of Georges' son bringing it back from the war.

'Marc had a casualty on board, an older man no hospital would take. He'd been badly hurt, badly patched up. Everyone knew he was dying. It was just a question of time. *Madame* said she'd take him. Insisted. And so Marc drove him here in the ambulance. That man was in an even worse state than the ambulance. We carried him upstairs. *Madame* had prepared a bed. We stripped him bare and *madame* washed him and then dressed him in a pair of her husband's pyjamas. Nathan loved the good things. The pyjamas were silk, blue and gold. She said it was like having her husband back in the house again. She fed him and nursed him and read him stories, like a child. He loved Stendahl most of all. We found a copy of the *Le Rouge et le Noir*. You know it? A fine book. A long book. A big book. We read to him all summer, taking it in turns. We were on the final chapter when the man died. He was lying there on the bed and it was *madame* who was reading and she just carried on until the end because we both wanted to find out what happened.' He paused. 'Julien Sorel? You know about him?'

Billy shook his head.

'He's Stendahl's hero. He's a young man. He comes from a poor family. *Madame* and I liked him very much. He's intelligent. He has the best of intentions. But he falls between the church and aristocracy because he's so . . .' he shrugged, '. . . innocent. These people have power. They grind him down, like mill wheels . . . .' he mimed the motion with his fists, '. . . and he ends up under the guillotine.'

'He dies?'

'Yes. And then his lover gives him a final kiss.'

'On the lips?'

'Yes.'

'Of his severed head?'

Malin nodded. Then he looked up at Billy and at last raised his glass.

'So here's to Julien Sorel, my friend. *Madame* sees a lot of him in you.'

CHAPTER 30

The curfew ended at dawn. They left within the hour. The last item Hélène fetched from her bedroom was a red beret she'd always treasured. It had been a playful gift from Nathan. It was a little rumpled and could maybe have done with a wash but it was still stylish, a token of the good times. She put on the beret, studied herself briefly in the mirror and then came downstairs. She took a last look around, shut and locked the kitchen door, and then hid the key in case, as she put it to Malin, she ever had the good fortune to return. Malin, who'd already done the same to Valmy's stable, put his thin arms round her.

'*Courage, madame,*' he muttered. '*Allons-y.*'

They drove south as Hélène had suggested, taking the country roads, avoiding the villages. Hélène was alone in the cab. If they hit a road block, she'd try and bluff her way through. To warn of trouble ahead, she'd bang on the panel behind her.

From the cab, there was no access to the rear of the ambulance. Malin had left space for all five of them to sit on the floor, their backs against the bodywork, their legs outstretched between the stocks of food and rolls of bedding. A single rectangle of dirty glass shed a thin light over the box-like interior and Billy swayed with the motion of the vehicle as Hélène dropped a gear for yet another bend. Agnès appeared to be asleep. Maria, too, had her eyes closed but her lips were moving very softly, her hand in her husband's lap. Billy watched her for a while, then caught Malin's eye.

'I think she's saying her prayers,' Malin murmured.

Billy nodded and then he, too, shut his eyes. Malin, he was sure, was right. This was exactly what you'd do if events suddenly took charge of your life, if you found yourself in the back of a windowless cell, bumping down roads you couldn't see, past landscapes you could only imagine, your fate mysteriously in the hands of whatever might happen next.

Billy pondered the thought for a while, turning it over and over, and then – quite suddenly – he knew that this was the way it must have been for his dead father, a young man here in France, at the mercy of an incoming mortar shell, or clouds of choking gas, or a close-quarter encounter with an enemy probably as terrified and as lost as he'd been.

Days earlier, Billy told himself, my dad would have been on a train or in the back of a lorry, making his way inexorably towards the line of trenches where the slaughter began. There'd have been no way out. You enlisted. You did your training. You crossed the Channel. And, days later, there you were.

Because you were young, you naturally assumed you were immortal. Of course people died. Everyone knew that. But they were other people, unlucky people, careless people, not you. And then came the moment, that brief vivid splinter of time when everything turned upside down and – if you were lucky – it was over.

Was that the way it had happened to his dad? A whizz and a bang and another torn body in the mud at the bottom of the trench? Or had he been stretchered back to some casualty station behind the lines to take his chances with the rest of the nearly dead? In truth Billy would never know, but when he opened his eyes again Maria had finished with her prayers and appeared to have fallen asleep.

A couple of hours took them down towards Angoulême. It was a fine day, bright sunshine. A brisk wind tugged cloud shadows across the neglected fields of wheat and barley and from the driving cab Hélène was struck by the emptiness of this vast landscape. The last war, she thought, had thinned out an entire generation of Frenchmen. This one had shipped them all off to Germany.

She concentrated on her driving, nursing the old van along the maze of country roads, steering by the sun. A couple of times she risked thinking about Spain, and about the Portuguese border beyond. Maybe there was a way of keeping the ambulance, of finding an unguarded road over the mountains. In that case she could trade in her *Reichsmarks* for real money and keep going until they reached Lisbon. Lisbon was where Nathan had been headed as the Germans plunged into France. Lisbon was where you could buy yourself a ticket for anywhere in the world. Lisbon might take her back to a time she could barely remember.

She thought a little more about Nathan and about the ways a life abroad might have changed him but she knew that, in essence, when it came to the things that really mattered, there'd be no changing him. Like Malin, he'd always been very sure of himself. That confidence was something that had always attracted her and she was honest enough to acknowledge that Klimt had it, too. These were people who had no trouble looking at themselves in the mirror. They had a sense of purpose, a sense of direction that seldom let them down. It governed everything they did, every step they took, and to be in company like that had always been a special pleasure.

She smiled at some of the memories. Nathan in the box he always hired at the Paris opera, tossing flowers onto the stage below. Nathan on his feet in front of an audience of hundreds, welcoming Picasso to Paris. Nathan in bed. They'd made love in the afternoon in the slow winter months when Nathan could get back from the gallery and he'd never tired of her body. He was gifted in ways that had frankly surprised her and she was recalling an occasion in late January, with snow blowing softly against the bedroom window, when she saw the uniformed figures in the road ahead.

There were three of them. The uniforms were black. They were heavily armed. And when the tallest stepped forward, motioning her to slow down, her foot found the brake. At the same time she reached back, and banged the metal partition with the flat of her hand.

Boches, mes amis. Prenez garde.

The ambulance came to a halt. The soldier was approaching her side of the cab. Already she could see the silver flashes on his collar. SS. *Merde.*

She wound the window down. The soldier motioned her out of the cab. He wore an officer's cap and he was clearly in charge. The other soldiers had unslung their rifles and were taking a lively interest in the ambulance.

The officer asked for her papers. He had good French. Hélène fetched them from the cab. He unfolded her ID papers and matched the photo to her face.

'You've come far?' He was eyeing her beret.

'Far enough.'

'How far's that, Madame Lafosse?'

'Maybe eighty kilometres? I don't know. A nice day like today I haven't been counting.'

'And where are you going?'

'Angoulême.'

'Why?'

'I have friends there. They need help in the fields.'

'What sort of help?'

'Anything. I don't mind.'

'Show me your hands, Madame Lafosse.'

Hélène extended both hands. The officer peeled off a glove.

'May I?' He took her hand and held it for a moment before turning it over, palm-side up. Looking at his face – quizzical, amused – Hélène realised he was toying with her. This isn't about my hands at all, she thought. He's not interested in whether or not I'm used to manual labour. He wants to touch me, before whatever happens next.

She enquired whether she was permitted to drive on. She might not have the hands of a navvy but her friends still needed help.

With the barest hint of regret he shook his head, then turned on his heel and signalled to someone further down the road. For the first time, Hélène recognised the wings and radiator of a car parked in the entrance to a field. It was a Mercedes, like Klimt's, but dark green. It began to nose into the road. Moments later it came to a halt in front of the ambulance. The driver's door opened and a tall figure alighted. She stared at him. The pale eyes. The thin mouth. The carefully pressed uniform.

Huber.

He barely spared her a glance. Instead, he was looking at the ambulance. She had taken care to lock the doors at the back.

'You have a key, Madame Lafosse?'

She nodded, said nothing. She felt physically sick. All her careful plans. All her fantasies about Lisbon. About Nathan. Now this.

At a word from Huber, the officer got into the cab. The key to the rear door was with the ignition key. The officer extracted the keys and got out of the cab. Huber took Hélène by the arm and she accompanied him to the back of the vehicle.

'What may we expect to find, Madame Lafosse? Would you care to tell us? More friends perhaps?'

Hélène didn't react. She could think of nothing to say. She wished Nathan was here. He'd know what to do, how to charm these people, how to recognise the traps they were setting and turn disaster on its head. Instead, she was rooted to the spot. They know, she told herself. These people are God. They know everything. About everyone. And by the time you recognise that simple truth it's far, far too late.

Inside the ambulance, Billy could smell the fear. It was a distinctive smell, not loose bowels as you might expect, but something even earthier, a mix of sweat and despair. Maria's knuckles were white. She was clutching her husband's arm and tears were pouring down her face. Her husband's eyes were shut, his head tipped back against the thin metal side of the van, the image of resignation. Even Agnès appeared to accept that her war was over. Only Malin seemed still engaged, his eyes flicking left and right.

Earlier, before they'd left, he'd had a brief exchange with Hélène. He'd wanted to bring Nathan's shotgun, claiming that it might be good for the odd rabbit, but she'd said no. Now he was softly cursing the lack of a weapon. Anything. Anything to avoid arrest.

The murmured conversation in the road had come to an end. Billy heard the scrape of a key in the lock. Then, abruptly, both doors swung open and he found himself staring at the barrel of a rifle. Another soldier stepped into view, his rifle readied. Then came a third face, his face pale beneath the peaked cap.

'*Papiers?*' The officer had a hand extended.

No one had any papers. The officer ordered them out onto the road, and then looked to Hélène for introductions.

Hélène shook her head.

'I've never seen them before,' she said. 'I picked them up back there,' she gestured vaguely behind her.

'More labour, perhaps? For your friends in Angoulême?'

'Of course. They might even get paid.'

'Nice story, *madame*,' the officer's smile was icy. 'Fine effort.'

A word to a third man, also an officer, and the little party in the middle of the road was pushed roughly towards the field entrance where the Mercedes had been parked. Billy was at the back. From time to time he could feel the barrel of the gun between his shoulder blades. His mouth was dry. He felt the first prickles of sweat on his face. Behind him, he could hear one of the Germans talking to Hélène.

The gap in the hedge led to a meadow. The grass was knee-high, lush after the recent rain. An Army truck was parked beside the hedge, more soldiers smoking in the back, and in the next field Billy caught sight of a herd of cows. Somerset, he suddenly thought. An afternoon's ramble with Mum.

The sun was hot now. Butterflies darted along the hedge line and there was a murmur of bees. The little group had come to a halt. The officer shouted at the soldiers in the back of the lorry. Two of them jumped out. One collected what looked like a wooden stake and slung it on his shoulder. The other had a big lump hammer and a spade.

The officer led them deeper into the field and then marked a spot with the heel of his boot. The soldier with the spade began to dig while the other one unshouldered the stake and watched. From down the lane came the cough of an engine and the grinding of gears. Seconds later, the ambulance bumped into the field and came to a halt. The soldiers gaped at it. Then one of them began to laugh.

The older of the two officers silenced the soldier with a look. Then he beckoned Billy towards him. Hélène was to serve as translator.

'I need to ask you some questions,' he said. 'Before we start.'

'Me?'

'You, Herr Angell.'

Billy stared at him. The realisation that this man knew his name also sparked an exchange of looks between Agnès and Malin. She'd been right all along. A spy. They should have shot him last night while they still had the chance.

'This brother of yours, Herr Angell. What's his name again?'

'Douglas.'

'And he really exists?'

'Yes.'

'You'd be prepared to swear that? At the price of someone else's life?'

Billy said he didn't understand the question. Hélène translated. The officer shrugged, then nodded at the nearest soldier. The soldier took Pablo by the arm and forced him to his knees. Pablo was looking at his wife. Then he crossed himself, his lips moving wordlessly as he stared at the boots of the officer.

The officer unholstered a pistol and circled Pablo.

The same question. The same translation. Do you have a brother, Herr Angell?

'Yes.'

The single shot raised a flock of pigeons from the nearby trees. Pablo slumped to the ground. Blood gushed from his mouth and began to puddle in the moistness of the grass.

Maria had fainted. At a word from the officer, a soldier ran to the back of the ambulance, returning with one of the jars of water. He tipped the water over the woman's face. She shook herself like a dog and began to whimper, pawing at her husband's corpse.

'Another question, Herr Angell. Your brother did what in the war?'

'He was in the Navy.'

'And then what?'

'He became a diver.'

Maria was on her knees now, still staring at her dead husband. Another prayer. This time the officer shot down through the crown of her head. She rocked sideways at the force of the blast, collapsing beside Pablo, her knees drawn up to her chest. Billy could smell the sourness of the cordite. It caught in the back of his throat, a horrible taste. He was aware of the soldiers watching him, of the officer's eyes on his face. He couldn't stop looking at the two bodies in the grass. I did that, he told himself. Me.

The wooden stake was ready. One of the soldiers went to Agnès and tried to escort her across. He had a loop of rope in his other hand. She shook her head, refused to move. When he went to push her, she spat in his face. Two more soldiers leapt from the back of the lorry and helped drag her across. She was screaming at them now, lashing out. A wild kick caught one of them on the side of his knee. He broke off to rub it then drove his fist into her face. She screamed again, pain salted with fear. Blood was pouring from her nose. The officer yelled for more men. It took five of them to lash her wrists and secure them to the stake.

Hélène was watching her every move. Her face was pale. Then she glanced at Billy and shook her head.

'*Untermensch*,' she said.

Agnès made another attempt to break free but the fight had gone out of her. Alone at the stake, her whole body seemed to have slumped. The soldiers had formed a firing line ten paces away. The officer motioned Billy and Hélène towards them.

'Herr Angell. Your brother again. He's in the Navy. He's a diver. He swims onto a beach. Tell me why.'

'To take samples.'

'And why would he do that? The truth please. Only the truth will save this young woman's life.'

Billy stared at her. She returned his gaze, unblinking. Blood was still dripping from her chin but her head was up, her eyes blazing, her legs braced.

'*Espion*,' she hissed.

The officer was smiling.

'Is she right, Herr Angell? Is she right that you're a spy?'

Billy closed his eyes. He didn't want to look anymore. This was more terrible than anything he'd ever seen in his life. More terrible than Hamburg.

More terrible than the Rear Gunner. More terrible than trying to nurse Les Hammond back through the freezing night. Because he was suddenly God. Because he'd suddenly acquired the power of life and death.

'Herr Angell? Your answer please. Are you what this young woman says you are? Are you a spy? And, if so, what does that tell us about this brother of yours?'

Billy swallowed hard. He was on the edge of an enormous pit. Below him was a cauldron of fire. One misstep, one false move, and it would all be over.

'No,' he said. 'I'm not a spy.'

'Are you sure?'

'Yes.'

The bark of the rifles rippled out across the fields. Agnès hung on the post for an instant or two before the weight of her body, riddled with bullets, dragged her slowly earthwards.

Billy turned away, sickened. Me next, he thought. And not before time.

CHAPTER 31

An hour later, Hélène and Billy were in the back of the Mercedes, heading north again. Huber occupied the passenger seat in the front beside the driver. Malin had been spared a bullet. Arrested for being a Jew without either papers or proper registration, he would be taken separately to the holding camp at Pithiviers. From there, Huber promised, he could expect a railway journey east with lots of company and plenty of time to think. The soldiers, meanwhile, had retrieved the dead bodies and carried them back to the ambulance. Once they were all inside, they emptied half a jerrycan of petrol over the interior and tossed in a grenade. As the van erupted, Malin watched his precious clock being consumed by the flames. He didn't appear to hear Hélène's shouted farewell.

There was no conversation in the car. Twice Hélène asked where they were going; both times Huber ignored her. The destination turned out to be Tours. In the middle of the old town, close to the cathedral, the Mercedes turned in at an impressive pair of wrought-iron gates. Billy was in limbo, a place where neither space nor time mattered. The Mercedes? The passing landscape? The occasional touch of Hélène's hand on his arm? The unspeakable image of Agnès' slow death slide? None of this made sense any longer. This was the darkness of deepest space. If he felt anything at all, he felt dead.

Two sentries saluted their arrival. Huber emerged from the car first, gesturing to his passengers in the back. Moments later, Hélène and Billy were escorted into the building. Steps led down into a basement. There was a sudden chill in the air and it felt damp. Doors opened left and right onto miles of shelving. The shelves were full of files, each one carefully labelled.

At the end of the corridor was a bigger room. It was empty. No files. A thin beam of sunshine through a window high in the opposite wall brought a sparkle of light from the tiled floor. Billy realised that the floor was wet. The walls were tiled, too. In white.

Hélène was staring at an iron bedstead in the very centre of the room. The legs appeared to be anchored to the floor. In the far corner a length of hosepipe was neatly coiled beside a tap and a pile of carefully folded towels. There was a heavy smell of bleach.

He exchanged looks with Hélène and nodded at the bedstead. The metal door had clanged shut behind them. Hélène put her finger to her lips and gestured upwards.

'*Mikro*,' she mouthed.

Billy thought he understood. He wanted to talk. He wanted comfort. He wanted the touch of another human being. He wanted some small hint that he might have imagined this nightmare, that the action might come to an end, and the house lights might go up, and that the audience would be on their feet the moment the curtains parted again.

Nothing. Just the slow drip of water from the tap.

After a while the door opened to admit an orderly in a white coat and a pair of rubber boots. He didn't look French. He might have been German, or even Polish. He was late middle-aged. He had a big mournful face and a luxuriant moustache that nearly hid a hare lip. Billy watched him uncoiling the hose pipe until it reached the bedstead. He might have been working in a hospital: careful, meticulous, painstaking.

His work done, the man fetched three chairs from a neighbouring room. He arranged them in a shallow semicircle three paces from the bedstead. Then he turned to Hélène and gestured to the pair of them: who's first?

Hélène shrugged. The orderly shot her a look. Then he was gone.

Hélène and Billy sat in silence. After a while, Hélène took Billy's hand and gave it a squeeze. He looked at her but she didn't say anything. The hose was hanging over the bedstead and there came the slow drip of water from the end. Billy stared at it. Drip. Drip. Drip. It was mesmeric. It penetrated his skull. It seemed to sum up everything that had happened. It was implacable. There was no turning it off. It would continue until the end of time. Drip. Drip. Drip.

The door opened again. It was Huber, the officer. With him was the orderly in the white coat.

Huber told Billy to take his clothes off. Hélène interrupted. She said that wouldn't be necessary.

'Why is that, *madame*?'

'Because I know the truth about this man's brother. And whatever you do to him you can never be sure whether he's lying or not.'

'So what do you suggest, *madame*? That I listen to you? What if you're lying, too?'

'I have no reason to lie.'

'Do you want me to test you on that?' He glanced across at the orderly. 'Our friend here can perform some interesting tricks. Put the pipe in one end, collect the truth from the other. Eh, Günther?'

Günther permitted himself a gloomy nod of agreement. It seemed to suggest that with time and patience anything would be possible.

'Then start with me, Herr Huber.' Hélène was already unbuttoning her dress.

Huber hadn't expected this development and it showed in his face. Billy was horrified.

'Me,' he said. 'Start with me.'

He was wearing a baggy shirt with only one button. He slipped it off and let it fall to the floor. Günther, confused, was awaiting a decision. Huber hesitated. Then, from nowhere, another figure appeared in the room. He was medium height, neatly dressed. He looked like a successful businessman or a solicitor with a reputation to protect. Billy, naked from the waist up, stared at him. Polished shoes. Carefully manicured hands. Oiled side parting. What possible connection did a man like this have with what was about to take place?

'*Oberführer* Schellenberg,' Huber offered a reluctant salute. This man was the last person he wanted to see.

Schellenberg was looking at the bedstead. He didn't bother to hide his distaste. He asked Billy to pick up his shirt. His English was good.

'Put it on,' he turned to Hélène. 'Your dress is undone, *madame*. We have to get you back to Paris.'

Huber raised a voice in protest. Billy hadn't any idea what he was saying but Schellenberg took absolutely no notice. He had the manners of a born hotelier. He shepherded Hélène and Billy out of the door and back along the corridor to the stairs. His driver, thankfully, had mustered the good sense to stock the car with a snack or two. He was a gentleman in most respects, murmured Schellenberg, but he sincerely hoped nothing untoward would test the man's martial skills.

He paused at the top of the stairs. He was looking at Billy.

'May I take it that we understand each other?'

Yet another Mercedes. Billy sat in the back, his hand in Hélène's as they drove out of Tours. He could feel the tension in her body. She sat stiffly upright, her gaze fixed, her eyes unseeing, and from time to time a deep shudder seemed to ripple through her body. There was a glass partition between the front and the rear of the car. Billy could see Schellenberg and his driver chatting together, the way good friends might, and after a while Schellenberg lit a small cigar. Hélène blinked. She reached forward and tapped on the glass. There was a panel in the partition. Schellenberg reached back and slid it open.

'*Madame*?'

Hélène asked him to leave the panel open.

'You like the smell of cigar smoke?'

She nodded.

'May I offer you one?'

'No, thank you.'

'Mr Angell?'

Billy shook his head. He'd never smoked in his life and didn't intend to start now. The smoke curled back into the passenger compartment. Hélène slumped a little deeper into the seat, her head resting on the leather squab. Her eyes were closed and she seemed more relaxed. Within minutes, she was asleep.

She jerked awake an hour later. They were trapped in a queue of traffic behind a tractor in a small village three kilometres short of Chartres. Despite a chorus of horns, the farmer was refusing to pull over. Billy had a sudden image of the bedstead and the hose pipe and the gloomy attendant in the white coat. He was still looking at the man on the tractor. Brave, he thought. Or maybe just foolish.

Schellenberg was at the partition again. He wanted to direct Billy's attention to a package of sandwiches stored in the back.

'Help yourself,' he said.

Billy declined. Hélène was staring out of the window. She appeared to recognise this place.

'A favour, Herr Schellenberg?'

'*Madame?*'

'Can we make time to visit the cathedral?'

Schellenberg asked her whether she meant Chartres. She nodded.

'You wish to go inside?'

'Yes, please.'

'You think it will be open?'

'It always used to be. Unless you've put a lock on it.'

Schellenberg smiled, and said nothing. Then he softly closed the partition.

They were in Chartres within minutes. The bulk of the cathedral with its twin spires rode above the city, dominating everything below. They parked in the old town and the driver unlocked the rear doors. When Hélène appeared to have difficulty getting out, the driver extended a gloved hand. Billy slipped into step beside her as they crossed the empty cobbles and made for the main doors. There was nobody about.

'You've been here before?'

'I was at school here. In a convent. We sang in the cathedral every Sunday, morning and evening.'

She'd stopped. She was looking up at the stone-work and the tracery, soft whites and greys in the late afternoon sun. Billy asked whether she'd enjoyed the convent.

'I hated it.'

'And the cathedral?'

'That, too.' She spared him a glance. 'How wrong can you be?'

The doors of the cathedral were indeed locked. Schellenberg peered at a notice in German pinned to the woodwork. Then he checked his watch and muttered something to the driver. The driver disappeared.

'God in his pomp, *madame*,' he gestured upwards. 'I'm afraid it might be necessary to wait.'

The driver was back within minutes. The iron key was huge. Schellenberg weighed it in his hand for a moment and then slipped it into the lock. The big oak door swung open without difficulty.

It took several seconds for Billy's eyes to adjust to the gloom. The space seemed – was – cavernous, huge. Stone pillars soared towards the vaulted ceiling and when he looked up he caught a flicker of movement.

'Bats.' It was Schellenberg. Like Billy, he was gazing up towards the roof.

Billy felt the touch of Hélène's hand on his arm. 'See?' she said.

Billy followed her raised finger. The last of the

afternoon sun was bursting through the central stained glass window above the west door. Christ was enthroned at the top, where the sides of the window met in an arch, and the countless panels below splashed a multitude of colours on the cathedral floor. Billy took a step backwards. The pattern on the stone flagged floor fascinated him, concentric circles whorling inwards, tighter and tighter.

'It's a labyrinth, Billy. We're lucky they've taken the chairs away.'

'Labyrinth?'

'Pilgrims came here from all over Europe. The last thing you walked was this. Round and round until you got to the middle.'

'And what did you find?' He was peering at the labyrinth.

'There used to be a plaque. They melted it down for cannons during the Revolution.'

'And underneath?'

'Nothing. They dug and they found nothing.'

'A waste, then? For the pilgrims?'

'Not at all. It's the journey that matters, Billy. Not the destination.'

'They taught you that at school?'

'They did. And you know something? They were wrong.'

She took a final look at the stained glass window. Chairs were stacked in the side aisles, adding to the sense of space. The cathedral stretched before them, the distant altar bathed in a soft yellow light.

'*Viens* . . .'

Billy followed her down the aisle, aware of footsteps behind him. Then she stopped and knelt.

'We must talk to God,' she said. 'About what we've done.'

Her lips began to move in a silent prayer. Billy was on his knees beside her, his head bowed, his hands clasped together. He hadn't the words to describe how he felt, to atone for the part he'd played in the meadow, to make any kind of peace with what had happened. And so he recited their names, the way you might list a collection of friends you'd casually mislaid, except that he knew they'd gone forever, in the most terrible circumstances, and that he'd betrayed them.

'Agnès . . .' he whispered, '. . . Maria . . . Pablo . . .'

He repeated the names twice more, a conversation with himself, and then he lapsed into silence. It had been this way in the Friends Meeting House with Irene. Except then he'd been on better terms with God.

He looked up at the altar, still distant, still beyond reach, and then he stole a sideways glance at Hélène. Her head, like his, was erect. And tears were pouring down her cheeks.

They reached Paris in the early evening. Schellenberg directed the driver to the 16th *arrondissement*. Expecting delivery to another part of the German intelligence empire, Hélène awoke to find herself outside her own apartment building. It was Schellenberg who opened the rear door and helped her onto the pavement.

'You want me to collect something?' She was still confused.

'I'm inviting you to stay the night, to sleep in your own bed. The alternative might be less than agreeable. Herr Angell?' He indicated that Billy should join her. Then he extended his hand to Hélène. '*À demain, madame.*'

Until tomorrow? Her confusion deepened. Billy wanted to know where they were, what might happen next. The Mercedes was already pulling away.

Hélène watched it slow for the intersection at the end of the road. Then it was gone. She looked round. Were they under surveillance? Were there German eyes behind the closed shutters across the street? She had no idea.

'This is where I live,' she told Billy. 'Or used to.'

There was a new concierge. He was young, watchful, plump. Plump was unusual these days in Paris.

'Madame Lessault?' Hélène enquired.

'Madame Lessault doesn't work here anymore. An illness in the family, I understand. And you would be . . .?'

'Madame Lafosse. Apartment four.'

'Ah . . .' he recognised the name but he didn't get up. 'You have a key?'

'Of course.'

'Then welcome . . .' he nodded towards the lift.

Hélène didn't move. She wanted to know about an *Abwehr* officer named Bjorn Klimt.

'I know *Oberst* Klimt, *madame*. Also *Sturmbannführer* Huber.'

'He's still living here? In my apartment? *Oberst* Klimt?'

'Yes.'

'He's up there now?'

'Regrettably not. He left two days ago. He had luggage.'

'And *Oberst* Huber?'

'He was here yesterday.'

'In my flat?'

'Yes.'

Hélène nodded. Klimt leaving, she thought. With luggage.

'Do you happen to know where *Oberst* Klimt has gone?'

The concierge shook his head. His phone rang, shrill in the early evening calm. She had a thousand other questions she would have liked to ask anyone but this toad of a man. About how Klimt had looked. About how he was weathering the storm that had beset them all. About whether or not he'd been meeting with Huber.

Hélène took the stairs. Billy followed her. On the top floor she paused at the first door. For a moment she thought the locks must have been changed but then, with an effort, she managed to get the door open. The faintest scent of cigars brought her to a halt. Maybe he's come back, she thought. Maybe he's ghosted past the concierge desk while the fat little bastard was looking the other way.

'Bjorn . . .' she called. *'C'est moi.'* Nothing.

She stepped into the apartment. At once she knew that something was wrong but it was a moment before she realised exactly what. She was staring at the bare walls in the hall. Her pictures had gone. Every single one. She went through to the big sitting room. The pictures here had belonged to Nathan. The Cubist take on a rock off the Costa Brava, the work of a pupil of Picasso's. The delicate nude in charcoal she'd loved so much. The water-colour of Chartres Cathedral, glimpsed from the wheat fields miles to the north. Nathan had left them to keep her company on her rare visits to Paris. They were warmth. They were candles in the darkness. And now they too were gone.

She sank onto the chaise longue, her head in her hands. Huber, she thought. Emptying her life of everything that mattered. First Klimt. Then the tiny tribe of lost souls she'd gathered under her roof at the chateau. And now her precious paint-ings, stolen by the man who'd made it his business to take everything else away from her.

Billy had settled beside her. He took her in his arms, told her everything would be all right, assured her that she'd done her best.

'You really think that? Leaving? Going south?' She wanted to believe it.

'They'd have come for you anyway,' Billy said. 'You're right. They know everything.'

She nodded. The ambulance had had no wing mirror, an oversight on the part of Georges' son. They must have been following me, she thought. They must have been tracking me the whole way, making their plans, laying their traps, readying themselves for the moment when three men in black uniforms stepped into the road and added yet another chapter to the history of Occupation atrocities. How could you fight people like this? For whom a human life had no significance?

She remembered the soldiers in the back of the truck laughing when the ambulance appeared in the field. They knew, she told herself. They were part of all that. They knew exactly what was going to happen next. Load a gun. Pull a trigger. And then find someone else to kill.

Billy wanted to know about Klimt. Had she been expecting to find him here?

Hélène shrugged, then held up her forefinger and circled the walls and the ceiling before tapping her ear. Huber obviously had access to the apartment. There'd be microphones everywhere. It took a while for Billy to understand. No more conversations about Klimt.

Klimt. She struggled to her feet. They had a secret place they'd created in case they ever had to leave messages for each other. It had been Klimt's idea. Parquet flooring had been laid throughout the apartment. In the corner of the

378

bedroom, he'd loosened one of the wooden blocks and scraped out a small space beneath it. She found two knives in the kitchen and knelt there now, using the knives to prise the block free. Billy watched her lift the wooden block and extract a folded sheet of paper. She replaced the block, returned the knives to the kitchen and went back to the sitting room.

The note was brief. She'd always had problems with Klimt's beautiful handwriting but at least he'd written in French, which helped. Line by line, she managed to decipher it. At the end of the message he said she'd always be in his heart. He regretted nothing. The space they'd made for each other was the one thing he'd take to his grave. The rest, he wrote, was *absurde*. Without meaning.

Billy was looking over her shoulder. He wanted to know what Klimt had said, where the note might take them. She got up again and fetched a pencil from the escritoire. Another of Nathan's precious heirlooms, she thought. Mercifully spared the attentions of Huber.

She rejoined Billy on the chaise. On the back of the note she wrote four words. *Klimt thinks he's finished.* Billy stared at it. Then held his hands wide. *Why?*

'I don't know,' Hélène shook her head. Then she turned the note over, her whole body beginning to rock, and she reread the final lines, Klimt's meticulous hand blurring in front of her eyes.

Billy tried to comfort her again but it was

hopeless. She began to howl with grief, with a bottomless despair that seemed to extend to everything she'd ever cherished. After a while, empty, she sat in the silence as the last of the daylight died over the rooftops.

'It's over,' she said, not caring who might be listening.

PART IV

CHAPTER 32

Next morning, *Oberst* Bjorn Klimt found himself delivered to an address in the 12th. He'd spent the last two days and nights at his stuffy office in the Hôtel Meurice waiting, he suspected, for just this summons. The note from the office of the *Sicherheitsdienst* had been typically lacking in detail. Dress in a decent suit and bring a change of clothes. Nothing more.

The SD were the coming force. Everyone in what remained of the *Abwehr* knew that. Brush fires on the margins of the sprawling Nazi intelligence empire had become a conflagration. The *Abwehr*, including Klimt himself, had long depended on their boss, the maverick Admiral Canaris, for a degree of protection. But Canaris, who was a wily old fox in every other respect, had never hidden his distaste for the new breed of Nazi zealots and when a couple of remarks about Hitler himself reached the wrong ears his days were numbered. Could a man who viewed the Führer as a carpet biter really be trusted to protect the Reich's inner secrets?

The answer, as Klimt knew only too well, was

to anoint someone else to stand guard at Hitler's door. Heinrich Himmler, head of the SS, had been doing just that since the days when the Brownshirts were running riot. Years of obsessional manoeuvring had given him more power in the corridors of the Reich than anyone else except his beloved Führer. One more little push and Canaris would be history.

The address in the 12th lay behind high stucco walls near the Château de Vincennes. Wearing his best suit, Klimt was escorted to the front door. A pleasant young man in the uniform of an SS *Sturmbannführer* was waiting for him in the marbled hall. He introduced himself as Busch. He led the way up a flight of stairs to the second floor. The door at the end of corridor was already open. Busch knocked twice and stepped aside to admit Klimt. The figure at the window turned to greet him. They'd met twice before, once at an SD gathering in Munich, and once to celebrate Canaris' birthday at a restaurant in Berlin. To Klimt's certain knowledge this man at the window and the boss of the *Abwehr* had been good friends. They'd even met on crisp Berlin mornings to ride together in the Grosse Tiergarten.

'*Oberführer* Schellenberg,' Klimt saluted.

Schellenberg waved him into an armchair. There was no desk in the room, no filing cabinets, not a single sheet of paper to indicate Schellenberg's standing in the SD. Since Reinhard Heydrich's assassination in Prague, this man had been leading

Himmler's *Sicherheitsdienst* from one triumph to another, pecking at the carcase of the carefully discredited *Abwehr*. Not someone you'd ever underestimate, thought Klimt. Assume the winning smile and the gentle handshake were genuine and you were already in serious trouble.

Schellenberg wanted to apologise for a man called Huber with whom he understood Klimt was familiar.

'I know him, yes.'

'The man's a clown. He doesn't know the meaning of excess. I understand he's helped himself to some paintings belonging to a friend of yours.'

This was news to Klimt. What paintings?

Schellenberg tallied them from memory. A study in charcoal. A rather nice watercolour. And a Cubist piece not altogether to his taste.

'They will be returned intact,' he said. 'You have my assurance. My apologies to Madame Lafosse.'

Klimt accepted the gesture with a nod. Was that why he was here? To put Hélène's life back together?

'And what about the *Mona Lisa*?' he enquired.

'*La Gioconda* is another fantasy of Huber's. He's an asset in a number of ways but he knows nothing worthwhile about fine art and even less about believing rumours that might have . . .' he permitted himself a tiny frown, '. . . repercussions.'

'Meaning?'

'Meaning he heard that you were in attendance at a nightclub recently with Madame Lafosse. That you danced together. And that you sang to her in

English. That never happened, *Oberst* Klimt. As I've had the pleasure of explaining to *Sturmbannführer* Huber.'

'He took offence?'

'He decided that you were unreliable. I have his correspondence on the matter. His reports run to far more pages than they should. Brevity and Huber were never best friends.'

He sighed and turned to gaze out of the window again. Klimt was trying to anticipate where this conversation might be headed next. Never take anything at face value, he told himself. Especially someone as subtle and gifted as this man.

'We have a problem, *Oberst* Klimt. May I be candid?'

'Of course.'

'We're in danger of losing this war. The Americans and the British will be knocking at the gates of Rome within months. Mussolini will fold. The Russians are feasting on our armies in the east. Winning a war on one front is enough for any nation. Winning a war on two is, to be frank, impossible.'

'So what should we expect?'

'A second front. Obviously. The Allies have the resources to cross the Channel and give us a bloody nose. Stalin can't understand why it hasn't happened already and in some respects neither can I. It's getting a little late in the year for adventures like that so I'm guessing the spring of next year, as soon as the weather settles down.' He paused. His fingers were drumming lightly on the arm of the chair. 'Which brings us to Mr Angell, *Oberst* Klimt. Your thoughts?'

Klimt leaned forward. He'd filed his report in the aftermath of letting Dieter Merz have a sniff at the English flier. The report had been addressed to *Abwehr* headquarters in Berlin but somehow it had ended up on this man's desk. Yet another sign that the days of Admiral Canaris were numbered.

'I think Mr Angell is genuine,' he said carefully. 'I've taken the steps I described to check his story and nothing he said raised any problems.'

'Story?'

'His service background. The fact that he's been flying with their Bomber Command.'

'So why did he jump from the aircraft? When it was perfectly serviceable?'

'Because he'd had enough of the war.' Klimt gestured at the space between them. 'Maybe he thinks the way you think, sir. Maybe he thinks the war's already half over and that there's no point spilling more blood.'

'And what about his brother? You believe that, too?'

'Yes.'

'You really think they plan to give us a bloody nose at Dunkirk?'

'I think it's more than possible. The English can be tougher than you think. The evacuation hurt them. Where better to put the record straight?'

Schellenberg accepted the point with the faintest

smile. Klimt was in the dark now. There was something else coming. He knew it.

'Let's assume you're right, *Oberst* Klimt.'

'Not me, sir. Billy Angell.'

'Of course. Let's assume the boy really does have a brother. Let's agree the English really do intend to land at Dunkirk. I can see every good reason why that might happen and so do my *Wehrmacht* friends. You might be interested in Erwin's view in this respect.'

'Erwin?'

'Rommel. The Führer intends to place him in overall command in northern France. He will be our man on the ramparts. It's not a job you'd recommend to anyone. Construction has been slow. The coastline is long. He'll need thousands of mines. Millions of tank traps. And all this at a moment when we have other pressing demands to meet. More fighter aircraft. More U-boats. More special projects. Anything to pluck victory – or maybe survival – from the jaws of defeat. No nation, least of all ours, has a limitless supply of steel, of labour, of oil. And so we need to concentrate our forces. Make a decision on the invasion site. Take a gamble or two.'

'And Rommel's views?'

'He thinks two landings. One in Normandy. Basically a feint, a diversion. Then the main thrust.'

'Where?'

'Calais. Because it's closest. But you know something else? His worst nightmare?'

'Dunkirk.'

'Exactly. The terrain is better. The beaches are flat. It has port facilities. It's closer to Antwerp, too. Port facilities will be the key to everything. Land a couple of armies and you have to keep them fed. We're talking millions of tons of fuel, of ammunition, of replacement equipment. War is voracious. It eats everything in sight. And so you need somewhere to land all that stuff. Otherwise the beast will starve to death.'

Klimt began to relax. Thus far, he and Himmler's favourite son appeared to agree on everything. Maybe there was room for him in the SD. Maybe his days at the Château de Neaune weren't quite over. Maybe.

'So what do you want me to do, sir?'

'I want you to do a job for me, an important job. We could call it an errand. We could agree it's a sort of favour. Whatever the word, it has to remain absolutely confidential. You've brought a change of clothes? As we requested?'

'My suitcase is downstairs.'

'Excellent.' He glanced at his watch. 'This afternoon we will fly you to Madrid. Tomorrow morning, you're booked through to Lisbon. You'll be staying at the embassy overnight. You'll love the place. The views are sensational and the food's even better. They'll have another ticket for you. On Thursday morning you'll fly to England.'

'England?' For a split second Klimt wondered whether this was some kind of code word. It wasn't.

'I know you speak the language, *Oberst* Klimt. More importantly, the people you're going to be meeting are aware of your allegiance to Admiral Canaris. These are intelligence people, people like ourselves. The fact that you're *Abwehr* makes you their kind of Nazi.'

'And what do I do? What do I say?'

'You enquire about the prospects for peace. Or, more precisely, you enquire about the possibility of opening unofficial negotiations.'

'With whom?'

'With whomever we decide to delegate. Don't worry, *Oberst* Klimt. We're not asking you to undertake the negotiations yourself. We're just asking you to test the water. You'll be talking to fellow professionals, fellow spies if you like. You'll have a great deal in common. They'll take a long look at you and I daresay you'll do the same.'

'And afterwards?'

'Afterwards you come back. Same route. Possibly the same flying boat. The arrangements are in place. You'll have a *laissez-passer*. But only on the strict condition that no word ever leaks out. Do we understand each other?'

'Perfectly.' Klimt wondered whether this was a hint from Schellenberg to bring the conversation to an end. He decided to ignore it. 'One question, sir.'

'By all means.'

'When would these negotiations take place?'

'During the winter, *Oberst* Klimt.' The smile again.

'That way, with a successful outcome, the issue of the invasion will no longer matter.'

Both men got to their feet. There was an exchange of handshakes. Young Erwin Busch downstairs, said Schellenberg, would be accompanying Klimt to Lisbon. He had the authority of the SD to resolve any issues en route.

'One last thing I ought to mention, *Oberst* Klimt.' They were at the door now. 'There is, of course, a possibility that you might not come back at all.'

'You think they'll arrest me?'

'I think you might desert. It might be a temptation. I say no more than that.'

Klimt held his gaze. They had to talk this thing through.

'And if that did happen?'

'Then life would get extremely difficult.'

'For whom?'

'For Madame Lafosse, *Oberst* Klimt. *Bon voyage,*' he extended a hand. 'And good luck.'

CHAPTER 33

The soldiers arrived several minutes before midday. Billy was still in the big double bed. He and Hélène had slept together for mutual comfort more than anything else, and now she'd gone to a neighbouring apartment to ask for milk and maybe something to eat. Billy lay back, hearing the stamp of boots on the staircase in the depths of the building below. The pillow and the sheets still smelled faintly of cigar smoke.

Hélène was the first into the apartment. She had two eggs in a bowl and a hunk of bread. Behind her came two soldiers. A taller figure lurked in the background: long leather coat, peaked cap, SS collar flashes. He followed the soldiers into the apartment and gave the bedroom door a gentle push. Billy, naked, was trying to clamber into his pants. He looked up. Huber.

A car was waiting at the kerbside below. From the window, Billy saw Hélène being escorted across the pavement. Once dressed, he was hustled down four flights of stairs and marched past the concierge's desk. The concierge, once again, was on the telephone. Huber tossed him the key to the apartment and followed the soldiers onto the street. Two women across the road scarcely spared this small moment of drama a glance. Hélène was already in the back of the car. When Billy joined her, she took his hand.

'Bad,' she murmured.

Huber was in the front of the car. When Hélène asked where they were going he ignored her. They drove at speed towards the middle of Paris, the tyres thrumming on the *pavé*, the driver swerving to avoid thickets of cyclists. The Gare de l'Est, like all the mainline stations, was heavily guarded. The driver made for a side street and came to a halt beside an entrance that led directly onto one of the platforms. Another officer in SS uniform was waiting. He opened the rear doors and spoke to Huber. Huber nodded and then turned to Hélène.

'Say your goodbyes, *madame*. Herr Angell is leaving us.'

'Where are you taking him?'

'Somewhere safe. Not pretty perhaps, but safe.'

Billy was staring up at him. He understood none of this. Then the other door opened and a gloved hand reached in and hauled him roughly out. Not a word of farewell. Not a kiss. Not a touch. Not even a glance. As he crossed the pavement he tried to look backwards but the car was already on the move, the paleness of Hélène's face no more than a memory.

★　　★　　★

Klimt's aircraft flew into the blinding sun. The pilot, who turned out to be a friend of Dieter Merz, had invited him to ride up front in the cockpit. The Ju-52 roared south, over the greenness of central France, the fields shadowed by a scatter of clouds. A third propeller at the end of the long silver nose of the aircraft played tricks with Klimt's eyes and after a while the steady beat of the engines lulled him into drowsiness.

Somewhere below them, he thought, lay Hélène's chateau. His eyes closed, he could picture the scurrying of pheasants beside the bridle path, hear the bark of a fox in the small hours of the night, feel her body beside him, watch the tiny rise and fall of her chest as she slept. One day, God willing, life might make another space like this for both of them. The thought made him smile.

The pilot woke him two hours later. He gestured at the blue shadows on the far horizon. The roar of the engines was deafening.

'The Pyrenees,' he mouthed.

On the train Billy shared a compartment with two soldiers and a trio of passengers. Two of them, both men, were asleep but the woman between them kept stealing glances at Billy. He was handcuffed to the smaller of the two soldiers and his attempts to start a conversation with the man had taken him nowhere. The soldier was young and he'd made it plain that he didn't speak

English. When Billy nodded at his watch and tried to ask how long this journey might take he simply shrugged.

'*Ich verstehe nicht*,' he grunted.

After a while, the woman unpacked a packet of sandwiches from the wicker basket that served as a handbag. There was cheese in the sandwiches and Billy thought he caught the tang of mustard. She was well dressed and ate with a fierce concentration, staring out of the window as one village after another slipped by. Scruffy-looking brick-built houses. A chicken pecking in the dirt. A pair of pyjamas blowing on a washing line. Billy was thinking about his father again. Given any kind of choice, he was beginning to prefer his dad's war to this one.

Finally the woman turned away from the view. There was one sandwich left. She leaned forward, offering it to Billy.

Billy was looking at his guard. The young soldier shrugged.

'*Essen Sie*,' he said. '*Während Sie noch können.*'

Billy was confused. The woman was smiling.

'Eat,' she said. 'While you still can.'

The aircraft carrying Klimt landed in Madrid in the late afternoon. A change of planes in Barcelona had robbed him of his seat in the cockpit and he found himself wedged beside a fat businessman from Düsseldorf who picked his nose throughout the flight. Mercifully, the moment the aircraft came to a halt in front of the terminal building he struggled to his feet and made for the exit.

Klimt watched him through the window as he stood on the tarmac waiting for his bag to be unloaded from the back, then his attention was caught by another figure hurrying towards the plane. It was Erwin Busch, Schellenberg's young assistant.

He climbed aboard and settled himself beside Klimt. A morning meeting at the German embassy in Madrid had meant an overnight flight down from Paris. As soon as they'd refuelled, they'd be off for the last hop across to Lisbon. The journey normally took three hours or so. Plenty of time to catch up on lost sleep.

Klimt nodded. He wanted to know more about this young man.

'We'll be together tonight?' he enquired.

'Of course,' he smiled. 'My boss insists I look after you.'

It was dark by the time the train arrived. Billy peered out of the window, trying to make out the name of the station among the press of passengers waiting on the platform. The woman with the sandwiches had got off at Stuttgart, offering him a tiny nod of farewell as she gathered her possessions and left the compartment.

Stuttgart, as Billy knew only too well, was in south-western Germany. A city full of factories, he'd bombed it on a number of occasions and had a healthy respect for its flak defences. Now, as the train finally came to a halt, he caught sight of another name on his list of ops. München.

The station seemed enormous. Looking up, he could see the night sky through sizeable holes in the roof canopy. Bomb damage, he thought. I might have done that. The soldier was tugging him across the concourse. At the sight of the handcuffs, the crowd parted in front of them. Out of uniform Billy could have been anyone and he was glad to be spared the attentions of strangers.

Back in England, he'd once met a Flight Engineer who'd bailed out of a crippled Sterling bomber on a trip to Duisburg. He'd survived the jump, only to find himself surrounded by angry German farmers. They'd given him a beating before handing him over to the local police. Manacled, like Billy, he'd been shipped east to a *Stalag* deep in Poland. He'd later managed to escape but his memory of that journey across Germany had never left him. The farmers had been bad enough, he'd told Billy, but I can't abide being spat at.

Now, they were out of the station. An Army van was parked at the kerbside. The young soldier saluted the officer waiting beside it and unlocked the handcuffs. To the best of Billy's knowledge, all the POW camps lay much further to the east. So where were they going?

He tried to put the question to the officer. He was an older man with tired eyes and a skin tone Billy had last seen in the mortuary in Bristol.

'No one's told you?' His English was good.

'No.' Billy shook his head.

'Then let it be a surprise.' He bent to open the rear door. '*Kommen Sie.*'

Klimt and Busch ate on the waterfront in Lisbon. They'd walked down the hill from the embassy in the warmth of a velvet evening, and now a waiter Busch appeared to know well took them to a table in the depths of the restaurant.

'I always ask for privacy,' he told Klimt. 'Hard to find in this city.'

It was already late and the mid-evening diners had begun to drift away. Klimt didn't bother with the menu. When he asked for recommendations, Busch didn't have a moment's hesitation.

'*Arroz de marisco*,' he said. 'Rice with anything that swims. You want to taste the sea? These people make it happen.'

The waiter brought a carafe of white wine. Klimt had never tried Alvarinho before. It was ice-cold and decidedly flinty. Huber in a bottle, he thought.

Busch was talking about the chaotic *Abwehr* set-up in Madrid. He'd arrived at that morning's meeting with a thick file of reports from SD agents in the field, information he'd need when it came to cutting out the dead wood at the heart of the Canaris operation. The real challenge, he said, was patrolling the fine line between negligence and corruption, but either way he had a list of placemen who'd soon be answering questions in Berlin.

Lisbon, he said, was the Wild West, lawless, riddled with spies, full of rich pickings. If you didn't mind who you betrayed you could make yourself very rich without a great deal of effort. People he'd once respected had fallen for what he called 'the Lisbon handshake' and the knowledge that their days were numbered had caused some consternation.

'This city has grown fat on the war,' he gestured out towards the busy street. 'Our people like the sunshine, the women, the casinos, the nightlife. Money and influence buy you anything here. The place is a kasbah. The Arabs were here for longer than we ever think. They certainly left their mark.'

Klimt could see the attractions. He was thinking of Hélène. Late afternoons on the beach, an hour or two in bed, then a gentle stroll in the last of the sunshine before finding a restaurant like this. If the war ever came to an end, he'd try and make it happen.

Busch was pouring more wine. Klimt wanted to know why Schellenberg had chosen him for the mission to England.

'I'm *Abwehr*,' he pointed out. 'It makes no sense.'

'On the contrary. The Chief has a suppleness of mind. He hates to be trapped by convention. In my view that's important. Good people are hard to come by. And he thinks you're one of them.'

'The Chief?'

'*Oberführer* Schellenberg.'

'You've worked for him for long?'

'Fourteen months. Since Heydrich was murdered.'

Klimt nodded. The Butcher of Prague had been the founding father of the SD. His *Einsatzgruppen* had left a trail of blood across Eastern Europe and a team of Czech and Slovak irregulars had finally shot him in an ambush.

'Schellenberg must have come as a relief after Heydrich.'

'He was. Is. It's a pleasure to work for such a man. And an education, too.'

He started to describe the chaos that was the Nazi administrative machine, the warring empires, the rival fiefdoms, the constant struggle for survival as reputations were lost and won.

'Berlin is a jungle,' he said. 'A lot of these people are animals. They're not stupid. Far from it. Underestimating them is the quickest way to earn a bullet. But most of them, up here . . .' he tapped his head, '. . . live in the bunker. They're underground people. They're creatures of darkness. They never look outwards. Other countries are fair game for invasion but their interest stops once the shooting is over. The world beyond the Reich is a mystery.'

'And your Chief?'

'*Oberführer* Schellenberg is different. He's aware. He has a taste for other countries, other cultures. He makes it his business to understand the enemy, not merely crush him. Which is why he's so keen to open the channels to London.'

Klimt was toying with his wine glass. There was

another question here, and he was determined to raise it.

'Schellenberg told me he thinks the war is lost. Was he serious?'

'It's not as simple as that. We know how war works. It's not just a question of will, as some of our people believe, it's also a question of figures, of computations, of resources, of drawing up a balance sheet and doing the sums, and taking a hard look at the figure on the bottom line. The Chief has done that. And the implications are troubling.'

'He thinks the war has turned against us?'

'He thinks there may be a peace to be had.'

'Roosevelt is insisting on unconditional surrender. You know that.'

'Roosevelt is a politician. These people bend with the wind. Just now they have the wind at their backs. That may not last forever.'

'Meaning what?'

'We have the best scientists in the world, the best engineers in the world.'

'You mean secret weapons?'

'Of course,' Busch nodded. 'You'll know about the flying bombs. And soon, God willing, so will the English. But there are other toys on the shelf. And if we enter negotiations, we may have a stronger hand than you might think. This is conjecture, of course. But when did people like us ever speak a different language? Imagine the world you want to live in. And then make it happen.'

Imagine the world you want to live in. And then make it happen.

Perfect. The waiter had emerged from the kitchen with a bowl piled high with steaming rice. He deposited it carefully between them. Prawns and flakes of white fish swam in a tomato broth. Klimt could smell garlic and paprika and lemon. Two plates arrived, and an enormous spoon.

The waiter asked Busch whether he needed to be served. Busch shook his head. They would help themselves. He smiled across the table and nodded at the food.

'You're ready?'

Klimt nodded, and reached for his glass.

'A toast,' he said. 'To the world we want to live in.'

They'd been on the road for nearly an hour when Billy felt the van begin to slow. Traffic had been light when they left the city and now nothing moved in the blackness of the night. There was thunder in the air and from time to time jagged forks of lightning speared the distant horizon.

The driver had only the dim glow of the masked headlights to grope his way forward but he'd anticipated the turn that would take them off the road. They swung left. Billy sensed trees right and left. Then came a fence of some kind and up ahead, very faintly, a light in the darkness. The lightning was closer now and Billy could feel the thunder in his bones.

The van was slowing again. They were among

buildings, darker shapes against the night. Finally they came to a halt. The light was moving. A guard held a lantern to the driver's window. At a shouted command, the doors were opened by unseen hands and Billy was dragged from the van.

He stood in the darkness, gazing around. He could faintly make out a pair of iron gates. They seemed close enough to touch. One of the gates creaked open and he stepped towards it. Then his attention was drawn to lettering above the gate. He stared at it for a moment, trying to make sense of the shapes. Then came another flash, an explosion of light, and he had time to register three words.

Arbeit Macht Frei.

He turned to the officer who'd sat beside him throughout the journey. He wanted to know what the words meant. He wanted to know where they were.

'Dachau, my friend. I wish you luck.'

CHAPTER 34

K limt landed on the grey waters of Poole
Harbour shortly after one o'clock the
following afternoon. The flying boat had
been delayed by head winds over the Bay of Biscay
and the American crew had distributed sick bags
in anticipation of rougher weather ahead. Klimt
gazed out of the window as the flying boat taxied
towards the landing pontoon. He'd spent most
of the journey in conversation with an English
missionary returning from West Africa, and had
been impressed by her tolerance. Her ministry, she
told him, had taught her a great deal about what
people the world over had in common. And one
of the things they held most dear was a yearning
for peace.

Just so, thought Klimt. For reasons he didn't
understand, he was the first passenger invited to
step onto the pontoon. There was a chill in the
air and the strength of the wind filled the harbour
with whitecaps. One of the American crew escorted
him to the landward end of the pontoon where a
car was waiting. Beside it stood a tall, raw-boned
figure trying to control his flailing hair. The *Abwehr*

had a pre-war subscription to a number of English magazines, all part of a bid to understand the enemy, and Klimt paused before accepting the outstretched hand. This man might have stepped out of the pages of *Country Life*, he thought. With his baggy trousers and tweed jacket he could have been a gamekeeper on some northern moor, or a giant ghillie in Scotland.

'The name's Moncrieff. A pleasure to meet you.' The handshake was surprisingly light. 'Call me Tam. Everyone else does.'

Klimt followed him to the car. There was a woman behind the wheel and Moncrieff opened the passenger door before stepping back.

'Meet Miss Barton. She's German. Her first name is Ursula. She'll make you feel at home.'

Klimt settled himself in the seat. The car was tiny. Moncrieff had to crouch in the back to avoid the roof. Klimt asked the woman in German whether they were going far. She shook her head.

'You know Bournemouth?' she said.

Half an hour's drive took them around a bay thick with pine trees and Klimt caught glimpses of a long curve of beach that would have been golden in the sunshine. The road dipped briefly to sea level and then Ursula dropped a gear and the little car was grinding inland up a long hill. Houses on both sides of the road reminded Klimt of the wealthier Berlin suburbs and he was about to ask the woman which part of Germany she came from when she slowed for a tight turn into a drive.

Invisible from the road, the house was enormous. Denied natural light by the surrounding trees, it seemed to brood. The overhang of the tiled roof shadowed the upper windows, and the oak front door, with its heavy iron hinges, belonged to a small castle. This is where a certain kind of owner might hide his family secrets, Klimt thought. Have the intelligence people moved in for the day? Or do they live here?

The door opened without warning and Moncrieff led the way inside. Refreshments, he announced, would be available as soon as cook was happy that the scones were done. Would Klimt prefer jam or clotted cream or both?

Klimt settled for jam. He'd never cared for cream.

Moncrieff strode from the room. Ursula apologised for the chill and invited him to sit down. The room, wood-panelled throughout, was dominated by an enormous fireplace. All that was missing was a stag's head and a stuffed fish or two.

Ursula enquired about his journey. It was the briefest courtesy. Klimt had barely started telling her about his first taste of Lisbon when she interrupted him. She was still speaking German. Her accent suggested Bavaria, or maybe the Black Forest.

'You're Schellenberg's man. Am I right?'

The question took Klimt by surprise, so sudden, so abrupt. As with every conversation in the intelligence world, you were best advised to tread carefully. How much did she know already about

Walther Schellenberg? Why might Klimt best avoid the traps she and her colleagues had doubtless prepared?

'I'm *Abwehr*, as you probably know.'

'Indeed, Herr Klimt. My question was about Schellenberg.'

'*Oberführer* Schellenberg heads the SD. The SD are no friends of my organisation. You're probably aware of that, too.'

'Exactly, Herr Klimt. So you'll excuse us for . . .' she frowned, '. . . a little confusion in this matter. Schellenberg has a reputation for gamesmanship. He always thinks three moves ahead. He has an extensive network of contacts, people he counts as friends, people he appears to rely on. They used to include Admiral Canaris. Am I right?'

'Yes.'

'But no longer?'

'I doubt it.'

'Doubt it, Herr Klimt? You'd know, surely.'

Klimt was beginning to weary of this conversation. He'd come here to test the waters on behalf of Walther Schellenberg, not to find himself interrogated about his professional loyalties.

'Schellenberg is in charge of the SD,' he said again. 'He has the backing of Himmler. That gives him exceptional power. Admiral Canaris is a man of honour. That can be a handicap in the regime I serve.'

'So Schellenberg's top of the heap? Is that what you're saying?'

'Of course. Even Canaris knows it.'

'So I repeat my question, Herr Klimt. Why you? Why not someone from the SD? Someone home-grown? Someone from within the organisation?'

Klimt didn't have time to answer. Moncrieff was back with a tray of scones. Behind him, a smaller figure carrying a huge silver tea pot. He put the pot carefully on the hearth and extended a hand as Klimt got to his feet. Klimt had recognised the face the moment he'd walked in. Guy Liddell. Director of Counter-Espionage. A spytaker of acknowledged genius.

His handshake was warm from the teapot. He was happy to speak German if Klimt insisted but he'd prefer to stick to English.

'*Kein Problem.*'

Moncrieff arranged the four armchairs in a loose circle. Klimt and Moncrieff sat down. Ursula distributed plates and scones while the Director poured the tea. The Director was the last to take a seat. Klimt could hear the wind howling down the chimney. There was an exchange of glances and then the Director cleared his throat.

'We all know why we're here, Herr Klimt. This evening we'll take you to London for detailed discussions. In the meantime, there's another matter we need to clear up. Tam?' The Director turned to Moncrieff.

Moncrieff produced a sheet of paper from his jacket. He needed spectacles to read.

'Billy Angell is in Dachau.' Moncrieff looked up. 'Billy Angell? Name ring any bells?'

Klimt was looking at the sheet of paper.

'This is some kind of message?'

'Yes.'

'Where does it come from?'

Moncrieff glanced at the Director.

'SD headquarters in Paris, Herr Klimt,' the Director said. 'With the compliments of our old friend Walther. And he didn't even bother to code it.' He paused. 'Now why would he send a message like that?'

'I've no idea. Who was it addressed to?'

'Me, Herr Klimt. Which is why it feels . . .' the Director smiled, '. . . a little personal. We're making enquiries, of course. Trying to find out who this man might be. But in the meantime we thought you might be able to shed a little light on the situation.'

Klimt held his gaze for a long moment, then shook his head.

'I've never heard of him,' he said, reaching at last for a scone.

Billy lay in the bottom bunk, staring at the rough wooden planks inches above his head. The hut was enormous. There were four tiers of bunks. They stretched down one side of the hut and up the other. In the heat of high summer the stench was overpowering. Hundreds of bodies. Thousands of bodies. Millions of bodies. Mysteriously gone.

Earlier he'd watched them leaving, an endless file of grey ghosts stumbling into the dawn outside, but when he'd tried to join them he'd been sent back to his bunk. No explanation. Nothing. Now, alone, he started scratching himself. He'd been scratching all night. The mattress was thin hessian. Straw poked through. The bunk reeked of piss and there were bugs in the straw of the mattress and every time Billy moved they found more flesh to feast on. He thought they were bed bugs. Tiny black things. He caught one but then lost it again.

Last night, in the reception centre, a prisoner who seemed to be an orderly had stripped him naked and shaved his head before dusting him with powder. No one spoke English. He'd asked for water, begged for something to drink, but no one took any notice. The orderly had thrown him a bundle of old rags and gestured for him to get dressed. A pair of baggy striped trousers with caked shit in the seams around the crutch. A garment that looked like a pyjama top, also striped. And a pair of ancient boots. There was only one button on the pyjama top and no laces for the boots. Already, he could smell himself.

The orderly had taken him outside. He'd shuffled across some kind of parade ground, asking for water again. The orderly had ignored him. There was a strange smell in the air, sour, sweet. When the second of the huts loomed out of the darkness the orderly had pushed a door open. The invitation was wordless. Sleep where you can.

A truly terrible night. Men snoring. Whimpering. Talking to themselves. And then, with the first glimmer of dawn at the windows, came a sudden bark of laughter. Billy tried to close his ears. Madness.

Alone in the emptiness of the hut, Billy's eyes were closed. He was trying to wish this place away. He wanted to wake up somewhere else, somewhere safe, somewhere he could smell fresh air, wash himself clean, talk to people who might speak his language. Then came the sound of the door opening and a shouted order.

'*Raus!*'

The guard wore the uniform of the SS. Billy was still dressed. He stumbled towards the door, scratching again, and followed the guard out. The brightness of the sunshine hurt his eyes. He gazed round. An infinity of barrack huts stretched away towards a distant fence, each one perfectly placed. Someone must have sat down at a drawing board and planned all this, he thought. Someone must have drawn a set of straight lines and worked out how many bodies each carefully pencilled oblong could hold. Layer after layer of prisoners for whom the regime had no place. The geometry of hell, Billy thought, for a community of ghosts.

The camp appeared to be empty. Maybe the prisoners worked elsewhere. Or maybe they just evaporated in the hot sunshine. Then, in the distance, Billy made out a flicker of movement. Two men were pushing a trolley loaded with what

411

looked like firewood. Beyond the wire was a building bigger than anything else in sight. Smoke curled from the tall brick chimney and Billy caught the smell again. Greasy. Sweet. Pungent.

He and the guard were making for a cluster of buildings at the entrance to the camp. Beyond lay some kind of factory. The guard paused at a door and knocked three times before letting himself in. The room was small. The woman sitting behind the desk was wearing an SS uniform. She was running to fat. She had a squint and her hair, iron-grey, had been flattened by the cap which lay on the desk. Billy was staring at her hands. They were the hands of a much smaller woman and she obviously took care of her nails. On the little finger of her left hand she wore a silver ring bearing the death's head insignia.

The guard was explaining something in German and at once Billy had the feeling that his very presence offended this woman's sense of order. He'd arrived in the dead of night, stolen in under the wire, and she knew nothing about him. Not a single detail.

'Your name?' She was consulting a list. She spoke a little English.

'Angell. Billy Angell.'

'Engel?' She couldn't find him.

'Angell.'

'*Ja.*' She looked up. '*Englisch?*'

'Yes.' He asked for water. Said he was very thirsty.

'*Wasser?*' She made the request sound bizarre.

Billy mimed a drinking motion. She didn't appear to understand.

The guard departed with a smirk. The woman pulled a drawer open and produced a handful of cloth badges. Billy found himself looking at a neat line of them laid out across the desk. They were triangular, in different colours.

'Every prisoner has to wear one,' she touched the front of her uniform. 'Just here. So you must help me, Herr Engell. You must choose. Maybe this one?' A perfectly manicured fingernail found the red badge. 'That means you're a political prisoner.'

'But I'm not.'

'Ach, so . . . this one?' This time it was black. 'That's when you don't like work.'

'I love work.'

'Maybe you fuck other men? You want the pink one?'

Billy hesitated, then shook his head. He asked about the violet badge.

'For crazy religious people, Herr Engell. Witnesses for Jehovah. *Ja?*'

'Not me.'

Billy was still staring at the desk. There were two badges left, a blue one and a brown one, but he'd always hated being labelled. Beside the line of badges was a white armband. Printed across it was the word *Blöd*.

'What's this?' he nodded at it.

'You don't know? You don't know what *Blöd* is?'

'No.'

'It means idiot. Fool. A simple person. We have many Polish here. Many *Blöd*.' She threw her head back and laughed. Terrible teeth.

Billy was putting the armband on. She stopped laughing.

'You're a *Blöd*?'

'Yes.'

'You want to wear that?'

'Yes.'

She couldn't believe it. She shook her head. Then she began to laugh again, her huge chest heaving, her little hand slapping down on the desk. The *Engländer*. A self-confessed *Blöd*. Priceless.

Billy asked again for water. She was drying her eyes. Then she returned the badges to the drawer, pushed back the chair and hauled herself to her feet.

'*Komm*,' she said.

She nodded at the door. There was a path outside. She motioned for him to follow. At last, he thought. At last someone who understands me. At the back of the building was another door. Peeling grey paint. She opened it and stepped back. It was a primitive lavatory. No tap. No basin. Just the toilet bowl. The stench was overwhelming.

'*Wasser, Herr Blöd*,' she gave him a playful punch on the arm. 'Drink as much as you like.'

CHAPTER 35

Klimt was driven to London, sharing the back of the car with the Director. It was a bigger car this time, befitting the Director's status, and Ursula – once again – was behind the wheel. She drove fast, eating up the miles, barely slowing for the interminable military convoys heading south.

'Our American cousins, Herr Klimt,' the Director announced softly. 'Once you wake these people up, life can become difficult.'

'You're telling me they're hard to control?'

'I'm telling you they're like children. Impossible to get to sleep again.'

They drove to an address in the maze of streets east of Marble Arch. Klimt had been to London on a couple of occasions before, back in the thirties when Admiral Canaris was keen to alert his contacts in Whitehall about the growing Russian threat in the east, and he recognised some of the bigger stores in Oxford Street. Beyond Selfridges, Ursula took a left turn. Minutes later, Klimt was following the Director into a tall red-brick house with a uniformed sentry at the door.

A jowly fifty-something was waiting for them in a reception room on the first floor. He looked like a senior civil servant a little past his best. His eyes were tired behind the rimless glasses and the baggy grey suit badly needed a press. His handshake was soft. The Director introduced him as Passmore. Time, it seemed, was precious.

The Director busied himself with a decanter of sherry while the two men sat down. Passmore spoke fluent German without a trace of an English accent. He said he was on his way to an airfield on the edges of London. This evening he would be joining a party of principals en route to Washington and he'd be happy to deliver any message Klimt might like to impart. Principals was an interesting word.

'These people hate surprises, Herr Klimt. You should assume I know a little about you already. What exactly do you have for us?'

Klimt was familiar with British understatement. 'A little' meant a great deal. He began to outline an unease in certain quarters of the Reich about the future course of the war. No one liked negotiating from a position of weakness but anyone who lived in the real world couldn't fail to conclude that a great deal of blood was still to be shed. Perhaps in vain.

'Whose blood, Herr Klimt?'

'Ours. And yours.'

'And the Soviets? Our allies?'

'Of course.'

'You appreciate they'd have no truck with a conversation like this?'

'Yes.'

Passmore nodded. He hadn't touched his sherry. He wanted to know whom he might expect to be representing German interests in any negotiation.

'Possibly *Reichsführer* Himmler.'

'With Hitler's blessing?'

'I suspect not.'

'We're assuming Hitler's dead?'

'We're assuming the negotiations are conducted without his participation.'

'Or knowledge?'

'That too.'

'So where's the guarantee that Himmler can deliver on any kind of agreement? Assuming that these negotiations ever take place?'

'There'd be ways and means.'

'Is that an assumption, Herr Klimt? Are you making it up? Or have you something a little weightier to put on the table?'

Klimt had already gone beyond the limits of his brief and he suspected that Passmore knew it. At last Passmore put the glass to his lips and took a tiny sip of sherry. Then he checked his watch.

'Ten minutes, Herr Klimt.'

Klimt looked at him quizzically. 'Ten minutes for what?'

'Ten minutes for you to come up with something new. I'm not entirely sure how much you know about Herr Schellenberg's previous efforts in this respect but it might be helpful to remind you of conversations he had with some of our people in Zurich. This is recent history, Herr Klimt. January to be precise. I was rereading the transcripts only this morning. Nothing you've just said has added anything new. Not one jot. Not one tiny particle.'

Passmore chose not to disguise his irritation. It showed on his face, in his voice. He put the sherry to one side and leaned forward. The situation, in his view, couldn't be clearer. If Schellenberg, or Himmler, or even the Führer himself were prepared to settle for unconditional surrender then so be it. Otherwise there was still a war on. Best to see it through to the end.

'No matter how messy?'

'Your people started it, Herr Klimt. Ask the Czechs. Ask the Poles. You reap what you sow. But you're right. Messy doesn't do justice to what we're all about to face.'

'You don't think there's a better way?'

'Of course I do. I've just mentioned it. It's called unconditional surrender. Is this some kind of surprise, Herr Klimt?'

Klimt accepted the rebuke with a shrug. The Director had been taking discreet notes, sitting on an upright chair in the shadows. Now he got to his feet. The conversation was obviously at an end.

Klimt was still looking at Passmore.

'Do you think I'm here under false pretences? Be honest.'

'I've no idea why you're here, Herr Klimt.' Passmore offered a thin smile. 'Perhaps that's a question you should be asking yourself.'

One of the orderlies took Billy Angell to the library block. No one had explained why but he seemed to have been chosen for special duties. Shelves of books and a rack of party newspapers and magazines sat uneasily with everything else he'd seen in this terrifying place but he assumed the library was for the use of the camp's staff.

Another woman appeared to be in charge. She was young and sullen and reminded Billy of a thinner version of Agnès. Her English, to his surprise, was good.

'You speak no German?' She was eyeing the *Blöd* armband.

'No.'

'A pity. Maybe we should teach you. Either German or Polish. You sleep with the Poles. You work with the Germans. How lucky to have a choice. A moment, please.'

She left her desk and disappeared through a door in the corner. Billy caught a brief conversation but he didn't understand a word. Then she was back at the open door.

'In here please, Herr Angell. As a place of work this has its advantages. You will assist with material refurbishment. Most of the prisoners do factory jobs. Some go to quarries to break stones. Others dig all day. In summer, we keep the

419

windows open for the breeze. In winter we have a stove. I suggest you keep that in mind.'

Material refurbishment? Billy stepped across. The room was small and dominated by a table. An old man was bent over a pool of light from a lamp at his elbow. He was thin, frail. Striped shirt. Striped trousers. Not a hair on his shaven head. He didn't look round.

The door closed. The old man didn't move.

'Sit down,' he indicated the chair beside him. Billy froze. He recognised the voice. It triggered a thousand memories, all of them bad.

'Malin? Malin, is that you?'

The old man nodded, then looked round. Something had happened to his face. It seemed to have caved in. Then he saw the armband and attempted a smile of welcome. No teeth.

Billy didn't know what to do.

'Sit down,' Malin said again, this time patting the seat.

Billy did as he was told. The old man had a collection of watches in a cardboard box at his feet. He was working on them one by one, easing off the casing, exposing the movement inside, making tiny adjustments with a collection of specialist tools.

Billy had a thousand questions to ask. It seemed an age since they'd been dragged into the field by the SS, a thousand years since they'd been forced to watch the slaughter of the Spanish couple and of Agnès, but the moment Billy began to talk Malin put a finger to his lips and gestured upwards. *Mikros.* Even here.

'Tell me about the watches,' Billy said hopelessly.

'They come from prisoners. The ones that work are sold. The ones that don't I mend. Use a man as best you can. Efficient, don't you think?'

He spat the word out. The same old Malin. He had two magnifying glasses, one of which he gave to Billy. It was scratched and smeared but the innards of the exposed watch began to make sense as Malin talked him through it. Material refurbishment, thought Billy. That's what the woman had meant. He followed the explanation as best he could but something told him that there was going to be more to this conversation than the beginnings of an apprenticeship in watchmaking. He was right.

'I had a brother, too,' Malin said. Billy felt the lightest pressure of the old man's boot on his. Play along. Pretend.

'You did?'

'Karyl. He was older, as well. Just like yours. I was frightened of him to begin with but it turned out he was a real softie. He used to take me sledging when the first snows came. And when we were older he taught me how to drink. That was a brave thing to do with my parents around but Karyl never cared. He led his own life, that boy. He wrote his own script.'

Billy had the magnifying glass to his eye, watching the old man coaxing the movement to life. He had the skills of a surgeon. After everything he'd

421

been through, there was barely a tremor as he eased the tension on the mainspring.

'My brother was the same,' Billy said. 'We fought like cats and dogs when we were young. He knew I was scared of spiders and he used to collect them in a matchbox and put them in my bed. We shared a room upstairs. My mum would come up when she heard me screaming but I never told on him. Not once. I think he respected me for that.'

'The screaming?'

'The not telling. He was a tough guy, my brother, and he knew from the start that I was a weakling but in the end it didn't make any difference at all. He went his way and I went mine. He even came to see some of the plays I was in. I knew he didn't much like the theatre and all that showing off but I loved him being there.'

'You must miss him.'

'I do. Especially now he's gone.'

'Gone?'

'He died.'

'You never told me that.'

'You never asked.'

'So what happened?'

Billy went through the whole story. The Navy. The diving course. The long, unexplained absences overseas. The fact that his brother's fiancée didn't even know what he was up to. Then the moment arrived when she answered a knock at her door and found herself looking at a naval officer with the worst news in the world.

'He just disappeared,' Billy said. 'And no one thought to tell us.'

'Why not?'

'Because it was supposed to be secret. Because no one was supposed to know what really happened.'

'And?' The old man was looking at him now, his work put to one side.

Billy smiled at him. In some small way, this felt like redemption. Do your duty. See it through. No matter what.

'He was looking for a beach for the invasion,' he said. 'And he found it.'

'Where?' Billy felt another tiny tap, this time on his ankle.

'Dunkirk,' he said.

'And he really did die?'

'Yes.'

'Then I'm sorry, my friend,' his eyes were misty. 'It's a terrible price to pay.'

CHAPTER 36

After Passmore left, the Director approached Klimt with the decanter. Moncrieff, he said, was about to arrive from the office. They knew a decent restaurant down the road. Reliable grub even in this time of austerity. Nice people. Klimt nodded. He felt he owed this man an apology. Not least because he'd so obviously let him down.

'Not at all. Our friend from the Foreign Office was right. Walther's putting nothing new on the table. But that's hardly the point. When it came to making this trip, I'm not sure you had any choice in the matter.'

'Meaning?'

The Director smiled, said nothing. Moncrieff arrived shortly afterwards, clumping up the stairs and announcing himself at the door. The table was booked for half eight. Best to make a move.

The restaurant specialised in offal. Klimt chose lightly spiced sweetbreads. The Director settled for braised pig's head with black pudding. Moncrieff stuck with home-made faggots under a glistening roof of pork crackling, which was evidently his favourite. The war, they all agreed, had done wonders for the British diet. How many people had ever eaten this stuff before?

'The French love it,' Klimt pointed out. 'The whole beast? It's a way of life.'

This was no man's land, a conversationally useful place to be. Over a bottle of Mouton Cadet, they shared memories of pre-war Paris and asked Klimt for updates. Was the Boeuf sur le Toit in the 8th still open? Could you still get a decent cassoulet at Allard? Was it still possible to attend midnight mass at Notre-Dame and then feast on borscht and vodka on the Left Bank? And – most intriguing of all – how did the nation's new masters cope with the language? And all those Frenchmen?

'Most of them we shipped to the Ruhr,' Klimt pointed out. 'Germans don't let anything go to waste.'

'The whole beast, Bjorn?' A gentle smile from the Director. It was the first time he had called Klimt by his Christian name. From the *Abwehr* file, Klimt knew that this man's nickname was Roly. Might he return the compliment?

Moncrieff was roaring with laughter. The whole beast. Guts and all. An army of Frenchies on the Ruhr. Lovely.

Klimt smiled. He liked these people. He admired their style, their wit, their seeming insouciance. Take them at face value and you were in danger of missing how good they were. Schellenberg thought them the best in the world, unmatched for guile and sheer originality, and he was beginning to sense that the Chief was seldom wrong.

The main course arrived. The restaurant was small and intimate. Moncrieff sawed at his crackling. Klimt speared a lightly sautéed sweetbread. The Director watched them both, an indulgent father hosting a rather special family get-together.

'Why did Walther really send you?' he asked Klimt after the waiter had departed with the empty plates.

'You want the truth? I'm not sure I know.'

'But he had a reason, surely.'

Klimt nodded.

'And you must have thought about it.'

Nodded again.

'So . . .? Care to give us a clue or two?'

Klimt bowed his head. This was dangerous territory and they all knew it. The social courtesies were over. They'd stepped out of no man's land. Ahead lay the minefield where motive underpinned the usual tissue of half-truths. One false step, Klimt thought. One careless remark.

'Schellenberg wants to be Emperor,' he said lightly. 'Canaris refuses to bow the knee. Everybody knows it's only a question of time but Walther is an impatient man and so is Himmler.'

'You've met him? Little Heine?'

'Several times.'

'What's he like?'

'He's a believer. To people like him, the regime is a faith. He lives in the Dark Ages. He's read the runes. He's also very ambitious. He's been studying the map for years and he knows the way to the top.'

'Meaning?'

'He has the power and he means to keep it. He's not as damaged as Goering. He's not as clever as Goebbels. He's not an oaf like Kaltenbrunner. But he's single-minded and he's very good at keeping his ear to the ground. Maybe that's why he prizes Schellenberg so much. Schellenberg understands *Ausland*. Schellenberg is fluent in *Ausland*. *Ausland* doesn't frighten Schellenberg, unlike so many of our brethren.'

Ausland meant abroad. *Ausland* meant sitting in a poorly lit London restaurant with the taste of sweetbreads on your breath.

'That makes Himmler a realist, surely.' The Director was turning his empty glass in his hand.

'Of course it does. Which is why Schellenberg can get clearance for expeditions like mine.'

'You're sure you have his blessing? Himmler's? You're certain he knows you've made the journey?'

'I can't imagine Schellenberg would take the risk otherwise. Himmler hates surprises. He's a nervous man. Ask him to make a decision, any decision, and you'll grow old waiting. He also lives in a world where everybody is expendable and Schellenberg knows that. No . . .' he shook his head, '. . . I'm here because Himmler wants me here.'

'A shame you've failed then.'

427

'Indeed.'

'Will there be repercussions? How will you report this evening's conversation?'

'I'll tell Schellenberg the truth. I'll tell him I sat down with the enemy and the enemy told us to get fucked.'

Moncrieff was filling his pipe. He glanced up, a broad smile on his bony face.

'Brave man.'

'But it's true. And if I'd been listening to me, I'd have said exactly the same thing. Fucked is perfect. Fucked is exactly where we are. In our business you get a feel for the minor key, for what's really happening under all the crashing brass. The gangsters have been in charge for years. And it's starting to show. These are people who stumbled out of the wilderness and led us to the Promised Land. Now even they are beginning to understand that violence only begets more violence. Have either of you been to Hamburg recently? Or Cologne? Or Lübeck? The band's still playing. The music's as loud as ever. But you wouldn't want to be a German anymore.'

Klimt accepted a cigarette. The last thing he'd intended to do was to make a speech but the truth was that he believed every word of what he'd just said. Did that make him a traitor? One of the army of defeatists that were filling the concentration camps? Or was there some kind of comfort or maybe even redemption in acknowledging the facts? He didn't know.

'You'll be going back then?' Moncrieff was lighting his pipe.

'Of course.'

'To face the music?' He smiled.

'A pleasure. As always.'

'Anything we can help you with? You're booked at the Savoy, courtesy of the wicked enemy. Will the one night be enough?'

'I'd like to stay for two. I'm not here often.'

'Of course. Our pleasure. Need anything fixing up?'

'I'll be all right. A little sightseeing. Then home.'

Moncrieff nodded. He'd see to the booking on the flying boat back to Lisbon. Arrange a lift down to Poole. Then he was struck by another thought. He turned to the Director.

'By the way, sir, I made some enquiries about the Angell chap. Turns out he was with the bomber boys, jumped out of a Lancaster last month coming back from Saint-Nazaire. No one seems to know why.'

'Anything wrong with the aircraft?'

'Not a damn thing. There's talk that he might have a problem . . .' Moncrieff tapped his head, '. . . up here.'

'Bailed out?' The Director was frowning. 'That's desertion, isn't it?'

'Technically, I imagine it is.' Moncrieff turned to Klimt. 'Any chance of getting him back?'

Night again. Malin seemed to have influence in the camp. He'd arranged for Billy to change huts. It was the same four tiers, the same fug of unwashed bodies, the same straw mattress, but at least he had company.

Malin had a nearby bunk. They were close to the door that stayed open as dusk stole across the camp. 'Supper' had been a thin soup of hot water flavoured by rotting vegetables. Malin had made friends with fellow Poles and had somehow laid hands on an extra slice of black bread to mop up the remains of the soup. To Billy's surprise, he was hungry.

The old man always referred to Hélène as '*Madame*'. He asked what had become of her. Billy said he didn't know. They'd both been arrested in her apartment in Paris. They'd shared a car as far as a big railway station. Then she'd been driven away.

'Gestapo?'

'Grey uniforms.'

'Could be SS. Could be anyone. A German isn't a German without a uniform.' He was staring at his empty bowl. 'How was she?'

'Upset.'

'That boyfriend of hers? Klimt? He wasn't around?'

'No.'

'Shame. She loved that man. I know she did. God always allows you one mistake in life. That may have been hers.'

'But he looked after her, surely. He looked after all of you.'

'God?'

'Klimt.'

'That's true.' Malin looked up. 'Did you ever talk to him? Properly? Klimt?'

Billy held his gaze. The chateau by the river, he thought. Klimt's pilot friend. The trouble they'd taken to check every rivet in this story of his.

'No,' he said. 'I didn't.'

Malin said nothing for a moment. Then he gave Billy a squeeze on his arm.

'You're learning fast, my friend. Which is probably just as well. *Madame* told me a lot about you. Before it all went wrong.'

Hélène had never been in prison in her life. For the last two days she'd occupied a single cell in the camp they called Ravensbrück. It lay in the flatlands north of Berlin. From the back of the car the landscape had the pallor of death.

At the reception centre outside the main compound they'd treated her with something close to respect. Unlike every other prisoner she'd glimpsed, she'd been allowed to keep her hair and her own clothes. They were all women here, no men. She'd been assigned a short, stocky Jew from Lübeck, a woman of some education, to attend to her.

The woman's name was Ruth. She brought hot rolls in the morning, wrapped in a copy of *Völkischer Beobachter*, and she stayed for a chat. Hélène didn't know whether she was a plant, a trap, whether the cell was equipped with a micro-phone, but in any case she didn't care. She had no one to betray, no secrets to share except the burning conviction that this life of hers was over.

She'd been a fool at the chateau, kindling false hopes. She'd been crazy to believe that Klimt, fine man as he was, could guard her door forever. They lived in a time of darkness and now the darkness had won.

She'd worn her beloved beret on the train and in the car. She had it still. Alone in the cell, she sat on the cold concrete of the plinth and twisted it this way and that. She was grateful to have been spared the camp uniform but the days were long and the nights were worse and she was beginning to be afraid of her own company.

Listening to Ruth, she sometimes wondered whether she might be able to swap this single cell for a bunk in one of the hutments. Ruth lived with more than fifty other women. She'd made friends. The women looked after each other. Like any family they had their fallings-out but Ruth said the hutment was a place she looked forward to returning to. Because they were women, she said, and because they'd all coped with worse in their lives, they laughed a lot, despite the food and the stinking latrines and some of the female guards who'd put most men to shame. One day, said Ruth, they'd wake up to a horde of Russian soldiers chasing the Germans back to Berlin. Given the Russians' appetite for anything in a skirt, liberation might be a mixed blessing but nothing lasted forever and in the end they'd be free again.

Nothing lasted forever.

Hélène didn't believe her. This lasted forever. Not the cell. Not the wash of grey dawn light that brought her sleepless nights to an end. Not the cockroaches that scuttled across the floor. But this. This feeling of shame, of worthlessness. She'd never had a problem with self-esteem. She'd always known exactly who she was. Hélène Lafosse. Wife of the maverick Nathan Khorrami. Chatelaine of a neat little estate in the depths of the Touraine. Owner of the famous Valmy. Lover of a man who happened to be a Nazi. Friends in Paris had sometimes questioned the seeming contradictions in her busy life but she'd never felt the need either to explain or excuse the way she was. True, she'd made an accommodation with the New Order, with the hard-faced men in uniforms, but she'd also played mother hen to a brood of needy children who'd stepped out of the night and knocked on her door, and asked for shelter. Jews. Misfits. *Résistantes.* Refugees. They'd come and they'd gone. Until Billy Angell.

Was he the reason everything had fallen apart? On balance, she thought not. The Germans had swept into France. They had the country by the throat. It was in the nature of things that round every corner lurked the possibility of disaster, of arrest, of torture, of an early death. In her case that possibility wore an SS uniform and answered

433

to the name of Huber. Huber was the fate that lay in waiting. And she'd been a fool to expect anything else.

And so she sat alone, head bowed, twisting the beret this way and that. Soon, she thought to herself. Please God.

CHAPTER 37

K limt was awoken by the blast of a tugboat's air horn on the river. They'd lodged him at the Savoy as a gesture, as Moncrieff had put it, of solidarity. Wars are *Scheisse*, he'd said last night as they'd parted company outside the hotel. But we're all in it together.

Indeed. Klimt dressed for breakfast. He ate alone at a table by the window, watching the traffic hurrying over Waterloo Bridge. Barrage balloons hung in the smoky air and the river was stirred by tiny waves. An officer in the uniform of a Major General was sharing his eggs and bacon with a woman who appeared to be his wife. They were effortlessly intimate, sharing tiny courtesies, and Klimt was envious.

At the desk, before he made for the street, Klimt enquired about the National Gallery. Might it be open this morning? The answer was yes. Many of the finest paintings had regretfully been evacuated for safe storage elsewhere but sufficient of interest remained to fill an idle hour or so. The gallery was a five-minute stroll away. Be sure to watch the traffic. Klimt thanked the receptionist and left.

Out on the pavement he paused before heading up the street towards the Strand. He knew they'd have a tail in place, maybe two. They'd also be at the front desk within minutes, quizzing the receptionist on the nature of Klimt's enquiries. Best stick to the National Gallery.

At this time in the morning, it was nearly empty. The washrooms were in the basement. He locked himself in a cubicle for five minutes and then returned to the marbled entrance hall. No sign of a tail. Outside, he hailed a taxi and asked for Waterloo Station. They were there in minutes. Another cab took him to the Tower of London. Only in the third cab did he give the driver his real destination.

'You're looking for Persepolis in Berkeley Street. It's an art gallery.'

Klimt sat in the back as they headed west. As far as he could tell he was alone. No tail.

The art gallery occupied the ground floor of a handsome three-storey townhouse. The biggest room was at the front. Thickly carpeted, it was lit with crystal chandeliers suspended from an ornate ceiling. There were bowls of rosewater on every surface, crimson petals, obviously fresh, and dishes of what looked like cashew nuts for clients who might be peckish. Cashew nuts were hard to find in continental Europe. Even the best hotels in Paris had trouble laying hands on them.

Klimt took a catalogue from a pile at the desk. It seemed that Nathan Khorrami had hosted a soirée only last week in honour of an English artist named Andrew Prebble. There were a dozen of his pictures in the catalogue. All of them had been sold.

The woman sitting behind the desk was Italian – crisp white blouse, tailored skirt, absurdly good-looking. She smiled up at Klimt and asked if he was interested in anything in particular. She had a light American accent. He shook his head and then enquired whether the owner ever appeared at this hour in the morning.

'He's upstairs, sir.' Her hand was reaching for the phone. 'You want to have me call him?'

Klimt shook his head. Maybe later. He began to look at the pictures, moving from canvas to canvas. Khorrami had a good eye. That was evident at once. Some of the modern stuff was deeply original, splashes of colour against a textured hessian-like background, and he had a real feel for the interpretation of seascapes. A series of watercolours showcased an estuary setting, a gauzy evening light bathing a line of soft green hills, and he was still wondering where this place might be when he moved into the next room.

It felt like a boudoir, no natural light, heavy wall hangings in rich reds and golds. There was the scent of lemons in the air and in the far corner a parrot eyed him from a big wicker cage. It shuffled from claw to claw, eyeing this stranger.

'Fuck the Boches,' it squawked.

Klimt smiled. Another of Nathan's talents, Hélène

had once told him, was for gestures that might take you by surprise. She hadn't been wrong.

He gazed round. There were fewer pictures on display here and they were all portraits. A baker extracting a tray of loaves from his oven. The face of a priest, half hidden in the confessional. An old man gazing in bewilderment at a goldfish bowl. These were intimate studies, all the work of the same hand, and Klimt was trying to decipher the scrawled name in the bottom corner when his attention was drawn by another picture.

It showed a woman standing at a first-floor window looking out at a landscape of rolling meadows. The view beyond the window was nicely done. A buzzard was riding the hot air from the fields below and the cloudscape was magnificent. But what drew him in was the woman. She was naked but for a red beret. She was tall with a generous figure. The artist had caught her face in quarter-profile. Klimt took a step closer, examining the room itself. The oak chest of drawers. The fleur-de-lis pattern on the wallpaper. The shape of the window itself, the lower sash half open. No doubt about it. Hélène Lafosse.

'You like this picture?' A deep voice. Almost a chuckle. Foreign inflection.

'Very much. Is it for sale?'

'Regrettably not.'

At last Klimt looked round. This had to be Nathan Khorrami. He was small and broad and heavily tanned. He had a big Jewish face made for company: a wide, fleshy mouth, and laugh lines round his eyes. He wore a pair of belted grey trousers and a black cotton shirt open at the neck. Highly polished leather shoes, not cheap.

'You're German?' he enquired.

'Yes.'

'Here on business?'

'Yes.'

'Not an easy thing to do, my friend. You've come from South America, perhaps? Brazil, maybe? Argentina?'

Klimt didn't reply. He wanted to know more about the picture.

'Tell me about the artist,' he said.

'An Englishman. Andrew Prebble. He lives here in London. He's too old for the war. His good fortune, my friend. And mine.'

'It's a life drawing? From a model?'

'He did it from a photograph.'

'I see.' Klimt was staring at the picture again. 'Beautiful.'

'The picture?'

'The woman.'

There was a brief silence, broken by the parrot. Fuck the Boches. Khorrami tossed it a cashew nut and told it to behave. Then he took Klimt by the arm. Intimacy came naturally to this man and he walked Klimt back towards the big room at the front.

'Let me sell you something else,' he said. 'You like landscapes? I have something very special.'

They paused in front of the estuary watercolours. Klimt said they weren't to his taste. Khorrami feigned disappointment. Something else, perhaps?

Klimt shook his head.

'The picture of the woman with the beret,' he said. 'Why *The Stolen Hour*?'

Khorrami gazed at him for a moment, then stepped across to the desk where the receptionist was pretending not to listen.

'Francesca? You want to explain this title to the gentleman?'

'Of course, Mr Khorrami.' She looked up at Klimt. That same melting smile. 'I guess it's that special time of the day. Late afternoon? Early evening? When everything feels just right? For both of you?'

'Perfect.' Khorrami was beaming down at her, his thick fingers resting lightly on her shoulder. Mine, he was telling Klimt. All mine.

The phone rang. Francesca listened briefly to the caller, then whispered a name to Khorrami. He nodded, made his excuses and disappeared upstairs.

Klimt had noticed a comments book lying on an occasional table in the corner of the room.

'May I?' He nodded at it.

'Of course. It was there for the soirée last week. The artist who does the portraits was our guest of honour. Andrew. Mr Prebble.'

Klimt began to leaf through the book. There were pages of comments, most of them effusive.

The evening must have drawn hundreds of guests. 'Peace in our time' read one comment. 'The face is the window to the soul' another. Then, on the last page, he noticed a third, fuller hand, black ink.

A tribute to your untiring genius, mon vieux, and your good taste in women, as well as fine art. Comme toujours. Roly.

Klimt looked up. The receptionist was on the phone again, her back turned. Roly was Guy Liddell. Roly was the Director. Roly was the spy-catcher who appeared never to have heard of Hélène Lafosse, of the Château de Neaune, of Billy Angell. Klimt toyed briefly with removing the page and folding it into his pocket but decided against it. Commit nothing to paper. Keep everything in your head.

Keep everything in your head. One last look at the canvas, he thought, and then I'll go.

It was Ruth who interceded on Hélène's behalf. She'd earned the trust of the SS *Über-Lagerkommandant* who helped run the camp. She'd knocked on her office door an hour after she'd taken her lunch. At that time of day, she was close to being human.

'It's about prisoner Lafosse,' Ruth announced.

'*Ja?*'

'She needs company. She's depressed. I've seen it before. It's a medical condition.'

'I have orders to keep her in her cell. It's for her

own good. She won't be with us long. A week at the most.'

'Really?' This had never happened before. 'Why?'

'I have no idea. These kinds of orders, you ask no questions.'

The *Über-Lagerkommandant* looked up. The interview was plainly over. Ruth hadn't finished.

'Lafosse is a danger where she is,' she said. 'That's my opinion.'

'A danger to whom?'

'To herself. Depression plays tricks with the mind. If you want to keep her safe let me take care of her.'

'You think you can do that?'

'I can try,' Ruth risked a smile. Safe was a word that mattered in circles like these. Play safe. Stay safe.

Within the hour Hélène had been released from solitary confinement. Ruth walked her across the parade ground to 'C' hut where she lived. The *Kommandant*'s office had arranged for the temporary reallocation of a prisoner who slept in the bunk above Ruth.

Hélène's arrival in the hut caused a stir. This was a woman in civilian clothes. A woman with a stylish beret, for God's sake. And she wore no badge. Ruth had done her best to pave the way. She said she'd talked to the newcomer. Hélène was French. She lived in Paris. She was a nice woman, a little quiet, a little afraid. Ruth had no idea why she'd been arrested in the first place but she wouldn't be with them long. Make the most of her. Make her welcome.

That night, Hélène found herself the centre of attention. She was grateful for countless little acts of kindness but she had no appetite for either food or conversation. Later, long after the lights had gone out, she heard a whisper in the darkness and rolled over to find herself staring at a face just inches away. Ruth appeared to be asleep.

Hélène had noticed the woman before. She was tall, and even thinner than the rest of the prisoners. She wore a violet-coloured badge on her striped uniform. Ruth said she was deeply religious, a woman of the cloth. She'd been arrested by the Gestapo after preaching a street sermon outside Goebbels' birthplace in Rheydt. The sermon had been about the iniquities of propaganda.

Now she wanted to warn Hélène about the countless ways this place could kill her. Never upset the guards, especially the Ukrainians. Never trust any meat, especially in summer. And never stray into the forbidden zone.

'Forbidden zone?'

'By the wire. Fifteen metres. The guards are in the tower. They get bored. They'll shoot you.'

Hélène nodded, said she understood. The woman was staring at her. Huge eyes in the darkness. She didn't want to end this conversation. She had lots of other things to tell her, special secrets that would keep her safe. Hélène said another time. She was grateful but she was also very tired. Please leave me alone.

The woman vanished. Hélène rolled over, her face against the wall. She was using the beret to cushion her head against the prickles of the straw through the thin mattress. She closed her eyes. She wanted no more of this. Try very hard, and she could still catch the faintest scent of cigars.

CHAPTER 38

They came for the old man at dawn. Billy, already awake, heard a murmur of voices outside. Then the sound of the door opening at the far end of the hut and the stamp of boots on the wooden floor. One of the guards had a flashlight, sweeping from bunk to bunk until it settled on Malin. He appeared not to be surprised. He got up without protest. The footsteps receded. The door closed. Silence again.

Roll call was at seven. The filth on the window was pebbled with rain. A pair of orderlies appeared, shouting at the prisoners, holding the door open as they stumbled out into the murk. With the orderlies was another man whom Billy hadn't seen before. He was wearing an SS uniform and he spoke a little English.

'Engell?' Billy nodded. He was all but alone in the hut now. 'You come with me.'

Billy followed him to the door. Outside, the other huts were emptying fast. On the parade ground prisoners were forming themselves into untidy ranks, hut by hut. Billy recognised a face or two from his own hut and made to join them. Then came a tug on his arm.

'This way, *ja*?'

The SS man pointed to a distant stand of pine trees. They appeared to be outside the wire. The rain was heavier now. Behind him he could hear a guard bellowing at a prisoner. He wanted to look behind him but something told him not to. With a growing sense of dread, he splashed through the puddles towards the wire.

Two sentries guarded the gate. Billy stepped through. On the other side were the trees.

'The path. To the right.'

Billy spotted the path. There were wheel marks in the mud. Ahead, through the trees, he glimpsed a low brick building. A chimney soared above it. No smoke.

'Now left.'

A narrower path. No wheel marks. He trudged for maybe a hundred metres, his head down, trying to shield his face from the rain. Branches were lashing above his head, the forest bending and groaning in the wind from the east.

'Here.'

Billy stopped. Looked up. A line of wooden gibbets had been built among the trees. There were crude 'T' shapes maybe three times his height. From either arm of the 'T' hung a body. Heads lolled at odd angles. Tongues protruded between parted lips. Eyes gazed sightlessly into nowhere. And with each new gust of wind, the bodies swayed. Billy stared up at them. It was beyond comprehension. He couldn't take it in.

'This one.'

The SS officer was pointing to the left. Billy didn't want to look, didn't want to know. It had to be Abel Malinowski. And it was. Billy stared at his sunken face, at the gape of his toothless mouth, at the faded yellow star pinned to his thin chest.

'Roll call takes an hour,' the officer said. 'And so we wait.'

At Ravensbrück, the rain had stopped and the first fingers of sunlight were creeping slowly towards the camp. Roll call was over and the prisoners were preparing for the long trudge to the factories beyond the wire. This was to be Hélène's first day of proper work. The women in the hut had prepared her for it. Ten hours repairing uniforms for the Eastern Front. An entire day bent over a looted sewing machine, darning bullet holes, mending tears in the heavy serge fabric after a bayonet thrust, preparing the grey tunics for yet another luckless soldier. Hélène had expressed a polite interest in these accounts. She knew the women meant to be helpful but she'd never much cared for sewing.

The prisoners had formed themselves into a long file. The camp gate was half a mile away. Hélène still had her beret but she'd hidden it at roll call in case the guards took it away. As the line of

447

prisoners began to shuffle forward, she could feel it tucked into the waistband of her skirt. A lone splash of colour in this long grey caterpillar, she waited for her chance.

It came minutes later. They'd left the huts behind them. Ahead lay the main gate. To the right, no more than thirty metres away, was the fence. The fence was high, topped with barbed wire. Sentries patrolled outside and more soldiers manned the guard towers. Hélène could see insulators on the sturdy fence posts and the electric wires strung between. Fifteen metres, she told herself. The forbidden zone.

For whatever reason, the column of prisoners had come to a halt. This appeared to be routine. Women turned to talk to each other. One of them took a look at Hélène's face and asked her whether she was all right.

'Yes,' Hélène said.

Above the camp, the clouds were parting. She tilted her face to the sun, felt the sudden warmth on her skin. She had the beret in her hand now. She was smiling. She was glad it was nearly over. Then she started to run.

Billy, soaked, was numb. It felt as if he'd been standing here among the dripping trees for most of his life. Every turn of his head, every attempt to avert his gaze, every bid to look at anything but the hanging line of bodies had prompted a word of command from the officer. Look at the old man.

Look what you've done. Just look. Now he wanted to know what happened next.

'Next? We go back.'

'Where?'

'There,' he jerked a finger towards the building with the chimney. 'Every day we have bodies we must burn. You will help with this one.'

'Me?'

'You. Soon the old man will be stiff. Easier to deal with . . .' he smiled, '. . . *ja*?'

Billy closed his eyes. All he could think about was the mortuary at Bristol Infirmary. More broken bodies. Irene. Countless others. He couldn't do it. He knew he couldn't. He'd done his best. He'd tried to play the part. But in the end he'd failed. There was no more room in his life for any of this madness. It was over.

The officer studied him. Water dripped from the peak of his cap. He appeared to have expected this moment.

'You want to talk to someone? Someone with better English than me?'

'Yes, please.'

'*Kommen Sie.*'

They retraced their steps through the trees. The sentry let them back into the camp. Roll call was over and Billy could see the prisoners shuffling into columns for the march to work. Ahead lay the camp gates and the guard house. The officer told Billy to wait outside. He didn't appear to think he was worth keeping an eye on. He stood alone in the rain.

At length the officer reappeared and gestured for Billy to follow him. A corridor led to an office at the end. The office was bare: two filing cabinets, a desk and a big map of the camp on the wall behind. At the desk sat a figure Billy recognised. SS uniform. And a faint smile when he saw the *Blöd* armband. Agnès, Billy thought. And the Spanish couple. And the soldiers laughing in the truck.

'You're ready, Mr Engell?' Huber had a pad at his elbow. Billy nodded. This man was waiting to take his confession. He'd probably been here for hours.

'I've been lying,' Billy whispered. 'None of what I said is true.'

CHAPTER 39

Klimt left London next morning, Ursula Barton driving him down to Poole for the flying boat service back to Lisbon. Klimt sat beside her and they passed the journey speaking in their own language, conversing like old friends. Ursula, as he had suspected, came from a village in the Black Forest. She'd married an Englishman before the war. When he'd turned out to be a bad lot she'd been obliged to send him packing and find herself a job. Her native German had, after considerable vetting, enabled her to secure a secretarial post at MI5 and she quickly won a promotion to find herself working under diplomatic cover at the British embassy in The Hague. She'd been there when Walther Schellenberg, a rising star in the late thirties, had pulled the Venlo stunt.

Klimt knew all about Venlo, a town on the Dutch/German border. Two British military officers had been lured into a trap and kidnapped. The operation, meticulously planned, had come from Schellenberg's fertile brain and the results of the subsequent interrogation had ended up on desks in Berlin. The very boldness of the operation had won the admiration of Hitler. He loved giving the British a black eye and young Walther Schellenberg was on his way.

'The Führer used to call him his "Benjamin".' Klimt was smiling. 'In the *Abwehr*, we used to keep an eye on him. He was exotic. He was an original. The old bruisers couldn't stand him, of course. A man who didn't smoke, scarcely drank, had no taste for a brawl? Unthinkable.'

They parted in good humour at the pontoon in Poole Harbour. Within the hour Klimt was airborne over the English Channel, anticipating the moment when the bony ribs of the Brittany coast would appear beneath them. The flight was full, a dowdy mixture of military personnel, businessmen and other figures in unremarkable suits who were probably fellow spies. Klimt was sitting beside a lean American Major who, thankfully, had no interest in making conversation. He'd guessed already that Klimt was a German and had retired behind the pages of *Picture Post*.

Erwin Busch, Schellenberg's young attaché, was waiting at the flying boat terminus beside the Tagus. He'd spotted Klimt's name on the passenger manifest. The Chief was in town for a series of meetings and would be staying overnight at the embassy. This evening he'd proposed an outing to the casino in Estoril, down the coast. Erwin had booked a private room where they could talk. Afterwards, if he cared to, Klimt might gamble.

Gamble? Klimt stood in his bedroom at the embassy. The view over the city was, as promised, sensational. The flying boat had finished refuelling and was taxiing slowly into the river for the next leg of its flight down to the coast of West Africa. He watched it come to a halt while the pilot ran through the last of his checks. Then it began to move, faster and faster, tugging a long 'V' across the blue waters of the estuary until the pilot hauled it into the air. The big white bird performed a graceful turn to the south before Klimt lost it in the haze. I should be on that plane, he thought. With Hélène.

Erwin drove Klimt to Estoril. The casino stood at the top of a carefully tended stretch of grass that ran down to the waterfront. Erwin assured Klimt that Estoril was a party town. Lots of women. Lots of businessmen on the make. Lots of locals peddling worthless information to anyone they thought might be a spy.

Schellenberg was waiting for them in the private suite overlooking the gambling floor. He must have been in the sun because his face was lightly tanned and he seemed relaxed. He sent Erwin away for drinks. A glass of white wine for himself. Bottles of Sagres for Erwin and Klimt.

'So tell me . . .' he said, nodding Klimt into a chair.

Klimt did his best. He'd met with a senior diplomat. His name was Passmore. He had the ear of the mighty.

'What did you say?'

'I said there might be a chance for talks.'

'For peace?'

'For the fighting to stop.'

'And?'

'He told me unconditional surrender.'

'Nothing else?'

'Nothing. Either we lay down our arms or the war goes on.'

Schellenberg nodded. None of this appeared to come as a surprise. Erwin was back with a tray of drinks. Klimt studied his glass of lager. Then his head came up again.

'Madame Lafosse.' He was looking at Schellenberg. 'When do I get to see her?'

'Sadly, you won't.'

'Won't?'

'No. Madame Lafosse died this morning. She appears to have taken her own life. It's not uncommon in the camps.'

'How?' Klimt was staring at him. 'How did it happen?'

'She ran towards the wire. She knew the rules. She knew about the forbidden zone. It seems she threw down her beret before the guards opened fire. She was warned, of course. They always shout.'

'And then?'

Schellenberg glanced across at his attaché. Apparently Erwin had talked to the people at Ravensbrück.

'We believe she crouched beside the beret,' Erwin said. 'At first she refused to move. When the guards came to drag her away she died on the wire.'

'Shot?'

'Electrocuted. My sympathies, Bjorn.'

Klimt was trying to absorb the news. War was supposed to harden you to shock, to pain, to grief. He was staring at Erwin Busch. The beret, he thought. The canvas in the gallery. The hawk riding high above the fields beyond the bedroom window. And the searing jolt that would have brought such a life to an end. Impossible to imagine. Impossible to accept.

Schellenberg was reaching for his wine.

'You met our friends from MI5?'

'Yes.'

'What else did you discuss?'

Klimt shrugged. His mind had closed down. He could think of nothing but Hélène hanging on the wire. A death like that was supposed to be quick.

'Angell, perhaps? Young Billy?'

'Angell?' Klimt was trying to focus, trying to think.

'Yes. Did his name come up?'

'It did. Because you sent them a message. About Dachau.'

'And?'

'They wanted to find out what I knew about him.'

'And where did that lead?'

'I told them I'd never heard of him. They made

455

some more enquiries. It seems he has a problem. A mental problem. That's why he jumped from the aircraft.'

'You believed that?'

'Absolutely. It's what he told me. He'd had enough of the war. He'd seen too much. He was finished. Thank God he found Hélène.'

'And the rest of it? The story about his brother? Dunkirk? That was true too? You believed it?'

'Of course. You know that.'

'Indeed.'

Schellenberg motioned to Erwin. Erwin opened his briefcase and extracted a folder. Inside was a long telex. Schellenberg gave it a glance and then pushed it across.

'From Huber,' he said. 'In Dachau.'

Klimt studied the first page. This was a transcript. It must have come from a recording. It seemed jumbled, slightly chaotic. He could sense the moments when Billy paused for breath, trying to remember a fact or a name or a date. The prompts from Huber were remarkably few. A textbook confession.

'*Ein Spiel, ja?*' *Spiel* meant 'game'. Schellenberg's voice was soft. In situations like these, he had the touch of the master. Deft. Silky. Implacable.

'You were at the chateau,' he said. 'You must have known.'

'I didn't.'

'I don't believe you.'

'Believe what you like. It makes no difference.'

'That makes you stupid. You've never been fooled before. Why now?' He nodded at the telex. 'Why this?'

'Because the story was very clever. And the boy was very good.'

'So you never suspected? Not once?'

Klimt held his gaze.

'I made some extra enquiries in London,' he said at last. 'And Huber's got it right.'

'But you didn't know before?'

'No.'

Schellenberg nodded but Klimt knew he didn't believe him. In every possible respect he was finished.

Schellenberg motioned to Erwin again. A second file. Inside, a single sheet of paper.

'Read it please.' Schellenberg was uncapping a fountain pen. 'Word about your expedition has reached the Führer. Alas, someone has to pay for this. In blood.'

'Me?'

'Read it.'

Erwin passed the sheet of paper to Klimt. In three short paragraphs, immaculately typed, it detailed how *Oberst* Bjorn Klimt had taken it upon himself to make contacts through *Abwehr* channels with key politicians in London. How he'd tried to pave the way for separate peace negotiations. And how he now admitted that this act of defeatism should warrant the harshest punishment.

He looked at the proffered pen. He knew he would be signing his death warrant.

457

'You sent me, Walther,' he murmured. 'You know you did.'

Schellenberg said nothing. His eyes never left Klimt's face. Erwin was looking at his hands. Klimt knew it was hopeless. He shrugged and took the pen. It was a Montblanc. A thousand dollars, at the very least. Nathan, he thought, probably had half a dozen.

Klimt read the confession again. Another little victory for the SD. Another scalp to hang on Himmler's belt.

Schellenberg still had the pen. Klimt took it and scribbled his name at the foot of the page. The nib moved sweetly beneath his fingers. Done.

Erwin took the confession and blew the ink dry on the signature. Then Schellenberg asked whether he might have any special requests.

How quaint, Klimt thought. The condemned man. He gave the question some thought.

'Billy Angell,' he said at last. 'Send him back.'

Erwin scribbled himself a note. Then Schellenberg produced a package from his own suitcase. Klimt recognised the torn wrapping paper. This was the bundle of *Reichsmarks* he'd negotiated on Hélène's behalf for the services of her stallion.

'We recovered the money from Madame Lafosse's apartment,' Schellenberg said. 'I'm proposing we go downstairs. You might care to place a bet or two. Roulette might be amusing. Winnings to the Winter Appeal.'

Another game, Klimt thought. They never stop.

Not in my world. Not in Walther Schellenberg's. Not in London. The Winter Appeal raised money for the armies in the east. These were men who'd be frozen to death by Christmas.

Klimt nodded his assent. Schellenberg gave him the money. Klimt wanted to know how much.

'One hundred and twenty thousand *Reichsmarks*, give or take. Enough for a blanket or two, Bjorn.'

Klimt said nothing. He followed Erwin downstairs. There was an empty chair at the crowded roulette table and he wondered whether that was pre-planned. Schellenberg had a reputation for attention to the smallest details. Truly a survivor.

Klimt took the seat. Erwin wanted to know how many chips to buy.

'Spend the lot.'

'All of it?'

'Yes, please.'

Erwin glanced at Schellenberg. Schellenberg offered the faintest nod. Erwin picked his way between the tables, heading for the cashier's window. Klimt was looking round. He'd already spotted three men taking an unusual interest in him. They were all wearing civilian suits but the military haircuts gave them away. He's got the place surrounded, Klimt thought. More men on the exits. And doubtless a car waiting outside. In Walther's world you left nothing to chance.

Erwin returned with a cardboard box full of chips. Play around the table had stopped. Gamblers were staring at the contents of the box.

The croupier was looking at Klimt.

'You want to place a bet, sir?'

'I do.'

'How much?'

'The lot. Everything.'

'On what?'

'Red.'

The croupier was looking troubled. A bet of this size? Crazy.

'You know the odds?'

'Of course I do. All my life I've known the odds.'

The croupier shrugged.

'Place a chip on red, sir. This will signify your entire holding. Are you sure this is what you want to do?'

Klimt nodded. He was looking at a woman across the table. A stranger. Beautiful. And she was miming applause. His eyes returned to the croupier. The croupier spun the wheel and released the ball. The ball circled the wheel and danced from number to number as the wheel began to slow. Finally it came to a halt.

Klimt smiled. Black.

CHAPTER 40

Billy Angell was released from Dachau concentration camp three days later. Erwin, who handled the arrangements, had him flown to a Spanish airfield at Algeciras. From there he was delivered to the British at the heavily guarded crossing point into Gibraltar. An accompanying note from SD headquarters in Berlin presented *Oberst* Klimt's compliments to the Director of Counter-Espionage at MI5 and requested safe passage for Wireless Operator Angell back to England.

By now, MI5 knew that Klimt was dead. The Director convened an emergency meeting ahead of Angell's arrival. Enigma intercepts had revealed that Agent Thesp had been blown. Under heavy interrogation, presumably at Dachau, he'd revealed every detail of the Dunkirk plant. The issue now was whether the Germans had managed to turn him.

Making space for a double agent was an opportunity as well as a hazard. Double agents could themselves be turned, thus becoming triple agents. But would Billy Angell ever want to set foot in Germany again? Or even France?

Ursula Barton, with her fluent German, was alarmed by the decrypted material. Billy, she said at once, must have had a difficult time. People he'd got to know at the chateau had been killed in front of him. A survivor, a Pole, had met a similar fate at Dachau. He'd grown fond of Hélène Lafosse and she, too, had disappeared without trace. For an ex-Quaker with a troubled conscience, the secret world probably had limited appeal.

'So are we sending him back to Bomber Command?' This from the Director. 'Would they even want him?'

There was no consensus around the table. The Director announced that they'd await his arrival for the full debrief. Only then could they make any kind of decision about where Angell's future lay.

Two hours later, Ursula knocked on the Director's door. Billy Angell, she said, lay heavily on her conscience. It had been her decision to suggest the original approach, and she bore as much responsibility for what had happened as anyone else in the organisation. With this in mind, she'd commissioned a bit of additional research in the military archives.

'Archives?'

'Here, sir.'

She slipped a folder onto the Director's desk. He quickly scanned the contents, then looked up. He was visibly shocked.

'Christ', he said. 'So what do we do now?'

★ ★ ★

462

Billy Angell found himself on a converted bomber for the flight back to the UK. Six hours in the air extinguished any flicker of a desire to fly again. The smells, the roar of the engine, the intense cold were all too familiar. Another world he was only too happy to leave behind him.

A car was waiting for him at an RAF airfield on the north-west edge of London. He knew he was going to meet the people from MI5 again. They'd told him so at Gibraltar. Indeed, they'd treated him with a degree of respect. A secret agent stepping in from the front line. One of ours. Billy gazed out at the interminable suburbs in the last of the sunset. If they'd only known, he thought.

Ursula met him outside a house in Mayfair. He'd never been there before. She took him inside and then up to a spacious reception room on the first floor. Expecting trouble from the start, Billy realised she was making a fuss of him. A pot of tea, even a slice of jam sponge.

'Home-made,' she said. 'And you're looking at someone who hasn't baked a cake since the war began.'

Billy was waiting for the inevitable. Any minute now, he knew he'd have to face the rest of them. Tam. The instructors who'd briefed him before his flight to France. Maybe even the Director. Everyone, in short, whom he'd failed. When Ursula enquired whether he was ready for the post-mortem, he shuddered at her choice of phrase.

'Of course,' he said.

In the event, it was only Tam and the Director. To his relief, they seemed to know the whole story already. They even knew about Dachau, and about the morning they'd killed the old man, and when they went through his confession, the account he'd offered Huber, there wasn't a hint of reproach. Operation Aurore, they told him, had been a brave attempt. But, all too sadly, it had ended in failure. Failure, to Billy, hardly did justice to the past few weeks but he was grateful, none the less, for their forbearance.

The debrief over, the Director asked him what he wanted to do. Billy had thought a great deal about this very question over the past couple of days.

'I have a friend in Devon,' he said.

'She'd look after you? For the time being?'

'He. His name's Don.'

'I see . . .' An exchange of glances around the table. Tam had evidently kept Don's existence to himself.

Ursula was the first to mention his mother. They'd been in touch with her, told her just a little about the circumstances surrounding Billy's return. Your son's been exceptionally brave, they'd told her. And we feel he might appreciate a bit of a rest.

'So what did she say?'

'She said she'd be very glad to have you home.'

'And Ralph? Her new husband?'

'She never mentioned him.' The Director steepled his fingers. 'We'd be very happy to run you down. Somerset, isn't it?'

They left the next morning. Ursula was at the wheel. A night's sleep in a bedroom upstairs in the Mayfair house had made Billy feel a little less nervous and he was happy to let the glorious scenery slip by in silence. Proper conversation, he suspected, was something he wouldn't be risking for a while. Not even with Don.

His mother was pleased to see him. The hug felt genuine. She was still clinging to him when Ursula waved goodbye and got back in the car.

For the next few days the huge house felt like a convalescent home. Ralph was away, tending his factories in the Midlands, and his mother – sensing his reluctance to talk – mostly left him alone. To Billy, her cooking had always been wonderful. Food from the estate – eggs, meat, fresh vegetables – appeared on the table every evening. They ate in the kitchen, just the way they'd always done at home, and as the days extended to a full week Billy began to feel that a return to normal life might just be possible.

Then came the moment when his mother sat him down in the sunshine on the terrace. There was something they had to discuss. Something important. Billy fought the urge to say no. He was gazing over the estate towards the distant hills that led south to Cheddar Gorge. He didn't want to talk about the chateau. About Hélène. About Malin. About the constant pressures of pretending to be someone else. His acting days were over. From now on he wanted to be as small and unremarkable and insignificant as possible. He didn't want either attention or applause. Just getting by from day to day, if it ever happened, would be miracle enough.

'It's not about any of that, Billy.'

He looked at her. For the first time he realised she was crying.

'What is it, then?'

'It's about your father. Your dad.'

'But he's dead.'

'No, he's not.'

'He must be.' Billy was staring at her. 'You told me he was. You've always told me he was. He died in the war. In the trenches. Before I was born. That's what you said.'

She shook her head, wiped her eyes, blew her nose. Dad, she explained, had been terribly injured in a battle during the war. It was true that Billy hadn't even been born. In fact she was seven months pregnant when the Army people allowed her to visit him.

'Where was he?'

'In a big hospital. It was near Southampton. It was where they brought all the injured soldiers across from France.'

'And how was he?'

'Terrible. He was in a terrible state. He'd lost a leg and his right arm but he had no face, Billy. It had gone. All of it. In some ways he was better off dead.'

Better off dead.

Billy nodded. Said he understood. It was true. That's exactly how you'd feel.

'So what happened?'

'They tried to patch him up. They did their best. At least they got him so he could eat, feed himself, breathe properly.'

'But what do you do without a face?'

'They made him one.'

'*Made* him one? How do you do that?'

His mum did her best to explain. She described the metal mask they'd made, how it fitted, how it stayed on. Two years had passed by then. The war was over. Then came the moment when they'd asked him whether he was ready to go home.

'What did he say?'

'He said no. He said he couldn't face any of us. Not strangers. Not you. Not even me. He was ashamed of himself. He didn't want people looking, asking questions. He just wanted to be left alone.'

Alone. Yes.

'He stayed in the hospital?'

'Not that one. Not the big one. Another one. Smaller and much closer. A special sort of hospital. For men like him, soldiers who'd been so badly injured.'

'Where is this place?'

'High Cross. It's half an hour away.'

'And he's still there?'

'Yes.' Billy's mother took his hand, stroked it. 'Would you like to meet him?'

★ ★ ★

They went next day. Ralph had bought Billy's mum a car, a little Morris, and she picked her way through the country lanes until they slowed for a turn into a sweeping drive. The hospital was smaller and more intimate than Billy had been expecting. It faced south, bathed in the mid-summer sunshine, and Billy caught the bright golden twinkle of light on the faces of the men in wheelchairs, relaxing on the terrace. They were all wearing masks, every single one of them. Billy had been in a production like this before the war. Greek tragedy. *Oedipus*.

The Morris came to a halt. Billy's mum knew the way. The hospital was as bright inside as out. She led Billy through a warren of corridors, greeting nurses by name. A staircase led up to the first floor. Single rooms, left and right. One of the doors was open.

She paused outside, peeked in, then turned to Billy.

'He's expecting you,' she whispered. 'But I think he might be asleep.'

She was smiling and Billy realised that she must have been hoping for this moment for years.

He stepped into the room, nervous about what he might find. The curtains were half pulled against the brightness of the sunshine. The room was a decent size. A cat lay curled on his father's lap. His dad was a small man, thin. He was wearing trousers and a soft blue shirt. One leg was out straight, supported on a padded foot rest. One sleeve of the shirt was knotted above the elbow. But it was his dad's face that drew Billy's attention.

His mask lay on the carpet beside the chair, exposing what lay beneath. His mum had been right. There was nothing left. No nose. Half an ear. No lips. No eyelids. Just a hideous face-shaped tangle of scarring, shiny in the afternoon light. Without a face, thought Billy, you were no one. Small wonder he'd opted for a home like this.

His dad's eyes were open. They were filmy, the lightest blue. Billy retreated to the corridor, shocked.

'He's awake? He can see me?'

'He's blind, Billy. He can see nothing.'

'Shall I wake him up?'

'Of course. That's why you're here.'

Billy tiptoed back into the room, trying not to make any noise. On the chest of drawers was a nest of photos. Back when they'd met, in that first year of the war, his mum had been the prettiest bride. She'd worn a simple white frock for the wedding and she clung to her handsome soldier boy. He, too, was a looker: strong face, neatly pressed uniform, full head of hair, and a proud smile for the camera.

Billy stole a glance at the figure in the armchair, overcome by the contrast. Then he went back to the photos. Many were of him. As a baby kicking on a blanket. As a toddler straddling a wooden horse. On a beach playing sandcastles with his mum. He thought he remembered that day. He went out into the corridor again with the photo.

'Clevedon?'

'Weston-super-Mare, Billy. Your dad used to give me money for ice creams.'

'Strawberry,' Billy said, 'With a dollop of cream on top.'

He looked in at his dad again. He still seemed to be asleep.

'Why so many photos?' he said. 'When he can't see?'

'They're for me, Billy. To remind me who we were. Sometimes you don't want to keep up with life. Sometimes it's nicer to live in the past.'

'So why didn't you let me visit before? When I was young?'

'We thought it would frighten you.'

'We?'

'Me and your dad. We still took decisions together. That was nice.'

'And now? Does he know about Ralph?'

'Yes.'

'You told him you were going to get married?'

'Yes.'

'And what did he say?'

'He said he was glad. He wanted to buy us a present but I said no. Me and Dad were divorced after the war. That was his decision. He wanted me to start a new life. He thought I waited far too long.'

'Has Ralph been here?'

'No. He thinks it would make him jealous and he's probably right.'

'*Jealous?*'

'Of what we had. Of what we have.' She nodded at the photos. 'You.'

The figure in the armchair was beginning to stir. A thin dribble of saliva found its way down the remains of his chin. His good arm twitched.

'There's a towel under the basin, Billy.'

Billy fetched the towel and knelt by the armchair, mopping gently at the wreckage that had once been a face. His father was awake now, his good arm reaching out for contact. The claw-like hand found Billy's arm, clutched it tight. Then the hand tracked upwards, across his chest, the fingertips mapping Billy's chin, his lips, his eyebrows, his cheeks. The voice was a croak. It came from deep in his throat.

'Son?'

Billy nodded. The figure in the armchair had become a blur. Agnès, he thought. The Spanish couple sprawled in the meadow. Malin's body hanging in the rain under the trees. And now this. My dad. My real dad. Back from the dead. He gave the bony hand a squeeze. The end of the journey. The very middle of the labyrinth.

Magic.